DREADNOUGHT

A NOVEL BY MICHAEL COLE

SEVEREDPRESS

DREADNOUGHT

WWW.SEVEREDPRESS.COM

ISBN: 978-1-923663-10-7

CHAPTER 1

The night sky slowly changed to light gray as the sun prepped for its daily arrival to the western world. To Jordan Burch, it usually meant he had another two or three hours of sleep remaining. He'd stayed up late the previous night making sure everything was packed and ready to go. He always hated feeling rushed on the last morning of a trip, and the hurried feeling of trying to have everything accounted for to bring home. He liked it simple: grab the bags, get in the car, leave, and dread going back to work.

He would really dread it this time. His yearly trip to Falk's Tale Resort was his safe haven from a lifedraining existence in accounting. That, and sleep, which he felt he was getting less and less of these days.

He groaned as his fiancée jostled him back and forth.

"Come on, come on, get up," Elena said. Jordan rolled onto his back and stared up at the twenty-three-year-old college cheerleader. Her hair was undone, her nightie hanging low, the goods underneath properly getting his attention. If she was suggesting what he thought she was, maybe being woken up early wasn't such a bad thing.

He managed to crack a smile. "Yeah?"

"Let's go out paddle-boating one more time," Elena said.

That smile vanished. "Huh?"

"Oh, come on, I really love it," she said. "I really enjoyed being here, and I'm already missing it." Jordan rolled back onto his left side. Elena tapped his shoulder.

"What?"

She giggled. "What do you mean, 'whaaaat'?"

Jordan rolled back, then squinted to look at the clock. "Jesus, babe, it's five o'clock."

"Five-*ten*."

"Oh, *much* better," he said.

Elena sighed. This was the end of their third visit to this resort. Like him, she enjoyed simple quiet trips to get away from the rest of the world, and during their final day, she spent the evening feeling sad that it was ending. Even now, with just a few hours until their departure, she wasn't quite ready to let it go. Jordan, on the other hand, was a 'rip the Band-aid off quick' kind of guy. As usual, he already had the bags packed, intent on waking up, getting in the car, and going home. He wouldn't even stay for breakfast, always stating that it's easier to stop at a drive-through.

Elena jostled him again.

"Seriously?" he said. "You're like my four-year old niece. 'Uncle Jordan, wake up. You said you were gonna take me out on da boat.'"

"It works, doesn't it?" Elena said, smiling.

Jordan threw his head back on the pillow and stared at the ceiling. "I gotta pee." He rolled over the side and stumbled into the bathroom. In the long minute it took to relieve himself, he could hear Elena fixing some coffee. The girl was damn determined.

He stepped out to the aroma of brewing French roast.

"Great. Now we'll have to wash that before we leave."

"Oh, boo-hoo, it'll take ten seconds," Elena said.

"And the mugs," he said.

Elena strutted up to him and stood up on her toes, leveling her eyes with his. She rested the tip of her finger on his chin. "It's a quarter after five. An hour out there, and we'll still be more than on track for your schedule of getting-home-at-a-decent-time. Even more-so than if you slept in."

He stared at her, one eye still crusted half-shut. "What's in it for me?"

"Time well-spent with the love of your life," Elena said.

"Not good enough."

She smiled. Banter—it was a good sign. She slowly closed in and placed a kiss on his lips. A longer, wetter one followed, while simultaneously, she worked his hands over to her thighs. That other eye was open all the way now.

There was no mistaking what she was suggesting. Now, all of a sudden, a little morning exercise didn't seem like such a bad thing.

"I suppose . . ." he kissed her again . . . "I'll get . . ." *kiss* ". . . enough sleep . . . when I'm dead."

"Good!"

His next kiss fell on nothing but air as Elena dashed for the closet. She grabbed a light jacket and changed into her shorts, then made a rush for the door.

"Wha—holy crap! Hang on!" he said, fumbling for something better to wear. Elena stopped halfway out the door and looked back at him.

"Last one into the water is a rotten egg!" she said. She took off running toward the beach.

"Jesus . . ." He fumbled with his ragged T-shirt in favor of his tank top, pulling it over his face, only for the collar to bunch up under his chin. Still drowsy and with the shirt completely covering his face, he stumbled through the living room, ultimately faceplanting against the closet door. "Son of a bitch!" He ripped the shirt off and threw it on the floor. He checked his forehead. No blood, but he'd be lucky if he didn't see a bruise in a few hours. He threw on the tank top, figured he'd stay in his pajama shorts, then hurried outside.

What was the point of making coffee if we weren't gonna drink it?!

He hastened out onto the front lawn overlooking the beach. It was still somewhat dark, with barely enough light to make out the layout of the resort. There were six rental houses, lined up in a slight arch along the beach. At the farthest end to his right was the main lodge for Falk's Tale, where the owners kept the paddleboats and supplies on standby. Their house was directly behind that.

He could see the dock, due to a small porchlight at its end.

Jordan noticed Mr. Falk's big boat was not there. Interesting that he'd be out this early. He often took tourists out to various dive sites, though that seemed unlikely at this hour. Then again, Jordan knew very little about diving. Or the ocean, for that matter, other than it was very big. He and Elena lived a couple hundred miles inland, and only saw the ocean when they vacationed here at the resort. He heard boat horns in the distance. Many of the local fishermen usually set out around this time. Probably what Falk was doing, as he did fish occasionally to supplement his income.

He looked out at the water, surprised to see a large gathering of seagulls everywhere. They didn't seem to mind Elena's presence, as she eagerly pulled her kayak into the water.

"Holy shit! What's your rush?" he jogged over to the kayak rack in front of the main lodge and grabbed for paddles.

"Rotten egg!" she laughed, pointing at him.

"What was the point of me tagging along if you were gonna go off ahead?" he muttered. Luckily, she grabbed an orange kayak, which was easy to see even in this light. He reached up along the kayak racks. *The blue one was the forty-pound one, right?* Caught off guard by the eighty pounds, his hands slipped, and the small boat fell on his head. "Fuck!" He remembered—the green one was the mid-weight one. His displeasure could be heard in a groan. *She better be a fireball in that bed when we get back!*

Elena paddled thirty feet out before finally stopping to look back.

"Jeez, slowpoke! Kick up 'em heels and drag that sucker on out!" she said between cackles.

Jordan scowled, then bitterly dragged the kayak out onto the water. The distant horizon was turning bright now. He could see the outline of the clouds, as well as a few large boats way in the distance. There was something soothing about listening to the boat horns. Elena paddled gently, not going too much farther while she waited for him.

The crack of dawn allowed him to see the shoreline a little better. He brought the kayak to the edge, then got ready to step in it. The seagulls were really intent on gathering now. Their numbers had doubled in the last few minutes, with little concern for the six-foot human walking between them.

"Okay, come on! Out of the way," he said, as though they would listen. A few scattered off, uncovering the long black thing in the sand. He thought it was a surfboard at first, until he saw the weird, stringy residue dancing with the tide on its far end. The object was about six-feet long and dagger-shaped. "The hell?" He touched his fingers to it, feeling its rubbery texture. He gazed at the open ends where the residue was and saw the fleshy strings. This was once part of something—something alive. Or rather, *dead.*

Jordan noticed the seagulls converging on something just ten feet down the beach. Curious, he took a look, scattering the birds with his paddle. They took to the sky, revealing another black object. He knelt and scraped some of the sand away. It was identical to the other in color and texture, but this one was rounder in shape, almost like a flower petal. As he brushed the sand away, he struck something else. There was something bony resting in the sand, half out of the water. It was pinkish white, lined with four-inch pointed objects. Teeth! He was looking at a ravaged jawline.

Jordan jumped up and stepped back. His eyes went from the jaw to the black objects . . . then he finally made the connection. Fins. Flippers. He was looking at the shredded remains of a killer whale.

The water rolled back, rolling smaller, unidentifiable pieces of bone and meat . . . and a fully intact eyeball with a white pupil that gazed back at him.

"What's going on?" Elena asked. Her fiancé didn't answer. It was hard to tell from where she was, but it almost looked as though he was getting sick. She heard him coughing and turned around.

Water splashed against her back as the tide rolled in. She kept watching Jordan. He was looking okay now, composed.

Another wave hit her back. Gosh, the ocean wasn't this alive when she started out. She shook it off and focused on her fiancé.

"Babe? You okay?"

"I'm good," he said. "There's just . . . there's something dead in the sand," he shouted back. "You might want to . . . Babe?"

He was looking right at her. Elena noticed he was pointing a finger, then realized it wasn't her he was pointing at. There was something behind her.

Something splashed, and she felt the jolt of impact on the underside of her kayak. She shrieked, her boat fishtailing toward the shore. As her bow pointed out into the ocean, she saw a large swell in the water. There was something under there. Something huge! The swell erupted like a bubble, spraying water in her face.

"Jordan! There's something in the water!"

There was a spray of water, like mist.

The sun's rays streamed across the Atlantic, giving the water a golden appearance. Only the water around her kayak was red. There was blood all around Elena. The large mass thrashed from underneath, rising like an uppercut. The kayak flipped, flinging Elena into the water.

Jordan sprinted into the water.

"Elena! Babe! Swim!" he shouted. Submerged up to his chest, he paddled out. His fiancée broke the surface and frantically swam toward him. "Come on! Come on. Almost there." He spit water with every word. By the time he reached her, he saw the ocean was full of blood. He almost panicked, thinking it was hers. Then she grabbed him, and it was clear she was all intact.

They glanced back, seeing the thing's big mass rising from the water. Its mouth opened, revealing huge cone-shaped teeth.

"Good Christ! An orca," he said. It rolled under the surface, its tail lashing up with no fluke. Only a bloody stump.

The two lovers backpaddled, gasping as the mammal raised its head again. It was covered in horrible gashes, as though it had visited a slaughterhouse. Its underside was torn open. Its left pectoral fin was missing. Its lower jaw was almost split down the center, as though someone had taken a buzzsaw to it.

Their feet were touching the sand bottom now, though they needed to stand on their toes to keep their noses above water.

Elena cupped her mouth, unable to take her eyes off the phenomenon as they backed toward the shore.

"My God! Jordan, what happened to it?"

"I have no idea. Let's just get—WHOA!" He fell backward, as though the seafloor was yanked from under his feet. Elena reached for him, only to trip over the same mass he did. Once again, she was underwater. She opened her eyes, then froze. The need for oxygen could not overcome the fright from seeing the skeletal corpse of another butchered orca directly in front of her. Its body was nothing but a deflated mass, with only bits of bone holding it together. The only recognizable part was its head, which was split wide open, revealing skull and brain matter.

Her scream erupted in a flood of air bubbles. Jordan lifted her to her feet and dragged her back to the surface. They kept going, even after crossing the shoreline. People in other rental houses rushed outside, startled by the screams, horrified to see the dying orca rolling with the waves.

Elena and Jordan collapsed on the grass, their hearts racing. Together, they stared in shock, unfazed by the blinding sunlight that streamed over the pod of dead killer whales lining the shore.

CHAPTER 2

When Dakota McCullough woke up to the sound of a ringing phone, his first temptation was to reach for his department radio, for a six-a.m. call usually meant something serious was going down. The realization that there was no radio triggered frustration, which quickly shifted into grand amusement.

Oh, right. I'm not the sheriff anymore.

He was glad he remembered before looking at his phone screen. Even after seven months, he still had the contact listed as Dispatch. For as long as cell phones existed, the department was always listed under that name. The thought of changing it, or even removing it from his list, simply felt weird after two decades.

He answered the call and placed the phone to his ear. "Hey, Maggie. I thought with retirement I wouldn't have to suffer wakeup calls from you anymore."

"Oh, you're funny, Dakota. How've you been?"

"Just dandy. Livin' the dream."

"That's good. You've earned it. Sorry to wake you up, though I figured you might've been awake already."

"That bored at the office? Don't worry, it's Saturday. I'm sure there'll be something to keep you busy. Then again, it's Gallant Bay. Not much goes on around here anymore."

"I consider that a good thing. Anyways, no, I'm not making a social call."

"Well, shit. I was ready to feel flattered."

"Don't worry, sunshine. There's still room for flattery. You're being requested for a towing job."

Dakota sat up. "A towing job? This early? Don't tell me some idiot got into a boating accident."

"No, no. Nothing like that, Sheriff—Dakota. Sorry. Still getting used to the change."

"Same."

"The location's at Falk's Tale Resort. It's an unusual situation. Dead killer whales have washed up. Or rather, the remains *of dead killer whales."*

"Really? What the hell happened?"

"Not sure yet. You'll see for yourself when you get there, but from what I hear, they're pretty effed up. Shall I let them know you're on your way, or should I pass the gig on to somebody else?"

"The sheriff heading over there?"

"That's correct."

"Yeah, I'll take the job. Is the County paying, or the Falks?"

"Actually, it's the University of Florida."

"Florida? What's their involvement? It's a little chilly up here for them, don't you think?"

"I guess you've been working on your snark during your newfound spare time, haven't you?"

"Have to justify my retirement somehow."

"Oh, it's justified, sir. To answer your question, they've been tracking this pod. One of their people has been notified and is en route to the location as we speak."

"Wait . . . one of their people? Did they happen to mention who it was?"

"I believe it's the same woman who was doing research here three years back."

"Oh, I'm *definitely* going! Thanks, Maggie. Don't work too hard."

"All right, Sheriff—Dakota. Damn it!"

With a laugh, he gave his farewell and hung up. Next came the morning routine of getting dressed and brushing his teeth. The shower could wait for later, since he was going to be cleaning up whale remains from the Falks' beach. The oddity started to weigh on his mind.

"Dead killer whales. A whole pod? What the hell happened?"

His first thought was poachers, but even that didn't make sense. Even the most experienced poachers with the best equipment would not be able to take down a whole pod. Maybe a couple at best and the rest would flee. Killer whales were not dummies. They knew how to get away from a vessel. The only other feasible explanation as to how an entire pod got butchered was that they stayed to fight. Dakota had never heard of an orca attack on humans.

As unlikely as that possibility seemed, everything else was even more unfeasible. Sharks would not stand a chance against killer whales for a second. Other predatory whales, even if it was in their nature to attack orcas, would fail at such an attempt. Even the mighty sperm whale often found itself the victim of orca pod ambushes.

I guess I'll know when I get there.

With that thought came the acknowledgement that he was no longer sheriff. The puzzle-solving instincts were still primed and ready to be put to use. There was no need for the detective work. He was a retiree making beer money with odd maintenance jobs and fishing. At least, whenever there were fish. The Gulf of Maine had seen better days. Lately, he'd be lucky to get thirty pounds of mackerel. Whatever catch he brought in was infested with illness.

Probably the reason the marine biologists are in the area.

He finished running a toothbrush over his teeth then went to the bookshelf where he usually stored his keys. He stopped to gaze at the many photos lining the upper shelves. After retirement, it had become part of his new routine to look at Glenn. To the left were the grainy photos of him wrapped up as a little peanut. Twenty-seven years later, Dakota could not get enough of those chunky cheeks. The line of photos progressed through the years, displaying memories of Glenn on a swing set, getting on the school bus, high school graduation, his graduation from the police academy, ultimately to his ceremonial picture after being inaugurated as sheriff.

The worst part of the campaign had been the dozens of questions directed to him by the local news sites. People asked why he wasn't running endorsements for his son. He thought the answer was obvious: because they were family. If he had endorsed Glenn, it would have forever tainted his image. He would have been thought of as the kid who only got the job because of his daddy.

Despite his best efforts, that fear still became a reality. Glenn won the election in a landslide, but even his supporters admitted it was only because of the familiarity of his name. Without his father's legacy, it was highly unlikely that the twenty-seven-year-old Glenn McCullough would have won election, especially considering his opposition. When Lieutenant Martin Willis lost to a candidate twenty years his junior—and with twenty less years of experience—he could not take it. He accepted the election results, but publicly stated it would be a cold day in hell before he worked under someone as inexperienced as Glenn. On December 30, Dakota was not the only one who chose to retire early.

What should have been a great day in Dakota's life soon became a memory he often suppressed. After the high of victory faded, Glenn quickly understood he did not win election on merit. From day one, he faced comparisons to his father from both his staff and the public. Though he never explicitly expressed resentment toward his father, it was evident in his demeaner and his actions. Or rather, the lack thereof. About a month in, the phone calls stopped. Whenever Dakota took the initiative and called his son, something always 'came up' to interrupt the chat. After a while, Dakota quit trying. He wanted to keep in touch with Glenn, but each conversation always contained the question "Making any motion toward that house in Boca Raton?"

Dakota had mentioned moving south many times during his last few years leading up to retirement. Forty-nine years old, his joints and back were sending painful signals of their wear and tear. The cooler weather of Maine made the arthritis flare up like Fourth of July fireworks. Dakota knew Glenn well enough to know the meaning behind the statement, "I know you're staying here to keep an eye on me, because you don't think I'm capable of running this department myself." His many attempts to offer advice did not help in deterring Glenn from that mindset.

He grabbed his boat key and stepped outside.

The morning sunlight was bright, the sky nearly cloudless. The sun rose early during the summer months, much to the delight of early birds like himself. He embraced the flat blue ocean ahead of him. The Atlantic was in a good mood today, just the way he liked her. A thing of beauty she was, until her rage was ignited. He had seen the ocean go from tranquil and silent to a rushing fury in less than an hour. His wallet and home insurance certainly had felt the latter part on plenty of occasions. So, the better the Atlantic's mood, the more he liked it.

It was a sentiment felt by many others that morning. Dakota was not the only early bird taking to the water. Roughly seven hundred feet northeast of his position were two kayakers. Despite the blinding sun, he could see their waving hands.

Dakota waved back. Ricky Cox and his live-in girlfriend, Ashley Thomas, were probably the only twenty-somethings he ever knew to enjoy getting up before the crack of dawn. It made sense, however. Both were professional fitness instructors. To get their own workout in before work started, they had to get up long before their customers. Dakota never complained, for he enjoyed their greeting whenever they passed by during their morning routine.

Even at this distance, he could make out the gold star symbol on their T-shirts, part of the logo for Gold Star Fitness. The kayaks were as purple as their clothes and had the same gold star logo on the forward decks. They believed heavily in merchandising, which also served as marketing.

After a few moments Ricky and Ashley resumed their exercise, rigorously slicing their paddles into the ocean. Before long, they were specks in the distance.

There was another couple heading out to sea. Reflecting the sun's light was the white hull of the *Autumn Bliss*. Up on the flybridge was Kelby Dryer. A sixty-year-old fisherman with forty-five years of experience, he joked that he spent more time on the water than on land. His family had joked that he would never see a happy marriage unless he found someone who equally loved the ocean. So, Kelby did just that.

Patty was on the main deck sorting through bait and netting. She jumped when her husband abruptly blew the boat horn.

"What's the big deal?" she shouted.

Kelby pointed to the dock. "Look who it is, Patty."

When she spotted Dakota, her frustration faded into pure joy. "Sheriff! Good to see you up this morning!"

"Morning, Mr. and Mrs. Dryer," he shouted back. The boat was slowing and angling toward his dock. A chit-chat was inevitable. He hurried down to his dock. The *Autumn Bliss* came within twenty feet of the end. Kelby turned the bow north and killed the engine.

"Morning, Sheriff! I see you're all dressed and ready to go. Heading out for some fishing?"

"Ha, no." Dakota hesitated before saying anything else. Every time someone called him sheriff, he debated whether he should correct them. Like with Maggie, it was a force of habit for everyone. Hell, he still responded whenever he was addressed by that title. It had practically taken the role of his first name at this point. He let the issue slide in favor of redundant small talk. "Just doing a small favor for the Falks. What about you guys? Trying your luck yet again?"

Kelby's expression soured. "You know how bad it's been out there lately."

"That I do."

"We've made our living fishing in these waters as long as either of us have been alive," Patty said. "I'm not willing to accept that all the fish have moved on."

"It's not that they've moved on, hon." Kelby took a breath. "They're dying. You've seen it, haven't you, Sheriff?"

Dakota nodded. "I have."

"Then you know something strange is going on. This isn't normal. Fish don't just turn up dead in mass for no reason."

"Kelby, the sheriff isn't the sheriff anymore," Patty said. That remark got a laugh from Dakota. At least she spared him from saying anything. Judging from Kelby's tone, he was probably hoping Dakota would start an investigation into the matter.

"I know that," Kelby said. "But he's still got influence around here. Maybe he can arrange a town hall meeting or something. Or maybe call some buddies at the EPA." Kelby looked at the former sheriff. "You've still got connections, don't ya?"

"Why don't you say something to the new sheriff?" Dakota said.

"Well . . . I don't . . ."

In his twenty-seven years of law enforcement, Dakota became an expert at reading tones and body language. The way Kelby's voice trailed off and the way he broke eye contact made it clear that he remembered he was talking to the 'incompetent sheriff's' father. Kelby was an opinionated guy, but he knew when it was best to keep his mouth shut.

Dakota didn't judge. Kelby and Patty's concern was genuine. They loved these waters and their gut instinct told them something awful was happening. After all, the ocean was their livelihood.

He sighed. "Listen, there's people here from the University of Florida. They're doing some research up here. I happen to know one of them. I'll ask her if she'd be willing to run some tests on some fish I caught."

"That'd be much appreciated, sir," Kelby said.

"You're a blessing to this community," Patty said.

"Aw, shucks. You guys might make me blush."

The Dryers laughed. Kelby started the engine back up and eased on the throttle.

"Well, I'll spare you the indignity. Hopefully, we'll catch something worth selling today. Thanks for your help, Sheriff! Have a good day!"

The Dryers gave a final wave then cruised northwest to their normal fishing grounds.

Dakota watched the vessel shrink in the distance, his eyes unfazed by the oncoming rays. He looked to his left breast. No tin badge was pinned to him, yet people still looked to him to solve their troubles. And he obliged. No wonder Glenn was always pissed at him.

He boarded his own watercraft. The *Pilgrimage* was a vessel that professional fishermen could only dream of owning. In fact, a few even tried to purchase it off of him. Dakota had planned his retirement early and knew much of his activity would be spent on the water, so he saved his money and bought the best boat on the market. It was sixty-five feet from bow to stern. The flybridge stood twenty feet over the waterline. Its cargo hold was capable of storing ten-thousand pounds of catch, ranging from tuna to swordfish.

The deck was mostly clear, aside from some netting and four black fuel drums. With the boat's diesel capacity of twelve-hundred gallons, Dakota always needed to keep spare fuel on hand. The *Pilgrimage* was as hungry as the fishermen in this coastal town of Saw Ridge, and she was a fast consumer.

With a twist of the key, he awoke the vessel from its slumber. With the moorings untied, the *Pilgrimage* was free to journey into the ocean. He wouldn't have to go far out yet. The Falk's Tale Resort was only five miles north. Once he secured the whales to his towing line, then it would be time to trek further out. Whale and dolphin corpses bloated after a few hours on the beach and needed to be towed out to sea before they literally exploded. Soon, they would sink to the bottom and become food for the ocean's inhabitants below—those that were still alive.

Dakota looked to the waterline. A brown disc-shaped creature lay in the sand. A fourteen-inch flounder. They made for good fishing all year round. Like with the commercial market, sport fishermen complained of little catch these past several months.

"Looks like it didn't take me long to find a sample." He climbed down to the main deck and scooped the poor fish up with an expandable net bag. The flesh was discolored, the gill line brown. The creature had probably been dead for half a day. It was bony, but not from decay. If the fish hadn't died from an illness, then probably from starvation.

It was a job for the scientists, not a lawman. Former lawman—one who was running late for his towing job.

He climbed back to the flybridge and steered the boat north.

CHAPTER 3

"You didn't see what caused this?"

"For the fifth time, Deputy, NO!"

Sheriff Glenn McCullough closed his eyes and exhaled slowly. He reminded himself that this gentleman Jordan Burch was from out of town, thus he probably didn't know that he was the sheriff. Of course, his tan uniform shirt ought to have differentiated him from the deputies, who wore olive green shirts. That, and the fact that Deputy Andrew Zolnai and Deputy Ben Denham had repeatedly referred to him as 'Sheriff' while on the scene.

All of the carcasses were lined up on the waterline, drawing the attention of the other vacationers. The stench of water-soaked meat and organs permeated the air.

Deputy Denham walked several meters past the main lodge. "They're all over the place, Sheriff! Hard to tell, considering a few of them are effed up beyond all recognition, but I'm estimating we've got seven."

"Sounds about right."

Elena clung to her fiancé and tucked her face into his chest, refusing to look at the horrific aftermath behind them. "There was that one under the water that I tripped over. And the one that was still alive."

"They both have been washed ashore by the current," Glenn said. "Mr. Burch, when you guys stepped outside, did you notice any large vessels in the area?"

"A bunch, all in the distance. Is that unusual? Isn't this a coastal town?"

"I'm just trying to get a full picture of what happened."

"Oh! Well, that's easy. Let me spell it out to you in laymen's terms. My fiancée and I were about to go kayaking. She went out first and ended up getting knocked over by a dying killer whale. When we got ashore, we saw that the beach was full of remains. That sums it up."

"You didn't see anything that might've caused it?"

"No. Now, if you don't mind, we'd like to go home. We've got a long drive ahead of us."

Without waiting for an answer, the lovers walked past the sheriff and approached a woman standing on the lodge porch. Tris Falk, a brown-haired woman of forty with a classic hour-glass figure, held out a hand to accept the key to Jordan's cabin.

"Hope you enjoyed your stay overall. I'm sorry it ended this way."

"Yeah, me too." Jordan looked at Elena, who was tearing up. He groaned. "I'm gonna be dealing with this for the next several hours."

"Well, thank you for coming. Hope we can see you again in the future." She retained her business smile until the patrons were in their vehicle. "Apparently, it's considered bad customer service to have dead orcas wash up on your beach."

"Don't you get it, Mrs. Falk? *Clearly,* you're responsible for the wildlife in the area," Glenn said.

"I guess so! Good thing it wasn't a bunch of great whites that showed up. Imagine the blame I'd get for that!"

Glenn chuckled, then looked to the main dock. "I see Jacob's already out for the day. Does he normally leave this early in the morning?"

"He's got some divers who contracted him to take them to the *George Crest* wreck site. They wanted to get going bright and early."

Glenn adjusted his ballcap to block the sun. "Well, they definitely have the sunlight for it. I'm assuming he would've called had he seen anything unusual."

"Obviously, Glenn. I alerted you the split-second I found out about these whales. You'd already know if we spotted any strange activity around here."

"Yes, of course." Glenn exhaled sharply through his nose. It was the only way he could keep from sighing. He always believed being thorough was crucial to any investigation, and that every investigation should be taken seriously. Apparently, he was the only one who felt that. Even Deputies Zolnai and Denham were nonchalant about this situation. Sure, it was interesting. It wasn't every day that a pod of six-thousand-pound orcas was found in pieces like wood chippings from a chipper. But it wasn't national news. Had a human been found in this condition, then everybody would be up in arms about determining the cause.

The sound of a honking horn drew his attention to the driveway. The irritable Jordan Burch was yelling out his window at a Ford Escape which pulled into the driveway in the exact moment he tried speeding out.

"Get the hell out of the way!"

"Oh, go sixty-nine a polar bear!" the driver replied. She parked in an empty slot and stepped out. When her eyes met the sheriff's, her bitter expression transformed into one of joy. "Glenn! Long time, no see!"

"Dr. Lehnert! Good to see you, ma'am."

"Oh, quit the 'doctor' and 'ma'am' stuff. You know better. Call me Siena." She walked to the beach and gave him a hug.

"Your wish is my command, Siena."

She looked at his badge. "So, *Sheriff*, I see things have changed a bit since I last saw you."

"A few things, not all of them good," he said.

Siena's eyes widened. "Everything all right?" She stepped back. "Oh, no. Is your father all right?"

Glenn raised his hands to calm her. "Whoa! No, no, no! I guess I need work on my sarcasm. I was referring to *them*." He tilted his head toward the dead orcas. "My first murder case is an odd one."

Siena eased up then chuckled. "Oh, sorry. Thank goodness." She laughed a little harder. "I used to get on your dad's case about those fast-food drive-throughs. Warned him he was on track to put himself in an early grave. How is he, anyway?"

"He's good. Retired, obviously."

"Still in town?"

"Yep." Glenn tried to think of something more to say. His mind instead fixated on the fact that his tone expressed disappointment. Irritation flooded his senses like a rising tide. *Dad's always talked about moving, except he won't.* Guilt followed the sentiment. His father did well in raising him. If Glenn had an issue, it centered around ego. It had been over half a year, and he was still in his dad's shadow. The effective police policies in force were already set by the previous administration. It was when something needed adjusting that the public expressed discontent with his leadership.

Awkward silence took over.

Siena cleared her throat and looked at the beach. "Yeah—so, I'm curious to find out what happened. I've been tracking this pod for two years."

"Why don't you take a look?"

"Sounds good."

"Hey, Glenn? Call in a consultant?" Tris Falk asked.

Their walk stopped after two steps. Glenn turned to face the lodge owner. "She's a marine biologist from the University of Florida here on another matter. I've asked her to inspect the situation and see if she could offer any advice."

"Oh. Okay."

"Tris! How are you?" Siena said. "You probably don't remember me. I stayed at your resort a few years back when my university sent me to do research up here."

Tris thought about it for a moment. 'Dr. Siena Lehnert' Glenn had called her a minute ago. Then it hit her. "Oh! Holy crap, I do remember! You brought that big boat that was a little too big for our docks."

"Yeah, sorry about that. I was just hoping to find a cheap spot where I could take to the water whenever I pleased. Made my work a hell of a lot easier."

"Oh, no worries. We made it work," Tris said. "I didn't know you were back in town."

"More work. As you know, it never ends." Siena looked at the line of cabins lining the beach and the various people moving about. "How's business? Looks like you're doing well for yourselves."

"It could be worse," Tris said. She looked to the sheriff. "So, should I assume this'll take a while? I wasn't anticipating actual forensics to deal with dead whales."

Glenn wasn't in the mood for nosiness. The only reason he tolerated it from Ms. Falk was because it was her property. It was additionally frustrating because she wasn't usually the type to ask questions. If there was an issue, she usually reported it and let the cops do their work.

"It's illegal for anyone to kill orcas. If this was done by people, I want to know about it. Is there a problem?"

Tris shook her head. "Not at all. It's just that I already had your office hire a contractor, who's probably already on his way."

"Beg your pardon?"

"Come on, Sheriff. I don't want these things stinking up my property. I have clients here who are eager to enjoy the beach. Hard to do that when it's lined with blood and guts. Jacob's gonna have to comb through the sand, dredge the shallows in case there's other remains . . . I'd like to get started sooner rather than later."

"Be nice if you said something."

"When your dispatcher didn't object, I figured it was fine," Tris said.

"Ma'am, I need to conduct an investigation."

"Sorry. I simply figured they got diced in a boat propellor or got mauled by a group of sharks, or something like that. My usual contractor is out of town and Jacob's busy, so I called your office to ask if they had anyone who could help. I certainly didn't think it was anything worth looking into."

Another exhale, followed by a deep breath. Glenn nodded and forced a smile. Getting the shape of that grin right was a struggle that rivaled getting a druggie's hands behind his back.

"I'll make this as fast as I can." He walked alongside the marine biologist to the water line. "What do you think, Doctor—Siena? Could sharks have done this?"

"Unlikely," Siena said.

"Well, Doc, we're looking at an unlikely scenario," Glenn said. "We've got a pod of killer whales that have been butchered. Can you assure me that we don't have to worry about a killer fish? I ask because anything that could do this to a pod of whales could do worse to someone swimming in the water."

He heard one of the deputies chuckle. Denham most likely, since he quickly looked away when Glenn glanced over. Was thoroughness really this frowned upon by all his deputies? Glenn refused to let himself get distracted by their silent judgments.

"Sharks, even great whites, usually avoid killer whales like a sheep would a wolf. Killer whales on average have ten feet of length and three thousand pounds of mass over them. Size matters in a fight, no matter how sharp your teeth are. Also, orcas are technically dolphins, not actual whales. That's an important fact to consider, because like other species of dolphins, orcas act in packs. Great whites and most other sharks are loners. The odds of any species of shark causing this much damage to these creatures is zilch, despite what you might see in the movies."

Glenn nodded. "Understood. What about other orcas? Would they attack each other? Judging by those jaws, I'd say they're more than capable of doing this kind of damage."

Another snicker. Glenn spun on his heel and looked at his deputy. "Something funny, Denham?"

"Not at all, sir," the scrawny, scruffy-faced deputy said. Glenn stared at him, unsure whether he should address the failure to match up to grooming standards. Then again, he'd have to have a meeting with half the department. He swore that under his dad's tenure, everyone respected the rank of sheriff. Now, it seemed everyone showed up and did their own thing.

He ignored it for now in favor of focusing on the current case.

Siena was kneeling by the nearest corpse. She clenched her teeth as she took in the extent of its many injuries. There were multiple wounds that would have been individually fatal. The fluke was gone, the stomach torn open. The right flipper was missing, as was the whole right side of its face. The flesh on the other side was tattered. Even if it could still swim, infection would have led to an agonizing death. Then again, that might've been preferable to whatever did occur. There was more. The dorsal fin was gone, depriving the mammal of the ability to regulate its body temperature. Siena almost attributed the injuries to a boat propellor, which could have explained the damage to the fluke and fins. As the creature drifted with the current, sharks and other fish could have picked at it, creating the other wounds. It would have made sense if it wasn't for the most unusual injury.

Numerous tears, all averaging two inches in width, stretched in various lengths down its body. Some were as short as a couple of inches, while others ran the length of its upper body.

"Strange." She looked down the shore at the other relatively intact corpses. "Have you or your deputies noticed these lacerations on any of the others?"

Deputy Zolnai raised his hand. "Yes, ma'am."

"The exact same as these?"

"Pretty similar," Zolnai said. "They don't follow any particular pattern. Some are more lateral, going from the back to the stomach."

"That's strange." Siena removed a pen from her pocket and pressed into one of the cuts. "Almost three inches deep." She checked another cut. Same depth. "I've never seen anything like this before. Boat propellor wouldn't have made these kinds of lacerations. And they're not consistent with shark bites."

"I'm worried it was poachers," Glenn said. "It's the only thing that makes sense to me. They could've taken a machete and slashed these poor things."

"I don't think so, Glenn. There's no market for orca meat, and they don't produce oil like large whales do. It'd be a waste of time and resources for anyone to do this. Plus, there's another issue." She waved him over to stand by her, then ran her pen through the wound again. "This cut is not made by a razor blade. See how the meat is tattered all along the edges? Whatever did this had a sharp point but did not have a blade for cutting. Something dull sliced this flesh."

"Dull? Like the back edge of a knife?"

Siena shrugged. "Your guess is as good as mine. But it wasn't done by a human unless you have some crazed maniac on the loose. Even that would not likely result in this." She removed a few plastic vials from her kit and took tissue samples from the orcas.

"What's that for?" Glenn asked, walking beside her.

"I'd like to test toxicity levels."

"I don't think these guys died of a drug overdose."

"No, but I'm still curious. If there's dioxin in their system, then maybe whatever happened here is somehow related to the reason I'm up here."

"And that is?"

"I've been sent up here to study the toxicity levels in the local waters. Whole schools of populations have gone missing within the past month. Such a fast change is not the result of overfishing. Surely, you've received letters of concern from the local fishermen."

"I have," Glenn said. He didn't say anything further. Better to stay silent and be thought a fool than speak and remove all doubt. The EPA had contacted him two weeks ago regarding concerns of the dwindling fish populations. He had his own staff test the local waters and found minimal trace of poison. Anything beyond that was not his jurisdiction.

This led to further comparisons to his father, who would have travelled well beyond the jurisdictional boundary to get to the bottom of the matter.

Siena's expression grew increasingly serious. She didn't like grilling the sheriff. She knew he was a nice young man, but it was clear his ambition outmatched his skill. There was a possible ecological disaster unfolding in his own hometown, and he was clueless as to what to do about it.

"So, what have you done about this?"

"What is there to do?" Glenn said. "Can't arrest the ocean for fish turning up dead. We've done tests and found nothing."

"What about the fish themselves?"

"Fishermen won't give them up. They discard the dead ones and only keep what they can sell."

"Well, you'd probably be interested to know that there have been reports of people getting dioxin poisoning in various states along the Northeast coast. There're still investigations pending, but each case has a common thread—they've gotten sick after eating fish. The markets that have been checked have provided their invoices. Each case traces back to fish brought in by local fishermen *here.*"

Glenn swallowed. "I never heard about this."

"Then it's a good thing I said something, because you will."

Glenn turned and looked at the water. He couldn't hold the stone-faced expression any longer, and he didn't want Siena to see him go pale.

"We'll run more tests. I'll speak with some of the local markets and see if I can collect some—oh, you've got to be kidding me!"

"What's the matter?" Siena asked. Glenn gestured at the sixty-five-foot vessel approaching from the south. The biologist shrugged. "What's the matter? It's just the contractor."

Glenn sighed. "Why'd Dispatch call *him*?"

"Call who?"

He hesitated to answer. Thinking out loud always got him into trouble. His back was against the wall now.

"Dad."

"Oh . . ." Siena's hands began to quiver suddenly. Was this excitement or dread? She hated mixed emotions. When she arrived in town, she convinced herself to avoid the coastal properties as much as possible. No point in reliving the past.

Looks like I don't have a choice.

***

The shoreline of Saw Ridge lived up to its name. The coastal town was made up of a series of jagged coves and small peninsulas. From high above, it resembled the toothy edge of a handsaw.

Dakota embraced the mist of saltwater against his face as he drove the boat north. As far as he was concerned, retirement was a double-edged sword. On the one hand, the sense of freedom was priceless. It took a few weeks of getting used to, but Dakota loved not having to report to an office Monday through Friday. Better yet, he could enjoy his off time without worrying about receiving any phone calls from the station. No more internal drama between staff. No more criminals, not that crime was bad in Saw Ridge, but sometimes the fishermen got a little rowdy.

It was the worst during times of economic hardship. The fishing community did not have the luxury of bi-weekly paychecks. Their income was based on the catch they brought in. Like in every industry, fishing had its highs and lows, and not all fishermen were financially savvy enough to plan for the lows. On more than one occasion, he was forced to arrest desperate people in various acts of desperate crime. In one case, a young fisherman with a family of four was caught trying to sabotage another resident's boat. It was a tactic of reducing the competition. Unfortunately, it landed him six months in jail—six months he could have been grinding out at least a modest income. It resulted in his own nightmare coming true. The house was foreclosed on and he and his wife forced to live in a van.

In another case, he arrested a fisherman who was using illegal drift nets and traps to bump his numbers up. That offense could have resulted in a simple fine had Dakota not seen the dead dolphins that got caught. Wildlife Services did not take well to this. It was two years of jail time and the removal of that gentleman's fishing license. The irony was that a year later, many new schools of mackerel had moved into the area, leading to a boost in productivity.

These memories made Dakota grateful not to be sheriff anymore. This year was looking to be the hardest ever for Saw Ridge. Men were in competition to get jobs at the local grocery stores. When proud men were close to blows for a part-time bagging position, he knew they were aching.

Looking at the boats in the far distance, it was easy to imagine the tension that currently seized the town. Dakota felt a tad guilty for the odd jobs he took over the last several months. With his pension from the county, he was more than well off for the rest of his many years. Even more so in twelve years, when he would start withdrawing from his Roth IRA. He felt like a rich man in a crowd of starving people. He knew they could use the work. Yet, he couldn't bring himself to turn the jobs down.

With retirement and middle age came loneliness. Dakota was a man who always planned for the next task, but he never braced for the reality of what this new stage of life would bring. He had no wife. His son hardly spoke with him. He felt heavy. A lack of purpose had a way of weighing on a man.

Ever since he was a child, purpose was never an issue. There was always a new goal to work toward. Unlike most kids, he enjoyed school for the most part. Then at twenty-one, he completed the police academy and scored a job with the county.

Two months in, he became a shining star, not only with the department, but the county as a whole. The silver ring on his right hand was a reminder to always act fast and use your head. Every year, he had the ring cleaned.

Bell Greany, the wife of a film producer, was thirty-seven weeks pregnant, and accompanying her husband who was looking to build a film set in a neighboring county. During their drive through the town to get to their location, the baby decided it wanted to come early.

It was a young Dakota McCullough who responded to that call. He delivered the baby before the ambulance even arrived. The fun didn't stop there. The poor little guy was not breathing. Slapping his rear didn't help. The kid was suffocating on his own gunk. When Dakota learned CPR, he figured he'd use it eventually, but on an adult or a teen. Not a freshly born child. Twenty-eight years later, he still remembered the sensation of trembling hands holding the tiny thing. Two fingers pressed into the baby's chest. In the blink of an eye, the little guy went from silent to wailing like a police siren.

The EMTs arrived afterward and later confirmed that the odds of the baby's survival would have been slim had he not acted. Grateful for the young deputy's actions, the film producer moved his set into Saw Ridge. The town saw economic prosperity for the rest of the year, then an increase in tourism in the years that followed. The film that was produced was a moderate success, but it was enough to draw people to the county. Vacationers were always looking for a place to charter a boat and fish. Why not do it while also seeing the shooting locations for *Waterspout*?

Since then, Dakota knew that every shift meant something. Every time he put on that badge, it meant a life saved. Now, he woke up to an empty house. There was no purpose except waiting for death. Every relationship failed miserably. Glenn's mother left after he was born. Getting the letter from her cousin was one of two major low points in his life. The other was when he was literally left at the altar. The rehearsal had gone smoothly, the bridal and groom parties all dressed up, and over a hundred people were seated and ready to witness the grand event. The music came on and everyone turned to see the bride walk down the aisle. Instead, it was one of her work friends, wearing regular clothes, rushing up to the altar to whisper the bad news to Dakota. Wanda had run off with someone else.

Getting back into law enforcement was not an option. His joints and back couldn't take the duty belt and heavy vest any longer. Genetics had not been kind to him. Two slipped discs had played havoc on his nerves since the age of thirty; he kept them in place through moderate exercise. All he had were these odd jobs.

Speaking of odd jobs . . .

His self-reflection came to an end when he saw the line of white cottages to the left. Seven twenty-foot docks protruded from the beach, and farther south was a long pier that lined up with the main lodge. He couldn't see Jacob Falk's boat, but he could see some of the killer whales. Maggie from Dispatch was not kidding—there really was a whole pod of them dead. Not just dead. *Butchered.*

Glenn was easy to spot. He was a tad shorter than the deputies, and always stood with his right thumb tucked under his belt. Dakota's favorite feature was the brown hair and pointed widow's peak, an exact match of his own.

As excited as he was to see his son, it was the woman standing beside him that made Dakota's heart flutter. It was the first time he'd seen Siena in three years. From the looks of it, she hadn't aged a day. She was the same gorgeous strawberry blonde that broke his heart before departing for Florida.

He didn't prescribe well to the 'I have to leave. My job won't let me stay' mentality. She claimed she didn't want to continue the relationship, but Dakota knew a lie when he heard one. Unfortunately, calling it out was not the best judgement.

Tris Falk was waiting at the main pier. He brought the boat alongside it and tossed her the mooring.

"Good morning!" he said in his usual happy-go-lucky voice. "I'm here to shovel roadkill for the county."

"Hi, Sheriff. Dakota. Good to see you."

He gave her a hug. "Good to see you, too. Don't worry, everyone still calls me that." He looked past her at the actual sheriff, who seemed to be deliberately looking away. Embarrassment and stress. Dakota had both experienced it himself and seen it in others. The office of the sheriff had highs and lows, and Glenn was going through the latter.

"So, they just turned up dead?"

"That's correct," Tris said. "Not sure what caused it. Scared the hell out of my clients. I have people waiting to enjoy the waters. It's a hot day, and they pay decent money to be here. I'd like this beach cleared as soon as possible. Glenn and the doctor have taken tissue samples and recordings of the, uh, injuries. Not sure what the endgame is, but I'm not a cop."

"Well, leave it to me. I'll have your beach sparkly clean in no time." He marched onto the sand.

Right away, Deputy Zolnai approached him with open arms. "Hey! Boss! How are you?!"

"Hi, Andrew. I see you still have that mustard stain on your collar."

Zolnai looked at the neck of his uniform shirt, then smiled nervously. "Whoops! I forgot all about that. I'll get that neatened up this weekend."

Now, Glenn had completely turned away, in the way someone did when they were muttering something to themselves. He had probably instructed Zolnai to clean up multiple times before.

Denham approached and shook hands with him. "Good to see you again. Why don't you visit us at the station?"

"Why the hell would he visit your ugly face?" Zolnai said.

"Hey, at least I manage to keep the mustard on my hot dog!"

"Denham, you look like you could use a hot dog." Dakota tapped the deputy's slim belly. "Jesus, you look like a teenage girl that's been purging."

"Happens naturally. Side effect of my wife's cooking."

Dakota laughed along with his former employees, then turned to look at Siena. As he'd determined when approaching the shore, she looked exactly the same. She wore the same white button-down shirt and gray trousers as before, and she still had that single freckle below her left eye. The only difference was that her hair was cut low, just below the ear. He used to think short hair would not work on her, but now he was eating those words. It looked great on her.

She was looking back at him, her mild shakes exposing nervous anticipation.

He stepped forward and pointed a finger. "You!"

Siena stepped back, her mouth dropping. "Uh, hi, Dakota. I'm just here to—"

"You have any idea what you've stolen from me? The hole you left in my heart?"

"I—can we talk later?"

"No, I want an answer now."

"But what's done is done. I'm sorry, Dakota . . . I can't change what we went through."

"What? 'What's done is done'? That takes nerve to say. Every winter, I feel the loss. I figured if you had the balls to show up here, you'd have the curtesy to make things right."

Now, Siena was getting defensive. "Make things right? What do you want from me?"

"Isn't it obvious?" Dakota crossed his arms. "I want my Green Bay Packers sweater back."

Siena froze, then absorbed the words. She looked down, face beet red. How could she not have expected that?

The two of them broke into intense laughter.

"Well, I'm sorry for the damage I caused," she said after several moments. "I figured since they've been playing like shit lately, that I've been doing you a favor."

"Oh, God. Don't remind me. Worst part is that in a little over a month I'll have to suffer through it again," Dakota said. He stepped up to her and smiled. "How are you, Siena? Or should I call you Doctor? Professor?"

"Oh, Dakota, you know not to bother with the formalities. I'm good. How are you? I know better than to call you sheriff anymore."

"I can't complain." He looked at Glenn, who pretended to be studying the corpses. "For the most part."

Finally, the sheriff looked at his father. "Dad. How you feeling this morning?"

"A little stiff. Comes with age."

"Oh, quit being so dramatic. You talk like you're seventy years old," Siena said.

"I feel like it, especially if I've been sitting too long. My knees have practically formed their own band. Clickity-clack!"

"So . . . do you have any theories on what happened here?" Tris said. She was making an effort to be her usual polite self, while making her true desire evident: 'Can you finish up so I can get back to business?'

"We're trying to figure that out," Glenn said.

"No, I was talking to . . ." She tilted her head in Dakota's direction.

Glenn clenched his jaw and nodded. "Oh. Pardon me."

Dakota approached the nearest carcass, studied its injuries, then proceeded to the next one—if the next one could even be considered a carcass. It was pretty much a heap of pieces barely held together by strings of flesh.

"The only thought I had coming here was poachers, but looking at this, it just doesn't make sense. One orca, maybe. A whole pod? Not a chance in hell."

"Nothing else adds up," Glenn said. "And it's plenty possible that a poacher did this. They could have been armed with high-caliber rifles and shot these orcas first, then diced them up."

"That's a decent thought," Dakota said. He walked to one of the more intact carcasses. "Except, to kill these things quickly, they'd have to plant a headshot. I don't see any bullet hole in this one here. And what's the endgame? Unless we're dealing with a crazed maniac, there's no motivation for killing orcas."

"What about this one here?" Glenn said. "Half its face is missing. Maybe it was shot and . . ."

"There'd still be traces of the bullet hole," Dakota said. Glenn tucked both thumbs under his belt. It was the only way he could keep himself from crossing his arms and looking too obviously frustrated. Dakota knew better. "There is another possibility."

"What's that?" Tris asked.

"Maybe these guys died first and then got butchered."

"How could they have died?"

"Maybe it has something to do with whatever's causing the fish population to nosedive. Maybe they died, then drifted to shore. In the process, they got nibbled on by sharks and other fish."

"There is merit to that theory," Siena said. "I'm taking samples to test for toxicity. However, I'm not sure if that's what happened. Many of these injuries are inconsistent with all known marine life in this area. There isn't much here to indicate shark bites, that's for sure."

"We're going in circles," Glenn said.

"Over killer whales," Tris added.

Dakota continued walking along the shoreline. He stopped near the open jaw of one of them, then removed some pliers from his tool belt.

"Find something?" Deputy Denham asked.

"Couple things, actually." He lifted a small, bony object that was embedded in the orca's jawline. It was a couple of inches long, broken off at the stub. It was curved and pointed, like a cat's claw. "Siena, you recognize this?"

She took it from him. "No. Too big for a bird. Doesn't seem to be a tooth, though it seems to have high-calcium density." She looked at the jaw. Something black was sticking out of the gums. "Is that . . . metal?"

Dakota raised a small black sliver from the orca's teeth. "Yep. That's not nearly as weird as what's stuck on the back tooth." He reached down and pried another black object free. This one was more rubbery than solid. He bent it in his grip and ran his fingertips over it. "Carbon fiber."

"Wait? These guys were messing with the power line?" Denham said.

"That's what it looks like," Dakota said. "Any word from the power company? No reports of surges or outages? No issues with the lighthouse over on Lockhart Island?" Glenn shook his head. "All the same, you might want to get divers out here to inspect it. Two boating units should head out. Have one study the drop off with underwater cameras, and someone else should check for electric currents by the cable. Don't want to send divers down just for them to get zapped."

"I'll volunteer for that duty!" Zolnai said.

"What? To get zapped?" Denham said.

Zolnai punched his shoulder. "No. To inspect the water, genius."

"Well, I'm driving the boat. You'd be in England before you find the cable." The two men walked to their squad car.

Glenn opened his mouth to intervene but stopped himself. These idiots were following orders from someone who was not their superior. However, he didn't know what to say. He had no alternative plan of action. All he could contribute was a delay in the investigation.

Zolnai sat in the driver's seat and waved to the group. "See ya, Sheriff."

"See ya," Glenn replied. Zolnai's grin faded, his brow wrinkling. Rather than admit his mistake, he shut the door and drove off.

"Hey! Mind if get myself *in* the vehicle first?!" Denham yelled, half hanging out the passenger side. Zolnai slowed long enough for his partner to secure himself in his seat, then sped off for the police dock.

Dakota laughed. "Some things don't change."

"I guess not," Glenn said. His tone lacked the humor of his father's.

Dakota's smile shrank. "I was just giving recommendations, not orders. I'm not trying to step on your toes, kid."

"Dude, you mind . . ." Glenn controlled his voice. "You mind not calling me that?"

"Sorry. Force of habit. Didn't think it was condescending. You *are* my kid."

Realizing he was only digging himself a deeper hole, Glenn walked to his vehicle. "Sorry. Got a lot on my plate."

"That's part of the job, son. I warned you about this when you decided to throw your hat in the ring."

"Right." The sheriff opened his car door. "Good to see you again, Siena. Don't let him bother you too much."

Dakota waved as his son drove off. *So much for the joy of seeing you.* There was no weight like the misery of your own kid resenting you.

He turned his attention to Siena. Unlike Glenn, there was actually a hint of joy in her eyes. A faint hint, but it was there.

What's on your mind, Doc? Happy to see me but don't want to admit it?

"Well, I better get to work. You probably have things you need to work on, so don't let me hold you up."

"No, not at all," Siena said. "Just let me take a few more measurements, and . . ."

Dakota waited for the second part of that sentence, which never came. "And?"

"I was hoping to talk to you."

"Most ladies do."

She scoffed. "Wow, you! You really haven't changed a bit, have you?"

"Maybe. I'm as handsome as ever, smart as ever, and right as ever. What were you hoping to talk to me about?"

"Can you help me talk to the fishermen about getting fish samples so I can test them for dioxin?"

"Talk to them? Why me?"

"I figure they might listen to you."

"No need for that. I actually have some samples on my boat," he said. "There's a flounder that washed up. Pretty much the only thing I've caught in a week."

"Oh, good. If you don't mind . . ."

"It's all yours. Do whatever mad scientist stuff you want with it."

Siena rolled her eyes. "I don't think tissue samples qualify as that. Uh, you mention you haven't caught anything in a while?"

"Correct."

"Where are your fishing grounds?"

"About six miles out due east," he said.

"Would . . ." Siena's voice trailed off. "Would you be willing to take me out there? I'd like to take a look with my underwater drone."

"You don't have a boat? I figured the university would have supplied you with some decent toys."

"Oh, they do. Only Dr. Berman gets to hog them up. She's got the boat and is doing research at the Submarine Canyon."

"Ah," Dakota said. He cracked a small grin and looked Siena in the eye. "I suppose I could take you out."

Siena narrowed her gaze in her best attempt to look stern. "On the water."

"Right. On the water." That smile failed to waiver. "Sure there's nothing else you want to talk with me about?"

"No."

"No? Nothing else on your mind?"

"Just the assistance with research. I figured you're retired, so you have the time."

"Of course," Dakota said. "Anything to contribute to science."

CHAPTER 4

"All right, you epic dumbass." Deputy Denham held the ignition key in place, glancing at his partner before turning it. "Anything else we forgot before we head out there *again*?"

Zolnai rolled his eyes at what he perceived as an overreaction. So what if he had forgotten the amprobe rod at the station and only realized it when they were on the water? Not like they would be doing anything special in the meantime. Usually, they were driving around mindlessly in these early morning hours.

"What's the rush? Got a date?"

"No, but in case you haven't noticed, Glenn's a little more impatient today than usual."

"No shit. He doesn't know what he's doing," Zolnai said. "You think he got elected because of his resume?" Denham looked across the pier in search of other officers. "Oh, stop being such a wuss! Even if someone heard you, what are they gonna do, rat you out? To whom?"

Denham nodded. "Fair point." Never in his fifteen years as a cop had he seen a leader so universally despised by his staff. There was no personal disdain felt toward the young sheriff, but when going from Dakota to Glenn, it was impossible not to notice the decline in leadership quality.

He started the boat and took them out to the location. Twice, he checked the drawer for some Tylenol. Frustration accompanied the pain.

Ugh. Not a summer cold!

It was a slap in the face, for the summer was usually his reprieve from getting sick. For whatever reason, his immune system and the ocean didn't mesh well. It was only May through August when he didn't get sick. September through April was a long stretch of hell, January and February being the worst. Every year, he caught at least five colds. This was July! His break from this nonsense.

It was worse. He recognized the pressure between his eyes.

If this is a sinus infection, I might have to kill someone.

"It doesn't make sense."

Speaking of which . . .

"What doesn't make sense?" Denham said, keeping his eyes on the horizon.

"The carbon fiber. Why would orcas mess with a power line? I've heard of sea animals getting curious about these kinds of things, but not do anything like this."

Denham could not even pretend to be interested. "I don't know."

"Sharks make sense. They bite things all the time. That's how they inspect things. Sharks are scavengers as much as they are hunters. You learn about this stuff watching nature shows."

Denham closed his eyes. *Oh, my freaking lord! Is he* trying *to make this migraine worse?*

"But whales? Well, the doctor said they're not whales, but you know what I mean. They don't usually do shit like this."

"I don't know," Denham said. Those were the only words he could manage that were not a threat to Zolnai's physical health. For a couple of minutes, he was graced with silence. During that time, his sanity began to reemerge. The wind against his face was soothing. Better yet, there was a packet of ibuprofen in the cabinet near the flare gun. He took it dry and continued driving.

In ten minutes, they reached the cable. The plan would be long and tedious, checking every few hundred meters for electrical surges, starting with the first buoy marker.

Zolnai dipped the rod into the water, held it there for ten seconds, then looked at the LED screen on the handle.

"All good here," he said. Denham took the boat further east. A *thump* echoed through the hull. "Jeez, Deputy! Watch your driving. You damage these buoys, then the county will be all up Glenn's ass. Then you'll really see him in a cranky mood."

Denham waved him off.

The next spot produced the same results. No electrical discharges, meaning no breach in the underwater cable. Same with the next, the next, and the next.

With each inspection, Denham's headache lifted a little more. Usually, ibuprofen had iffy results, especially with dulling sinus headaches. Maybe it was not so severe after all. Maybe it was simply a minor cold.

Maybe I should stop stressing so much, then I wouldn't get sick so often.

"Hey! Look who it is!"

"Who?"

Zolnai snorted. "You blind? Up there to the left?" He waved. "Good morning, Mr. Falk!"

Denham snapped out of his droning existence and looked to the huge boat coming in from the northeast. At its helm was a man in his late fifties with a Detroit Tigers ballcap covering his balding scalp.

"What's going on, Officers? Trouble with the cable?"

"Not that we can see," Zolnai said. "You know those orcas that washed up on your beach?"

"Yeah, Tris told me through the radio. I was out before they showed up."

"Up and at 'em early today, aren't ya?"

"Well, I got some divers with me. They wanted to get a peek at one of the wrecks this morning."

"Yeah? Which one?" Zolnai said.

"*George Crest.*"

"Hope they paid you extra." Zolnai stood on his toes. "You didn't leave them at the wreck, did ya? I don't see anyone aboard."

"Ha! No, these fellas are actually pleasant. They're below, getting dried up. So, what do killer whales have to do with the power cable?"

"We found a little hint that they might have bitten it," Zolnai said. "Carbon fiber in its mouth. Weird, illogical, but it was there. So we're checking for electrical readings. So far, so good."

"Gotcha." Jacob pointed at the helmsman. "He talk?"

"When he feels like it." Zolnai playfully tapped Denham's shoulder. "He's a little under the weather. Nothing a little chicken soup won't cure."

Denham groaned. *Duct tape over your mouth might work wonders.*

"Well, good luck, Deputies. I better get back." Jacob waved and throttled ahead.

"Good day, mister!" Zolnai leaned against the gunwale and glared at his partner. "Gosh, can't even muster a hello? He's a nice guy."

Denham considered arguing but had the self-control to hold back. Zolnai wasn't wrong. Jacob was simply giving them a nice hello, and all he did was sit there like an angry teenager who was dragged to a boring family function. The good news was his headache was lifting.

"Yeah, I suppose you're right."

"I'm right?" Zolnai stepped forward and put a hand on his partner's brow.

"The hell you doing?"

"Just seeing if you have a fever. For you to admit I'm right, you *must* be sick."

"Oh, shut up." He smacked Zolnai's hand away, then resumed driving the boat. After a few moments, he cracked a smile. "Smart ass."

Thump!

"Oh, great! There you go not paying attention to where you're going," Zolnai said. "If you busted a buoy, then we might as well chew on that power cable ourselves."

Denham throttled back. "I don't know what I hit."

"Not a lot of options. We're traveling above the cable. Nothing but markers out here."

"Except the next one is up there." Denham pointed ahead. Zolnai gazed east and saw the big red ball floating a couple hundred feet ahead of them.

A few additional thumps echoed through the hull. Zolnai looked over the side. "Huh?"

"What is it? What do you see?"

The deputy reached over the side, his feet nearly coming off the deck. When he straightened himself out, he had a big purple kayak in hand. He leaned it against the side and backed away in disgust.

"Damn." Zolnai shook his hands. Tiny droplets sprinkled Denham's pantleg and slowly rolled down. They were not water.

Whatever this slimy residue was, it was all over the kayak.

"Smells like shit. What the hell is it?" Zolnai said.

"The better question is why the hell is a kayak drifting all the way out here?" Denham said. "We're a mile and a half from shore."

"There's *two* people I know of that would come this far out this early, actually," Zolnai said. He was sweating now. He turned the kayak over so the seat was facing inward. On the forward deck was a gold star symbol, with the words Gold Star Fitness underneath it.

CHAPTER 5

Dakota watched the floating corpses slowly drift toward the horizon. Had the orcas all been relatively intact, it would have taken several trips to tow them out. With many of them in literal pieces, he was able to do it in one.

Siena was on the deck, prepping her drone. It was an expensive-looking piece of equipment, a little bigger than a truck tire. It had little mechanical arms sticking out the sides, giving it the appearance of a big crab.

"Sorry for the stench. Happens when you deal with fish and, well, dead killer whales," he said.

Siena shook her head. "Oh, stop. You don't need to apologize for that."

"Oh. Well, I guess I'll stop." He climbed down and dropped the anchor. "If you haven't already guessed, we're here."

"This is where you usually fish?"

"Yep. Whenever I *do* fish," he said. "I try to leave most of it to the community most of the time."

"Have other people who fished around here reported the same luck?"

Dakota glanced to the north. "We can ask them after you do your dive."

Siena looked and saw the big white boat two thousand yards in the distance. "Who are they?"

"I think it's Kelby and Pattie Dryer. I saw them earlier taking off for some trawling. Nice people. Struggling right now, though. Much like everyone else." He watched Siena test the arms of her device. They reached out, then recoiled. Again, he was reminded of a crab's motions. "Will it turn red if I boil it?"

"No," Siena said, chuckling. A few moments of silence took over while she worked. "So, when did you get a fishing license?"

"Pretty much as soon as I retired."

"Got bored that quick, huh?"

"Maybe. I don't know."

Siena switched on her control module, then looked up at him. "You don't know? Is that regret I'm hearing?"

"I—don't know." He shrugged. "I mean, I knew it was time to retire. I'm just starting to doubt if I'm meant for the life of a retiree. At the same time, I'm not fit to go back to regular work. I joke about feeling eighty years old, but honestly, that's really how I feel. It was time to hang up the badge and gun."

"You need a hobby. There's always knitting."

"Look who brought her sense of humor up from Florida," Dakota said. "Then again, I remember you didn't used to joke a lot. I recall the Dr. Lehnert that showed up here three years ago had a boring, schoolteacher attitude. Didn't believe in fun, until someone I know convinced her to come to the Swordfish Bar for some music and beer."

She grinned. "It was the only way I could get rid of the creep. I couldn't call the police, so I was screwed."

"Then we got a few beers in ya, and WHOA! Suddenly you were up for shots, schooling everyone in darts, giving the guys a hard time for ordering wings with mild spices."

"I spent four years in Texas. They eat jalapenos like pickles down there. I guess it manned up my taste buds. It pained me to see grown ass dudes eating like girls."

"Right . . ."

"Yeah, 'right!'" she said. "Don't think I've forgotten the look on your face when you tried the spicy wings. I had to make you regret hounding me for a date somehow."

"Did it work?"

"Unfortunately, no. It was like you took it as a personal challenge." She stood up and lifted the drone.

"So, how 'bout a trip to Swordfish after we're done here?"

"No."

"Gosh, it's like an exact replay," he said.

Siena cleared her throat. "I'm seeing someone."

Dakota's smile gradually fell. "Oh . . ."

"Yeah." She looked away, feeling embarrassed for him. The poor guy was probably both sad and humiliated. Wanting to move away from the subject, she put her drone in the water. "I guess I should have said something before. I was hoping to avoid this all together . . . What are you doing?" He was standing still with his arms crossed, watching her. When no answer came, Siena pressed again. "What is it?"

He grinned. "You're lying."

"I am not!"

"Oh, yeah. Now I know for sure. Definitely calling bullshit on that."

"It's not bullshit. I've been seeing this guy for eighteen months. His name is Frank. He works at the university. He studies desalination in the polar ice caps and its effect on the local wildlife."

"Every word you say is proving my point further."

"What?!"

"Desalination, Frank, eighteen months . . . you had this whole story scripted in your mind. Want me to hire you an agent?"

"You don't . . ." The control module nearly dropped from Siena's quivering hand. She juggled it around until she secured a grasp on it. She closed her eyes, sucked in a breath, then sneered at him. "No, it's true! I'm seeing someone. We're talking about moving in together."

"Yeah? Your place or his?"

"What does it matter?"

"Ah, I see."

"See what?"

"You're off script now. You didn't originally plan on adding 'moving in together' as part of the narrative, so now you're scrounging for details."

"I . . . you . . ." Siena stammered. She looked up and prayed for strength. "Dakota, I'm seeing someone. I'm sorry if that hurts you." She sat on the deck with the module and activated the thrusters. After a few moments, she felt brave enough to peek at Dakota. The prick still had that grin on his face. Nothing was going to convince him that she was seeing Frank.

Together, they watched the monitor. The drone cruised through a hundred feet of depth, then reached the bottom.

It was like gazing at a miniature desert. The only sign of life was scattered patches of seaweed, reaching for the sun's light.

Siena steered the drone in a three-hundred-mile radius. The spotlights, along with the natural illumination provided by the sun, offered ample visibility.

"Odd. I haven't seen a single living thing so far," she said.

"Plenty of dead ones, though," Dakota said. Siena turned the drone to the right. Dead crabs lay belly-up, their shells pale from lifelessness.

"Still craving crab legs?"

Dakota shook his head.

Several yards north, the drone crossed a school of dead mackerel. Bacterial growth and fungus reached from their raw flesh like tendrils. Dakota was no wildlife expert, but he knew bodies and rates of decay. Part of the job was inspecting a house due to a horrid smell, which unfortunately led to him discovering the rotting body of someone who'd died unexpectedly. People, dogs, cats—he'd seen enough death in various stages of decay.

These fish had been dead for at least a week.

"Fish don't randomly die in large numbers," he said.

"No, they don't. Something's killing them." She hit a few buttons on her module. A second camera angle popped up on the screen, showing a third arm stretched from the drone's right side.

"What are you doing?"

"Taking water samples," Siena said. "Your son might have to get in touch with the EPA. I suspect there's been some sort of toxic spill nearby."

"Nobody's seen or heard anything. The only major factories are several miles inland."

"Doesn't mean they're not willing to go several miles out of their way to dump toxic garbage. As long as it saves money."

"I don't disagree on the merits, but if a company boat arrived in our waters, somebody would have seen them by now." Dakota watched the barren underwater wasteland on the screen. "And here's another question: Where's the dump? There's hundreds of dead fish here, but I don't see any barrels."

"They have to be nearby," Siena said.

"I'd agree based on what we're seeing, but we've got a pretty good view. I don't see any barrels."

"Maybe the company knew they were causing damage and removed their barrels before anyone could pin the ecological damage to them."

"Siena, it's not like they'd be stupid enough to use marked containers," Dakota said. "Plus, as hard as it is to dump this shit without being seen, it'd be ten times more difficult to clean it up."

"Well, there's no other explanation," Siena said. "Unless there's a carrier with a massive immune system carrying the waste along like a virus, I can't think of any other explanation. Look, it's a large area. We'll have to keep looking."

"You make it sound like you're expecting me to chauffeur you all day."

"I do."

"Well, shit. I guess I should've packed a sandwich," Dakota said.

"Somehow, I think you'll survive. It'll give you a chance to shed some of that gut."

Dakota looked at his midsection. "What gut?!"

"Oh, look at you go, denying the fact that you've added a layer or two of insulation since we last saw each other." Siena's face twitched in her attempt to keep from laughing. "It's all right. Happens when you get old."

"Wait a minute! You said I wasn't getting old."

"I've adjusted my opinion."

"You're one to talk. You're only, what? Three years younger than me?"

"Wouldn't guess that if I saw a picture of us standing next to each other."

He studied his gut some more. "Gee whiz! The nerve of you, woman! Come into my town, give some bullshit story about a supposed boyfriend, then call me old, fat, *and* ugly?! Going a little out of your way to make me feel undesirable. Guess what? I have feelings too. I might have to take comfort in some pizza tonight."

"Oh, shocker. You mean you still haven't learned to use your stove?"

"Good God! All the guns are out now, aren't they? Now you're going after my cooking skills. Just so you know, lady, I make one hell of a stir fry!"

"Do you now?"

"Damn right."

Now Siena was fully laughing. "Now *I'm* the one calling bullshit."

"Had to distract myself somehow after you dumped me. They say to do something constructive."

"Well, you've constructed that," she said, pointing at his gut. It felt good to lay on the punishment. Dakota was not truly fat but getting him obsessive about it was better entertainment than any Hollywood film she had seen lately.

The former sheriff checked his reflection in the cabin mirror. "Fine then. I'll get a Bowflex. Get my muscles back up to normal size."

Siena tucked her face down. She had just gotten control of her laughter, only to lose it again.

"Normal size?"

"That's right, baby." He struck a bodybuilder pose.

"Uh-huh."

Mimicking an Austrian accent, he bent his arm and pointed forward. "Yah, I see da lighthouse over der," he pointed behind him, allowing his bicep to flex, "and da harba's back der." His eyes suddenly widened, and he pointed to the monitor screen.

Siena squinted. "What kind of pose is that?"

"No . . . der . . . I mean THERE! The drone!"

She turned to the screen. "Ah, fuck!" Right in front of the drone was a mangled net which lay along the seafloor. She turned the joystick, only to see the image slant to the right. "Damn it! See what you made me do?"

"Hey, I didn't ask you to watch me. By the way, the way you were watching me . . . almost looked like you were checking me out."

"More like studying a bizarre specimen," she said. She applied power to the thrusters, turned every which way, attempted to reverse, none of which helped. All she accomplished was getting the drone even more tangled. "Son of a bitch. Berman's gonna kill me. What the hell is a net doing down here anyway?"

Dakota leaned forward to look. "Hmm, hard to tell from this angle, but it almost looks like a trawl net."

"I'm no fisherman, but it seems like it doesn't do much good trawling without a net."

Dakota studied the screen for a few more seconds, then took the module from Siena.

"What are you doing?"

"Trying to get a better view." He twisted the joystick. The image shook as though the drone was caught in an earthquake.

"You even know what you're doing?"

"I'm just trying to turn the camera."

"Listen, caveman—you're putting the drone in reverse. Gimme that." She took the module away and flicked a smaller joystick. "This one controls the camera." She rotated the image and zoomed out as far as possible. "It's a big net. Probably got ripped. It's a shame people feel the need to dump their garbage here."

"I'm not so sure it was dumped." Dakota pointed to the bottom left corner. Tangled in the net were a few unlucky fish. "This net hasn't been here long, or they'd be dead. And with things the way they are, no way would any fisherman leave a catch behind, no matter how meager it is."

"Is it theirs?" Siena asked, pointing to the white boat in the distance. Dakota stood up and looked. Siena watched his brow wrinkle and his eyes squint. "Everything all right?"

"I don't know. It's weird. They've hardly moved."

"Maybe they're taking a break."

Dakota shook his head. He reflected on when he saw the boat several minutes ago before they launched the drone. The bow was pointed east. Now the boat was facing south and drifting to the right.

No way would Kelby sit around for this long, not with his finances hurting.

He hoisted the anchor and climbed to the flybridge. As he steered the boat north, he adjusted the channel to the local frequency.

"Autumn Bliss, this is the *Pilgrimage.* Just a heads-up, I'm coming your way. Copy." He lowered the mic.

Nothing.

"Hey, Kelby. Wake up. Better not be screwing around over there. If you're on deck, that still technically counts as indecent exposure." He chuckled to himself and awaited a response. "Kelby, you there? Pattie?"

Again, nothing.

"Is everything all right?" Siena asked.

"I . . . don't know." He kept his eyes on the *Autumn Bliss.* A strange odor filled his nose, growing stronger as he got closer. It was a smell of sewage. Ammonia.

The *Autumn Bliss* remained adrift, the bow now pointing southwest.

"Kelby? Pattie? You up there?"

Siena climbed to the flybridge, then shivered after laying eyes on the vessel. "Please tell me that boat normally looks like that."

Dakota shook his head.

Multiple grooves marked the white paint. A section of guardrail was missing along the port bow, along with a chunk of the gunwale. The damage brought to mind a time when Dakota was remodeling his kitchen. He used a piece of plywood for the pantry door, but ended up ripping one of the corners off, leaving a semicircular gap with a jagged edge.

The odor intensified. No doubt it was coming from the boat.

"What is that?" he said.

"I don't know. Bait?"

"I've smelled bait and dead fish. Doesn't quite have that strong of an ammonia smell." He circled around the transom. Nobody was on deck. The flybridge was empty, the sides appearing oddly wet. Whatever coated the console was able to reflect the sun.

The line dangled freely from the outrigger. The end was frayed, as though it had snapped.

Snapped? They don't bottom trawl. Kelby might be desperate, but he doesn't believe in tearing up the ocean floor.

Twice more, he yelled for Pattie and Kelby. At this distance, they would have heard him if they were below.

The deck was a mess, with equipment rolling loose. The upper edge of the transom was chipped, the window to the galley shattered.

His eyes returned to the *Autumn Bliss'* bridge. On the console, the speaker mic dangled loose. Laying on the deck was a pistol.

"Take the wheel. Pull us up next to it," he said. Siena took the helm and did as instructed.

Dakota slid down the ladder and dropped the anchor. Next, he went below into the cabin. When he came out, he was strapping his duty belt over his waist. In the holster was a nine-millimeter Beretta 92.

He reached over the portside and secured a grip on the *Autumn Bliss.*

"What should I do?" Siena asked.

"Just wait there."

With one hand resting on the pistol grip, he began inspecting the boat. Much of the deck had been peeled back like an onion. Broken screws had rolled to the trolling pit, along with pliers and other small tools for net mending.

He turned to look at the flybridge. Instead, his eyes went further up to the crosstree. It had been snapped at the center, the two halves dangling from the outrigger.

Dakota unsnapped his holster and proceeded to the cabin entrance. When he saw it open from the *Pilgrimage,* he had assumed it was simply open. Now aboard, he was close enough to recognize that the various shards of wood spread out over the deck were, in fact, the door.

He leaned against the frame, peeked inside with caution, then entered. The interior was a wreck. Chairs, glasses, and a fire extinguisher lay on the back end of the room. The rear wall was heavily marked and dented.

These items had been thrown. There was no Kelby or Pattie. Only a strange slime and its vile odor remained.

He stepped outside and waved to Siena. "Call the sheriff. Have them get out here right now."

She nodded and reached for the radio. "Dakota, what happened?"

"I don't know." He turned his eyes to the strange grooves along the superstructure. Long, extended incisions, unlike anything he had ever seen. Except the lacerations on the killer whales.

CHAPTER 6

The Atlantic Submarine Canyon was home to many different species, including dolphins, whales, fish, shrimp, and squid. Fifty miles east of the Northeast Channel, it was the deepest region along the U.S. coast.

A massive trench, it was twelve miles wide at its widest point and stretched for thirty-two miles, as if a massive scalpel had been taken to the ocean floor. One-point-five miles deep, it was a black abyss far from the sun's reach. The only light came from the natural illuminations of the deep sea wildlife, and the spotlights of visiting submersibles.

Two bright beams swept over white igneous rocks.

At the helm of the deep sea exploring submersible *Century Cross*, Dr. Linda Berman carefully studied the scenery. Like the many other trenches in the four oceans, the Submarine Canyon was formed from tectonic activity over the course of millions of years. As a dense tectonic plate collides with another with higher density, it bends downward, resulting in a trench.

It was her second visit to this trench, and her twelfth dive into the hadalpelagic zone. Her deepest dive had been to the Puerto Rico Trench. Over five miles down, the pressures were eight-hundred times greater than those at sea level. Most of her colleagues quivered at the thought of such a crushing dive. One tiny breach in the hull would result in implosion for anyone inside.

Pressure was never an issue for Linda. Once the submersible was under the water, the danger was already present. Even at fifty feet, a breach in the hull still meant potential drowning. A faulty rudder could send the vessel into a rock formation or the edge of a reef. It was no different in the trenches, except it was darker. As far as she was concerned, nature prohibited humans from visiting these deep dark worlds. Conducting these dives gave Linda a mischievous feeling, much like what she felt as a teenager when she first took her dad's car for a joyride without his permission. At age thirteen, she figured out the code to the lock on his liquor cabinet. At seventeen, she and her friends skipped school in favor of taking her uncle's boat out. The best part of that daring trip came a week later at a family gathering, when he mentioned something about his fuel gauge being inexplicably low. Not even a hint of suspicion came her way.

Linda had matured a tad once she graduated with her Ph.D.

A tad.

Still, she enjoyed the thought of doing something she was not supposed to do. Perhaps it was a natural instinct to rebel against authority or parental figures. What authority had more clout than Mother Nature herself?

Yeah, you thought your frigid temperatures and crushing pressures could keep me out. Well, now you know different.

The thrill did not last long with today's trip, however. It was not an explorer's attitude that brought the biologist to the Submarine Canyon, but a conservationist one.

Whenever Linda visited places she wasn't meant to, she always knew to clean up after herself and erase all trace. Unfortunately, others were not so careful. In this case, it was not only carelessness, but selfish entitlement.

She extended the submersible's arm to the sediment. A flick of a switch triggered a whirring sound. "I got the sample."

"Good." Pedro, a graduate student from the University of California, was trying to conceal the fact he was shivering.

"Too chilly here? Missing that warm weather back home?"

"That and the sunshine."

"There's light here," she said, waving her hand along the glass.

Pedro shook his head. "All I see is a world of ocean ready to cave in on me at any moment."

"Better get used to these environments, Pedro. You chose to go into research."

"I chose to study the effects of pollution on the ocean, I wasn't thinking of going to the earth's natural gravesite."

"Hate to break it to you, dude, but it's only cheap lowlifes that dump their trash in relatively shallow areas. We're not talking beer bottles or Keurig cups here. Somebody dumped something that's causing all sorts of hell. According to Siena's reports, it's gone all the way through the Gulf of Maine."

"It doesn't make sense," Pedro said. "Why haven't we found anything yet?"

"It's a decent-sized trench. Practically a needle in a haystack. We've got over thirty miles of deep sea to explore, and that's just the length."

"Which leads me to another question: if the dump site is down here, then how is it affecting the Gulf? We're talking over two hundred miles. Would the toxic waste really infect the waters that far out?"

Linda stared into the darkness. "It'd have to be a very bad deposit, that's for sure."

She applied thrust, steering the submersible southeast. Pedro panned the spotlights back and forth. Their imaginations played tricks on them, making every rock appear like a toxic barrel or cannister. Instead, the only clue they found was dead fish.

For over an hour, they searched. They passed through small crevices, peered their lights across long valleys filled with rocks and dead sea creatures. Sharks, white in color, lay dead along the rocks, their bodies picked apart by small squid.

"So far, the only thing we've seen alive down here have been squid."

"It makes sense," Linda said. "Cephalopods, particularly squids, have special immune cells we call hemocytes. It's likely part of the reason they have existed for so many hundreds of millions of years."

"I'm afraid cephalopods are not my field of study," Pedro said. "Enlighten me on what hemocytes are, please?"

"They're part of the immune system. They detect foreign bacterium, bind to it, and eat it. Basically, a white blood cell. The squid down here have probably been eating the infected prey."

"You'd think it'd give them a bad tummy ache."

"They don't have much of a choice. Either they eat what they're given or move on. These squid are fairly small, so there's nowhere for them to go." She sighed.

"You feeling sorry for them?" Pedro asked, grinning.

"Sorry for them, because they might have to be collected and destroyed. In all likelihood, they're carriers for the toxin that's down here. That's something for the government to decide. Our job is to determine the extent of the damage."

Pedro tried to stretch his legs. "Well, if we figure out who's responsible, I'd like to be the first one to punch him in the face for making me sit down here for hours."

Linda snickered. She glanced at the oxygen and power gauges.

"Well, kid, you're in luck for today. We need to start heading up for a recharge. You can stretch your legs in about a half hour."

"You'll get no arguments from me." He took the stick and rotated the *Century Cross* starboard. The spotlight swept over another dead shark, a few rock shapes that resembled miniature volcanos, and then a large, white object.

A chill ran up his back.

A smaller section of this object extended from the big, rounded part, like a giant lever. Long, cone-shaped objects lined this lower section. Teeth. A mouth . . . a mouth that was ten feet from engulfing the submersible.

"Holy Mary! Mother of God!"

Pedro banked to port, bashing the submarine against some unseen object concealed in the dark. Alarms flashed.

The center screen lit up, flashing one word nobody wanted to see this far down. *Damage.*

"Pedro! Pedro! Calm down!" Linda took control of the vessel.

The assistant released the joystick and gripped the edge of his seat. He caught his breath and allowed the professor to take control.

Linda ran a diagnostic.

Left arm damage. Left rudder damage. Thrusters intact. Lights functional. Oxygen levels at thirty percent.

"We're fine. A little banged up, but we're fine." She looked over at her assistant. His head was pressed against the back of his seat, his teeth clenched, eyes wide open. After a long exhale, he relaxed himself.

"Sorry. I turned and saw those huge teeth. I . . . I guess I just reacted."

"Don't apologize. It scared the bejesus out of me, too," Linda said.

"What the hell is it?"

Linda faced the sub toward the big open jaw. The lower jaw was skeletal and white, while the larger upper part retained a little bit of its flesh. In life, the thing had a large, rounded head full of adipose tissue called melon, whose function modulated the animal's echolocation, and a waxy organ called spermaceti, which helped with buoyancy. In past centuries, the species had been hunted to endangerment by fishing crews for its oil and wax. Now, another of its kind had perished.

"It's a sperm whale."

"What's *left* of a sperm whale," Pedro said. Measuring from the edge of its spine to the tip of its head, the thing was a mature one. Probably fifty feet. He swallowed, retaining his bile after seeing some of the squid feeding off its deflated head. Behind it was a series of broken bones, void of flesh. "Doctor, what the hell happened to it?"

Linda shook her head. She was as flabbergasted as he was.

"I don't know. It looks like it's been . . . eaten."

"By those things?!" he said, pointing at the cuttlefish.

Linda steered the sub over the skeleton. Bone fragments had spread for several yards, like twigs from a dying tree.

"No. It would take something a lot bigger and stronger than those cuttlefish beaks to do something like this."

"Something big? What's big enough to kill a freaking sperm whale?"

For several moments, Linda sat silent. "I don't know. Whatever it is, I don't want to be in the same place as it."

Pedro gulped again and panned his light into the distance. Now, every shape in this canyon was full of menace. Every shadow cast by the rocks gave the appearance of a hungry beast, ready to lash out at the uninvited visitors.

“Where do you think it’s at?”

CHAPTER 7

The Saw Ridge first response harbor was located in a U-shaped cove on the north end of town. It held four county police boats, two EMT response boats, and one tugboat. Dakota McCullough was no stranger to this little harbor. If he had a dollar for every time he stepped on one of those police boats, he wouldn't need a police pension.

What he was a stranger to was being the interviewee in a police investigation. Fifteen minutes after Siena placed the radio call, Glenn and two divers arrived and began their investigation. For three hours, Dakota and Siena waited while they searched for any bodies under the water. After no results were produced, Glenn allowed his father to tow the boat to the county harbor where they could conduct a more detailed inspection.

He stood on the pier beside Siena while his son did his work. There, they had a better view of the damage. The scratches on the hull, while following a fairly distinguishable pattern, were random in length. Even more strange were the large indentations on the underside, as though the tips of a giant branch-cutting tool had been pressed into it.

Much of the slime residue had dried, but the smell was as loathsome as ever. Dakota, having investigated more than his fair share of vile crime scenes, was not unnerved by the odor, but it was enough to quell his appetite for lunch. The residue was on the outriggers and the dangling ropes.

Two forensic officers were on site, taking samples of the slime substance and combing through the vessel for any trace of bodily fluid. Glenn was standing on the flybridge with the Dryers' revolver in a gloved hand. The cylinder was open, the cartridges removed.

"Each one has been fired," he said. He shook his head. "No sign of any bullet holes on the deck or anywhere else. Whoever, or whatever, he was shooting at was outside the boat."

"And it chased him and Pattie inside the structure," Dakota said.

The sheriff climbed down to the pier with the weapon in one hand and the camera in the other. He had taken so many photos of the vessel, it nearly felt as if he was preparing a sales portfolio.

"One of the guys found a wallet inside. One hundred bucks cash, three credit cards, and a gift card. The fuel tank is three-quarters full, and the spare drum is intact. From what we can see, nothing's been taken."

"If I may, Sheriff?" Siena picked up her test kit. "I'd like to take a sample of this substance before the remainder of it dries up."

Glenn looked at it, then nodded. Every detail of the boat had been documented and photographed. Any change to its condition would be easy to track.

"What do you think it is?"

"That's what I want to find out."

"Nothing I've ever seen before," one of the forensics officers said.

"Well, whatever it is, it's loaded with ammonia," Siena said. She put on gloves, pulled out a few glass vials and a cotton swab from her kit, then approached the boat.

Dakota and Glenn watched from the pier. The father could sense his son's stress levels rising.

"First homicide investigation?"

"I've been on a few. You know that."

"No, I mean as sheriff. First time in charge of one?" Dakota said.

Glenn bit his lip, not wanting his answer heard by his staff. "Yes." It was barely audible. When he noticed a couple of deputies watching from the shoreline, he realized answering that way was worse. He might as well have put his lack of confidence on a billboard.

"What about the kayaks?" Dakota said.

"I still have people searching," Glenn said.

"Until they turn up, you'll want to keep a unit on the water and a couple of deputies walking a beat on the shoreline."

"They won't turn up if they're deceased."

"Oh, they might," Dakota said. "If they died and sank, they'll bloat in a matter of hours. Better if one of the guys finds them than a tourist."

Glenn nodded. For a moment, he forgot he was taking advice from his dad and not his boss.

"I know how this works," he said.

Dakota closed his eyes. *I did it again, didn't I?*

Another police vessel entered the harbor. On deck were Deputies Zolnai and Denham. Leaning against the transom was the purple kayak with the gold star.

The McCulloughs approached the dock and helped them moor the boat.

"Anything?" Glenn asked.

Denham shook his head. "No, nothing. We searched every inch of water between the lighthouse all the way to the south bend. There's no sign of them at all. No sign of the other kayak, nothing."

"Did you happen to cross by Gold Beach?" Dakota asked. "They drive a white Chevy pickup."

"Yeah, it's still there," Zolnai said.

"I took the liberty of calling the Gold Star Gym," Denham said. "The manager there says they never showed."

"Four missing persons inside of four hours," Dakota said. He leaned over the side of the police boat for a better look at the kayak. "You found it with that residue on it?"

"Correct," Zolnai said.

Dakota looked at Glenn. "Well, now it's official. These are related. And judging by the markings on the *Autumn Bliss*, they're related to whatever happened to the orcas."

Glenn groaned. "Four missing people, likely deceased. No valuables taken. Mass murder of marine life. You ask me, everything points to a homicidal maniac."

"Not sure," Dakota said. "If somebody wanted to knock off the Dryers, why wreck their boat to do it? Not to mention the fact that Kelby got off six rounds. I saw the interior. Practically a dozen items were thrown toward the entryway. We know for a fact that the intruder got aboard."

"Perhaps he had a firearm, too," Glenn said. "Some killers are crack shots. Maybe he picked off Kelby and went after Pattie."

"There's no blood, though," Dakota said. "A guy willing to cause this much wreckage isn't going to worry about some DNA evidence. Assuming it was a human."

Glenn scoffed. "Dad, pardon me for questioning your expertise, but I don't believe there's any sea life capable of doing this kind of damage. It'd have to be a pretty big animal, and the only big things I've seen around here are whales. Considering their anatomy, even if they did attack, they wouldn't cause this kind of damage." He turned to face Siena. "Right?"

"It wasn't a whale or a shark."

Glenn nodded. "That's what I thought."

"But we might be dealing with an organism."

Glenn felt his stomach tighten. "An organism?"

"This residue is biologic secretion of some kind. Only thing I can think of off the top of my head are cephalopods. Some species produce mucus from their suckers."

"You're telling me a big octopus did this?" Glenn said.

"I'm not saying anything," Siena said. "Most cephalopods are relatively small. Even the giant squid would have a hard time doing this kind of damage. Not to mention the statistics and feeding habits. There's never been a confirmed attack on humans, let alone an appearance by one of those creatures."

"Good, because I'm not humiliating myself in front of the public by telling everybody there's a kraken on the loose," Glenn said.

"This isn't funny, kid," Dakota said. "I knew the Dryers, and Ricky and Ashley. They often brightened my mornings when I saw them out on the water."

"I'm doing the best I can, Dad." He sighed and stared at the *Autumn Bliss.* After a moment of pondering, he lifted his radio mic to his lips. "Unit One to Dispatch."

"Go ahead."

"Pass on to second shift when they get here, I want a boat patrol conducting patrols between the lighthouse and the south bend. It's very likely we have deceased persons in these waters. Put out a warning to all fishing vessels in the community."

"Copy that."

Glenn clipped his mic, groaning. "First, a freaking pollution issue, now this." He looked at his dad. "You picked a good time to retire."

"Says you."

Glenn looked at one of the deputies on shore. Both were looking away, attempting to stare off into the distance as if neither of them had muttered something.

He dug his keys from his pocket and went to Boat One. "I'm gonna conduct a few more passes. Thanks for your help, Dad. You too, Siena. If you find something, you mind letting me know?"

"Sure thing," she said.

Glenn gave a thumbs up and started the boat engine.

"Want me to go with ya?" Dakota said.

"That's fine. Thanks." Glenn backed the boat out, then took it into the Gulf.

Siena packed her samples into her kit and stepped ashore. "That's it for me as well."

"Guess that means you're ready for me to take you back," Dakota said.

"No need." She looked at a small hill to the south, then glanced at the deputies. "Falk's Tale Resort is just a little ways in that direction, correct?"

"Yes, ma'am. Not even a half mile."

"Good. Don't want to leave my rental car on the Falks' property," she said. She picked up a case with the flounder Dakota had brought. "Okay, then. Time to go back to my hotel and prepare for getting my ass ripped by Linda."

"Don't look at me. I didn't make you lose the drone," Dakota said.

"Your antics did," she replied.

"Oh, come on. How was I supposed to know there was a net down there?"

She smiled. "It's all right. It's not the first time we've lost some equipment. That said, I need to get to work analyzing my samples."

"Sure you don't want me to take you over there?" Dakota asked.

"No, thank you. I've been on that boat all morning and afternoon. I could use a little stroll. That said, I better go. I wanna get this call to Linda over with, then give Frank a ring."

"Oh, Frank." Dakota grinned. "Aren't you a little old for imaginary boyfriends?"

"Dakota . . ." She closed her eyes and allowed the tension to recede. "I'm sorry about your friends."

He nodded. "Me, too." He watched her walk up the hill and disappear on the other side.

With nothing else to keep him here, Dakota boarded the *Pilgrimage* and backed it out of the harbor. The entire time, his eyes were fixed on the *Autumn Bliss*.

Turning the boat south, he watched the deceitfully peaceful ocean. The sparkling blue waves, which normally brought to mind warm feelings of paradise, now brought chills. Even the prettiest garden sometimes covered a grave. This bay, which brought joy to thousands of people every year, now concealed four deaths.

And a mysterious killer.

CHAPTER 8

"Ready to go?"

Andrew Palace looked up at the late afternoon sky. Of course, it would start to rain as they were about to set out for their job.

He lowered his eyes to his partner, Erica Lupo. "No."

The buttermilk blonde grabbed him by the shirt and pulled him aboard the company boat.

Andrew stepped to the console. Even on the helm, the weather service had made sure their logo was seen. NDBC–National Data Buoy Center. Was this to advertise to their own staff?

Every day, he asked himself the exact same question. Nowadays, he kept it within the confines of his own mind. Up until a couple of months ago, he'd said it out loud. Eventually, his co-workers, namely Erica, got sick of hearing him spout the same thing over and over again. She agreed with his general point: the repair techs were the unsung heroes of the weather service industry. The public only ever thought of the talking heads who pointed to a green screen. Not only that, but the company could not even give them a boat with a decent canopy. All they had was a windshield and a small overhead for the cockpit, nothing that would keep its operator dry.

Despite all this, Erica found the constant complaining more tiresome than the work itself. Each conversation with Andrew was as predictable as a Hallmark Christmas movie. It was as though his brain was on a loop, playing the same lines from the same conversation over and over again. The only difference was the date, and occasionally the subject.

Andrew unmoored the boat then looked out to the horizon.

"Where's this buoy at?"

"Five clicks straight out that way," Erica said, pointing due east.

Andrew gazed at the horizon, then at the weather above it. The bright sunny weather that blessed the Saw Ridge coast earlier had been eliminated by an invading army of storm clouds. A gentle breeze touched his face. Only for another twenty minutes would it be gentle. Once those clouds got closer, that wind would be like the arm of an enraged beast, lashing at everything that stood before it.

"Looks like it might come down rather hard."

"No. Billy said it's only supposed to be scattered showers."

He glared at her, then pointed at the sky. "Does that spell scattered showers to you?"

Erica looked, then shook her head, frowning. "I guess he misjudged the buildup."

"Oh, you're shocked? Like the weather service is ever right," Andrew said. He groaned, then started the engine. "It must feel great to have a job where you're wrong all the time. You know, if you and I ever screwed up, made a miscalculation or whatever, they'd treat it like it was the end of times. Most of these guys don't even use the readings from these buoys. They just use the weather app on their phones."

"If you don't quit whining, it's gonna be the end of times for you," Erica said. She pulled her utility gloves on and inspected the winch, visibly not in the mood for his griping. Andrew took the hint and steered the boat into the Gulf, straight in the direction of those clouds. A distant sound of thunder echoed from behind those dark gray mountains. No wonder Erica was in a mood. She did not want to be out here, either.

"Scattered showers, my ass. Besides, if they lost the signal to the buoy, how do they know what the forecast was?"

"They only lost the signal at noon," Erica said. "Plus, there's other buoys."

"Yet, it's still so important that we pick it up right now." Andrew pushed the boat to its maximum speed. The sooner they reached that thing, the sooner they would be done and out of the rain.

The next several minutes were full of silence. Andrew spent that time sulking. The clouds were getting darker. His estimate of twenty minutes for the wind to intensify was way off. It only took six.

A flash of lightning traveled along the sky like a ghostly eel. Heavy rain was inevitable.

It didn't matter to Erica. She was dressed in her insulated diving suit. It would be a quick dive into the water to unhook the anchor chain and apply the red marker to keep it afloat for installation.

Over the next twenty minutes, the sky grew darker, the ocean livelier. Nothing an experienced diver couldn't handle, but Andrew was not looking at it from that perspective. Crummy weather made him wish he was stretched out on his sofa at home with Netflix on the TV.

Today had *to be my on-call day.*

Rain pelted the boat.

"Son of a bitch." Erica crowded into the cockpit with him.

"Move. You're taking up all the space."

Her eyes widened. "You saying something there?"

Andrew smiled. "Yeah, that came out a little worse than I intended, didn't it?"

"That it did, mister." She chuckled, not taking genuine offense. Despite being annoyed by his frequent whining, Erica did have a soft spot for the maintenance tech, even with that so-called mullet.

"What's it matter to you anyway? You're already getting wet."

"Doesn't mean I enjoy getting shelled with rain." She reached for the instrument panel and flicked on the spotlights. She panned one around like a search and rescue boat probing for shipwreck survivors. "It could be anywhere."

Andrew glanced back and forth. "I don't see the blinking light . . . You sure it's in this area?"

"Yes, I'm sure. It's on the map."

"That thing is probably as accurate as the weather forecasts." He hugged the side in a futile attempt to keep out of the rain while Erica panned the port bow spotlight left and right.

The twenty-five-minute trip to reach the buoy turned into fifty.

Now, it was Erica that was complaining. She got on her phone to the office and sneered like a wildcat when they put her on hold.

"Pick up, damn you. I swear, if they don't take me off hold, I'll—AH!" She jumped as a bolt of lightning streaked within ten feet of their boat. "JESUS!"

Andrew's attempt to cover his mouth and look away failed to conceal his laugh. "If they don't take you off hold, you'll 'AH' them to death?"

Erica closed her eyes and regained control of her temper. The rain pelting her head made such a feat nearly impossible. Only the sight of yellow-painted steel several meters off the portside kept her from snapping.

She hung up and tossed the phone on the console. "I see it. It's over there."

"Finally." Andrew turned the boat and increased speed. He had already been out here twice as long as he intended. "Get your facemask and shit on. Hook the thing up and let's get out of here."

"Don't have to tell me twice." Erica pulled her goggles on, checked her rebreather, and stood at the transom. She watched for the teepee shape of the buoy as they drew closer, specifically waiting for the yellow light to blink. If even its standard functions failed, then the entire system must have lost power somehow.

Something was off about it. Its pointed top was compressed into the platform, giving it more of a mushroom shape.

"Wait a minute . . ."

"We've waited long enough," Andrew said.

"No, I . . ." She bit her lip. The stupid idiot's brain was clearly dysfunctional to a degree. Every so often, he'd take a common figure of speech literally. "I mean, something's wrong with the buoy."

"Well, duh. Hence we're out here."

"No, what I mean is it . . . looks different." She aimed the spotlight at it.

Andrew brought the boat alongside the thing then dropped the anchor. "What the hell? It's . . . crushed."

"Crushed. Splintered. Smashed."

"What the hell could do that to these buoys? They're not made from thin metal."

"I don't know. Fishing boat, maybe," Erica said.

"Hate to see the boat that struck this thing that hard. They'd be lucky to make it back to shore."

Erica wiped the rain from her forehead as she kept the light centered on the buoy. The thing was crushed, yet almost looked as though it had been pulled apart. Her mind could not settle on a proper description for what happened to it, let alone hypothesize what caused it. The top, while crushed, looked to have been twisted into a corkscrew. Several grooves lined the flatter parts.

Were those there before?

A raindrop struck Andrew's eye, sparking a series of curses. "Girl, can we play detective later? I'd like to get out of here."

"Yeah. Hang on. Keep the light on the thing, will ya?"

"Sure." He took control of the spotlight and kept it pointed. Every few seconds, the buoy moved out of view. "Jeez o Pete's. The thing won't stay still. How much range of motion do the anchors allow?"

"Shouldn't be much."

With her supplies in hand, Erica hit the water. She swam to the buoy, which seemed to be moving away from her. Andrew was right; the thing was moving way more than it should have.

Fighting a vigorous sea, she reached the platform. Miraculously, the loop for the towing cable was still intact. She attached the clip, then waved to Andrew to toss her the floatation marker. It landed a couple of meters shy of her. She couldn't blame him for this one, for the buoy was floating freely. She swam to the marker, grabbed the cord, and returned to the buoy.

A moment later, she was underwater. Her flashlight found the chain, dangling freely from the platform. It was swinging back and forth. *Weightless*. Erica lowered the golden stream. Two meters down, the anchor chain was broken, the final link folded inward. The tips of the remaining half-link were narrowed, as though a pair of giant pliers had been taken to it.

That's not possible. THAT'S NOT POSSIBLE. What the hell could break that chain?

A thunderous *crack* echoed through the ocean. It was a crash that made Erica shudder. The storm must be getting really ferocious if even the ocean could not muffle its thunder.

She returned to the surface and waved to the boat. "I'm coming back!" Andrew didn't answer. *Probably didn't hear me.*

The spotlight had moved away from her, now pointing to her left. The bum was probably cowering in the cockpit. Next time she set out with him, she would make sure the idiot brought a raincoat.

Midway back, she stopped. *Is something off with the boat, or is it just me?* She removed her goggles and aimed her light.

It wasn't just her. The boat was tilting oddly to starboard. Farther and farther, it went.

"Good Christ . . . Andrew! What's going on?"

The boat continued to teeter until she could almost see the full underside. The edge of the keel and the propellor came into view. The way it tilted defied the laws of physics. This was not caused by the waves, or else the boat would rock back and forth.

This was more as though the boat was being *pulled.*

In the blink of an eye, the boat rocked toward her. It was not the oddity of its intense swaying that made Erica freeze, but the brief but perfect view of the deck and cockpit.

It was empty.

"Andrew?"

Huge waves swept her back toward the buoy. The boat's rocking did not slow but intensified. It brought to mind stories of haunted houses, in which inanimate objects would randomly shake in place and settle in an impossible position.

In this case, it was a twenty-foot boat. Teetering back and forth as though on an invisible fulcrum, it smashed both sides of its cockpit against the water. The spotlight shattered and fell free of its prop. Smashing glass overcame the roar of thunder.

With her back pressed against the buoy, Erica could do nothing but keep her light fixed on the oddity. The beam swept over the white hull. It wasn't all white. Something red had risen from the waterline. It was long and relatively thin—if a foot-and-a-half could be considered thin.

Panning the light left, she saw another one. Then another.

A flash of lightning revealed a wider view. On this side alone were four of these weird slithery things. On the starboard side were four others, their tips bent over the gunwale. Together, they resembled a giant ribcage, but one made of rubbery things that resembled giant nightcrawlers.

The hull compressed under their combined might. Like the buoy she floated away with, the boat imploded, the engine spewing smoke, the fuel tank filling the air with diesel.

All at once, it stopped. The boat rocked in place, swinging by its anchor line.

Erica held her breath and remained perfectly still. The next several seconds were spent questioning her sanity. What she just witnessed was impossible. Those things were organic. Alive—that, or part of something alive. Whatever it was, it was huge. And hungry.

Andrew's nonexistence took new meaning now. Erica held still. Maybe she could blend in with the buoy and remain unseen. She kept holding her breath in an attempt to calm herself down. Her heart drummed in her chest. She could feel the blood pulsing throughout her body, down to her toes. The tension only increased. Her legs strained, pressing against each other. An odd chill crept up her back.

Erica's eyes widened. Only when she aimed her flashlight down did she realize these sensations were not figments of her imagination. Like a python, the long red thing coiled around her legs and up her back. The constricting of her ribs prevented her from screaming. She tried anyway. It was not vocals that escaped her lungs, but blood.

Next came the sensation of pointed objects ripping her flesh from the bone.

CHAPTER 9

The innards churned, the meat peeling like the skin of an onion. Over the next few minutes, they were a mishmash of various parts with little identity.

"Ha!" Dakota plunged the spatula into the frying pan and stirred. "Can't cook, my ass!" He added some seasonings to his stir fry and conducted a smell test. "Yeah . . . well, maybe a little spicy, but I can cook, damn it!" He added the peppers and onions, then searched the kitchen counter for his phone. "Gotta have some music for the chef to work his magic."

He searched a few options, then decided on Pavarotti's "Cielo e mar." Swaying to the rhythm of the music, Dakota continued stirring. After a minute, he was humming along with the song. Three minutes in, he was completely in the moment, singing along with Luciano Pavarotti.

"Qui nell'ombra, ov'io mi giacio, coll'anelito del cor … Vieni, o donna, vieni al bacio … della vita e dell'amor …"

As the music reached its climax, he looked up, arms out, and sang as though on stage. "Ah! Vieeeeeeeeeeeeeen!" The high-pitched blast of the smoke alarm cut his tune short. "Oh, shit! Shit! Shit! Shit!"

He reduced the heat to a minimum, opened a window, then fanned the smoke in that direction. After that, he pulled a chair toward the hallway wall so he could reset the fire alarm, which continued to scream at him.

"You know, the way they set these damn things, it takes more effort to reach them than it would to put out a freaking structure fire!" He pulled the thing off the wall and pressed the button. "Thank you, now I can think." He stepped down, fanned the rest of the smoke out the window, then looked at the burnt ingredients sizzling in too much olive oil.

"Hmm. Well, good thing nobody was here to see that."

As if on cue, there was a knock at the door. Dakota closed his eyes.

"Oh, good. I was worried I wouldn't have an audience." With a sigh, he approached the door and opened it.

On the other side was Siena Lehnert. She smiled, nervously but genuinely. "Hi."

Dakota smiled, too. "Hi."

Siena sniffed, then looked past him into the house. "On a mission to prove me right about the cooking, are ya?"

"I don't know what you're talking about, woman."

"Really? I saw the fumes coming out the window. Gave a thought or two to calling the fire department."

"Aw, just a little extra heat. Nothing to worry about."

"Yeah? I'm not sure your smoke alarm would agree."

Dakota raised his eyebrows. "You heard that, huh?"

"That, the cussing, the singing leading up to it . . ."

"Melts your heart, doesn't it?"

"More like fries it, like whatever's burning in that kitchen. Thank goodness you didn't pursue opera." She looked up at the rolling clouds. "So, you gonna let me stand out in the rain?"

"I don't know. At the moment, I seem to be enjoying it," Dakota said.

"Guess next time I should wait for better weather to make fun of your singing and cooking."

Dakota smiled and let her in. Siena knew right where to hang her coat. The house had not changed much in the three years since she last saw him. Maybe a little cleaner, except for the kitchen right now.

She peeked at the charred remains in the skillet. "Good God, Dakota! How 'bout a little stir fry with your olive oil?!"

He scratched his head. "A little much, huh?"

Siena took a look in the fridge. "Thank goodness you prepared for your failure by having extra ingredients. I can't let this slide. I'll salvage this for you."

"That why you showed up unannounced? To poke fun at my cooking skills?"

"Would you believe me if I said I smelled this disaster from across town and felt the need to rescue you?"

"Only if you said it smelled good."

She sniffed. "It probably did at some point."

"What really brings you here?" Dakota said, leaning against the counter.

"I thought you'd be interested to know that I ran some tests on that flounder you gave me, as well as the orca samples, and that strange crap that was on the *Autumn Bliss*."

"Let me guess, they contain a cellular connection."

"Only in the sense that the cells are loaded with pollutants."

"Pollutants? That would explain why the fishing around here has gone to shit. You think it's that slime stuff? That looks like waste material of some sort."

"It contains strong traces, but it's organic. Closer in nature to the secretion from octopuses, as I hypothesized earlier."

"Really? I thought you were being facetious."

"I was."

"You still sound wary, like you don't believe it," he said.

She shrugged. "I guess that's because I don't. Or, at least I'm having a hard time wrapping my head around it."

"Why not? There're giant squids in the ocean, aren't there? Isn't there the colossal squid? Sounds big to me."

"Don't believe what you saw in *Twenty Thousand Leagues Under the Sea*," Siena said. "The giant and colossal squids are big, but not nearly as big as they're often portrayed in fiction. Not nearly big enough to collapse a boat. The longest mantle length on record is two-point-twenty-five meters. With the arms outstretched, it was twenty-five feet. Big, but not 'mythical sea monster' big. And it's so rare that they'd appear, it's hard to imagine a squid is what wrecked the Dryers' boat."

Dakota looked at the ocean. "What does the sheriff have to say about this?" Siena froze, skillet in hand. "You did inform the sheriff, right?"

"Of course, I did," she said.

It was then that Dakota understood her hesitation. "He didn't answer."

"Probably busy with other things," she said.

"Like shirking his responsibilities and hiding at home," Dakota said.

"I did send him an email and asked the office to shoot him a text so he looks at it. I didn't mention anything about squids." Siena continued rinsing the dishes. "I'm sure the poor guy has a lot on his mind right now."

"He's about to have more." Dakota yanked his phone out and started texting.

CHAPTER 10

When Glenn initially heard the chime of his phone, he tensed. Had to be the office giving him more bad news. His spirits lifted when he saw that it was his father, only to fall again when he read the text.

"Important info in your email. Please read and respond to Dr. Siena Lehnert."

"Sir, yes, sir," he muttered. He hated this feeling. Even seeing his father's text made him jump. It was as if he, along with the rest of the community, still saw Dakota as the legitimate sheriff. Like the good deputy he no longer was, Glenn begrudgingly checked his email. There it was, a message from Dr. Lehnert.

Toxicity report finds common trace in slime, orca remains, dead fish, and water samples. I advise your people look for any kind of leak or any suspicious boating. Pollution confirmed in Gulf of Maine and Submarine Canyon. Email sent to EPA.

Like clockwork, the next email was from the EPA. asking him to have divers investigate the nearby areas. With such a broad area showing traces of dioxin poisoning, they were requesting local departments to assist in narrowing down the search area.

The entire afternoon was spent searching for bodies, to no avail. By six, the general public had gotten wind of the issue. The families of Ricky Cox and Ashley Thomas were breathing down his neck, understandably distraught over the disappearances. Like in many of these cases, it was the unanswered questions that drove loved ones more insane than the possible deaths themselves.

He arrived home at seven, having abandoned the search when the storm rolled in. His people couldn't find anything in ideal weather; it would be impossible to find anything in the wind and rain. Naturally, the families of the Dryers and the kayakers did not take kindly to this news. Some were clinging to the hope that their missing loved ones were somehow still alive. The local newspaper did not help at all. They bombarded his phone as much as the families, demanding action.

The jacket and hat were tossed on the rocking chair. Glenn yanked off the uniform shirt, kicked off his boots, then sank right into the couch. What followed was one of those nights when Glenn McCullough found himself staring at his living room wall.

For the next hour, he scrolled through Netflix and Hulu in search of anything that would help take his mind off the job. Instead, all it did was make his brain fixate on the issues even more. A polluted Gulf, a dying economy, a citizenry that was getting increasingly desperate, and now four disappearances.

He settled on scrolling through his tablet. Before he could browse his usual sites, the device pinged him to a few news notifications, all of which were local. He tried to avoid that annoying red dot as he browsed through eBay. The notification icon was an itch that had to be scratched, even if it meant opening up an old wound.

He succumbed to the urge and immediately felt the pain of that scab. The blood came in the form of the headline: *"McCullough: the Good and the Bad."* The text below was not a balanced critique of the current administration, but a detailed comparison of Dakota's time in office to Glenn's. Everything was there, from crime statistics and budget handling, to jail management and public safety.

The next headline was: *"Sheriff McCullough: The man haunted by his name."*

Usually, it was family members of criminals who carried the burden of their names. At least those people usually didn't have anything to live up to. There was nowhere for them to go but up.

Glenn quit after reading the first few lines of the article. He shut off his tablet and placed it on the shelf.

"You know what never fails you, Sheriff?" he said to himself. He marched to the kitchen and pulled a beer from the fridge. He cracked it open, started to walk away, then stopped. He watched the interior of the fridge, then at the last moment, caught the door before it swung shut.

A night like this needed three of these, for sure. Why make the extra trips?

Glenn grabbed two more beers and returned to the living room. Before the first swig was gulped, his phone started ringing. It was Dispatch.

"Four years, you can't go by fast enough." He picked up the phone and answered. "McCullough here."

"Sorry to call you at home, Sheriff."

"Part of the job." Hearing his own voice, he worried he came off as too sarcastic.

"We just got a call from the weather service. They're requesting our help."

"What the hell do they want?"

"One of their supervisors is coming into town. He's looking for a couple of his staff that apparently took a company boat out into the Gulf in search of a defective weather buoy."

"He sent them out in this weather?"

"They were supposed to be done before it rolled in. Apparently, they never checked back. He's asking for one of our deputies to meet him at the county harbor."

"Wait? This guy is making demands?"

"You know how these big-wigs are," the dispatcher said. *"Climb the corporate ladder, and soon enough, they think everybody on earth answers to them. To be frank, it kinda pissed me off, too. I thought I'd run it by you first before I send one of the guys over there."*

"I'd be lying if I said I wasn't tempted to tell him to fuck off," Glenn said. He looked out the window at the storm. The worst of it was ending, the torrential downpour reduced to a steady drizzle. Visibility would be dim, especially if any fog should appear.

He thought of the *Autumn Bliss* and the fitness instructors. The last thing he needed was another missing couple.

"Odds are these people just don't know how to handle a boat," he said. "Probably went out, couldn't find the buoy, then got caught up in the storm. Buuuuuut, we better make sure they get back."

"Copy. I'll send one of the guys."

"Actually, Dispatch . . ." Glenn stared at the empty living room. Only three beer bottles and a tablet were available to occupy his depressed mind. He had heard on many occasions that the best antidote to depression was to do something constructive. He wasn't enthusiastic about going out in this weather, but at least he would keep the deputies from getting drenched. ". . . I'll go myself."

"Oh! You sure?"

"Yeah, I don't want to send the guys out in this weather. I might not be good at much, but I can handle a boat pretty good. Plus, Boat One is the only one with any decent overhead."

"Whatever you say, sir. I'll write it in the log."

"Gotcha. Thanks."

He hung up, then reached for his uniform shirt, only to retract. He didn't want to wear that stupid thing any more than he had to. As long as he had the jacket and badge, he would be fine.

Three and a half years from now, this county will be somebody else's problem.

He found his keys, double-checked to ensure he had the boat key, then went out the door.

CHAPTER 11

It took twenty minutes for the smell of burnt olive oil and pork to air out of the house. Ten minutes later, a much more pleasant aroma took its place. Siena, with the proper amount of oil in the pan, gradually stirred in the ingredients. All the while, she eyeballed the bottle of wine that Dakota brought out.

Though he did not show it, he took great pleasure in watching her eyes occasionally go to the bottle.

"How much does Dr. Berman think has been dumped in the canyon?"

"I don't know. It's like finding a needle in a haystack," Siena said. "However, water and fish samples taken from that area are showing strong traces of chemical agents that weren't there before. It's pretty much a sure fact that someone's been dumping out there."

"And it managed to pollute the waters all the way over here?" Dakota said. "Seems a little far, don't you think?"

"Unless they've been dumping in the Gulf as well," Siena said.

"No way a big cargo ship would come into these waters unseen. It'd have to be a private contractor, and even that's stretching it a bit."

"It'd be an easy way for some of the fishermen around here to make some easy money," Siena said.

Dakota shook his head. "Doesn't add up. These people might go through drastic measures, but I don't see them intentionally polluting the waters and killing their very livelihood."

"Maybe they didn't understand what they were dumping," Siena said.

"It still begins with the initial dumping in the canyon," Dakota said. "Any company willing to go through such a measure to save a few bucks will not risk exposure hiring locals who might alert the police. They would use their own people."

"Fact of the matter is, either the dumpsite in the canyon is large enough to affect the Gulf of Maine, or the perpetrator is also dumping in your local waters."

Dakota sat on one of his dining room chairs and watched the steam rise from the skillet and drift past him into the living room.

"Or something's carrying traces of the toxin over here."

"Something? Like an animal?"

"You said the fish and whales tested positive."

"Yeah, but with varying degrees. Neither of them migrated from the canyon, I can guarantee that. It would have to be something with a hell of an immune system to get that level of exposure and make it all the way over here." She looked at the assortment of ingredients on the countertop. "Ah! I know what I'm missing. Water chestnuts. You have any?"

"The cabinet in the back room," Dakota said.

She laughed. "You still keep the canned goods back there?"

"Of course, I do. That's the way my folks had the place set up."

"Just because you were gifted your mom and dad's house doesn't mean you have to keep up with their illogical tendencies," Siena said. She turned the heat down and went down the hallway.

It was then that Dakota decided to open that bottle of wine.

"Wait for it," he whispered to himself. "Three . . . two . . . one . . ."

"Hey!" Siena marched back to the kitchen. Instead of water chestnuts, she held an underwater drone with crab-like arms. "This looks familiar, mister!"

Dakota filled two glasses. "I needed something to do this afternoon, so I took a dive and freed it from the net."

"And you didn't call me and let me know?"

"I figured you'd be stopping by."

Siena gasped. "You figured I'd be stopping by?"

Dakota smiled. Her shock *almost* sounded genuine.

"What? You think I believe you came here to warn me about the toxic waste in the water?" Dakota extended one of the glasses to her. "That's about as realistic as that whole Frank thing."

A new smile crept over Siena's face. Slowly, she accepted the glass.

"Did you at least believe it for a short while?"

He shook his head, then sipped his wine.

Siena ogled her glass, then downed it, then succumbed to the temptation that brought her to his house. She threw her arms around his neck and pressed her lips to his.

"Mmm. Oh, man. You're a bad girlfriend. Frank's gonna be so pissed."

"Oh, shut up, you goofball," she said between kisses. "I'm as good at lying as you are cooking."

The passionate coupling continued until the sizzling stir fry charred and the smoke alarms finally went off for a second time.

CHAPTER 12

If anything was going well for Glenn tonight, it was the clear roads. Most of the population was inside by this time, and with the storm raging, the town seemed barren.

Yet, somehow, every intersection greeted him with a red light. Most of them were right at the beginning, taunting him with the yellow light when he was still a few hundred feet out. Each time, he considered flooring it, only to remember his first major call as a deputy. Someone had attempted to catch the light when they were too far out, entered the intersection when the crossing lane was green for go, and smacked into the first car. It was the first body he saw, and still one of the worst. The image of the mangled, twisted pose of a regular everyday Joe was frozen in his mind. The randomness of accidents was sometimes not so random. For the victim, it was just another morning of going to work. For the impatient driver, it was a choice.

Glenn always made a choice when he saw that yellow light. Slow down and stop. No need to rush.

Now, if only I'd had a yellow light for when I decided to run for sheriff.

Like the driver, he'd made a choice. All the same, he had to live with it.

After a minute, the light for the intersecting lane turned yellow. For once, it actually served a purpose. A semi-truck was coming in from the right.

When his light turned green, Glenn eased on the accelerator, only to stop right away. The prick flew right through the intersection, honking at him as though he were the jerk trying to cut through.

"Son of a—"

His blood rushing, Glenn turned left, simultaneously pulling the cherry from the glove box. The fact that he was going in the same direction as the truck elevated the temptation to pull him over. He went as far as to flick the light on and raise it out the window. The rain hitting his hand made him reconsider. The truck deserved to be pulled over, and if it were any other night, Glenn probably would have gone after him. But he had more important things to worry about. There was a man waiting at the harbor and the possibility of two more missing persons. Such a thing would be the death of this town, and the county at large.

He put the cherry away and continued on.

After a couple of miles, the truck began to slow. The right turn signal soon came on, and the truck swung left, then hooked into a driveway.

Glenn groaned, then slowed to a stop. This was one of those drivers who had to take up the entire road just to make a turn. He squinted at the destination. Falk's Tale Resort.

"What the hell did they order that required a semi-truck to transport?"

He saw Jacob step out the back of the main lodge to greet the driver.

As soon as the road was cleared, Glenn's interest faded. He didn't know anything about running that resort. Maybe they ordered some new kayaks or paddleboards. Still, seemed strange that a truck that large was needed, but he had too many real concerns to occupy his mind.

Thirty seconds later, he arrived at the county harbor. There was a white truck in the driveway with the headlights on. Once Glenn parked, the tall, stocky individual inside stepped out. He was a slightly balding, but otherwise well-groomed man wearing a button-down shirt and slacks under his raincoat. Not exactly boating attire, but Glenn figured the guy was hoping it would be a quick trip.

After seeing the badge on Glenn's jacket, he stepped forward and extended his hand.

"Good evening, Sheriff. Thanks for coming out. I'm Ben Leever. I work for the weather service." He smiled briefly, then wrinkled his jaw to stay focused on the matter. It was the hundredth time Glenn had to endure someone being shocked that the sheriff was this young.

"I hear you have a couple of people out here, Mr. Leever."

"They should've been back already," he said. "GPS on their boat shows they're still out there."

"Does it normally take this long to recover a buoy?"

"Not at all," Ben said. "Unless you don't know what you're doing. And one of those fellas, well . . . frankly, I think there's a couple wires touching in his head that shouldn't be."

That sparked a laugh from Glenn. "Okay, let's head out there, make sure nothing's wrong." He led him aboard Boat One. The cockpit provided just enough room for the two of them.

"Whew! Glad we're going on this one. I was worried we'd be taking one of the other boats. Not a fan of getting drenched." He leaned to his left, then felt something press down under the weight of his arm. He looked over and realized he was leaning on a chemical fire extinguisher. "Whoa!"

"Be careful with that. I had one fall off and burst all over the damn place one time," Glenn said. "I asked the county to install a proper box for that. Instead, they hung it on that stupid little hook." He started the engine and took them out. "These people go out frequently?"

"It's their first time in this area, I believe," Ben said. "The GPS tracker on the buoy went dead for some reason, so they probably had a hell of a time finding it, even though it was listed on the physical map. Then again, who uses those things anymore, right?"

"Not me," Glenn said. He laughed nervously. "What I mean, though, is—these people—any chance they're not responding because they might be. . . you know? A thing?"

It took Ben a moment to comprehend Glenn's question. "Oh! No. If you saw Andrew . . . just no. Trust me."

Both men chuckled. Glenn appreciated the levity. At least this guy seemed to have a decent personality, despite his unpleasant interaction with Dispatch.

During the five-mile trip, the wind continued hurtling swells at the boat. Only eighteen-inches high, they were not anything Glenn could not handle, but unsettling all the same. The rain thumped heavily on the overhead and deck.

"God, I hope it doesn't hail," Ben said.

"Don't jinx it." Another swell struck the bow, spraying mist in both directions. Glenn swallowed, sensing his stomach starting to spin.

This is just great. Get seasick in front of this guy. After the day I've had, this would be the icing on the cake.

Keeping a straight, confident posture, Glenn discreetly opened the lower drawer to his right. He was no stranger to the water, thus he rarely needed Dramamine, but the increased turbulence brought by the storm was wreaking havoc on his insides.

His discretion did not pay off. Ben saw the package come out of the drawer. Right away, he inched back. "You all right, Sheriff?"

"Yep. Of course. I was just going to offer you one."

"Oh, no thanks. I took one an hour ago."

"Gotcha." Glenn no longer cared at this point. He took one right in front of Ben and carried on. For the rest of the trip, he kept his eye on the distance and took very deep and steady breaths. Slowly but surely, the nausea backed off.

Oh, thank God.

"Hey." Ben held his phone to Glenn's face. "We're just about there. A little this way." He pointed left, not knowing to say 'port' or 'north'.

Glenn turned the boat and switched on the spotlights. With an inner knob, he panned one of them back and forth, swinging a seventy-foot stretch of light over an angry black sea.

"Found it," he said. He pointed at a knob above the windshield's left corner. "You see that? Aim that light on the boat." Ben followed the instruction, allowing Glenn to focus on steering them closer.

"They found the buoy," Ben said. He leaned forward and squinted. "What the hell?"

Glenn saw it, too. "Do weather buoys normally look like that?"

Ben shook his head. He swung the light to the company boat. The cockpit was crumpled, the hull indented in several locations, marked with several weird grooves.

Glenn lined the police boat nearby, then stepped out with a flashlight. Ben followed.

"Andrew? Erica?"

Glenn shook his head. They had a clear view of the interior. Nobody was on this boat.

"They're not here."

"Where are they?" Ben, on the verge of panic, pulled a second flashlight from the cockpit and waved it over the water. Each time the stream touched the boat, it revealed a new detail. On the inner corner of the windshield was a wet glob of blood. Dangling from the helm was a hand, clenched tightly, the flesh around the wrist bone stretched like bubble gum. "Sheriff? What happened here?"

"Calm down," Glenn said. He swallowed, the nausea threatening to take over again.

Staring at the hand, he noticed another oddity. The helm was crooked. It had come partly off the console. There was no blunt force damage to the wheel. It had been *pulled* off. He looked at the stretched tendons and skin dangling below it.

He was clinging on for dear life.

Another swell shook the police vessel. It was all over for Glenn now. He stumbled to the starboard side, then retched his insides out. His action had a domino effect on Ben, who hurled over the opposite side.

Lightheadedness came next. Seasickness and shock were working together. Glenn stumbled to the cockpit with his hands out, shutting the door behind him. As soon as it latched, he fell against the helm.

Several deep breaths followed.

Don't pass out. Don't pass out, you asshole. Like it or not, you're the sheriff. Under the circumstances, you can get away with vomiting, but you will never live down passing out.

"Sheriff?"

"Hang on. Making a radio call." It was only a partial lie. Once he got control of himself, he would make a call to Dispatch. First, he needed to stop the room from spinning.

He resumed the breathing exercise, watching Ben in the rearview mirror. He was sweeping his light across the water in search of his employees. This administrative guy, still on the verge of panic, managed to be more composed than the sheriff.

Glenn forced himself to stand up straight. He fumbled for his mic, clumsily dropping it near his foot. He knelt, picked it up, then reached for the channel knob.

He felt reverberation under his feet. Something thumped against the hull. Not heavily, but enough to be heard. What was more audible was the sound of scraping. It stirred childhood memories when he lost at a baseball game and angrily dragged his bat along the sidewalk.

The left spotlight flickered, the sheriff catching the glimpse of a serpentine shape bending below the window frame.

Another scraping followed. On the starboard side. Then ahead, along the bow. Behind him. Above him. All over the boat, something was rising out of the sea.

"SHERIFF!"

He heard running feet come toward the cockpit. Glenn turned and opened the door. Ben was one step away, his eyes and mouth wide with fright. His hands reached for the sheriff's but found nothing, for he was yanked backward.

Glenn beheld the sight of red, rubbery serpents, their bellies lined with suction cups. Emerging from those suction cups were crooked, razor-sharp hooks. Like angry spirits, the tentacles danced over the boat, while two of them fought over the prize.

One wrapped itself under Ben's armpits while another pulled at his legs. There was a sound of gagging, then popping, such as when one cracked their knuckles, only there was a hint of splintering to this sound. Then came the raining of guts as the two halves of Ben Leever came apart.

Dangling flesh and entrails, the two snake-things returned to the sea with their prizes. Meanwhile, the others proceeded to invade the boat. Zeroing in on the vibrations coming from the front, they lashed.

Glenn threw himself back into the cockpit, wrestling his pistol from its holster. It took three tugs before he remembered to unclip the strap. He yanked the Beretta free and fired into the mass of squiggly tentacles. Two of his bullets hit the door frame, several more missed entirely, and those that struck rubbery flesh only seemed to enrage the beasts more.

It only took five seconds to fire all seventeen rounds. Lightheadedness and adrenaline clashed, warping Glenn's senses. All reason was lost. He squeezed the trigger a dozen more times before he finally reached for a fresh magazine.

He kicked the door shut, only for it to hit one of the tentacles and bounce back. Screaming with rage and panic, he got to his feet and threw himself over the door. The tentacle pushed back, as if it knew it was preventing him from latching it.

Finally, he pressed the muzzle to the tip and fired repeatedly. The thing recoiled, the door shutting behind it.

The boat shook. The engine groaned and died. In the chaos, Glenn failed to realize the other slithery appendages were constricting his boat.

An explosive impact sent glass flying into the cockpit. Glenn turned around and was immediately greeted by two invading tentacles. They lashed blindly. *Searching.*

A moment later, they found him. He jumped away from one, only to be batted by the other. Back and forth, they smacked him around. Now, the room was literally spinning.

He felt pressure around his midsection, then the pain of sharp objects entering his skin. His mind flashed to those hooks, like those to snare a fish.

"No! NO!"

He pressed his pistol into the tentacle and emptied the mag. Blood spurted across the room. The tentacle retreated, tossing him to the floor in the process. The other remained, smacking the walls in search of him.

Glenn fired, only to hear those empty *clicks* once again.

The tentacle found the wall, then worked its way down, right toward his face. All sense of reasoning was lost. Trapped and with nowhere to escape, Glenn threw his arms over his face and screamed.

His attacker raked against the wall and everything attached to it.

A metal object struck the floor. Suddenly, the cockpit was full of a burning mist. As soon as it appeared, the tentacle withdrew and disappeared into the ocean along with its brethren.

Glenn opened his eyes. The room was tan, as though it had morphed into a desert. Rolling on the floor was the chemical fire extinguisher.

He found the door and let himself out. The tentacles were gone, the boat slowly spinning in circles. All that remained was the rain and the pile of Ben Leever's guts on the deck.

This time, Glenn McCullough passed out.

CHAPTER 13

"How ya doin', Pedro? Hanging in there?"

Though he carried through like a good soldier, it did not take a PhD to know Pedro was less than eager to return to the Atlantic Submarine Canyon. Getting the twenty-six-year-old PhD candidate to smile felt as difficult as sending a rocket to the moon.

He steered the sub over a rigid series of spiked rocks, which created the illusion of flying over a giant porcupine.

"Someone asked me once if I would rather go into space or visit the bottom of the ocean. I used to say the latter, because the vacuum of space, just waiting to suck you out of your spaceship, seemed too inevitable." He shuddered after a creaking sound echoed through the hull. They were normal, simply fluctuations in pressure and underwater currents, but it didn't matter. Each time they occurred, Pedro thought the world was ending. "Now, I think different."

Linda snickered. "Oh, Pedro. You're so dramatic."

"Yeah? You remember that when you're doing one of these dives and something bumps you. You see those damn red alarm lights, then that automated voice echoing from this speaker up here, 'Hull breach.' Then you'll think to yourself, 'Pedro wasn't dramatic, he was spot on!'"

Linda laughed again. "Now I really think you're dramatic." She took the joystick and rotated the *Century Cross* to port. "Come on, Drama Boy. Let's get back to work."

They were moving northwest this time, toward the Northeast Channel. Last night, during a phone conference with Dr. Siena Lehnert, she learned of high toxicity levels in the Gulf of Maine. It was undoubtedly connected to what was happening here in the canyon. With that in mind, it made sense to backtrack and conduct a more detailed search of the northwest end.

Her suspicions were substantiated by the overabundance of dead fish lying about. There were twice as many here as anywhere else they had searched so far, indicating the level of toxicity was greater.

Linda tapped a few keys on the instrument panel, then extended one of the arms. "Water sample intake . . . complete. All right, let's keep heading this way."

"This is weird, Professor," Pedro said, looking at the pale white corpses in the glow of the searchlight. "It's like the aftermath of some extinction-level event."

"That's not too far off," she said. "What happened here is the equivalent of an underwater plague. Only this one was not natural, but man-made."

Pedro sipped on his water bottle. He did not want to ingest too many fluids. Having a full bladder all the way down here was not an appealing thought. Still, his dry throat was an equally distracting issue. That, and dehydration.

It was cold as ice here in the depths, his left hand shaking against the controls, yet he pressed the bottle to his brow as if to cool down. Every few feet, they came across another body. Tuna, squid, various deep-sea fish, and little salt and pepper dots that were shrimp.

"Everything's dead."

"Not everything," Linda said. She was looking to the upper left. Pedro leaned forward to see what she was looking at.

He shook his head. "I don't see it."

"You will."

"Don't see how—WHOA!" Several globs of pink and white flesh hit the visor. Tentacles, lined with suckers the size of silver dollars, stretched from each one. Little beaks extended from a tiny orifice, scraping against the glass. "Oh, Christ! Holy shit!"

They were all over the glass, completely obscuring their view of their surroundings. Tentacles swarmed the submersible like earthworms in a rainstorm, each one appearing to have a life of its own.

Linda chuckled, taking joy in this massive cuttlefish attack, which spurred Pedro further.

"How can you laugh? They're going to crush us."

"Relax, kid. These little guys are tough, but they're not nearly strong enough to break through this glass, let alone breach the hull. This thing's designed to handle a swarm of locals four times the size of these bad boys." She crossed her arms and leaned back. "Just give them a moment. They'll conclude we're inedible and move on."

Pedro's hand shook against the joystick as he kept the submersible level. The last thing they wanted to do was set down on that rugged seafloor. He swallowed, battling a wave of nausea. He loved the sea and all its creatures, but that did not mean he enjoyed literally staring into their gullets.

After what felt like an eternity, one of them finally broke free. Another followed, then another. The sub juddered as several others broke away from the top and sides. They glided through the reach of the spotlight, no longer appearing like violent predators, but graceful spirits—just uglier.

"See?" Linda said.

Pedro glared at her and that shit-eating grin on her face. "You suck, you know that?"

"Thus, my point is proven about you being dramatic."

After a brief pause, the two of them burst into laughter. Pedro wiped his sleeve over his forehead, brushing away the sweat that had accumulated.

"Man, that was freaky."

"You lived through it."

"Yeah, you're right. I guess I need to have more faith in the structural integrity of . . . these . . ." He instantly forgot what he was talking about, for his attention shifted to the cylinder-shaped object in the spotlight. "Doc?"

"I see it." Linda was all business now. She picked up her headset and moved the mic to her lips. "This is *Century Cross*. You paying attention to the monitors, Driver?"

The pause indicated that her second assistant, Ann Driver, had probably stepped away from the desk and was actively running back. It made sense; otherwise, she would have commented on the cuttlefish infestation. At least she kept her radio on her whenever she walked the decks of the research vessel *Tenacious Seeker.*

"This is Driver. I see it."

There was no mistaking the object. It was a barrel full of toxic waste.

Linda took the controls and moved the sub forward. Where there was one, there were others. That theory was proven within ten seconds. Another barrel came into view. The further northwest they went, the more barrels they spotted.

"Oh, my God," Linda said. Now she sounded like the one who was fighting nausea. Lying around each barrel were the bodies of rotting fish. Dead cuttlefish lay among the crowd, still clinging to the toxic meals that ended their lives. "Ann?"

"I'll get the captain."

"Have him alert the EPA and the Coast Guard." Linda applied thrust, minimum power. Everywhere they looked, there were barrels. Some were split open, revealing a greenish mixture in some, and a white mixture in others. Sludge, chemical mixtures, bleach, waste. All was toxic and was destroying this region of the ocean.

Pedro settled his light on one busted barrel and its contents. This one did not contain liquid, but solid materials. They resembled grenade shrapnel, each one having its own shape and size.

"They, whoever 'they' are, are also dumping metal and glass, and who knows what else."

Linda lowered the sub to the barrel and used one of the claws to pick up samples.

"We'll find out. I wanna get a vial of everything we find."

"That might take a couple of trips," Pedro said.

"So be it." She extended the port quarter arm, which opened like the scoop of a bulldozer, and shoveled a pound of the shrapnel waste. The upper lid shut over it, securing the find. "Got it. Let's continue on. Looks like these barrels form a trail that leads to that big hill up ahead. We'll head toward that."

Pedro stared at the large mound up ahead. From their location, it was nothing more than a distant black shape, one with a rigid exterior. It was another example of the strange deep ocean features formed by pressure from tectonic plates.

Linda slowly advanced toward it, keeping her eyes on the graveyard below them.

"This is the captain. You hear me, Linda?"

"Yeah Karl, I hear you. I'm assuming you're up to speed?"

"Correct. I'm seeing what you're seeing right now. Professor, they've had to have been doing this for a while to have dropped this much trash."

"I agree. I've collected some samples. We'll probably be headed up shortly to drop them off for the chemists. We'll give the batteries time to recharge, then head back down for more. Hopefully by then, the EPA will be here."

"Hey, Professor? Mind backing up about six or seven feet? Pan camera two to the left."

Linda considered asking why but decided not to bother wasting time. If Captain Karl Hubert wanted to look at something, it was for a good reason. She reversed the sub then rotated the camera. Before the lens captured the object, she spotted it with her own two eyes.

"Whoa."

"What the hell is that?" Pedro said.

The thing was like the metal waste from the one barrel, only this chunk was larger than the containers themselves. It was seven feet long, the edges appearing sharp enough to cleave a man down the middle.

"They're dumping large metal fragments down here," Linda said.

"Possibly. Except, that looks like a piece of hull."

"Hull? Like from a ship?" Pedro muttered. Linda resumed the trip up the path. After ten yards, they came across another large piece of metal lying near some barrels. The farther they went, the more miscellaneous shapes came into view. Long, narrow pieces of metal—guardrails. Large chunks of glass.

Pedro leaned over and put his hand over Linda's, forcing her to stop the sub. He adjusted his spotlight, settling it on a black V-shaped object. A boot.

Nobody said a word, for everyone, including those watching from the *Tenacious Seeker,* shared the same thought. They looked to that strange 'hill' in the distance. For the first time, Linda was nervous to advance the sub.

The closer they got, the more details took form. One end of this object was pointed, the edges gradually expanding as they looked further down its length. It was resting on its side, a large structure protruding roughly thirty feet down. The sub's occupants waved the spotlights down the length of its one-hundred-and-thirty-foot body. At its rear, a buzzsaw-like object protruded.

Linda's suspicion was confirmed. They were looking at a ship wreckage.

In life, it had stood forty feet high and was surrounded with thick guardrails and steel decking. It had been light brown in color, though much of the paint had faded from pressure and exposure.

Linda brought the sub to what remained of the main deck.

Pedro gripped the edge of his seat with one hand. "Do we really want to get closer?"

"Yes, you do," Karl said.

"Captain, are there any records of shipwrecks in this area? Any Mayday calls in the last couple of weeks that you're aware of?" Linda said.

"I already ran it through the computer. No and no. This is new."

She kept the spotlights fixed on the gaping wound in the deck. Huge shards of metal resembled tidal waves, cresting outward over the rest of the ship. Beneath this breach was the cargo hold, where a half dozen other barrels were stored.

"New update," Pedro said. "I think we've confirmed this is the ship that's been doing the dumping."

"But how did it end up here? And what in God's name did this?" Linda waved her finger at the metal folds.

"Probably from impact," Pedro said.

"Kid, I know what impact breaches look like. This was not caused by implosion. This was ripped *out*. Either it got pushed out from within, maybe from a fuel explosion, or . . . something pulled this apart."

Before Pedro could respond to that, Karl's voice came through the receiver.

"Guys, go around the other side. See if you can get the name of this thing."

"Hang on." Linda ascended and glided the *Century Cross* over the wreck, turning to face the starboard bow. The underside was bent out of proportion, the hull heavily marked with long incisions.

The white letters of the ship name had faded but were intact enough for them to read. *Alexandra Yale.*

"Stand by."

As they waited for the captain to check records of this ship, Linda and Pedro examined the keel. Six feet of steel had been heavily compressed by some sort of intense concentrated pressure.

"I had a pet bird once." Pedro stared at the strange gash as he spoke. "The thing was a terror. Absolutely hated its house. Once, it tried to bite the corner of the roof, which was made from aluminum. It wrinkled like skin around the punctures."

Linda brought the sub closer. Sure enough, just as Pedro described, there were two puncture wounds in the middle of this 'incision.' The analogy was spot on; it was as if a giant bird had bitten the keel of this ship.

"I'm back."

"What'd you find?"

"It's from Nova Scotia. Owner is Christopher Willis. Don't know much about the guy himself, other than the fact that he declared bankruptcy two years ago, but then managed to pay off his debts the following year."

"Looks like he found some under-the-table work," Linda said.

"Captain, has this ship been declared missing?" Pedro said.

"Supposedly, this ship is supposed to be out on the Flemish Cap right now, hauling swordfish. It last departed five days ago."

Linda was silent, staring at the indentations in the boat. The upper edges of the deck were crushed inward in several locations, each area lined with the same elongated scrapings.

Without saying a word, she initiated ascent.

Pedro was still gripping his seat. "You think I'm dramatic now?"

CHAPTER 14

For the first time all summer, the early sunrise failed to wake Dakota. He needed the rest after the vigorous night he'd had. It was not until Siena finally pried his arm from her bare midsection that he awakened. She did not do it out of contempt, but to allow herself to roll onto her back.

He kissed her cheek and smiled. "Morning."

"Hi." She was staring at the ceiling. "You have any idea how much I hate myself right now?"

"Should we go over again what a bad liar you are?"

She smiled then brushed his chin with her thumb. "Nah. You've made your point loud and clear."

Dakota chuckled. "I don't think I was the one that was loud."

Siena playfully tapped his face with her palm. She leaned up, only to lie back down. The bed was too comfy, and Dakota's presence too intoxicating.

"Can I ask you something?"

"Sure." A flutter of nervousness came over him.

"You're retired now. Why are you still living here?"

"You say that like Saw Ridge is a crummy place."

"Oh, no. Not at all, don't get me wrong. But you've made it clear that you've fantasized about leaving. I understand the winter here is hell on your joints."

Dakota's smile faded. He knew the real question behind what was spoken. 'Why won't you move to Florida with me?' It was a question he dreaded. Immediately, he felt his spirit being split in two different directions.

"I guess I've been here so long . . ." his voice trailed off. Now he was the bad liar. There was a hint of truth to his unfinished statement. He did enjoy living in Saw Ridge, but he never saw himself as the type to be cemented to one place, even after three decades.

Siena rolled to her left. Her sigh was barely audible, but Dakota picked up on it. This time, her regret was genuine.

"I'm not gonna be here long," she said.

He ran his hand over her shoulder. "I know."

"I told myself I wouldn't put myself through this again, but yet, here I am."

"Oh, quit being so dramatic."

She shook her head. "You're not going to leave, Dakota. I know you too well. You feel an obligation to this community, especially now of all times. Since Glenn's term has another three full years to go."

Dakota plopped his head on the pillow. This was not how he expected this morning to go. Sure, this conversation was inevitable, but he thought he could at least enjoy the morning-after sex. The mood was lost.

So much for trying for seconds.

"I don't know what to say."

"Just say the truth," Siena said. "You don't love me enough to follow me to Florida."

"Wait a second." He sat up, his eyes fiery. "You're pissed at me for not ditching everything and moving to Florida three years back?"

"You knew I couldn't stay."

"That lane goes both ways, lady. You knew I couldn't leave. I still had a term to fulfill. Normally, I'm not one for long-distance relationships, but I think with what we had, we could have made something work. And why is all this coming out now?"

Siena pulled the blanket up to her chin. "Don't worry about it. Forget I said anything."

"You're asking a little much there. No, I'd like to know. Why is this coming out now? You had all day yesterday."

She flipped over. "Because I remember how much I wanted you to come with me."

Dakota stared quietly, then cracked a grin. "The sex was that good, huh?"

"Ugh!" She faced away from him.

"Admit it."

Her next groan was an act. Finally, she relaxed enough to chuckle.

"Okay, maybe." She turned back, wrapped her arms around his neck, and kissed him passionately. "I do hate myself for putting us through this again. You're not going to leave. The people here still look up to you. More importantly, you're worried about Glenn."

Dakota groaned. "You know, it makes it difficult to get things going again when you keep mentioning my kid."

She scoffed, then rested her forehead on his chest. "That ship has sailed for now. Right now, I'm hungry."

"No wonder you woke up in a mood," Dakota said. He playfully pushed her away as though repulsed, then got up to get dressed. "Okay, your highness, how can I settle this need of yours? Eggs and coffee? An omelet?"

"Coffee first and foremost," she said, buttoning her jeans. "Honestly, all I need is a fried egg slapped on a piece of toast, and I'm good."

"You trust me with this cooking operation?"

"I am taking a risk there, aren't I?" She laughed. "Yes, I trust you to fry an egg."

"As long as you don't have high expectations for the yolk." Dakota stepped out into the kitchen and got the coffee pot going. While he waited, he opened the fridge and got the eggs out. His eye went to the window, which looked to the north. He could see the shoreline, and occasionally, a boat.

The boat he saw this morning held his attention. He recognized the green stripes of the county sheriff's patrol boats.

"What's this about?" he muttered.

"Don't worry, I'll help clean up this catastrophe," Siena said. She got to work picking up the stir fry skillet and scraping the contents into the trash.

"No, the guys are out on patrol."

"That unusual?"

"This early on a Sunday? They usually don't go unless something's going on. Don't tell me they're still looking for floaters." He walked to the front door.

"Dakota, you're not the sheriff anymore. It's not your concern."

"I'm just curious—a concerned citizen! There you go." He stepped outside with his old police radio in hand. Perks of being sheriff for twenty years, he got to keep some of his old equipment. "Zolnai? Denham? Is that you goofing around out there? Better not be lobster-diving on the job."

He watched the boat turn toward his dock and increase speed.

Siena stepped out the front door, coffee mug in hand. "Everything all right?"

"Not sure." He hustled to the dock, arriving at its end as the police boat arrived. Deputies Denham and Zolnai stood at the cockpit, both appearing forlorn. It was the same look the former sheriff had whenever he had to inform family members of a deceased person.

Denham finally made eye contact. "Sir . . ."

"What happened? Where's Glenn?"

"He went out on the water last night. Went to inspect a buoy with some guy from the weather service. Never returned."

"There's no radio response," Zolnai said. "We've been trying to reach him all night and morning."

"Buoy? Which buoy?"

"Second shift's log says Weather Reader Five, but none of us know which one that is or where it's at," Denham said.

"Weather Five. I know where that is. Hang on."

"Sheriff, uh . . . you're not the sheriff anymore. This isn't your responsibility . . ." Denham gave up. Dakota was already heading back in his house, and more importantly, there was no stopping a man from going after his son.

He dashed past Siena, grabbed his boat key from the computer table, then was right back outside. Siena was right behind him. There was no need for discussion. Glenn was in trouble and there was no way she would let Dakota go out there by himself.

On board, she freed the moorings and gave the okay for castoff. Dakota started the boat and gunned the engine, whipping past the police boat.

Denham and Zolnai looked at each other, then mutually shrugged. *Might as well follow him.*

CHAPTER 15

Glenn awoke from a strange nightmare involving smothering and worms. He flipped himself on his back and tapped his face. The sensation of slime on the deck did not help with the mental recovery.

He looked at his surroundings. The deck was a mess with slime all around. The hull had been peeled outward in various areas. The pilothouse was crumpled like a soda can, the cockpit wrecked and covered in chemical dust. A stench radiated from a translucent slime that coated the vessel. In the corner, a brownish-red splatter surrounded a thin ropy substance.

Then, in the blink of an eye, it all came back to him: the tentacles, the wrecked weather service boat, Ben Leever being torn in half, his entrails raining down.

Screaming, Glenn was up on his feet. He spun on his heel, found his Beretta, and loaded his final magazine.

The more his senses returned, the more pain he felt. His eyes and lungs were in agony, probably due to exposure to the extinguisher chemical. He leaned over the side and reached down for some water, only to retract. The slime was on his jacket sleeve, secreted by those enormous arms. Snakes, worms, tentacles—they had to be the latter. The memory of those suction cups triggered a flashback to Siena talking about cephalopods in the county harbor.

Last night, he was attacked by a giant squid.

Not nearly big enough to collapse a boat, she said.

Glenn watched the water, his eyes burning. The temptation was too strong. He needed to wash his eyes. Saltwater would sting, but it beat the burning of this chemical.

In a sweeping motion, he took a handful of water and splashed his face with it. The next couple of minutes were spent coughing. After regaining control, he stumbled to the cockpit and turned the ignition key.

As he feared, the engine was dead. Even worse, the radio had been destroyed. Five miles out, it would be impossible to get a signal on his phone. He was trapped in the middle of the ocean, with a colossal beast lurking below.

"Sweet Jesus, this can't be happening." The burning sensation in his chest worsened the anxiety. He paced along the deck and tried to think of a solution. Instead, he gradually descended into madness. He tried dialing several numbers on his phone, only to see the infuriating dots of a loading screen, followed by a *Call Failed* alert. The cherry on top of the cake came in the form of a dead battery. There was not much to begin with, since the phone had been attempting all night to get a signal.

The smell of the secretion, the sight of the rotting intestines and the infinite stretch of blue all around him worked together to overwhelm his psyche.

The outburst came in the form of kicking the pilothouse door. Only hanging by its top hinge, it easily collapsed into the cockpit's interior. It provided the release Glenn needed. He stood, eyes closed, then calmed himself down.

"Okay," he said to himself, "where the hell is it? How the hell do I get out of here?" He scanned the horizon. There were a few fishing boats in the far distance, none of which were remotely close enough to help. Even if he shot a flare, it would likely go unnoticed by them.

His eyes went to the weather service boat. *Is it functional?* The nearly broken helm was definitely not a good sign. Unfortunately, the only way Glenn could find out was to get aboard.

The gentle waves felt deceitful, as though the ocean were trying to tempt him into the arms of that huge squid. Or perhaps it was nature's way of telling him 'now is your chance to cross the water.' Glenn only knew two certainties: staying here was suicide, and so was going in the water.

Another mental breakdown threatened to consume him. It boiled his fragile mind, triggering small tremors in his hands. Only another glance at the service boat's cockpit prevented Glenn from snapping.

Its radio was intact. He was literally two-hundred feet away from his only way out of this predicament.

"Fuck it." He dug the inflatable life raft from the cockpit, pulled the ripcord and ballooned it to its full six-foot length. He dug through the cabinet and found the flare gun and two cartridges.

Glenn looked at the boats in the distance. "Would they see the flare that far out?" After a few moments of thought, a new thought hit him. "No. I'm eager to get out of here, but that thing will attack any boat who comes near. That's what happened to us last night." He looked skyward. "I need a damn helicopter. Or a goddamn battleship." He took another glance at the flare gun, then tucked it in his jacket pocket. If nothing else, it might be useful in fending off the squid should it reappear.

The time was now.

Glenn lowered the raft, touching its end to the water. The sight of ripples made him cringe. How sensitive was that creature? He thought of sharks and how easily they could detect vibration.

Are octopuses the same way? What about squid? . . . Was that thing a squid? Or an octopus?

"Big! That's what it is. Fucking big."

He leveled the raft, then gently lowered himself in. Every bobbing motion sparked chills. Should those tentacles appear, there would be no escape. There was no fire extinguisher holder that would save him out here.

Slowly, he pierced the ocean with the paddle. One stroke moved the raft outward.

So far, no monster.

Another stroke. And another.

Fifty feet of distance: one-fourth of the way there. More strokes increased that distance to one hundred feet. The closer he got, the more courageous he felt. The second half of the short journey was accomplished in half the time.

He got on his knees and reached for the maintenance boat.

Thud!

The impact came from underneath. Glenn fell on his back, his hands wildly scrambling for his weapons. The urge to scream took hold, though all he could do was babble.

It was here. His movements were detected. Any second now, those tentacles would snatch him out of the raft.

Another *thud* rocked the raft, knocking him about. He heard splashes from the other side of the rubber hull. He could not see the slimy tentacles yet.

He remained on his back, waiting for those ammonia dripping appendages to coil over the raft. Instead, nothing appeared.

The raft bumped a third time. Still, no tentacles appeared. His exhausted mind jumped to the only logical conclusion it could conjecture.

It's playing with its food. It knows it's freaking me out. Glenn stared at the clouds above. A headache, spurred by stress and his electrolyte imbalance, was the straw that broke the camel's back. *Motherfucker. It's doing this on purpose.*

Like a small fuse to a stick of dynamite, the fear burnt down. Instead of pure panic, he felt anger. He had survived the night and crossed the water all the way over here only to become fish food.

"Fine . . ." He held his pistol in one hand and the flare gun in the other. "Wanna eat me? FINE!"

Glenn propped himself on his knees and pointed both muzzles to the water, fingers on trigger, ready to apply pressure.

A splash hit his face.

Three dolphins hopped about, cackling to each other like the Three Stooges. One bumped the raft then ran off.

Glenn lowered the guns. It took a few seconds to compose himself before he managed to crack a smile. Even under these circumstances, after the horrors he had gone through, he couldn't help but find these aquatic mammals highly amusing. Like teenagers they were, or maybe drunken goofballs in a bar. Regardless, he was happy to see them and not a carnivorous kraken.

"Excuse me, kids. You're messing with police property and could be subject to a fine," he said. Calming down, he holstered his pistol. "I suppose if you guys are here, that thing isn't around, either. You guys would know, right? You use echolocation and all that? Oh, well. Anyways, keep an eye out for me, will ya?"

Some would say it was a waste of valuable time, but as far as Glenn was concerned, the flippancy was helpful. Already, he felt the stress and tension lift a bit.

It did not change the reality of his predicament, however.

Glenn lifted himself onto the maintenance boat. The sight of the helmsman's dangling hand gave him pause, as did the crumpled deck. Only when on deck did he notice the narrowness of the boat. It had been squeezed tight. Only by pure luck did a breach not form. The deck was a series of rolling hills, the sides bent inward. The beast probably stopped the attack only because there was no more food.

He rushed to the console and grabbed the radio.

"Hello. Mayday. Coast Guard? Garrison County Police Department? Anybody reading this?"

Nothing.

Glenn inspected the radio. The casing was cracked, the antennae above busted.

"Damn it!" He threw the mic down.

In the water, the dolphins clicked and cried. One, swimming a half-dozen meters off the starboard bow, started racing west, calling to its companions. The other turned and raced alongside it.

Glenn watched the three of them depart, their dorsal fins cutting across the water's surface like sharks.

"Am I *that* scary when I'm mad?"

A mountain of ocean rose between the three dolphins. Like a bubble, it burst into a series of crystalline waves. The translucence faded to red.

Fear returned with the sight of an enormous tentacle. Rising twenty feet in the air, it constricted one of the dolphins. Blood spurted from where the hooks tore into its flesh.

As quickly as it appeared, the tentacle vanished, delivering its prize to the squid's mouth.

And it was indeed a squid. This time, there was no rain, night, or the shaking of a boat to make Glenn question his eyes. It was broad daylight. The creature was real. Enormous.

Hungry.

He grabbed the radio again. "Come on, please work . . . This is Sheriff McCullough. Can anyone hear this transmission?" He tapped the device, then slammed his elbow into it, punishing it as if it purposely failed to work.

Something about doing that felt good. Needing a little extra release, Glenn hit it again.

The whole boat lurched.

Glenn fell to his knees, eye level to the dangling hand which still managed to hold on.

Numerous shadows swept over him. Drawn by his vibrations, the creature had returned to finish last night's snack. The tentacles, dripping fluid, arched over the boat.

Some crossed over from opposite sides, squeezing the already crumpled vessel. He heard a squeezing of metal followed by a heavy crack. Glenn was no engineer, but he did not need to be to know that was a breach in the underside. He could hear the water filling the engine compartment below him.

There was more intent beyond simply crushing the boat. One of those tentacles angled over the cockpit and wormed its way toward him. Hooks extended from is many suckers. They were twin hooks, like the tusks of a mastodon, except upside down and much sharper.

Glenn raised his pistol muzzle to his temple and gritted his teeth. Yet, even now, he struggled to squeeze the trigger and end it. He had spent a few Sundays in church, and though he never considered himself religious, he held a basic belief in the existence of Heaven and Hell. One lesson that always stuck out was the topic of suicide and how it automatically led to Hell.

Even now, with his blood like a raging river inside him, his senses overwhelmed, that fear still remained, for there was no escape from eternal torture.

Hellfire . . . FIRE!

Glenn looked to the splintering deck. In the middle was the big red spare fuel cannister. With his Beretta, he popped two holes into it. He fired the flare then tucked his head under his arms.

The cannister erupted in a volcanic display. The ball of fire hit the tentacles around it and clung to the flesh like napalm. The tentacles unwound and danced like burning demons worshiping a devil.

Glenn was on his feet, loading the second cannister into the flare gun. On the main deck, the fire enlarged. Next thing he knew, it was burning over the water. The smell of burning fuel registered in his mind. It was not just the gas cannister, but the main fuel tank. It had ruptured during the attack and was leaking into the ocean.

He peeked, saw the fire entering the crack in the hull.

"Oh, shit!"

He found a clean area of ocean near the bow and dove. Seventy remaining gallons ignited in the blink of an eye. The boat disappeared underneath an orange-and-black cloud.

More fire touched the tentacles, the vibration traveling far and fast. The only thing faster was the creature's retreat.

***

"What in the name of heaven?"

Roger Wilkerson had worked near mines for twenty of his fifty-seven years. He knew what an explosion sounded like. Furthermore, he knew what a smoke cloud looked like. Over a mineral deposit, the occasional smoke trail was common. Out here, in the middle of the ocean, not so much.

"Holy shit, Dad!" His twenty-five-year-old son climbed to the bridge and gazed at the black, twisting tower to the northwest. Nick's thoughts were the same as his father and brother's. "Something blew up out there."

"No shit, Sherlock," Zach said. The youngest sibling, he tended to be the snarkiest. It was his only way to make up for being the least experienced in the family business. That fact was made evident by his constant attempts to sound smart by speculating. "Some assholes probably using depth charges."

"Depth charges wouldn't make such a big smoke trail, idiot," Nick said.

"Knock it off, you two," Roger said. "Zach, haul the anchor up. We're going over there."

"Shouldn't we call the police?" Nick asked.

"I will, but we're still heading over there. We're several miles out. It'll take valuable time for the cops to get out here." With that in mind, Roger grabbed his radio. "Hello, Sheriff's Office. This is Roger Wilkerson of the fishing trawler *Horizon Line,* reporting an explosion northwest of our position."

With the anchor line up, he drove the boat in the direction of the smoke trail.

***

"Dakota! HEY, DAKOTA?!"

"Hey, stop! They're calling for us," Siena said. Dakota stopped the boat and looked back at his former employees.

Denham was at the helm with the radio in hand. "You sure it's an explosion?"

"Unless you can give me one other explanation why there's a big cloud of smoke in the middle of the Gulf."

"Fair enough." Denham looked to the former sheriff. "Got a report of some kind of explosion over by Carrier Reef."

"I know where that is," Dakota said. He aimed the *Pilgrimage* northeast and put the throttle back in action. After a half-mile, he could see the trail of smoke up ahead. "Oh, Lord. Don't let that be Glenn."

***

For the second time in twelve hours, Glenn was knocked unconscious. This time, it was only for a few seconds. The body's natural reflex to inhale put water up his nose, triggering a gag reflex which shocked Glenn back to consciousness.

He awoke in a frenzy. The world around him was both bright and dark, cold and hot. Hell.

Up above was the orange glow of fire. Down below was the cold reef. It all came back to him. He had dived from the boat right before it exploded. There was no sign of the squid.

For the moment, being devoured was not his main concern. His lungs were aching. Much of the air had been knocked out of him in the blast. Everything had happened so fast, he had not taken a decent breath before jumping.

Glenn raced for the surface, emerging less than a yard from the ring of fire. The maintenance boat was reduced to scrap, the raft deflated, leaving nothing but his useless police boat.

It floats. Not entirely useless.

He swam along the literal ring of fire, while keeping an eye out for the squid. His memory flashed to those tentacles, encased in fire, swaying over the vessel. With that backflash came the hope that the injuries were enough to kill the thing.

"Who am I kidding?" he said to himself, spitting water. With that in mind, he deliberately stuck as close to the fire as possible. The creature had learned that fire hurt, and this bright orange glow meant it was still burning.

He reached the department boat and pulled himself aboard, nearly slipping on the entrails.

The sight of the brownish biohazard erased what little poise he had built up. It was a reminder that he was still stuck in the middle of nowhere. That thing would be back, and this time there was no escape.

Glenn stumbled into the pilothouse and slumped against the console. Just like last night, he was fighting to regain control of his stomach.

A heavy droning sound made him lift his head. He peeked through the broken windshield at the approaching vessel. It was sixty feet in length, equal to the height of the outriggers. On the port bow was its name: *Horizon Line*.

He knew these people. Roger Wilkerson and his two sons, Nick and Zach.

A brief feeling of joy was washed away by dreaded knowledge. They were over two-hundred meters away—more than enough distance from the dwindling flames.

"Hey! Anyone there?" Roger shouted.

Glenn raced to the edge of the boat and waved his arms. "NO! DON'T COME CLOSER! RUN! RUN, DAMN YOU!!!!"

"Hot damn! Look at that," Roger said, staring at the field of wreckage.

"The sheriff's here," Nick said. He looked at the officer, dripping wet, shouting at them. Whatever he was saying, it was drowned out by the thumping of the *Horizon Line*.

"His boat's messed up bad!" Zach said. "Look at that."

"He needs help," Roger said. "Hold on, Sheriff!"

He closed in on the police vessel, angling the *Horizon Line* to line its starboard side with that of the police vessel's. The closer they got, the more distinct the sheriff's cries became.

"No! Get out of here! THERE'S SOMETHING IN THE WATER!"

Roger looked at his equally confused son. "Head aft. Be ready to pick him up."

"Dad, maybe we should do what he says."

"He's soaking wet, bruised, and looks like hell. I'm not even sure he's in his right mind. He needs to get off that boat as soon as possible. Get aft! Help him aboard."

Nick climbed down and joined Zach at the starboard quarter. The boat drew to fifty meters. The sheriff's rants grew more intense.

"Run! Run! Go! There's a large animal in the water!"

Nick shook his head. "Something's wrong."

Zach scoffed. "Oh really?!" He waved his hand at the fire. "You mean boats don't explode every single day?"

"No, I mean I think we should do what he says."

"Oh, for chrissake! You're not believing this shit about a sea monster, are you?"

"Well . . ."

"Quit it. You need your head examined. The guy probably caused this and is playing dumb." He leaned over the side and stared into the water. "Oh no! Ahhhh! I see it!"

"Really?"

Zach shut his eyes and burst into laughter. "No! You dumbass! There's no sea monsters." He opened his eyes then cocked his head back. His laughter metamorphosed into a wailing shriek.

Under the water was a red snake-like creature, coiled like a spring. In a blur of motion, it unwound. Equally as fast, it was coiled again, this time around Zach's body.

Seeing his brother lifted ten feet into the air, Nick could do nothing but scream.

Roger turned around. He opened his mouth to speak, but nothing came out. Fright and disbelief filled his mind. In the span of a second, he went from initial shock, to questioning if what he was seeing was even real, to uncontrollable terror. The cracking of bones and his son's agonized howl gave his throat the boost it needed.

Like Nick, all he could do was scream.

Blood spewed from Zach's nose, his eyes bulging from their sockets. His jaw was wide open, cheeks peeled back, tongue wiggling in the center as though trying to imitate the other tentacles.

One rose over the portside. Another at the stern. A series of thumps and scrapes echoed from the keel. The *Horizon Line* rocked back and forth. More of these things were clutching the underside and shaking the boat.

The sprinkling of water made Roger turn around. Rising over the bow was a thirty-foot tentacle, its hooded tip bending down as though to gaze at him. It lashed blindly, crushing the instrument panel. The canopy snapped and fell to the side. Wet flesh slapped Roger's torso, knocking him backward.

He felt his heel slip over the edge of the flybridge. As soon as he realized he was in freefall, he smacked down on the main deck. Everything after that literally became a blur.

***

"There!" Dakota said. "I see him."

"What is that?" Siena said. "Something's happening with that other boat."

They remained silent, watching the event as the view gradually improved with proximity.

"You guys seeing what we're seeing?" Denham radioed.

"It's a damn squid," Dakota said.

There was no mistaking those squirmy appendages surrounding the second vessel. With binoculars, Siena could see the 'dots' on their undersides. Only from this distance did they resemble dots. In reality, they were suction cups as large as a seat cushion.

"Deputies, is Glenn responding to the radio?"

"Negative. We have no way of knowing whether . . ." Denham decided not to finish that sentence.

As it turned out, he did not have to. Sharp cracks echoed from the distance. The two deputies and former sheriff had enough experience with firearms to know what a nine-millimeter sounded like.

"He's alive," Dakota said. "Siena, take the wheel." Once her fingers touched the helm, Dakota dove to the main deck and collected his own nine-millimeter, the duty belt, and a Remington twelve-gauge shotgun. For good measure, he grabbed his fire axe.

He returned to the deck, resembling a pirate ready to raid a cargo ship.

***

With each squeeze of the trigger, the slippery wet Beretta threatened to fly out of Glenn's grasp. For the first time, Glenn understood the difference between shooting paper targets and moving ones. Though far larger, the tentacles were much tougher to hit. Each one seemed to have a consciousness of its own, yet like ants, they had a unified purpose.

They peeled the *Horizon Line* apart like an onion. Large fragments of hull came off the body, exposing the interior. Sparks spat from the engine like breadcrumbs before it sputtered to a stop. Two arms, thicker and longer than the others, wrapped themselves around the bow. Their tips were hooded, like the crest of a king cobra. And like cobras, they bared fangs, not from a mouth, but from dozens of suction cups.

The *Horizon Line's* bow imploded from the pressure, shaking the rest of the vessel. The tentacles tightened their grip. The shaking intensified.

Glenn watched as the stern began to rise. The squid was pulling the vessel downward.

On deck, Nick Wilkerson was pulling his father up the slope, meanwhile attempting to swat at the tentacles. He had a small fishing knife in hand. The first several slashes found nothing but air. Finally, he caught one of the arms. His hand jolted from the impact, failing to cut the thick flesh, and instead snapping the blade.

Glenn steadied his grip and centered the arm in his iron sights. The bullet found its mark, the slithery limb jolting from impact. It recoiled from its target, hovered over the air for a moment, then joined its brothers in tearing the boat apart.

The sheriff watched the helpless fisherman try to save his nearly unconscious father. Roger was moving, but clearly dazed from his fall. Nick grabbed anything he could and flung it at the monsters. Debris, bait, boots, lights, even his hat.

Like the tailgate of a truck, the transom was torn loose. A thunderous boom signaled a breach in the keel. A huge crack traveled up the starboard bow. Slowly, that crack widened. The boat was moments from splitting in two.

The sound of splitting metal was overtaken by a steady humming sound. Motors.

"Glenn!"

He turned around. Two boats—a police vessel and the *Pilgrimage.*

"Dad!"

Siena Lehnert was at the helm. Dakota was on the portside, leaning over to grab his hand.

"Come on, kid!"

Glenn stepped atop the gunwale and took his father's hand. With a single yank, he was aboard the *Pilgrimage.* He took a deep breath, silently appreciating the taken-for-granted luxury of a moving vessel, then snapped back into focus.

"There's still people on that boat," he said, pointing at the *Horizon Line.*

Dakota pumped his shotgun. "Siena?"

"Hang on." She gunned the throttle, putting the vessel on a collision course with the tentacles near the *Horizon Line's* port bow.

Dakota got on his radio. "Deputies, I want you to hold back. Those arms will snap your boat like a toothpick."

"I concur," Siena said.

"Holding back. Ready to provide cover," Denham said.

Glancing back, the McCulloughs could see Deputy Zolnai on deck, standing ready with an M4 Carbine.

The *Pilgrimage* charged, then came to a sudden stop. Tremors of impact shook the vessel as the bow smacked into two of the tentacles, knocking them down like trees.

The port bow scraped the side of the *Horizon Line.* On its deck, Nick Wilkerson was dragging his father to the side. Roger was conscious, but heavily dazed.

"Move, Dad! Get over the side."

"Hurry up!" Dakota said.

One of the arms moved over the gap where the transom had been and reached for the two fishermen.

"Oh, hell!" Dakota aimed his shotgun and fired at one of the enormous arms. The pellets landed in a tight group. The tentacle whipped backward, rolling like a millipede. Suction cups bulged, the twin hooks exposing themselves like tarantula fangs.

"Go! Go!" Nick pushed his dad over. Glenn reached and took the fisherman's hand and pulled him aboard.

Dakota fired several more shots, fending the tentacles off. Roger landed on deck, immediately falling to his hands and knees.

"Nick . . . where's Nick?"

"Get aboard, kid," Dakota said.

Nick propped himself over the side and reached for Glenn's hands.

The crack in the *Horizon Line's* starboard bow fully ruptured. The ocean surged into the vessel, pushing the two sections apart. The bow detached completely, the main body plunging.

Nick fell backward, landing in a mixture of seawater, slime, and his brother's blood.

A wet feeling came over his body, then intense pressure. Next thing he knew, his own blood was added to the weird mixture. His ribs plunged into his lungs, forcing blood out his mouth like ketchup from a bottle.

The crew of the *Pilgrimage* watched in horror as Nick was lifted off the deck and swung across the air like a kite.

Helplessness and terror overwhelmed Roger Wilkerson. Like the bow of his vessel, his psyche split apart. Logic and reason sank beneath the waves. He grabbed the sheriff by the coat.

"DO SOMETHING!"

Glenn tried to pry his hands off. "I can't."

Dakota fired the last couple of shells. The first spread went wide, the other struck another tentacle that passed in front of the intended target.

Nick let out a suffocating scream. The arm angled him downward, right for the deck. Like a child playing with a toy plane, it smashed him against the boat. Upon impact, his head disappeared in a red cloud of blood and brains.

Roger fainted, the sheriff catching him before he hit the deck.

Dakota dropped the shotgun in favor of the Beretta. "Gun it, Siena."

The helmswoman hooked the boat around and made a run for home. In seconds, they were fifty feet away. Then a hundred. One-fifty . . .

The *Pilgrimage* came to a dead stop. The bow lurched, the stern sinking. All hands lost their balance. Siena clung to the helm to keep from falling backward. Behind her, Dakota and Glenn were falling head over heels. The elder McCullough managed to grab ahold of some netting with one hand, losing his Beretta in the process. The weapon slid to the transom with Glenn and Roger.

Up on the edge were two tentacles, pulling the boat further down. Two others stretched over them, lured by the fresh meat that fell nearby.

Rubbery flesh folded over the edge of the deck, dripping slime onto its victim. Five feet of tentacle waved over him, displaying its suction cups, hooks, and other oddities that decorated it. Small black objects protruded from the sides of the arms. Spines, by the looks of them, except they did not match the texture of shell or bone. Nor did they contain any consistent shape. Some were flat and bent, others were rod-shaped. They were not extending from its skin, but rather *stuck* like thorns. Whatever they were, they glinted in the sun like glass.

Or metal.

"Glenn! The pistol!" Dakota shouted.

Glenn, on his back, saw the weapon near his right boot. He snatched it, chambered a round, and fired half the mag into the nearest tentacle. The second half was directed at the other. Small flakes of meat spurted from the arms, drawing blood. Despite brief pain, the tentacles were deterred only momentarily.

One of the tentacles descended on the sheriff, hooks extending.

"Here! Glenn!" Dakota removed the axe from his belt and slid it to his son. Glenn snatched it by the handle and swung it wildly.

The blade caught one of the suction cups. Its blade sliced through the inner edge of the rubbery meat and struck the hook at its base.

POP!

The hook fell free, the tentacle again lurching backward.

Glenn seized the opportunity by getting on his feet and grabbing Roger. As they ascended the deck, the waterline approached the edge of the transom. In moments, the ocean would freely spill over and flood the boat.

"Son of a bitch," Dakota muttered. This creature *knew* what it was doing. Instead of using brute force to tear the boat apart, it was using the path of least resistance by simply pulling it under.

The spare fuel drum slid down the incline, its edge scraping the deck. After several inches, it toppled over with a heavy *thud*. Dakota watched it roll to the transom, his gaze sweeping over his son and the unconscious fisherman. Standing out from Glenn's drenched clothing was an orange flare gun.

An idea came to mind. It was a risky idea, but desperate times called for desperate measures.

Dakota snatched the axe from his son's hand, yanked the flare gun from his waist, then threw himself at the spare drum.

"Dad! What are you doing?!"

Dakota ignored him, focusing his attention on the huge limb straight ahead. He smacked it away with the axe, then raised the blade over his head like a lumberjack. He brought it down with all his might, piercing the fuel drum. Gasoline gushed from the incision, coating the deck.

Dakota knelt down, his arthritis sending lightning bolts through his nerves as he lifted the fuel drum over the side. It splashed down in the middle of the horde of arms.

Below the slime-filled water was an immense red shape. At its rear, giant fins flapped like wings. The front was a mess of ropy tentacles, surrounding a jaw he could not see. What Dakota could see, however, were two enormous yellow eyes staring up at him.

"Have a look at *this*." He pointed the flare gun and fired. The fuel cannister erupted, spewing flames across the surface. The tentacles released their grip and retreated.

The *Pilgrimage* fell forward, the momentum making Dakota stagger.

Siena engaged the throttle. Soon enough, that pool of fire became a spark in the distance.

The group stood silent, waiting for any sign of the beast until it was clear it had given up the chase.

"Nice work, Sheriff. Is it dead?"

Glenn turned away, pissed at his deputy's slipup. What made it worse was his dad's nonchalant response to the title.

Dakota watched the water, radio in hand. "Not hardly. If anything, we just pissed it off even more."

"What the hell was it?!"

"A squid." Dakota's eyes went to the bony object lying on the deck—the twin hook from one of its suction cups. He was no marine biologist, but even he knew this was different from hooks found in normal cephalopods. "Some kind of squid."

CHAPTER 16

The sudden appearance of two boats brought every resident from the Falk's Tale cabins. The sight of boats on the ocean was not unusual, but the speed at which they were coming to shore, and the use of police sirens, sparked confusion and concern. People resting on the beaches sat up to stare at the incident, speculating as to what was going on.

Jacob Falk stepped out his front door, coffee mug in hand. In the distance, he could see the flashing lights following a larger vessel. His first thought was that a chase was in progress. Then the sixty-footer came into view. It was former Sheriff Dakota McCullough's boat. Not likely that he of all people would be fleeing the cops.

That realization only enhanced his confusion.

"Honey?"

Tris stepped out of the house. "Yes?" She saw the lights and heard the sirens. "Oh! What's this?"

"I have no idea, but they're both flying toward shore." After watching for a few additional moments, he hurried down to the *Great Valley* and got on the radio. "*Pilgrimage*, this is Jacob from Falk's Tale. You guys all right?"

"Negative, Jake. If you have anyone in the water, get them out now!"

"What's happening?"

"We found what killed those orcas. It's a large organism, a cephalopod of massive proportions. It's what killed the gym instructors, the Dryers, and at least five other people that we know of. Get everyone out of the water."

"Copy that. Listen, you're closer to my dock than the county's. Wanna bring it in here? I have room."

"Ten-four. Appreciate it."

Jacob disembarked and hurried to the shoreline. Four people were swimming in the shallows, while a few others were getting set up for the day on beach chairs.

"Everyone, out of the water. Now, please."

All eyes pointed in his direction.

"What? Why?" a teen swimmer asked.

"Police instruction," Jacob said. "They're reporting something dangerous in the water. I've been asked to keep everyone out until further notice."

"Wait a second." Another client hustled down from his cottage. Jacob could feel the man's temper rising like magma. "We have a dive scheduled for today. We already paid for it. Don't tell me this police stuff is going to cancel that."

"Sadly, it's looking that way," Jacob said.

"Oh, this can't be for real," another said. "This is such bull—"

"I'll knock a hundred bucks off the cottage price for the inconvenience, regardless of whether you return to the water. As for the diving fee, I'll refund it. Just please, for your own safety, stay out of the water."

The adjusted price tag made the angry vacationer think twice. "All right." The swimmers vacated the water and joined their families in the sand.

"Is the beach still okay?" one of them asked.

"Yeah, that should be fine," Jacob said. "Just make room for the first responders. We have a serious situation unfolding. Just don't panic."

"Hey, Jake? You still there?"

The resort owner returned to his boat. "Yeah, I'm here."

"Just a heads-up. There are police and EMS units en route. Should be showing up in your lot any minute now."

"Thanks, Dakota." He looked to the street. "I can hear them now, actually. Probably will arrive at the same time as you."

His theory was proven right. As the *Pilgrimage* and police vessel arrived at his pier, EMS and a sheriff's department Interceptor arrived in the Falk's front lot.

Tris sprinted around the side of the house to greet them. "Around this way." She led the EMTs to the main pier, where the *Pilgrimage* and *Extra Credit* were docked.

Dakota and Glenn were gently lowering an unconscious fisherman off the boat.

"Oh, Jesus!" Jacob said. "That's Roger Wilkerson."

"Where's his boat?" Tris said. She combed the *Pilgrimage's* deck with her eyes, then looked to the police vessel, which docked in front of the next cottage. "Where's Nick and Zach?"

Roger Wilkerson was beginning to stir as the McCulloughs lowered him onto a bench on the pier.

"Nick? Zach?"

"Don't talk, Roger," Dakota said. He stood straight and waved to the EMTs.

"What happened?" the supervising medic asked.

"He's in shock," Dakota said. "Possibly a concussion. He fell and hit his head."

"Okay." The medics crowded the patient and took his vitals. "Blood pressure's low. Heart rate is fine. There's signs of bruising on his neck and shoulders."

"You mentioned shock," one of the other EMTs said. "What happened?"

Dakota scoffed. "If I told you, you'd probably order a psyche evaluation for me. But here's the truth—there's a carnivorous organism in the water. A giant squid of some sort. You see that?" He tilted his head at his boat's transom. The medics could see the folds in the metal, resembling cardboard after it had been bent. "It almost pulled us under. It split Mr. Wilkerson's boat in half."

"And killed his sons," Glenn said.

Dakota grabbed his shoulder. "SHH!"

It was too late. Roger shot up, his face animated with twisted horror. "NICK! ZACH!"

"Whoa! Roger, rest easy, sir."

The fisherman wrestled the EMT off him and got to his feet. "Where are my sons?" The smell of the secretion dangling from the *Pilgrimage* answered the question for him. Recent memories played in his mind, repeating over and over as if on a Satanic reel.

Zach lifted into the air, the breaking of his bones loud and distinct. That image was followed by that of Nick, constricted by the tentacle, vomiting blood and being rammed into the deck.

Roger fell to his knees and sobbed.

"Come on." Dakota helped him onto the stretcher.

"Does he have any family in the area?" one of the medics asked. Dakota shook his head.

"I'll visit you later, bud. All right?" Roger did not seem to hear him. His face was buried in his hands as the EMTs carted him away.

Jacob, Tris, Denham, and Zolnai stood to the side, patiently waiting until the stretcher was loaded into the ambulance. Once they heard the doors slam shut, they approached the pier.

"Did I hear you right?" Tris said. "You said a giant squid attacked you?"

"Unfortunately, yes," Dakota said.

"Sheriff? You look like hell," Jacob said. "You all right, sir?"

Glenn looked at himself, soaking wet and with bits of chemical extinguisher caked into his shirt. "Could be worse, I suppose." He turned to face Siena. "I guess I owe you an apology, Doctor. I thought the idea of a giant squid causing all this mayhem was ludicrous. After what I saw last night, though, I'm eating my words."

"Don't feel too badly, Glenn," she replied. "None of us expected this."

"You're the one who said something yesterday. I didn't listen." He took his jacket off. "I never knew they could get that big."

"They don't. At least, present day species don't."

Everyone on the pier stared at her.

Dakota raised an eyebrow. "*Present day* species?"

Siena nodded slightly, uncertain if she wanted to commit to this theory. With the stares and silence, she knew she had passed the point of no return.

She gazed at the double hook she held in her hand. "I believe this creature belongs to a species thought to be extinct. Fossil evidence shows that it is the largest cephalopod ever on record. Makes the giant squid look like fish bait."

"What the hell is it?" Zolnai asked. "A super-giant squid?"

Siena shook her head.

"A dreadnought."

CHAPTER 17

The Falks were generous enough to allow Siena access to their home office. While the computer booted up, she helped herself to some water. Her hands were still quivering from the adrenaline rush. Not until today had she witnessed any human death, and Nick's was the worst anyone could suffer.

She felt Dakota's hand on her shoulder.

"You all right?"

"Yeah." She put a hand on his, then looked up at him. "I imagine you've seen more than your fair share of horrors, haven't you?"

"More than I care to remember," he said. "Never like this, though. Haven't had a sea monster wreak havoc on our town before."

The computer came on. Siena got on the internet and typed in a link to a paleobiology website. As she sifted through various pages of unrelated data, Glenn and the Falks walked in.

Siena found the files on the dreadnought. On the right corner was an illustration provided by 1960s researchers after the first fossil evidence was recovered.

"Here it is." She enlarged the image and scooted back.

Glenn studied the photo. It showed a creature that resembled the typical giant squid, with large bulging eyes, a massive beak that made him think of eagles, and ten enormous tentacles.

"You said it was prehistoric?"

"Or so we thought," Siena replied.

"How long ago did it supposedly go extinct?"

"Between one and three million years. Right around the time megalodons disappeared. I suspect the two species often competed for food. For all we know, they were mortal enemies."

"Looks like we figured out who the winner was," Dakota said. On the desk near the monitor was the hook. "I'm assuming they're distinguishable because of this."

"Correct. I guess some of my incessant chatter about marine biology stuck around after my last visit," Siena said.

"The tip matches the fragment we found in the orca jaw," Dakota said. "The poor bastard must've put up a hell of a fight. Probably bit with everything he had before he was bested."

"Also explains how that carbon fiber and sliver was in its mouth," Glenn said.

"Beg your pardon?" Siena asked.

"When it attacked, I had an up-close look. Its arms are littered with metal slivers, as though the thing tried to hug a junkyard," Glenn said. "Also explains all the lacerations we saw. Thing clawed them all over attempting to sink its hooks in them."

"Of course, you wouldn't need to see the hooks to know you're dealing with a dreadnought. Just the size alone will let you know you've met the devil himself."

"How big is it, exactly?" Dakota asked.

"Usually, for a giant squid, the mantle length is seven-and-a-half feet. With the tentacles outstretched, about forty-three feet. Females are larger, with a weight around six-hundred pounds." She scrolled down to another photo, with the giant and dreadnought squids on a chart for comparison.

"Holy sweet Savior," Tris said, beholding the graphic of the creature Siena just described, and the monstrosity that dwarfed it. It was like a mother and her toddler, except these were wholly separate species.

"From what we've estimated from fossil remains, the dreadnought has a mantle length of thirty-five feet. With arms outstretched, it can exceed two hundred feet."

"That *cannot* be right," Glenn said. "That would mean its arms exceed a hundred-sixty feet!"

"That's correct. Most squids have eight arms and two longer feeding tentacles, which are mainly used to catch prey. This one, though, seemed to use all ten as feeding tentacles."

"Marvelous." Glenn clasped his hands behind his head. "You mean to tell me we have a literal kraken swimming around in our waters? This shit is meant to be fairy tales for kids. TV stuff. Not real life."

Dakota grabbed him by the arm and leaned toward his ear. "Bring yourself together. You're the sheriff. If you lose it, everyone will."

"Like it matters," Glenn whispered.

Dakota looked him in the eye. *Everyone still looks to me for a reason, kid.* Now was not the time for this conversation. Knowing Glenn and his tendency to avoid issues, it would never be the time.

"Why is it here?" he asked Siena.

She rotated her chair to face him. "I received a message from Dr. Berman's assistant. They found a dumpsite this morning. The entire Submarine Canyon is completely polluted with all sorts of toxic waste."

"You're shitting me."

"You believe this thing was living in the Canyon all this time?" Glenn said. "I guess that would explain why it hasn't been seen until now."

"The pollution drew it out," Siena said. "Probably killed most of its natural prey. For all we know, it probably fed on some of the waste itself."

Tris winced. "They do that?"

"Squids are predators, but they're often scavengers as well. It's easier and requires less expenditure of energy. The secretion I found on Kelby's boat was rife with chemicals. Its immune system probably kept it alive all this time, hence it didn't die off."

"That would explain the metal fragments and carbon fibers," Glenn said.

"It's possible, assuming whoever dumped the toxic waste also dropped mechanical and electrical waste in the same area. Takes money to dispose of this stuff."

"Great. So, it's hungry and pissed off."

"Very much so," Siena said. "I tested the flounder your dad gave me yesterday. There's swelling in the brain, which causes heightened aggression. It's logical to assume that the dreadnought is suffering the same condition. That creature will attack any living thing it comes across."

"Oh, no." Glenn marched out of the room. The deputies were standing outside the door, waiting for further instructions. Glenn stepped out and pointed a finger. "Get on the horn to Dispatch. Get an emergency broadcast out. I want all boats grounded immediately."

"You got it," Denham said.

"What if they don't come in?" Zolnai said.

"I want all three boats on the water. I also want our drone in the air to seek out anyone not heading to port."

The deputy appeared to shrink several inches. "Wait . . . you want *us* on the water? Where that thing is?"

"That's your job, Deputy. It's what you're paid to do. Get on it." Glenn turned around to return to the office, only to see his father standing a few feet away. "You disapprove?"

"Not at all," Dakota said.

Glenn nodded, then walked past him. "Siena, what other knowledge do you have on this thing? Characteristics? Hunting patterns? I need to know it all."

"Unfortunately, my knowledge on this creature is limited," she said. "However, Dr. Lehnert knows much more. She'll want to see this for herself. I'll give her a call ASAP."

"Thank you. One other question: It emerged from the depths because of the toxic waste. But . . . why is it *here*?"

Siena thought for a moment, then shrugged. "I wish I knew."

CHAPTER 18

In years past, he had been nicknamed *Poseidon* for the mammoth bounty he hauled from the water. This nickname inspired the name of his vessel, the *Trident*. High and mighty, the seventy-foot vessel carried Alex Kelley across the Gulf of Maine, and often into the open ocean whenever he desired greater challenge.

In a single day, a single pass in populated waters would fill his trawl net with all kinds of fish. In the summer months, he could take dozens of people on a single trip to fish for stripers and Atlantic salmon.

Now, he was looking at an empty deck and an equally empty trawl net. Nobody wanted to fish in vacant waters. They took their business to the Florida Keys, Gulf of Mexico, and the West Coast.

"This is the Garrison County Sheriff's Department, relaying an emergency message to any boats fishing along the Jordan Basin or Jeffery's Bank. You are in imminent danger. Bring your boats to shore at once. A press conference will be held at three o'clock this afternoon by the sheriff and his advisors."

Alex gave thought to slamming a hammer down on the radio. His two crewmen watched nervously. Under normal circumstances, Alex was a friendly, reasonable guy who was easy to work for. Unfortunately, his recent stresses had brought out the worst in him.

Bobby Douglas leaned in toward Art Palley's ear. "You hear that?"

"Duh," Art replied. Both men turned away. "First his divorce, then his son gets sick, the poor lad can barely pay for the treatment. Then all the fish vanish. He can barely pay the bills, let alone an expensive intestinal transplantation."

"Shit, he barely pays us," Bobby said.

"You boys have something to say?" Alex's voice came out like thunder. The two crewmen separated and went to work mending the nets and prepping the few fish that came up with the previous passes.

"No, Captain," Art said. "We could hear the radio call and figured we were calling it a day early." When he heard no response, he looked up at his captain. Alex was watching the water, his hand clenching the helm. "We are heading in, right?"

"They are," Bobby said. To the northwest were two fishing boats who clearly received the message. Unless they were lucky enough to fill their tanks with ten-thousand pounds of fish in a few passes, no fisherman ever headed west before ten a.m.

More radio calls came in, from the Maine State Police, Harbor Master, and Massachusetts State Police. Whatever was going on, it had the attention of some major players. Soon enough, the Coast Guard would be involved in this operation.

A bitter Alex Kelley groaned. "This cannot be happening to me."

"Sir, if I may," Art said, reading his mind. "I really do not want to get caught disobeying police instructions. It's best if we bite the bullet and head in for today."

"It's not like we're catching anything anyway," Bobby added.

"To put it more delicately," Art glared at Bobby, "if they're serious, they'll confiscate any boat that defies the order. And frankly, I can't afford the arrest." He pulled down his sleeve to cover his prison tattoo. It was a time when he was a much different person. Having a child had a way of straightening some men out, and when Art looked into those little eyes, he knew it was time to grow up. The only reason that tattoo remained was to remind him of where he had come from. His life was not glamorous, but it was honest. Whether a police order was lawful or not, he had no intention of standing toe-to-toe with those enforcing it.

Bobby did not care. He just wanted to make money. By the looks of what today's trawls were bringing, it did not make a difference whether they stayed or went home. Either way, he would be living off value brand beans and rice, and maybe a bag of potato chips for the week.

A helicopter flew to the south. Sure enough, state units were patrolling the red zones, seeking out any fishermen that refused to head in.

The sight of the aircraft forced Alex to accept reality. There was no version of this situation where he came out on top. Even if he tried to defy the order, he would be caught.

"Anchor up."

"Already done," Art said. "You gonna go to that press conference?"

"You're damn right I will. This is bullshit." Alex turned the boat west and headed for port.

"Whatever's going on, it's probably serious," Bobby said. "I mean, hell, every state on the Gulf is ordering people out of the water."

"I don't give a shit what their reasons are," Alex said. "Unless the county decides to pay for Ted's procedure, this grounding will not go past today. I give you my word on that."

CHAPTER 19

By noon, the harbor was full of angry fishermen whose first actions were to call the sheriff's office or visit the front steps personally. Three o'clock was too late. They wanted answers immediately.

"Sheriff, the phones are ringing off the hook. It's like Saw Ridge is looking to riot."

"Tell them it's for their own safety, Dispatch."

"Sorry, sir, but you're gonna have to do better than that. These are bad economic times, and these people are claiming we're deliberately putting them on welfare."

"It's almost three," he said. "There's a conference in twenty minutes. Tell them to bring their concerns directly to me. Stop radioing me with this shit. McCullough out."

Glenn lowered the radio and tilted his head back. So much for his little break at home. A hot shower, a light meal, and a cold beer failed to ease his nerves. Everyone was questioning him, from his deputies to the secondary staff, and most of the townspeople. The local government was quick to give him grief for the decision. Even the drone footage of the wreckage failed to convince them to shut down the waters.

As he suspected, it was the testimony of his father that made them change their minds. Dakota McCullough's judgement was sound, even if his words were the exact same as Glenn's. It did not matter. They trusted him, not his successor.

A knock on his door made him jump off his couch. Had he not been stressed, he would have instantly noticed his father's truck outside his front window.

"Come in."

Dakota stepped inside. "Hey, kid. Came to see if you're all right."

Glenn sat back down and put a hand to his forehead. "What can I say? Either I condemn people to death by letting them go out there, or I starve them into poverty by keeping them grounded."

"No, you're making the right call," Dakota said. "And you're not the one starving them. Whoever's been polluting these waters are the ones to blame, not you."

Glenn nodded. "Dad, you're right."

"Of course, I am . . ."

"No, I mean—well, yeah, you're right about what you just said. But I mean you're right about something else. I shouldn't have gone for this job."

"Beg your pardon?"

"I'm fessing up. I wasn't ready for this job, and you knew it. You tried to warn me . . ."

"Whoa, whoa, kid." Dakota put his hands up and approached. "I warned you that it was a *tough* position. I never said you couldn't handle it."

"Oh, give me a break. Why else do you hang around here?"

"Glenn, I've lived here most of my life—"

"And spent much of that time talking about leaving," Glenn said. He took his breath and settled his temperament, for it was not his intention to start a fight. "I know you're looking after me. For a while, I resented it. Now, I realize you've kept me afloat so far this year."

Dakota sat down. "You need to take it easy on yourself. The past sixteen hours have not been kind to you. How are your eyes, by the way?"

"The shower helped." Glenn allowed himself to smile. "I used to say not-so-kind things about you whenever I saw that stupid fire extinguisher rocking on that little hanger. Who knew that little annoyance would end up saving my life?"

"I'm *that* good," Dakota joked.

"That you are. I owe you my thanks for pulling me out of shit creek." Glenn eyed the fridge in the kitchen. The temptation to down another beer would have broken him had the press conference not been twenty-seven minutes away. "I deliberately tried to keep any civilian vessel away from my position. I knew that thing would snatch anyone that drew near. Roger must've seen the smoke and tried to help."

"It's not your fault, Glenn. Like Siena said, this creature—dreadnought, as she calls it—happily lived over a mile deep. We should have never known it exists. But the canyon was poisoned, and this is a consequence of that."

Glenn nodded, though it did little to make him feel better.

"Where is Siena?"

"She's at my place. On the phone with her supervisor."

"Your place, huh?"

Dakota grinned. "Let's not get ahead of ourselves."

"Too late." The two of them laughed. It was a welcome moment of levity, which unfortunately came crashing down with the understanding that this situation was going to haunt the town. "Something's gonna have to happen about this squid, Dad. I can't keep these waters closed indefinitely."

"You're gonna have to," Dakota said. "You let people go out, and someone else gets killed, that *will* be on your head. If they defy your instructions, you have them arrested. I don't like it any more than you do, but this is an emergency. Have you spoken to the Coast Guard?"

"I have. They're sending an Island Class patrol boat and two response boats. I'm praying to God that they kill the bastard quickly."

"When are they getting here?"

"Don't have an exact time, but I'm told tonight." Glenn looked at his watch. "I better get going to Town Hall. Wanna come?"

"Yeah, sure. I'm no stranger to press conferences."

"I don't recall you ever being scrutinized."

"No, but I've never faced this exact circumstance. Life throws challenges at us, son. Some of us get it worse than others. That's just the way it is. But like you said, maybe the Coast Guard will solve all of our problems for us tonight."

"God, I hope so." Glenn shut off the lights and went out the front door. "I've texted Siena and asked her to make a statement at the conference."

"Yep, I'm gonna run home and pick her up," Dakota said. "We'll meet you there."

"Thanks. See you in a few."

CHAPTER 20

It was not Glenn's first press conference, but certainly his busiest. It was ten minutes till three, and already the Town Hall Center was filled with angry civilians who demanded answers when they recognized Glenn's personal vehicle go around the back. He parked near the town mayor's vehicle and stepped into the building. Several deputies waited, one of whom had a mustard stain on his uniform.

"Deputy Roark? What the hell happened to you?"

"Apparently, one of the crowd mistook me for a brat," the deputy quipped.

"They're pissed off, Sheriff," Denham said.

"Oh, gee. You think?" Glenn said. "I thought they threw mustard at him because they were in a *good* mood."

The door behind him opened.

"On the bright side, Andrew Zolnai won't be the only one with a yellow stain on his uniform."

The deputies smiled and welcomed Dakota and Siena.

"Hey, sir. Good to see you again. I see you brought a date to the party!" Roark said.

"Don't fill his ego," Siena said.

"So, what's happening?" another deputy said.

"Yeah! This is nuts. Is there seriously a monster octopus swimming out there?"

"A squid, but yes," Siena said.

"Hey guys, let's do this press conference, and then you can receive your instructions from your sheriff. I'm simply a supporting role, and a witness."

The mayor stepped into the hallway. "Sheriff, we're about to start."

"On my way," Glenn said. He squeezed through the group of deputies and found the door to the large room. Reporters spoke into their microphones, informing their audiences that the sheriff and his advisors had approached the podium. Camera operators turned to film the event.

Up in the corner, Glenn could see his face on the live feed of Channel Nine. In the bar on the lower screen were the words *Catastrophe in Garrison County. Over a half-dozen people presumed dead.*

"Clearly a headline to put people at ease," he said to himself.

Dakota, Siena, and the town mayor stood to the side and faced the crowd. The chatter in the room went silent as everyone turned their attention to the podium.

Here we go.

"Thank you everyone for being here. I'll get right to the point. At around five-thirty yesterday morning—"

"Hey! Turn your mic up!" someone shouted from the crowd.

Glenn could feel the blood rushing to his face. He adjusted the mic, tried speaking, only to realize it was completely off. He leaned down and found the switch, which triggered a loud squeal that made the room cringe.

"My apologies," he said, shooting a glare at the maintenance department on his left. *Assholes probably set me up to look like a moron on purpose.* "At five-thirty yesterday morning, multiple killer whales washed up dead at Falk's Tale Resort. Some were sliced up and down, others were in literal pieces, only identifiable through jawbone fragments and other such remains. Around seven that same morning, a kayak belonging to one of two instructors for Gold Star Fitness was discovered. The couple were last seen earlier that same morning by Dakota McCullough as he was responding to assist with the Falk's Tale call. Later on, the fishing boat *Autumn Bliss* was found adrift, heavily damaged, its owners Kelby and Patty Dryer, missing.

"At eight p.m. yesterday evening, I personally went out with a man from the weather service to check on a pair of buoy techs who had failed to respond to their calls. During that time, my vessel was attacked by a . . ." He paused, mentally preparing for the mockery and backlash, ". . . by a cephalopod of mammoth proportions."

Several reporters stood.

"Excuse me, Sheriff?!" one shouted. "A cephalopod? Are you actually saying you were attacked by an octopus?!"

"A large squid," Glenn said. "It killed Mr. Ben Leever that night. I was able to drive it off but was unable to radio for help. This morning, I was able to escape thanks to the efforts of Deputies Andrew Zolnai and Ben Denham, as well as Dakota McCullough and Dr. Siena Lehnert. Unfortunately, the fishing vessel *Horizon Line* was attacked in the process and two of its three crew, Nick and Zach Wilkerson, were killed. Their father is currently receiving medical treatment."

"Is this a joke?" someone called from the back.

"I wish it was. I saw this thing for myself. It's real and it's dangerous."

"Come on!" another said. "You're telling us a squid was big enough to take down the *Horizon Line*?!"

"Why haven't we heard of anything like this before?!" shouted another.

Glenn cleared his throat. "Given our evidence of its size and aspects of its biology, we believe this creature is a member of an extinct species known as the dreadnought squid. It's likely this creature lived in the Atlantic Submarine Canyon but was driven out due to a toxic spill. An investigation is under way. In the meantime, I am issuing an order for all vessels in Saw Ridge jurisdiction to remain in port until the crisis is resolved."

Dozens of people stood up in the back rows. Many of them still wore their overalls, rubber boots, and gloves. All of them were angry.

"Sheriff, you have no right!" one shouted.

"We don't fish, we don't get paid!" another said.

"You go out there, you won't live to get paid," Glenn retorted.

"Since when do you have the right to tell us what risks we can take, Sheriff?" The group turned to look at their new speaker. Alex Kelley approached the podium, stopping once he reached the row of reporters. He was a stone-faced man, his beard several days old. Most that knew him were aware he was the kind that shaved regularly, but recent events occupied all his time—the same events that fueled his need to be back on the water. Eyes burning with contempt, he awaited an answer.

"Sir, I understand your frustration . . ."

"You don't understand shit," Alex said. "Most of us don't have the luxury of riding daddy's coattails. In case you haven't noticed, it hasn't been a fruitful season. Some of us working folk need to spend every hour we can just to buy some Top Ramen. Others have more pressing financial concerns and are willing to assume the risks out there."

A series of 'hear-hear', 'damn straight', and 'listen to this guy', among others, echoed across the room. The journalists' energy quickly gravitated in favor of the fishermen. Cameras pointed at them. Journalists picked out individuals whom they intended to interview later. Pens struck paper; mouths spoke into voice recorders.

At this point, all Glenn wanted was cold beer and a couple of shots of bourbon.

He waited for the uproar to settle, then continued. "I have gotten in touch with the Coast Guard. A unit has been dispatched and should arrive in our local jurisdiction in a few hours."

"Will they kill it?" Alex asked.

"I hope so, but I can't conclusively say so," Glenn said. "This situation has never been contemplated. This creature is very large, cunning, and strong. It might be very hard to kill. That said, my order stands. No boats will leave the harbor until I declare it is safe to do so."

Another upheaval filled the room.

"I have medical bills, Sheriff!" Alex Kelley shouted. "You plan on paying for my son's operation? Somehow, I doubt it."

"That's right," another fisherman said.

"Are you mad? You could be killed," Glenn said.

"You're kidding, right?" Alex said. "Like fishermen have never died on the job before. If you weren't so green around the gills, maybe you'd know that, kid. Let *me* take care of this thing. I can probably have it cut into calamari rings by the end of tonight."

The crowd cheered.

"What does the former sheriff have to say about this?" one of the journalists asked.

Dakota took a step toward the podium, only to be stopped by his son.

"He and Dr. Lehnert have been advising me on the situation," Glenn said. "He has no legal authority on this matter. The buck stops with me. I will make an announcement as soon as the water is safe. In the meantime, anyone who goes out will be subject to arrest. Thank you, that will be all."

He turned on his heel and disappeared into the hallway, ignoring the barrage of questions.

Several deputies awaited in the hall. The only smiles that dared show themselves were nervous ones. Not a single one of them wanted to be there.

"Excuse me, sir?" Zolnai said. "Just so we're clear, you expect us to arrest anyone on the water?"

"Correct," Glenn said. "That means constant boat patrols. Stick to the shallows. The creature is likely to remain in the deeper areas. I want all three boat units out starting now. The Coast Guard will arrive by tonight. We have the best marine biologist around as a consultant. We're going to get to the bottom of this matter. You hear me?"

"Whatever you say, Sheriff," one of the deputies said. Sarcasm. Glenn knew to go to the back door or else risk snapping. Dakota and Siena followed him out.

The three of them embraced the fresh afternoon air. A cloud had passed over the sun, knocking the temperature down a couple degrees. Just enough for Glenn to collect himself.

"Siena, we didn't get a chance to talk. I understand you've spoken with your supervisor?"

"I did. Linda didn't believe me at first, but when I showed her that claw, her tune changed. They're awaiting the arrival of a Coast Guard and EPA unit at their present location, then they'll head over here to meet us. She's agreed to a Zoom meeting when we meet with the Coast Guard officer."

"Good. You guys can fill him in on this squid stuff," Glenn said. "My specialty is public safety. The sooner you guys and the Coast Guard can kill that thing, the better."

Dakota groaned. "I just hope the lieutenant commander won't get hung up on disbelief."

"Oh, trust me," Siena said with a chuckle, "Linda and I will have a hell of a briefing for him."

CHAPTER 21

At seven o'clock that evening, the fast response cutter *USCGC St. Helens* and two forty-five-foot response boats arrived two hundred yards outside of the county harbor. With a length of a hundred-and-ten feet, a beam of twenty-one feet, and a draft of seven feet, the ship was a force to be reckoned with. Its hull was constructed from thick steel, its superstructure and main deck from aluminum. Powered by two Caterpillar 3516 diesel engines, it could reach a maximum speed of twenty-nine knots.

The front of the vessel was outfitted with a twenty-five-millimeter cannon. Secondary weapons included two M60 machine guns to be mounted at any point on the ship.

Operating all these functions were fourteen enlisted crew, led by its lieutenant commander. Two of them lowered the *St. Helens'* Yamaha 90 into the water. The lieutenant commander stepped aboard and ordered the operator to start the outboard.

Accompanied by his father and Siena, Glenn awaited his arrival. He directed the Yamaha into Boat One's normal space, barking orders to his two response vessels through his two-way radio.

"Boat Thirteen, begin your patrol southward. Keep a forty-meter distance from the shore. Twenty-One, head north, one thousand meters, then circle back. If you see any boats out there, order them back to port."

Glenn helped him onto the dock, then shook his hand.

The lieutenant commander's presence was as commanding as his rank. At six-foot-seven, he towered over the young sheriff and his associates. His skin had a dark complexion, his face was clean-shaven, and his hair showed signs of thinning. Glenn estimated he was approaching forty. The combined power of age, experience, and physical presence quickly made Glenn feel insignificant.

"Sir, appreciate you coming."

"That's my job, Sheriff," he said. Despite his large stature and throaty voice, he managed to bridge the gap between being commanding yet personable. "First things first: I'm Lieutenant Commander Louis Fredrick. If it's not obvious enough, I'm the commanding officer of the *St. Helens*. My understanding is that there's unruly wildlife lurking in these waters."

"That's correct, sir," Glenn said. "It's already killed a number of persons. Wrecked multiple seacrafts. The whole county, especially the town of Saw Ridge, is in an uproar over this." He led Fredrick to a tent which had been erected over a picnic table. Dakota and Siena approached and extended their hands.

"Dakota McCullough, former sheriff, and Dr. Siena Lehnert, marine biologist," Glenn said. "Both have been instrumental in helping me solve this issue."

Fredrick's imposing charisma faded momentarily, replaced by a smile as he shook Dakota's hand.

"Long time no see, Mister McCullough," he said.

"Likewise," Dakota said.

"I'd ask if you're enjoying retirement, but from what I see, you've once again found yourself in the middle of this town's issues. That said, I see you've passed the torch. Must make you proud."

Both men looked at Glenn.

"Of course, I am," Dakota said.

Siena stepped in and shook Fredrick's hand. "Thanks for coming."

"My pleasure. Pardon me, ma'am, but I'm still confused by this. I've served in the Guard for sixteen years. While I don't consider myself an expert in this field, I've learned more than the average Joe about undersea predators. I've never had a situation regarding a giant squid. What I do know is that sightings are beyond rare—as in, you're more likely to be struck by lightning twice before seeing a living giant squid. None of the dead ones that washed ashore even come close to the creature that was described to me over the radio."

"I assure you, it's real, sir," she said.

"We have footage from the police camera aboard Boat Two," Dakota said. "We've uploaded it onto this laptop for you to see."

"I'm all eyes and ears," Fredrick said. They sat at the table, positioned the screen to block the evening sunlight, then played the recording. For the next several minutes, the lieutenant commander watched the enormous tentacles constrict the *Horizon Line* and crush it. Next came the attack on the *Pilgrimage* and the narrow escape. "I'll be goddamned."

"God had to be in a pretty bad mood when he created that thing," Dakota said.

"I see in this footage you guys unloaded several rounds and shells into the creature. What effect does small arms gunfire have on it?"

"It hurts it, but does little physical damage," Glenn said. "Its flesh is penetrable, but damn thick. Fire seems to have a better effect, though it's hard to burn the bastard when it's underwater."

"That's all right. Our cannon should easily make minced meat of the bastard. All we need to do is draw it to the surface."

"I'm not sure if you want to do that," Siena said.

"If you expect me to gun it down, I'm gonna have to," Fredrick said. He watched the marine biologist's expression. "All right, fine. How big is it, exactly?"

"Thirty-five-foot body length, two hundred overall," Siena said. That got a reaction from Fredrick. He looked at his ship, then envisioned an elongated squid creature that nearly doubled its length.

"Well, that's big." He looked at Siena. "You mean to tell me this thing has been hiding in the Submarine Canyon all this time?"

"Believe me, if it weren't for human interference, we'd all be blissfully unaware of its presence," Siena said.

"How many ships are responding to the situation over there?" Dakota asked.

"Two Sentinel-Class cutters and an EPA vessel. They're going to get more submersibles down there and make a gameplan to remove as much waste as possible."

"On that note . . ." Siena typed a few notes into her computer. She was right on time, as the Zoom screen was loading an incoming signal.

"Hello? Can you guys hear me? . . . Ah! There you are! Hello, Dr. Lehnert."

"Dr. Berman, thanks for meeting us. This is Lieutenant Commander Fredrick of the *USCGC St. Helens.* He'll be helping us with this situation with the dreadnought."

"They only sent one ship?!"

"An island-class cutter and two medium response boats," Fredrick said. "More than enough to handle this squid of yours."

"With all due respect, sir, I'm inclined to disagree. This creature has already sunk a vessel of equal size to an island-class cutter. If it gets ahold of your vessel . . ."

"You're referring to the *Alexandra Yale.* How do we know this thing sunk that ship?"

"I've uploaded images from our submersible to Dr. Lehnert. Doctor, can you show him, please?"

"Got 'em here." Siena had a tablet in hand. With a few swipes with her finger, she brought up the images of the sunken vessel, then handed the device to Fredrick.

He combed through the images, seeing the crushed hull, the ripped deck, and the puncture marks. "How'd it manage to do this?"

"Squids have a beak similar to an eagle's," Siena explained. "First, they grab ahold of their prey. If they don't choose to rip it apart with their claws, they drag it down toward the beak. Behind that beak is a tongue which is lined with rows of teeth that act as a sawing tool. A creature this size will make short work of a great white shark in about ten seconds."

"Or a killer whale," Dakota said.

"There's something to be said for that," Linda said. *"During our search yesterday, my assistant and I discovered the remains of a mature sperm whale. Though stripped of flesh, the state of the remains indicated that it had died less than a week ago. My belief is that the dreadnought retreated from the canyon, encountered it midway up, and had itself a meal. Then it met the Alexandra Yale."*

"What do you think happened there?" Fredrick asked. "You think it mistook the ship for food?"

"That's a logical theory, but I believe it's a little more sinister. To be honest, I believe that the dreadnought encountered the Alexandra Yale while it was in the middle of making its deposit. The creature identified the stuff that wiped out its habitat, which led to it seeing the vessel as an enemy."

"Wait . . ." Fredrick paused to keep from laughing. "You think this thing understood what the ship was doing?"

"Cephalopods are believed to be among the most intelligent creatures on earth," Siena said. "Keep in mind, we're dealing with a very large squid, with a large brain."

Fredrick considered the information and resisted the urge to argue. "All right. Let's assume that's why it sunk the ship. Why is it here?"

"Dr. Lehnert has sent me data on toxicity levels in the Gulf," Linda said. *"The levels are too high to be residual from the Submarine Canyon. There has to be a second dumping site somewhere around there. My guess is that the squid recognized the trail and followed it in search of other 'offending boats,' if you understand what I mean."*

"It thinks it's fighting off an invasion," Glenn said. "It's hungry and pissed. That damn company killed off its normal food supply, so it found a new menu. On top of that, it associates boats with the destruction of its habitat. Doesn't matter how big or small."

"Or how armored," Siena added.

Fredrick nodded. "I get your point. Sheriff, from what I've seen, I agree you've made the right call. We'll keep everyone on dry land until we come up with a means of destroying it. That said, if you're right about there being another dumping ground, we need to find it ASAP."

"And we need to figure out who's hiring these people to dump their garbage," Glenn added.

"The contractor has already been figured out," Fredrick said. "They paid for their crimes with their lives. Whatever company is doing this, it might be located in Canada, considering the residence of Christopher Willis."

"Begging your pardon, but Dr. Lehnert's findings have indicated high toxicity levels in Jordan Basin. A ship large enough traveling from Nova Scotia would have a hard time not being spotted."

"What are you suggesting, Sheriff?"

"I think there's another contractor, and they might be local."

Dakota shrugged. "It's possible. However, it's hard to know for certain. It would have to be someone with plenty of connections and resources. They'd have to have a large boat and a means of receiving shipments at night."

Glenn perked up. "Shipments, like on a semi-container?"

Dakota nodded, his stare growing increasingly inquisitive. "Yes. Does that ring a bell?" Glenn looked to the south. Dakota could tell he was not looking at the hill, but what lay beyond it. "The Falks?"

"I'll get back to you on that."

"Whoa, Glenn. That's a bit of a stretch," Dakota said.

"Hence I haven't made any accusations yet," Glenn said.

"Why do you think it might be them?" Siena asked.

"Last night, I was on my way over here to meet with Mr. Leever. Before I encountered the dreadnought, I had another near-death encounter. I almost got run over by a semi-truck hauling a thirty-foot container. It stopped at the Falk's resort. At the time, I didn't think much of it. But think of it: they have a large boat, a means of receiving cargo, an alibi. Probable cause would be a need to keep their business afloat. A resort like that must be costly, especially being on the coastline." Dakota, Siena, and Fredrick were all silent, each waiting for the other to make a statement combatting his implication. "Tell me, with all the economic hardships in this town, who here seems to be prospering?" He waited for an answer. "Anybody?"

"Son, they run a successful business. People come here from out of town. That late night shipment could've been anything. Cottage supplies, beds, kayaks, diving gear . . ."

"In a thirty-foot container?"

"Those trucks often make multiple drop-offs, Sheriff," Fredrick said.

"They make a lot of charitable donations to this town," Siena added.

Feeling outnumbered, Glenn lost the urge to continue. He faked a smile. "Ah, forget it. You guys are probably right. Ha, can you imagine the town's reaction if I actually investigated them?"

None of them laughed.

It was one of those awkward moments that made Glenn feel like he was shrinking. He cleared his throat and elevated his voice.

"Commander, if there's anything I can do to help, just say the word. Right now, all that matters is that we kill the dreadnought and make these waters safe again."

Fredrick nodded. "Thank you, Sheriff. First, we're going to do a sweep of the area and see if we can locate the creature on sonar. I can't guarantee we'll find it, considering the large area we'll have to cover."

"Also, keep in mind, it's been severely burnt by the flames," Siena said. "Sometimes animals, especially cephalopods, will lay low if they've been injured."

"Understood," Fredrick said. "Who knows? Maybe you've already taken care of the job for us."

"I doubt that," Siena said. "Cephalopods have extraordinary healing abilities. They can regenerate tissue, regrow lost limbs, even regenerate peripheral nerves and parts of the brain. Considering the damage it has taken, there's a chance it might avoid conflict."

"How long would that take?" Fredrick asked.

"With this species? I wish I knew. A day. A week. It's difficult to predict."

"Well, there's one definite factor, and that's that nobody sets out on these waters until we confirm it's dead or left the area," Fredrick said. "My response boats will patrol the shallows and keep anyone from departing. Sheriff, can I count on your department for support?"

"Yes sir. I already have patrols out."

"Good. Okay, that just about covers it." The lieutenant commander shook hands with the three, then nodded at Linda Berman. "Gentlemen, ladies, we'll be in touch. Dr. Berman, when your ship comes this way, please have your captain notify us so we can provide an escort."

"Will do. Thank you."

Fredrick boarded his Yamaha and set off for the cutter.

After waving goodbye, Siena turned to the computer screen. "Doctor, I've spoken with Jacob and Tris Falk. They have a vacancy in one of their cottages, and they have given the okay for you to stay there after you arrive."

"Thank you. It'll be nice to get off this boat for a day or two."

"When do you think you'll get here?" Dakota asked.

"Maybe in two days, after we're done assisting the EPA. I might have to make a couple of dives with them to help them locate the exact position of the Alexandra Yale. Shouldn't be too long, though."

"Okay, ma'am. See you then."

Siena ended the Zoom call and shut the computer down.

Meanwhile, Glenn kept his eyes to the south. He was deep in thought, nearly in a trance.

"Hey, kid," Dakota said. Glenn returned to the real world and turned to face him. Dakota hit him with a stern look. "Snap out of it. The Falks are highly respected around here. You go prodding around with half-assed conspiracy theories, you'll create an even bigger backlash than you're already facing."

Glenn nodded. "Absolutely." He chuckled. "I guess I have a lot to learn, don't I?"

Dakota's look softened. "About as much as I did when I was your age." He tapped Glenn on the shoulder, then joined Siena on her way to his truck.

"Taking her back to the hotel?" Glenn said.

Siena and Dakota looked at each other, then smirked.

"Yeah, sure," he said.

"Actually, I am going there," she said.

"Wait, what?! Why?"

"I have more work to do."

"More? Haven't you done enough? Including discovering an extinct species?" As soon as the words left his lips, he regretted not simply feigning indifference. He felt like a teenager on the verge of a breakup. His internal lie-detector was in the red. Glenn's was too, and he wasn't nearly as savvy as his father. Her motives were so obvious, she may as well have said them out loud. She was refusing to commit, regardless of how she truly felt.

It was a matter of 'why continue something when there's no chance of it working out.' She was a Florida resident, and he lived in Maine. In a sense, his father brought it on himself. Still, Glenn felt a little sorry for him. The poor man did not have the best track record with relationships, and in almost every case, he was not at fault when they fell apart. With Siena, there was something there that was special. There was a spark between them that was not present with the others.

Glenn felt the temptation to say something but decided it was better to stay out of it. He had bigger fish to fry at the moment.

"I'll be heading home, too. Got a big week ahead of me."

He got in his police vehicle, waved goodbye, then took off. In any other circumstance, he would have watched in the rearview mirror to catch a glimpse of their continued interaction. Instead, as soon as the engine started, his mind was on that property to the south.

He slowed the vehicle and eyed Falk's Tale Resort as he passed it. That storage garage was fairly large—large enough to store a shipment of illegal waste.

CHAPTER 22

The next several hours were spent communicating with the patrols through his radio and scrolling through his laptop and tablet. A cold beer went warm, the tab still on the bottle, as forgotten as the chicken patties on the plate next to it.

Glenn was single-minded in this self-appointed investigation. For hours, he searched companies that handled toxic waste of any kind. He found one that was dumping mercury in the rivers of Maine. For a moment, he thought he had his culprit—until he learned the plant had been shut down for several years. Most of the others had regular inspections confirming their respectable track records. The Ts were crossed and the Is dotted. Their hazmat disposals were recorded and properly monitored, paid for by the companies themselves.

Lack of results triggered a headache. However, his gut feeling did not let up. The trouble was the number of plants in Maine and the surrounding states. Too many to individually read up on in a short period of time.

He settled on a steel manufacturing plant in Westbrook. They had one CSB investigation in 2017 for a serious injury in a nearby neighborhood. Further research brought to light a hydrogen sulfide leak, which caused respiratory issues in two residents.

"Nothing to do with illegal hazmat disposal."

Glenn looked at his meal. Warm beer and cold chicken, not exactly what his stomach desired. He stood up and took the plate to the kitchen, yawning once he arrived. When he opened his eyes, he noticed it was dark out.

How long was I at it? He looked at the clock. Ten o'clock. *Damn. At least four hours.*

He yawned again, then opened the microwave. After hearing the clang of the rotating plate, he realized in his drowsiness that he'd placed the beer bottle in there instead of the chicken.

"Oh, shit!" He retracted the object. "Damn. After today, nuking my beer would've been the icing on the cake." He chuckled, then put the beer in the fridge. "There we go. Seems I'm always looking in the wrong place lately."

The wrong place . . .

"A Canadian ship . . ." He rushed back to the computer and began looking up companies with chemical plants in both the U.S. Northeast

Coast and Canada. An hour-long internet search followed until one caught his eye.

"Orion Plastic Company," he read aloud. He immediately did an internet search for any recorded offenses in the company's history. His efforts were futile. Every document he found suggested that none of the plants owned by the company had been subject to investigation.

He looked at the locations again, then shook his head. One was in Nova Scotia, the other near Dexter.

It can't be a coincidence.

Glenn was once again at a standstill. That gut feeling was roaring now, but he had nothing to go on except locations.

Frustration took its toll. He stepped outside for some fresh air. The night was refreshing, minus its reminder that he had to be up and at the office in seven hours. With that in mind, he considered the possibility that his father was right. Maybe this was a wild goose chase, led by a sheriff who was out of his league.

The only force stronger than drowsiness was his hunger. He had put off dinner all night in pursuit of this new obsession.

Glenn looked at his neglected vegetable garden. Most of the plants had wilted and died. Most had failed to produce anything. A few green beans lay in the soil, their texture withered and spotty, thanks to the ants that helped themselves. "Dad was right. Again."

Only a small tomato plant seemed to flourish. Glenn stared at the little green plant. *I don't remember planting one at the corner . . .*

Directly above it was the crooked limb of the main tomato plant. It was void of grape tomatoes, though the soil showed signs that some had fallen. A molded one lay near its center and had been seized by the ants, the seeds partially burrowed into the earth.

"Huh, no shit." It became clear what happened. One of the tomatoes had fallen. One of its seeds managed to survive and sprout and form a whole new plant.

An occupant leaves a dying entity, then forms a whole new, unblemished one.

He returned to the computer and typed 'Orion Plastic Company CEO'. The name that popped up was Gail Shingle. Glenn searched for any recorded controversies regarding this individual and chemical plant hazards.

The answer replaced his drowsiness with new energy.

"In 2004, she was head administrator of a metal manufacturing plant in Georgia. Plant was shut down after shipments were found in a deep lake in Blue Ridge Mountain . . . Son of a bitch! This person was forced out of the company, then years later founded Orion, and is doing the exact same shit. And they're using private contractors." He took a breath. "The Falks must still have that shipment. With my deputies and the Coast Guard doing routine patrols, it would be very difficult for them to leave unnoticed."

A session of brainstorming began. Glenn knew he did not have enough probable cause to get a warrant. A late-night delivery, regardless of the truck size, would not hold water with the judge. On top of that, the Falks had no criminal record.

These facts brought self-doubt. *Maybe I am reaching a little far with this.* But his gut would not let up. They would make the perfect contractors. They had a business, a way of laundering the money, a large enough boat to carry the cargo, a knowledge of the local waters, and were so well-liked that most people would not even think to suspect them.

"He would have to do it at night." He remembered Saturday morning when he responded to the orca situation. Jacob's boat was not there. According to Tris, he was taking divers out to the *George Crest* wreck. "Didn't Zolnai say something about passing him when they were checking the underwater cable?"

The dashcam footage had been uploaded at the end of the shift. As sheriff, he had access to it on his personal computers.

After typing in his code, he brought up the file, fast-forwarding to them arriving at the patrol boat.

Right away, he heard Denham's enraged tone. *"What do you mean you forgot the amprobe rod?"*

"I don't know! I thought I grabbed it," Zolnai replied.

"I see you remembered your donut!"

"It's delicious."

"I hope it is, you dumbass. Now we have to drive all the way back."

Glenn chuckled. "Andrew, you goofball. You'd fuck up a wet dream." He fast-forwarded through more footage, arriving at their departure. He skimmed through segments, stopping once he spotted Jacob Falk's vessel on the screen.

"What's going on, Officers? Trouble with the cable?"

"Not that we can see," Zolnai said. "You know those orcas that washed up on your beach?"

"Yeah, Tris told me through the radio. I was out before they showed up."

"Up and at 'em early today, aren't ya?"

"Well, I got some divers with me. They wanted to get a peek at one of the wrecks this morning."

"Yeah? Which one?" Zolnai said.

"George Crest."

"Hope they paid you extra." Zolnai stood on his toes. "You didn't leave them at the wreck, did ya? I don't see anyone aboard."

"Ha! No, these fellas are actually pleasant. They're below, getting dried up."

Glenn stopped the footage. "He came from the northeast. *George Crest* is *south*east of that location. And did they really dive that freaking early? I doubt it. Nor do I believe they were below getting dried off. If they were customers staying at one of his cottages, it would be more convenient for them to change there." He was guessing at that last statement, for Glenn did not know much about diving and divers' habits. What he did know was that there was enough reason to suspect these people of misdeed.

His predicament was the same. A judge would not sign off based on this circumstantial evidence. He needed something more. Something concrete. He needed to catch them in the act.

Glenn walked to his private office. It was rarely used, as he preferred the open space of the living room. However, it was still useful for storing some of his electronic equipment. Among the cords, old laptops, and radios was a box full of GPS trackers.

He held two of the devices, then considered the repercussions of his idea. It was risky, but it was the only sure way of determining their involvement in a timely manner.

If nothing else, it might help prove their innocence. As far as Glenn was concerned, that justified it.

He grabbed his keys and went out. It was late. With a little luck, the Falks would be asleep and never notice a prowler in their yard planting a tracker on their truck and boat.

CHAPTER 23

The night did not bring much sleep. The sheriff's secret deed had gone unnoticed. The only downside was the amount of time it took to walk from where he parked to the resort and back. He did not want to park near the driveway and risk being caught. By the time he got home, it was one-thirty. By then, his failure to eat dinner was wreaking havoc on his stomach. Dinner took precedence. Once his stomach was settled, he felt the slight feeling of regret. He had done something unethical. It felt right at the time, but now that the deed was done, he was questioning whether he should have done it.

What followed was maybe two and a half hours of deep sleep that made waking up almost impossible.

Like a good soldier, Glenn got in his uniform, and with two travel mugs full of coffee, he went to the office. He passed a quiet town on his way there. Many of the fishermen he usually passed were staying in for the day. The grocery store and coffee shop were relatively quiet, though that was common for a Monday morning.

The only activity he noticed was in Maple Park, where a few townsfolk seemed to be setting up a tent and some tables.

What was busy was the local newspaper, something that Glenn learned once he set foot in his office.

A series of articles had flooded his feed.

Sheriff saved by Daddy yet again.

Sherriff McCullough grounds fishermen. Will local fishing industry survive?

Mayor already reportedly considering pushing back on Sheriff's order.

Numerous Saw Ridge residents dead. Could Sheriff have prevented the fate of the Wilkersons?

Giant Squid in Gulf of Maine? Experts baffled.

Several researchers call into doubt Sheriff's claims about super squid.

"Yeah, assholes? Maybe you can see it up close and personal." He clicked away from the headlines. Why torture himself? He never had a grand opinion of mainstream journalists, whether they were local or national. It was all the same. It was not about being right or truthful; it was about being first. Get those clicks, make those headlines, sell those papers. The only ones with any credibility nowadays seemed to be independent journalists, and none tended to live near a quiet town like Saw Ridge.

His radio blared. *"Dispatch to Unit One?"*

"Go ahead."

"I just received a call from the Coast Guard. Lieutenant Commander Fredrick has asked if you were available to meet with him at the county harbor?"

"Yeah, I'll head over there right now." Glenn was immediately out the door, praying for good news from Fredrick.

***

Deputy Ben Denham was in a good mood. Monday was his Friday, and after the chaos of the recent weekend, he was ready for a couple of days off. He never cared that his 'weekend' was Tuesday and Wednesday. He had heard other first responders complain of how they missed having the regular weekend off. As far as Denham was concerned, as long as he had his two regular days off, and they were back-to-back, they could fall at any point of the week.

For Zolnai, on the other hand, it was only 'Thursday.' Even if it was his Friday, he would still act the same. Work was work, and he had more to do for the next twenty-three years.

If there was anything to be happy about, it was the fact they were spared boat patrol today. It was a long, drawn-out assignment that did not even offer the luxury of a decent phone signal. At least in the Interceptor, they could listen to podcasts or YouTube videos to pass the time between calls.

More importantly, they were nowhere near that gargantuan squid.

"I gotta say," Zolnai said. "My wife thought I was nuts when I first told her about that."

"In other words, it was an average day for her?" Denham said.

"Oh, you're funny. But seriously, she thought I was pulling her leg when I told her about the squid. Then she caught an internet video of the sheriff's press conference. All of a sudden, she's like 'Wait, you actually got attacked by a sea monster?' I'm like, 'Yep, almost died, too.'"

"Oh, nice one," Denham said. "Don't tell the sheriff that, since *he's* the one who almost died."

"Yeah, well it worked out in my favor. She thinks I'm a hero now. And boy, did she treat me well when she learned how I rescued the sheriff from the arms of the beast. Gosh, I've never experienced such vigorous . . ."

"Holy shit, man!" Denham put a hand over his brow. "Not information I needed to know. By the way, Dakota was the one who freaking saved Glenn's ass. Hell, we didn't go anywhere near the damn thing—something I have *no* problem with."

"Doesn't matter," Zolnai said. "My wife has a whole new appreciation for me. Hell, now that I think of it, I might put in for some overtime and go out and blast that squid into oblivion myself. I can only imagine the good treatment I'll get once she hears that I saved the town from the evil monster."

Denham kept his eyes on the road. The pressure in his sinuses made him avoid the main streets.

"Listening to your bullshit is not helping this migraine."

"You're still having problems?"

"Yeah. I might have to go to a clinic once I'm off and figure out what's going on. Probably some sinus thing. In the summer of all times, for god's sake." He found a side road on the outer perimeter of town and kept a steady pace. "All I want is to get through the day and go home."

"Did you take any Tylenol?"

"No. That stuff doesn't work for me when I have these sinus infections. Neither does ibuprofen."

"Have you tried the pharmacy over on Kingsley Avenue?" Zolnai asked. Denham shook his head, disinterested.

"What's the difference? Nothing works."

"I had a sinus infection two years back, and I'm like you. Almost nothing worked. But my wife stopped at this pharmacy and found this pain medication from Vicks that treats sinus pain. And it worked! It's not at the grocery store. We could only find it at this little place."

Now Denham was interested. He watched the road, contemplating this new information.

The very effort of thinking made the pain worse.

"All right, I'm willing to try anything at this point. I'm gonna continue this route and head over there when we come back around. Let's just hope we don't get any bullshit calls before we get there."

"Nah. That'll come this afternoon when the bars open. A lot of people would rather be on the water right now."

"Great." Denham nearly put his forehead on the steering wheel. "Thanks for reminding me."

***

When Glenn arrived at the harbor, Lieutenant Commander Fredrick was already ashore.

"Tell me some good news, sir."

Fredrick shook his head. "I wish I could. We could not locate the creature. If it's still in the area, I must assume Dr. Lehnert's theory is correct. It is taking time to heal."

"Damn it." Glenn looked over his shoulder, envisioning a town full of angry people. "Perhaps in the meantime we can focus our efforts on locating the dumpsite?"

"That's like finding a needle in a haystack, Sheriff. We have a large area to cover, and I only have one ship. Many of our available ships have been diverted south on other assignments. Our bigger cutters are over in the South China Sea to assist the Navy with the growing situation with China. Also, we're increasing our manpower in Alaska to intercept Chinese warships. There's more going on in the world than this dreadnought squid, unfortunately."

"I understand. What if I managed to narrow the search?" Glenn said.

"What do you mean?"

"What if I had a general idea of a specific region?"

Fredrick didn't answer. "Do you have something to go on, Sheriff?"

"Maybe."

Fredrick looked at the hill. "Please tell me you're not suspecting the Falks again."

"Listen, sir. I've spent all last night researching chemical manufacturing plants. I found one that operates in Nova Scotia and Maine. Guess what the CEO had previously been busted for doing?"

Fredrick was reluctant to answer. "Improper handling of hazmat waste?"

"Correct. Last time was in Georgia. They dumped materials such as dioxin, metals, plastics, various chemicals, used cables, and carbon fibers. According to reports, they paid unlicensed contractors under the table. Sound familiar?"

"Interesting." His tone was less stiff this time. "That makes sense, considering the *Alexandra Yale.* Still, that doesn't prove anything with the Falks. *If* they're using a second contractor, it could be anyone. Anywhere. There's more to the coast than Saw Ridge, you know?"

"That thing is *here*, though. Dr. Lehnert says it might be following a chemical trail similar to what ruined the canyon in which it lived. If that's the case, then it makes sense that somebody *here* is doing the deed."

It wasn't enough for Fredrick. His physical posture stiffened again, as did his tone. He had the look of someone who regretted this visit. If there were any future updates, they would likely be done through the radio.

"That's your department, kid."

"Sheriff," Glenn corrected him.

"I'll call you whatever the hell I want, *kid*." Fredrick stepped forward, his imposing presence and growly voice successfully making Glenn step backward. Intimidation was on full display, and Glenn knew it. "I'm telling you right now, you're making a big mistake. Kinda hard to believe you're the next generation of McCulloughs to be sheriff of this county. The last one had a lot of smarts, even when he was younger. I might not have jurisdiction over the town and county, but if I feel a high-ranking law enforcement officer is investigating someone without probable cause, I can take it up with the attorney general. Seeing how much I respect your father, I'd prefer not to do that."

The words had a bitter taste to them. Glenn felt like a cadet in the police academy, being called out by the instructor during class. The remarks were always the same. 'Just because your daddy is a big-time sheriff, doesn't mean you're hot shit, junior.'

"Believe me, it's for your own good. Unless you get something concrete, drop this obsession with connecting the Falks with what's going on out here. You have a gut feeling? Doesn't fucking matter, because your gut's not good enough."

"All right, all right." He sounded like a teenager getting chastised by a high school instructor. In an attempt to salvage his image, he grinned. "Yeah, I suppose you're right. I might be acting a little overzealous. Thanks for the brutal honesty."

The tactic worked, just as it did on his father yesterday afternoon. The slightest hint of a smile formed on Fredrick's face.

"You've been through a lot these past couple of days. I get that you're pissed that you nearly got killed by the squid and you want the people responsible for it being here to be brought to justice. And I'll give you credit: you did good with connecting the dots. It might be worth making a phone call to the state police to make an investigation on that plant you mentioned. The types of chemicals we found, along with the CEO's record, might be enough for a judge to issue a warrant. We just need to gather the evidence first. Should that go forward, we might get a lead as to what contractors they were using."

Glenn nodded. Everything Fredrick said made perfect sense. The issue was time, and the risk of coverup. Last time, the CEO was ratted out by the contractor, who was caught in the act. This time, the investigation would start at the source. All the CEO had to do was deny the claim and maybe make a few bribes. He doubted they used storage containers with any distinguishable markings that linked the substance to the company. At the end of the day, anyone could have dumped it.

"I appreciate it, Captain," he said. The two shook hands and went their separate ways. Glenn got in his car, watched the lieutenant commander return to his cutter, then eyed the road.

Is he right? Should I wait? What if there isn't enough to convict Orion Plastic Company, or any other guilty party? Interrogating a contractor might be the only way.

A beep on his GPS tracker stole his attention.

"No shit." The truck had departed during his conversation with Fredrick. It went west for a couple of miles, then turned north, then west again on some obscure side road. It was a route that bypassed the main part of town. Only a few residences were located that way. Otherwise, it was fairly obscure. "Where the hell could he be going?"

All of Fredrick's warnings, which Glenn genuinely had taken into consideration, dissipated like breath in a windstorm. Curious, he drove his police vehicle down the road, slowing as he neared Falk's Tale Resort.

Not only was the truck gone, but the trailer was, too.

"Why the hell would you need to take a trailer down Bernhardt Road?" Glenn could only think of one reason. *Getting another shipment, are ya? Big plant probably has a lot of waste to dispose of, and it costs big bucks to do it properly. A few grand for someone to toss it in the ocean, however . . .*

His heart thumped hard, his instinct spurring him to go after Jacob and catch him in the act. He nearly succumbed to that desire but managed to exercise a miniscule amount of self-control.

If they see a cop car, they'll depart without making the transfer. Plus, in case I'm wrong, I don't want to be accused of tailing this guy. If they just see an everyday truck, it'll be easier for them to assume it's just some random guy driving around. No big deal.

Glenn drove home, got in his truck, then followed the GPS signal.

***

Denham wished he had simply turned around and gone for the pharmacy. Two minutes after he decided to go, he got a call, or as he phrased it, a 'bullshit call.' Considering the mood he was in, he could have received a call to rescue the President of the United States, and he still would have considered it a bullshit call.

In this case, it was a drunk and disorderly. So much for waiting for the bars to open. A few fishermen had spent whatever spare change they had in the local liquor store and drank their misery away all through the night. A few did not bother with a typical breakfast. They woke up, slumped in the store's parking lot, and resumed their intake of alcohol. When employees arrived to open up, they asked the sweaty, vomiting scroungers to leave. They did not take well to this instruction. Fists were thrown, calls to the police were made, and as luck would have it, Denham and Zolnai were only three minutes away.

The effort to break up the altercation was thankfully quick. A couple of arrests were made and reports taken. After a bit of pleading from Denham, one of the other deputies agreed to write up the report and book the suspects.

"I'll write a supplemental later on," Denham said. "Anyone need me? No. Good. I'm gonna head out." He was back in his patrol car alongside Zolnai. "You jackass. You jinxed us."

"I resent that."

"Sure you do. Jesus, God. My head feels like it's gonna explode."

"Why don't you take a sick day?"

"Right. Call in sick right as the town is imploding in on itself. That certainly won't look like I'm trying to avoid unpleasant work duties." He started the engine and went north. "My phone is refusing to get a signal. You know the best way to that pharmacy?"

"Yeah." Zolnai pointed straight ahead. "Take this road up to Bernhardt, then take a left. It'll be a few miles outside of town."

"As long as this stuff you're talking about works, it could be on the other side of the county for all I care." He drove north, speeding to catch a yellow light. "Bernhardt is good. Hardly any stop signs or traffic lights. Nothing that should slow us down."

***

After twelve miles, Glenn slowed his truck. The signal stopped moving. Jacob had parked somewhere for a good while. Long enough to load something into that trailer.

It was just around the corner after the next intersection. Glenn carefully monitored his surroundings. Nobody was coming. Around here, a truck parked on the side of the road would not draw too much suspicion, unless somebody recognized it. Fortunately, Glenn hardly ventured this way in his personal time, so anyone who came by would probably not recognize his truck.

He stopped at the intersection and raised a pair of binoculars. He could just barely see Jacob Falk's trailer. There was another vehicle there—a semi-truck. There were no clear markings on it, meaning it could have come from anywhere. Its container was smaller than the other one, but it didn't matter. Glenn could hardly keep still. This was it! He was catching Jacob in the act. The guy that nearly got him killed would be brought to justice, and the town would no longer question his leadership ability.

Inching forward for a better view, he witnessed some large crates get hauled into the trailer. For the next few minutes, Jacob was in conversation with the trucker.

He snapped photos with his long-range camera. Faces and vehicles were captured. He even managed to get the license plate of the truck. Now, all he had to do was get a shot of the crate.

***

Denham arrived at Bernhardt and took a left. The smooth drive over the next mile would have put him asleep had he been in the passenger seat.

"Just keep heading this way," Zolnai said.

"I swear, if we get close and Dispatch radios with another bullshit call . . . " Denham muttered.

"Don't worry. Everyone else is getting ready for the event at Maple Park," Zolnai said. "Considering the financial state many of the fishermen are in, the rest will probably behave themselves to get a little free bread."

"Fair point."

"Don't worry. Besides, we're on Bernhardt. Nothing ever happens here. From here on, it should be smooth sailing."

Denham was too busy blowing his nose into a handkerchief to reply. Again and again, he emptied his sinuses, which seemed to have an endless supply of mucus.

"Uh, dude?" Zolnai said, concerned.

"I'm fine. Sorry, I was hoping this could wait."

"No . . . slow down."

"There's nobody here. I—uh, ah, eh . . .." He sneezed. "Damn it!"

"Andy!"

"What? OH!" Denham saw the truck parked at the intersection. He hit the brakes. "What the hell is this idiot doing? Sitting here. Dude! There's no stop sign. It's a two-way!"

"Wait a sec . . ." Zolnai leaned forward. "That truck looks familiar."

Denham squinted, studying the vehicle's make and model. "That's not the sheriff's truck, is it?"

Without waiting for answer, he stepped out of the vehicle and approached the driver's side window.

Glenn McCullough was so focused on his activity that he didn't notice the deputy until he was glaring through his window.

"What the—?!" The sheriff rolled his window down. "Denham? What are you guys doing here?"

For the first time, Denham was not intimidated by Glenn's authority. He recognized the device on the dashboard. Having seen the direction he was pointing the binoculars, Denham looked down the street.

"What's the matter?" Zolnai said as he approached. He could easily tell his partner was growing increasingly agitated, and it was not because of the sinus infection. "Sheriff? What's going on—oh . . ." He saw the tracking monitor. Before he could ask for further details, his partner went off.

"You're tailing Jacob Falk?!"

Glenn held up a hand. "This doesn't concern you."

"Oh, yes it does, goddamnit," Denham said. "This is against the law. Unless you have probable cause. Please tell me you have probable cause. I'm waiting."

"I . . ." Glenn's failure to come up with an immediate lie was his downfall.

"You son of a bitch. You realize how unethical this is?" Denham said.

"Deputy, there's a good reason—"

"Oh, shut up, Glenn. You're about as good of a liar as you are a sheriff."

"Give him a chance, Andrew," Zolnai said. "Sheriff, what's the idea?" Glenn's obvious reluctance to answer only made their perspective worse.

"I have reason to suspect he's the one dumping chemicals into the water."

Denham pursed his lips, struggling to not yell. Once he cooled down enough, he nodded at the truck. "You don't know who that is?"

"No. Do you?"

"That's a truck that delivers for Kroger. There's one up in Penobscot."

"Didn't you see the logo on the truck?" Zolnai said. "I've seen it in town once or twice. It's right there on its front left corner."

Glenn got out of the truck and stood up. That extra couple of inches made all the difference. The logo was somewhat faded, but still visible.

"Oh, shit. But why?"

"There's a food drive happening in town today to help with struggling families. The Falks are the ones who pretty much put the thing together," Denham said. "Didn't you get a notice from the mayor?" Denham already knew the answer. There was no more to be discussed. Denham took his badge off and looked to Zolnai. "Looks like you're driving. I'm officially resigning effective immediately. I'll return once someone better takes the oath."

"Okay . . ." Zolnai was more startled than outraged, and somewhat impressed with his partner's genuine virtue. Denham may have been the grumpy sort of guy, but he stuck to his principles.

They both entered the patrol vehicle.

"Take us around the side and roll down the window," Denham said.

Zolnai understood what he was getting at. He steered the car to where Jacob and the driver were. Both men turned, slightly unnerved to see the cop car pulling up. Zolnai brought the window down and leaned back, knowing his partner wanted to do the talking.

"Hey, Mr. Falk. You doing all right?"

"Yeah. You?"

"You might want to have a word with the sheriff back there. He's the one in the green Toyota, watching you."

"What? Why?"

"Might wanna ask him. All I can say is I'm going to file a report with the attorney general on your behalf."

The deputies departed, leaving a flustered Jacob Falk staring in Glenn's direction. Not even they wanted to witness the mild-tempered businessman go off.

***

It was one in the afternoon, and in the three hours Dakota had been assisting with the Falks' food drive, his mind was hardly on the task. The three calls he made went unanswered.

Siena was avoiding him, and he knew why. Twice, Dakota was asked by the other volunteers if he was okay. Even these people, whom he saw only now and then, could sense that he'd lost the spring in his step.

He faked a smile and took comfort in knowing he was helping the community. It beat sitting at home flicking through the channels.

Finally, around two he got a text. A long text, which meant this was a very good message, or a very bad one.

"Dakota, we'll talk later. I know you're busy right now. But first I should say I'm sorry. I succumbed to my urges and went to your place last night. I knew, even when I was doing it, that I shouldn't have. What's done is done, though, and I have to own up to it. I'm sorry for leading you on, but we need to accept that this isn't going to work."

Dakota started typing, then stopped when a second part of the message appeared.

"I got my next assignment. Once I'm finished here in Maine, I'm gonna conduct some research in the Gulf. Not too far from home, but way far from here. I had this fantasy that we could make this work, but it is what it is . . . a fantasy. I'm sorry. Call me a bitch if you want. We'll discuss it in person, but we HAVE to accept you and I can't be a thing. Frankly, I don't ever see you leaving this town. It needs you and you're good to it. More than they deserve.

"I'm sorry."

Dakota grunted. "I should call you a bitch, bitch."

"Beg your pardon?" one of the female volunteers asked, eyes wide.

Dakota looked at her and smiled. *Whoops.* "Not you. Just a buddy of mine yanking my chain." The lie worked and she laughed it off.

After she walked away, Dakota gave one last look at the message. "If nothing else, at least it was literate. Most text breakups are full of typos and are usually one sentence." He tucked the phone away. "On the bright side, at least the day can't get any worse. It can only go up from here."

He began the impossible task of trying to forget about it. It was surprisingly easy. Jacob Falk arrived late, his wife Tris with him, both more flustered than usual. The mayor and some press members were speaking to them.

"The hell's going on?" he said.

One of the journalists spotted him in the crowd and ran up to him. "Mr. McCullough! Can I get your opinion on the matter?"

"Uh, for the hundredth time, I'm not the sheriff anymore. My opinion is moot."

"Maybe not for long. There might be a vacancy in a few weeks after the attorney general finishes up his investigation."

"Beg your pardon?"

"Sheriff Glenn McCullough was caught illegally tailing Mr. Falk with a GPS. Former Deputy Andrew Denham has already filed a statement on the matter."

"What?!"

"Do you have any comment on the matter?"

It took Dakota several seconds to process this information before finally answering "No." He looked at the Falks and the mayor, who also spotted him in the crowd. Embarrassed, he turned around.

I was wrong. It DID get worse.

***

Glenn left the office early, but it did not save him from the backlash. If anything, it made it worse. His phone was constantly pinging with notifications from lawyers, staff at the AG's office, the mayor, and his own staff asking where he was.

Surprisingly, there was nothing from his father. Either he did not know, or he decided to leave the matter alone. Probably the latter, for the local press was already running with the story.

He poured himself a glass of Scotch and lifted it in a toast. "Well, I made a difference all right. To my shining example of how *not* to be sheriff." He downed the glass and started the next.

CHAPTER 24

Two days went by. During that time, Glenn mainly worked on boat patrol. The slow process of the investigation was excruciating. Since Monday morning, he'd kept his office and personal computers shut down. No sense in subjecting himself to the aftermath. He hardly even spoke to his deputies, leaving the general function of the department to the shift supervisors. Additionally, Lieutenant Commander Fredrick hardly got in touch with him, except for when he was obligated to give patrol updates.

The last forty-eight hours had been spent largely on the water, with the sheriff spending the time debating whether to resign. More importantly, what career should he pursue next?

His attempt at absence did not help with relieving tempers. At eleven o'clock that morning, he spotted a vessel attempting to sneak through the patrol lines. He switched on the lights and sirens and sped after the runaway vessel. After a hundred meters, the captain got the message and stopped.

It was the *Trident*, helmed by Alex Kelley. As far as Glenn could see, he was the only one aboard. He circled around the bow and guided the civilian back to port. There, he began the process of writing a report.

Alex Kelley stood on the pier, arms crossed, his face contorted into a snarl.

"So what? You're confiscating my boat?"

"That'll be the appropriate course of action," Glenn said. "You're well aware of the order. No boats on the water until we can locate and kill that squid."

"Oh really?" Alex said. "So it's all right for *you* to break the law. But for ordinary townsfolk who won't see a paycheck for weeks . . ."

Glenn lowered the pad and shot him a scornful look. "It is what it is, Mr. Kelley. I didn't invite the dreadnought here. Blame whoever drove it from the Submarine Canyon."

"Yeah, I heard they're already at the bottom of the ocean," Alex said. "By the way, have you ever issued an apology to the Falks?"

Glenn finished writing the ticket and handed the fisherman his copy. "I'm letting you off with a warning. I'm aware of your son's condition, sir. Last thing you need is another bill. Unfortunately, the only thing worse than mounting debts is death. Which'll certainly happen if you go out there."

The display of empathy did little to win Alex over. He took the warning then marched to his truck.

Glenn returned to his patrol boat and continued his route. The next hour was spent in silence. Even his father declined to message him.

Considering the way I've treated him, I can't really blame him. The guy's been in my corner since I took the job, but I didn't want to listen to the harsh realities.

Besides, Dakota had issues of his own. Even though it had been almost three days since Glenn last saw him, he could sense his depression. It was like a telekinetic force. If anyone else had assumed the position, he'd have left months ago.

The thought brought a fresh appreciation. His father was both a dedicated public figure, and even more of a dedicated parent. No wonder the town loved him so much.

"Coast Guard to Garrison County."

"This is Unit One. Go ahead."

"Just received a heads-up from the Tenacious Seeker. They're en route as we speak. We're hooking wide, traveling in the shallow waters near Yarmouth, then we'll angle toward Falk's Tale Resort. Should arrive in a couple hours. Dr. Lehnert has already been notified."

"Copy…" His voice trailed off. He forgot Siena had arranged for Linda Berman to stay at Falk's Tale. Right now, he was the last person they wanted on that property. He was actually surprised no restraining order had been written up. Then again, if one was, he probably wouldn't know it after ignoring most of his messages.

With nothing better to do, he resumed his patrol. Finally, a course of action could be determined. If nothing else, he needed to be present for that.

His phone buzzed. It was Siena shooting a text.

"Hey. Can you do me a favor?"

He texted back. *"Sure. What?"*

"Dr. Berman's boat will be anchored a few hundred feet off the Falk's Tale beach. Mind taking me to it? We have to go over our plan of operations."

He texted back, *"Sure thing,"* then continued on.

***

No sooner was Alex Kelley through the parking lot than he tore up the ticket and threw the pieces onto the road. For several miles, he filled his truck with a profane rant.

Thoughts of his son flooded his mind, lowering him into panic.

What do I do? Why did this freaking environmental hazard have to happen NOW of all times?!

Next came the usual routine of considering other jobs, only to realize it would take too long to learn something new and make money at it. His best bet would be to go out for a long haul, maybe fish around the Grand Banks. The problem was he could not even leave the damn harbor. He was stuck. Helpless.

His phone vibrated on his lap. Not recognizing the number, he ignored the call. Thirty seconds later, a voicemail notification appeared. Curious, he picked up the phone and listened to it.

"Hello, Mr. Kelley. I have a business proposition for you. Big money, if you're interested. I'll call back in a few minutes, since I'm calling from a payphone. Talk to you soon, hopefully."

A few minutes later, the phone rang again. Same number. Alex answered the call.

"This is Alex. Who am I speaking with?"

"Good afternoon, Alex."

He recognized the voice. "Why are you calling from a payphone?"

"Let's get to the point. I have a business proposition for you. The fee is five-hundred grand. You interested? Yes or no. Answer now."

To hell with the oddity of this call. Three-hundred thousand dollars?! Maybe luck was in Alex's corner after all.

"I'm listening."

"Just to be clear, this isn't legal."

"Figured as much, considering the way you're calling. Get to the point. What's the job?"

CHAPTER 25

It was two in the afternoon when Glenn returned to the county harbor. Five minutes later, he heard the scraping of tires on the pavement. Siena parked the rental vehicle and approached.

"Hi, Glenn. Thanks for your help."

"Not a problem," he said. "Give me a few minutes. The boat's thirsty and needs a drink." He picked up the gas canister and went to work. "Lieutenant Commander Fredrick gave me a radio call. They should arrive in ten minutes or so. I don't see them yet."

"They're a couple of miles off," Siena said. She waited quietly as he refueled the vessel. Then, as though to fill the silence, she finally asked, "So, how've you been? Haven't heard from you in the last couple of days."

Glenn sniggered. "You're kidding, right?"

"Yeah-yeah, I know." She waved a hand as though to say 'whatever.' "Personally, I think the town's overreacting a bit. I wouldn't call what you did ethical, but it's not like you put a gun to the guy's face." Glenn did not respond, which made Siena feel a bit uncomfortable. "Is that too naïve a way to look at it?"

"Maybe," Glenn said. "I don't know anymore. They're right, though. I was an idiot. Small county sheriff trying to play detective, seeking out a suspect that nobody else could believe was responsible. Well, time to pay the piper. Part of me hopes they remove me from office."

"Why?"

"Because I'm too much of a wuss to resign, I guess."

"That was not my meaning," Siena said.

Glenn finished refueling, then placed the cannister near the shed. "I'm in over my head, that's why. I don't think I even want to do this anymore."

"Let me ask you a personal question, since we're on the topic and have time to kill," Siena said. "Why did you campaign for the job to begin with? And be honest. If you say you were trying to follow in your dad's footsteps, I'll believe you. But I think there's more to it than that."

Glenn sighed, quietly thought over a dozen lies before settling on the truth.

"Ego. I hated being the guy always taking orders and wanted to be the one giving them. I guess I had a superiority complex. I saw how

Dad ran the department and how everyone respected him, and I wanted that for myself."

"Okay. How do you feel about that now?"

"To put it lightly, things did not play out the way I envisioned them," he said.

"That's because respect is earned," Siena said. "Let's face the truth. You only got the job because of your family name. You were not ready for the responsibility. And you thought you could boss the town into respecting your position. Any replies?"

"No, you just about nailed it."

"Good. The next step is you learn from this lesson. Don't pursue a case because of ego. Do it because it betters the community you serve." She put a hand on his shoulder. "I believe in you, Glenn. I wish I could stick around to help you out."

"Oh, right. I heard you're leaving soon," he said.

"Yep. In a couple of weeks. First, I'm gonna assist Dr. Berman with searching for any secondary waste dumps, then find the dreadnought. She convinced the university to let me stay for that. After all, this is a once in a lifetime opportunity."

"Once in a lifetime, huh?" He smiled. "That's what Dad thought when you first arrived in town."

Siena looked to the sky, wishing he had not brought Dakota up. "I tried to avoid him. I thought I could manage to work around here without running into him again."

"He smell bad or something?"

Siena laughed. "You know the deal, Glenn."

"If he left with you, how would you feel about it?"

"I—" her voice trailed off. "It doesn't matter."

"Let's not avoid the truth," Glenn said.

"He's not gonna leave this place, Glenn."

"Then he's a fool." Glenn climbed aboard the police boat then looked her in the eye. "He's had more than his fair share of failed relationships. For a guy who's such a great judge of character, he sucked when picking out partners. You, though, were the one he never got over. Probably because you were the only one who was worth something."

A warm feeling brushed over Siena. Her energy seemed to lift, her cheeks flushing somewhat.

"Flattery will get you nowhere, Sheriff."

They both laughed until a boat horn drew their attention. Approaching from the north were two large vessels. One was easily identifiable as the *USCGC St. Helens*, traveling a few hundred feet ahead of a second vessel.

"Right on time," Siena said.

The *Tenacious Seeker* was only a few meters smaller than the cutter. Its bridge stood at the bow, overlooking a main deck which ran two-thirds the length of the vessel. On the deck was the submersible *Century Cross,* secured by a cable attached to the crane.

Two people stood beside it, one of whom had a feminine figure.

"Berman here to Saw Ridge County. That you, Siena, that I see over there?"

Siena boarded Glenn's boat and took the radio speaker. "Yep, that's me."

"Good. Head on over. We have a lot of work ahead of us."

"On our way." She put the mic down and stepped aside to let Glenn take the controls.

"Time to better the community." He started the engine and headed off to meet with the vessel.

They aligned with the *Tenacious Seeker* three hundred feet from the Falk's Tale Resort. The crew secured ropes to the police vessel and helped its two occupants aboard.

Right away, Glenn recognized the familiar face he'd seen in Siena's computer monitor three days prior.

"Dr. Berman, good to meet you."

"Likewise, Sheriff. Feel free to call me Linda. I've been called doctor so much, I'm starting to feel I should be working in a hospital."

"Understood. On that note, just call me Glenn."

"Will do. Thank you for your help in this matter. I understand you encountered the dreadnought?"

"I owe Siena and my father for the privilege of being alive to talk about it," Glenn said. "With that said, I'd like to stop this thing before it kills anyone else. The Coast Guard hasn't been able to find it."

"It's been a few days," Linda said. "I imagine it's probably healed by now. I doubt it left the area."

"I agree," Siena said. "Lieutenant Commander Fredrick has been kind enough to provide me with regular water samples. There's still a steady trace of dioxin in most areas. The thing is secreting toxins with its mucus."

"Considering the lack of abundance in sea life around here, I imagine it will be getting hungry again soon," Linda said. "Tomorrow, we will commence our search. There's a good chance it might be hanging around the dump site."

"What makes you think that?" Glenn said.

"It probably expects more pesky humans will show up. My guess is that it plans to ambush them."

Glenn scratched his head. "Are these things really that intelligent?"

"You bet your ass they are." From the structure approached a strawberry blonde in her mid-twenties, walking alongside a young skinny Latino male, and a tall male with a dark complexion and a darker beard.

"Let me introduce you to my assistants, Ann Driver and Pedro Estrada," Linda said. "This taller, more handsome fellow is Captain Karl Hubert. Needless to say, he's in charge of the boat."

"Greetings, Sheriff. Hope you don't mind if we remain anchored out here until we set out for the expedition."

"No, that's quite fine," Glenn said. He turned to face Linda. "When exactly do you plan on starting?"

The marine biologist looked at the sky. "It looks like we're in for some mild weather tonight. Tomorrow, the forecast is looking clear. I'd like to set out tomorrow morning at oh-nine-hundred."

"Sounds good. I'll be joining you," he said.

"And do what, Sheriff?"

"A good stretch of these waters are my jurisdiction," he said. "If we find a clue that a resident in my county is responsible, I want to know. With a little luck, we'll find clues as to who's responsible."

Linda nodded. "I can't argue with that. Just so you know, the Coast Guard's already agreed to provide an escort."

"Great. Maybe we'll find the waste site and kill a prehistoric squid all in the same day. Two birds, one stone."

CHAPTER 26

"Five-hundred thousand?!" Art Palley immediately covered his mouth. Even in the privacy of Alex Kelley's home, there was a creeping fear of being overheard. "Is this for real?"

"Damn right it's for real," Alex said. "Like I said, it's a relatively simple gig. Pick up the explosives, load them onto the boat, then dump them at the waste site. Pow! We get paid and forget about the whole thing. Better yet, I already have the first step taken care of."

"You have the explosives?" Art said.

"In my trailer in the garage."

Bobby Douglas clapped his hands. "What's the split?"

"Three for me, one for each of you," Alex said.

"Hey!" Bobby said. "That's a little uneven, isn't it?"

"Captain's privileges," Alex said, raising a beer proudly. "Plus, I'm assuming more risk than the two of you. Should we get caught, I'll be fined or jailed to a larger extent."

"Not by that much," Art muttered.

"Listen, you two." Alex leaned forward, his newfound enthusiasm gone. "This is not a negotiation. To be honest, I was tempted to do this job myself and keep *all* the money. Reality is, I need a couple of extra hands."

"Hey, Captain, you don't have to justify it to me," Bobby said. "When do we leave?"

"Ten-thirty. We'll have plenty of cloud cover tonight. A little rain, but nothing that'll hinder the trip."

"And you know exactly where the location is?" Bobby said.

"I do. We'll be out and back in a couple of hours, tops." Alex sipped on his beer. "You guys have the opportunity to say no . . ."

Bobby broke out in a fit of laughter, spitting droplets of Budweiser. "No to a hundred grand? Fuck, I would've said yes to thirty." Alex swallowed, rocking his beer back and forth uncomfortably. Bobby cocked his head back. "Ah-ah, don't even think about it, you greedy bastard. The hundred grand's already been offered and accepted. That's the deal."

"Yeah, I know. Relax," Alex said. "Trust me, considering my use for the money, you're going to be the wealthier one once it's said and done." He stood up. "Get some rest. Tonight, we're heading out for Popham Furrow."

"Out in Jordan's Basin?" Art said.

"Yes. That bother you?"

"It's gonna be longer than a couple of hours."

"A couple of hours, six or seven, who cares? It's a figure of speech. Point is, we'll be back before daylight if we push the engines." Alex stood up. His face was starting to flush, a sure sign of rising blood pressure. "Or is that too much of a problem for the Boy Scout?"

Name calling. Art had misjudged his captain's mood. Despite the initial upbeat demeanor, his patience was still wafer-thin.

"Give me a break, Alex. This isn't the same as heading out and netting some shrimp. Look at it from my perspective: you invited us here where nobody can overhear us and tell us we're going to drop nearly a thousand pounds of explosives into the water in an attempt to cover up somebody's mess. That officially makes us accomplices of—who is it we're working for again?" Alex shook his head and walked into the kitchen. A frustrated Art threw up one of his hands. "You're not gonna say."

"Uh, dude?" Bobby said. "Why would he tell you if you're not going to take the job? More to the point, what difference does it make?"

"You don't care where the money's coming from?"

"Nope." Bobby downed the rest of his beer. "Does it make it more ethical if Mother Teresa asked us to do something illegal than, say, if Al Capone did?"

Art gave him a scornful look. "Do you even hear yourself?"

"I hear one-hundred grand, baby," Bobby said. "How can you turn that down?"

"Because I still believe in ethics." Art stood up and marched into the kitchen, finding Alex on a stool digging into one of the higher cabinets. He retracted the shot glass he kept back there. On the countertop was a bottle of whiskey.

For Art, this was getting worse with each passing moment. "Come on, Alex. You're better than this. And judging by the two empty beer bottles in your trash, and the way you're eyeballing that Southern Comfort, you're not comfortable with this, either."

Alex slammed the bottle down hard. "Listen, you chickenshit. I'm comfortable with whatever gets my son the treatment he needs. That end result is the only ethic I'm concerned with. If I have to burn down half the state to do it, I will."

"Good thing it's only bombs in water," Bobby added.

"Dude, will you shut up?" Art snapped. Bobby, though in plain sight, tiptoed into the kitchen, filled a glass with the whiskey, then 'snuck' back out. Art watched the pathetic idiot with contempt, then looked at his captain. "*That's* your crew, just so you know. He's already half-drunk."

"At least he's loyal."

"Loyal? Loyalty goes both ways. I would never ask you to do something so unethical." Art tossed his beer into the trash can then went for the door. "Do what you want. I'm out."

"Not so fast," Alex said.

Like an attack dog responding to an order from its master, Bobby jumped up to block his fellow crewmate. Art tensed, sneering at the younger man.

"Get out of my way, dude. You guys can't keep me here."

"Trust me, we wouldn't if you hadn't made such a holier-than-thou tirade about ethics," Alex said. "I know what's on your mind; you're going to the cops."

Art turned. "I am not. It's not any of my business . . ."

"Riiiiiight." Alex nodded to Bobby, who smashed the whiskey glass on the back of Art's head. The fisherman was unconscious before he hit the floor. Alex took a deep breath. "Sorry, pal. I'm not gonna let you ruin this for me." He looked at Bobby. "There's rope in the backroom. Tie him up. I'll use his phone to send a text to his wife that he'll be staying here a while."

"What'll we do with him after we're done?" Bobby said.

"First, I'm gonna see to it that my son's treatment is paid for. Once that's taken care of, Art can turn me in to the police for all I care." Over the next few seconds, his heart rate decreased, and his temper settled. He looked down at his unconscious friend with sympathetic eyes. A bit of blood oozed from the back of Art's head.

Alex grabbed his first aid kit from the bathroom and covered the wound with some gauze. Afterward, Bobby hogtied him and helped Alex drag him into the basement.

Somehow, doing this was the only part that made Alex feel a little uncomfortable. He felt like the maker of snuff films dragging his next victim into his dungeon. It only took a quick glance at his son's picture on the basement shelf to remind him why he was doing this.

Alex propped a water bottle and a straw near Art's head, then went upstairs with Bobby.

"I doubt he's gonna be our friend after this," Bobby said.

"Who can blame him," Alex said.

"Wait a sec. You just went on about what a chickenshit he is . . ."

Alex grabbed him by the shirt. "Bobby, I don't have the temperament for listening to your jargon. Fact is, if my family wasn't in this situation, I'd share Art's attitude." He let him go and inhaled deeply. "That said, what's done is done. You ready for this?"

Bobby rubbed his throat. "I guess." He spoke with the tone of someone who was second-guessing his decision, not because of the morals but his captain's increasingly hostile nature. "I hate to say it, but we're going to need an extra pair of hands. It's going to be hard for just the two of us to unload those explosive barrels."

Alex helped himself to a stiff drink. His crewman had a point. Alex had already collected the barrels in a trailer, and even with a dolly, they were extremely heavy. To make matters more difficult, he couldn't simply ask any random fisherman for his assistance. Should he make an offer to the wrong person, he could be facing a visit from law enforcement.

I need somebody who's bound to agree. Somebody financially struggling . . . somebody who's hurting . . . "I got it!"

Bobby grinned. "Who?"

"Get in my truck. We're going to pay a visit to Roger Wilkerson."

"Roger?! Why him?"

"He's the least likely to report us to the cops."

"You sure about that?" Bobby asked. "According to what I've heard, that chemical plant and these 'contractors' who dumped their shit are the reason that squid is here. You and I are being paid to cover it up. Why would he want to be a part of that, considering that thing killed his sons?"

"Easy. We'll just tell him we're being hired to kill the squid," Alex said. "He'll say yes in a heartbeat."

"Well, goddamn," Bobby said. He followed Alex to the doorway, then stared blankly as the reality of the situation finally started to sink in. *Shit. I never thought I could stoop this low.*

Alex opened his truck door, then noticed his crewmate wasn't there. "What are you waiting for?"

***

Roger sat in a dark living room. Two days prior, he was released by the hospital. Physically, he was fine aside from some minor bruising on the back of his head. Mentally, he was in a dark abyss.

His stomach growled, yet he was not hungry. His forehead ached, but he refused to take any medication. He was awake, yet he dreamt.

Every time he closed his eyes, he saw those frolicking tentacles. Nick was up there, wrapped in its clutches, the hooks digging deep into his body. Then *splat*! He was rammed into the deck.

Each replay of that memory sparked new shivers. Neighbors had come by to give their condolences, only to be faced with an expressionless man. Only when one was overheard suggesting that special services be called did he emerge from his trance.

"No!" he shouted, his eyes fiery, teeth crusted with tartar after being neglected for days. After a while, nobody bothered to visit. They didn't begrudge Roger's anger, but they did not know how to handle it. Besides, he did not seem to want the company. With no other family in town, it looked as if he was doomed to exist in his empty dark house all alone. Zach had still lived with him, though he was taking action toward getting his own place. Nick had moved in with his girlfriend two years ago. Roger had not spoken to her. He wasn't even sure if she knew Nick was dead. Most likely somebody told her after the sheriff's press conference.

Roger gave no thought to how she was handling it. As far as he was concerned, she could find herself a new boyfriend. A father could not replace his sons.

The clock struck seven-thirty. The sky outside was bright yellow as the evening sun's rays stretched horizontally. It was the only source of light in Roger's house, as everything was turned off, even the air conditioning. The combined forces of heat and humidity failed to stir him from his trance.

Same for the knocking at his door.

Roger could hear the voice from his front porch. "Hey, Roger. I know you're home. Open up."

He sat on his couch, staring at an empty fireplace. He recognized Alex Kelley's voice, but it didn't matter. He was just another person giving useless condolences, which only served as another reminder that Nick and Zach were dead.

In his sleeplike state, he never bothered to lock the door.

"I'm letting myself in," Alex called.

Another person was with him, speaking in a nervous whisper. "You sure we should do this? I don't wanna get shot."

"Quit being such a wuss."

The two men entered the house and found Roger seated on his sofa. Roger could see them in his peripheral vision but paid them no mind. They could have been homicidal burglars, and he would not have cared.

"Whoa," Bobby Douglas said. "Captain, I'm not so sure this is a good idea."

"Give me a sec," Alex said. He stepped in front of Roger and knelt. "Hey Rog. I'd ask how you're doing, but the answer's pretty obvious." Roger stared silently like a lobotomized mental patient. "Listen, I won't waste your time with formalities. I understand you're going through immense pain and there's nothing that can alleviate it. That said, there's something that might come the closest to making it right."

Roger's eyes shifted slightly. "Go away."

Bobby was backing toward the door. "I'm telling you, man . . ."

"Dude, will you chill?" Alex snapped.

Bobby bit his lip and stood silent, unsure which man he was more terrified of. Then he remembered he was potentially going to be trapped on a boat with *both* of them.

Lovely.

Alex saw the whiskey bottle on the table. "I'm sure you won't mind if I help myself to a swig." He took a drink from the bottle. "Listen, I'll go away, but there's something I want to tell you first. Bobby and I have accepted a job from . . . let's say a powerful individual that would rather not be named. We're going out tonight to kill that bastard squid." He kept an eye on Bobby as he spoke to make sure his nervous body language didn't get too out of hand. If Roger found out he was being lied to, he'd be more vicious than the dreadnought.

Roger sat up. "Kill it? How?"

"We have explosives that we're going to drop on its new hideout. New sonar readings have revealed the creature's been hiding in Popham Furrow. The Coast Guard unit doesn't have depth charges, but we do. I need an extra pair of hands, and I can't think of anyone better suited than you."

Roger's bloodshot eyes widened. "You're certain it's there?"

"May God strike me dead if I'm wrong."

Roger stood up. "Then what are we waiting for?"

CHAPTER 27

The light rain tapping on the roof did not help with Dakota's mood. The past few days had been lonely and frustrating. Respecting Siena's wishes, he did not message her, and he decided not to burden Glenn with advice. The kid needed to dig his own path out of the mess he was in. That's where the frustration came into play.

Three times over the last few days, reporters arrived at his front step to ask his opinion on the illegal tailing. Dakota declined to comment. He was often good with the press, but on these occasions, patience was not his virtue.

Even in their absence, the frustration had not completely subsided. He took his anger out on the chicken tenderloins in his skillet, batting them with his spatula. Ever the incompetent cook, he had poured too much of the marinade in with them. Smoke quickly filled the kitchen, something Dakota did not realize until he turned to reach for the refrigerator.

He went for the kitchen window to open it. In that time, the chicken started to burn.

Then the smoke alarm did its thing. Never was that blaring sound more annoying than it was tonight. Dakota propped the window open then went for the alarm.

"Come on, damn you. Oh, forget it." He yanked the wires free then tossed it in the trash. "I'll get a new one."

He looked at his dinner, its black color matching the skillet. Almost fifty years old, and he still could not break the habit of putting the burner at its highest setting.

"Looks like it's takeout once again." He grabbed the skillet, dumped its smoking contents in the trash, then tossed it into the sink. Cold water sizzled on contact, the steam mixing with the smoke. All the while, Dakota hoped the night's events would somehow trigger a repeat of Saturday. That night, he was certain she would show up. Today, it was a mere hope, and that hope was quickly deteriorating.

Dakota grabbed his keys and went for the door. He was still in the mood for chicken, but now it was the fried, unhealthy version he craved. Boneless wings and shrimp—perfect for the mood he was in. He got in the driver's seat and patted his gut.

"Might as well pack on the pounds."

He pulled out of the driveway and went north. In a couple of miles, he'd come up on Top Spring Road, which would take him directly to

The Wings Haven. At nine at night on a Wednesday, the roads were clear. The cloud cover completely blocked out the moonlight, leaving Dakota to the mercy of his headlamps.

He traveled along the coastline, watching one of the patrol boats pass by in the opposite direction. It was a police unit; the Coast Guard response boats were larger and had bulkier cockpits. The cutter was nowhere in sight. Two nights ago, he saw it heading south late in the evening. If they followed a similar routine, they were probably heading toward Massachusetts right now.

A mile up, he passed by one of the public harbors. Dozens of boats were docked, each one unused for days. Not that he could see them . . . oddly enough, the light posts were not working, coating the area in complete blackness.

"Huh. That's odd." He slowed to a stop, then looked at the road far ahead and behind him. The road lights were working, so it wasn't a power outage. It was as though someone had shut off power to the pier.

The investigator inside him began to stir. Unable to resist the urge, he pulled over and got out. Immediately, he heard the shuffling of feet on the docks and urgent whispering, including a "Shush!"

Flashlight in hand, the former sheriff set foot on the sidewalk that ran parallel to the line of boats and their docks. After walking a dozen yards, he spotted a vehicle up ahead. It had a trailer hitched, facing the pier. Its door was open, and a few feet past it, a two-wheel dolly rested on the concrete.

Dakota panned the flashlight in search of the owners. The lack of human presence made him nervous, for he knew somebody was here. Whoever it was, he suspected they were up to no good. Unloading contents from a trailer into a boat, under cover of darkness—when boating was not permitted—was not a sign of lawful intent.

"Good evening. Anyone there?" Nobody answered. "Whatever you're doing, I'd encourage you to reconsider. The Coast Guard will not take kindly to you sneaking out." His light went to the nearest boat. *Trident.* Alex Kelley's boat. "Oh, come on Alex. What the hell are you up to?"

Neither the captain nor his crew revealed themselves. They were hiding somewhere in this darkness. And that was the key word, hiding. Dakota had heard about Alex's family situation and personally saw his reaction at the press conference. It made sense that he would attempt to sneak out, maybe for a long swordfish haul.

Would he really hide like a six-year-old just to not be caught fishing? Dakota turned his light back to the trailer. *Unless there's something he doesn't want to be seen hauling aboard this boat.*

He stepped to the door and aimed his light inside. Four containers, fuel drums by the looks of them, stood two-by-two. Two circular indentations marked the empty space nearest to the door, indicating there were originally six. It made sense that Alex would be packing fuel for a long trip, except Dakota could usually smell the diesel in barrels like this. In fact, this had a different chemical smell.

That sixth sense of his went off. There was something illegal in these drums. Dakota stepped to one of the drums. Sure enough, it had a detachable lid. He raised it and aimed his light inside.

"Fuck me."

Hundreds of pounds of TNT were crammed into the drum. Near the top was a waterproof charge, wirelessly connected to a detonator.

Dakota turned around, ready to rush back to his truck. Before he could take a step, he was struck by a closed fist. He fell against the drums, his light falling from his hand. The stream bounced off the walls, illuminating the face of his attacker. To Dakota's surprise, it was not one of the *Trident's* normal crew, but Roger Wilkerson, of all people.

"Rog?"

"Sorry, Dakota. But you're not stopping us." The bereaved fisherman moved in to finish the job.

All sense of sympathy was out the window. Dakota had already righted himself; he sprang forward, wrapping his arms around Roger's legs. Like a wrestler, he slammed the fisherman into the pavement.

Running feet approached from his right. Dakota stood up just in time to intercept Bobby Douglas' haymaker. The younger crewmate gasped as the former sheriff kicked him in the stomach, putting him on his hands and knees.

Roger was already back up. Wasting no time, he plowed a fist into Dakota's groin.

"Ooooh! You fuck!"

A blow from behind put Dakota on the pavement. A kick to the ribs knocked any remaining fight out of him. Clutching his side, he looked up and saw a third figure towering over him. There was no light, but it didn't matter.

"I'm sorry to have to do this, but like Roger said, you're not stopping us." Alex Kelley kicked Dakota's head like a soccer ball. Now, the former sheriff found himself in a new kind of darkness—that of a dreamless sleep.

Alex did not usually get jittery, but when he did, he often felt sick. On this particular occasion, his stomach felt as though he had swallowed a pound of gravel. Twice tonight, he had had to turn to violence to complete this objective.

"Damn, Captain. That's Dakota McCullough," Bobby said. "We're totally screwed. We really should've thought this through before agreeing to this job."

Alex's soul-piercing stare could not be seen, but Bobby could sense it, especially when he spoke. "We did think this through."

"No, we didn't." Bobby clasped both hands behind his head. "Maybe we should have taken a night. Drawn up a better plan."

"No. The expedition sets out tomorrow. Thus, they might find the site. That's why our instructions are to handle this tonight."

"Expedition? What does blowing up the squid have to do with the expedition?" Roger said.

Alex looked at the former captain of the *Horizon Line*. He was standing near the trailer, the dropped flashlight revealing a disconcerted look on his face. Alex felt the hairs on the back of his neck standing up. Not only had he had to render two people unconscious tonight, but his lie was already at risk of being exposed.

"Nothing. Bobby simply meant that he didn't want to risk getting caught again," he said. "Now get some rope and some duct tape."

"Does he get a water bottle and a straw too?" Bobby joked.

"Not funny. Dakota is a good guy," Roger said. He tossed some rope to Alex. "It's unfortunate we had to do this. He'll understand, though, once we've killed the beast."

Sciatica in Alex's left leg started firing up. It tended to do that whenever he felt stressed.

"Yep." He finished tying Dakota up and moved him a few meters down the sidewalk. Meanwhile, Bobby went to his truck and shut off the lights. Like its owner, it was safe from view. Alex put a spare sweater under Dakota's head, gave a silent apology, then jogged back to the *Trident*. "Let's move it, boys. We've only got so much night ahead of us."

CHAPTER 28

Alex kept the motor running while he watched the next patrol pass by. He kept the lights off and ordered no movement on the deck. Despite his criticisms of the current sheriff, he had to give credit where it was due. These patrols were thorough and unrelenting. Considering the size of his motor, he needed to wait for the boat to be five hundred yards away before he could set out.

The deputies aboard the patrol boat did not seem to notice the *Trident's* engine. Alex guessed their minds were numb from boredom and repetition. He didn't blame them. Just the thought of coasting around the shallows for eight hours made him want to put his head against a propellor blade.

After a few minutes, the patrol boat was reduced to a little speck to the north. With no other boats in sight, he throttled out into open sea.

He was practically traveling blind. The lighthouse was farther to the north, and there was no other source of light ahead of him. With the spotlights and interiors off, the *Trident* had been swallowed in total blackness. It did not matter, for he knew these waters like the back of his hand.

Even the radio volume was kept to a minimum. Alex was so tense, he felt that the receiver might somehow be heard by patrolling boats. He had read on the internet once that stress and pressure had a way of messing with one's mind. He used to think that was mostly nonsense, maybe true for weak people.

Tonight, I hogtied two people after knocking them out. The stress and pressure made me do that. Does that make me soft?

With the thought came anger and a determination to justify his actions.

No! I'm not soft. I'm just willing to do what's necessary to protect my family.

His rationalization did not cover the reality that he would be coming home to. Even if this mission went picture perfect, he would be arriving at dawn in the best-case scenario. There was a good chance Dakota would be found by then, and the authorities would know exactly what happened.

"Then I'll dock somewhere else," he said out loud. "Head south toward Virginia. Get the money to my son's hospital . . ."

"What's that?" Bobby Douglas asked.

Alex whipped around, seeing his crewman standing at the bridge window. "Oh . . . nothing. Just want this over with."

"We're closer to that goal, boss. We're off!"

"Keep your voice down. Last thing we need is for your high-pitched squawking to draw attention to us."

"Can't be heard over this roaring motor," Bobby said.

Alex kept his eyes on the horizon, or rather, the blackness obscuring it. He could hear the faint reverberations of footsteps on the main deck. Roger Wilkerson was moving about, prepping the barrels.

He put the boat on autopilot and stepped out. The night air was as black out here as it was through the window. The only difference was the ambience of rippling water and the grumbling of the ship's motor.

Alex stepped to the edge of the fly deck and peered down at the six explosive barrels they had. It would be enough to ravage the ocean floor and anything inhabiting it, living or inanimate. He wondered whether the blast would be heard from shore, despite the vast number of miles in between. He had visited the countryside a few times. A few miles down, there was a copper mine. Every so often, he'd hear the echo of a dynamite blast. And that was with far less explosives than what he was carrying right now. Sound traveled faster and farther through water than in air.

Will it be heard?

It was one of many anxieties that were intruding his mind. Another was the sound of Roger Wilkerson moving about the deck. The man did not come unprepared for his intended mission. He brought aboard a high-powered bolt action rifle, a twelve-gauge shotgun, a .357 revolver, and a machete with a twenty-four- inch blade. Alex could not see those weapons where he stood, but just knowing they were aboard was enough to make him shiver. When he saw Roger load up his gear, Alex had second thoughts about this decision. The plan was to get an extra hand aboard his boat to unload the barrels. He never truly thought out what he would do if Roger discovered the truth of what they were doing. Sure, he planned to lie and say the creature was living down there, but if that didn't work, there was no plan as to how to handle the angry fisherman. Now it was a worse scenario; not only was he dealing with a slightly unhinged, grieving father, but one that was *armed.*

"The payload's in place," Roger said from the main deck.

"How can he even see down there?" Bobby muttered.

"He knows his way around a ship," Alex replied. They stood on the fly deck, watching the night air. There were no lights around them. They had successfully bypassed the patrol barrier.

The Gulf was practically theirs.

Alex monitored the speed and time. After about fifteen minutes they were a mile out. At that point, he returned to the helm and increased speed. Soon, one mile became two. At this point, Alex felt comfortable enough to turn on the wheelhouse's interior lights. He turned the vessel to port. There were several miles yet to pass before they reached Popham Furrow.

Again, the internal justification started running its course. Maybe the squid was in the furrow. It made sense, for it was the deepest part in Jordan's Basin. A deep, narrow trench, plunging an additional six-hundred feet below the rest of the basin. It was an ideal living space for a large predator—minus the toxic waste that he now knew was discarded there.

"Hey, Captain?" Roger called out.

Alex put the vessel back on autopilot, then stepped out. "What's the problem?"

"I thought I heard something. Starboard side, maybe a hundred meters out," Roger said.

Bobby stood on the fly deck, now visible in the interior's glow. "Okay, so that wasn't my imagination."

"You heard it too?" Alex asked.

"I thought that was implied by my statement," Bobby said. "Yes, I heard it."

"I would recommend using the spotlight," Roger said. The pump of a shotgun followed that statement. Next was the racking of a rifle bolt.

Alex took one last look left and right. Even though there were no lights, there was that odd fear that someone was nearby. Then he heard the splash, and that fear shifted to some*thing* being nearby.

He activated the starboard side rail spotlight and aimed it into the ocean. He swept it back and forth, then aimed it further out. The lingering glow brought the main deck to view, and the vengeful fisherman standing aboard it. Roger had his shotgun shouldered, his rifle slung over his shoulder, machete sheathed on his left hip like a pirate's cutlass.

"I saw something," Bobby whispered. He ducked, as if that would somehow make him invisible to any potential horror waiting out there. "Roger, can I have one of those guns?"

"With your boozy breath and jittery hands? I think not," Roger said through gritted teeth.

"Shh!" Alex pointed the light straight ahead. He shuddered after seeing something black break the surface. Roger quickly placed his shotgun on the deck in favor of the rifle. If the target were there, he would need something with longer range.

"Come on, you bastard."

"Shut up, Roger," Alex whispered.

"If it's there, we don't want to draw its attention," Bobby said.

Roger scowled at the two of them. "Why? Isn't this why we're out here?"

"It was supposed to be an ambush," Bobby said. He leaned toward his captain. "Boss, I'm having second thoughts about this. Maybe we should turn back."

"Shut up, you coward." Alex reached into his shirt pocket, pulled out a flask and handed it to his crewmate. "Maybe this'll help. Filled it when we left. Intended it for myself, but clearly you need it more."

Bobby did not hesitate. He snatched the flask and downed its contents at a speed that even surprised Alex.

Once again, he was questioning his decisions. Bobby was already wavering, the booze going straight for the brain. At least before, he was still somewhat useful. Now, he looked as though he would fall asleep on the deck at any point.

Great.

Another splash drew his eyes back to the water. Something again passed through the light source. This time, Alex was able to follow it with his light.

A sharp *crack* filled the air, making him jump. Alex looked down and watched Roger eject his empty cartridge and chamber a fresh one. Immediately, he fired another shot.

Something was thrashing at the end of the spotlight's reach. Bobby stumbled to the other side of the fly deck, unclamped the portside spotlight from the guardrail, then carried it over. With each step, he wavered. His nerves were calmed, but at the expense of his equilibrium.

He activated the spotlight, the stream waving across the night sky in his unsteady hands.

After several repeated attempts, the drunken sailor managed to aim it in the general direction of the ocean. Roger, fed up with his nonsense, climbed to the fly deck, rifle slung across his back. He yanked the light from Bobby's hands and aimed it at the target.

"Hey!" Bobby slurred.

"Shut up," Roger said. He matched the light's direction with Alex's. Together, they watched the struggling mass. "What is it?"

Alex tightened the clamp and locked the spotlight in place, then hurried into the pilothouse. When he returned, he had his binoculars in hand. He aimed them at the anomaly and watched. He saw red in the glowing water, stirred by a twelve-foot mass. Fins protruded from its side and back, its open mouth lined with teeth.

"You shot a shark," he said. "Well done."

"Hey!" Bobby raised the empty flask as though about to drink from it again. "At this distance? It was a good shot, though!"

"Shut up."

"Whoa!" Bobby pointed a tremulous finger at the sea. "Look at that."

"Look at what?"

"You dumb idiot. What were you thinking adding more booze to his rotted brain?" Roger said.

Alex squinted. "Wait . . ."

As it turned out, Bobby *did* see something. The water was alive with movement. Sharks, at least a dozen of them, converged on their dying brethren and plunged their teeth into its hide. Like flies buzzing around a corpse, they moved in, one after another, took a bite, then ran, only to circle back and wait for another opening in the crowd.

"Well, at least we served lunch for somebody," Bobby said. He put a finger to his chin and looked up. "Or is it a midnight snack?" He took a swig from the flask.

"Isn't that empty?" Alex said.

"Not anymore. I found the Scotch in your cabinet, so I took the opportunity to refill while you were distracted."

Roger stared at him, then at Alex. "You seriously brought him along for this? Hell, I'm doing most of the work down there."

"Hey! I've got seniority on this boat," Bobby said. "Besides, if you wanna talk about 'useless,' then I should point out you're the one wasting bullets on sharks."

"*My* bullets," Roger said.

"Yeah. Bullets that the entire coast can hear," Bobby said, spitting saliva. He stumbled to the guardrail and watched the feeding frenzy. "At least you're a good shot." He raised the flask. "Hey, fishes? Want a beverage with that?" He unscrewed the cap and tossed a few droplets out.

All at once, the sharks broke from their now-dead companion and darted off to the west, quickly disappearing under the water.

"Wow," Bobby said, taking a sip. "More for me, I guess."

Now, it was Roger's hands that were wavering. He held the rifle waist high, finger in the trigger guard.

"Why'd they leave? They weren't done."

"And why'd they leave in such a hurry?" Alex said. Fearing the worst, he retreated to the pilothouse and switched on the fish finder. A large blip had just passed underneath the boat. He had seen several large animals in the past. One time, a humpback whale passed a few yards under the ship, its mass taking up nearly a fourth of the screen.

This blip stretched from one end of the screen to the other.

"Oh, no, no, no. This can't be happening."

Roger rushed in and saw the reading. His face contorted into a bizarre mix of fear and excitement. "It's here." He rushed outside and went for the ladder. "Come on, Bobby!"

Alex dashed after him. "What are you doing?"

"It's right underneath us! We gotta drop the barrels! This is our prime opportunity!"

Alex peeked through the open window at a fallen picture of his son, which had likely been knocked over during Bobby's bumbling search for alcohol. He envisioned him in the hospital bed where he currently resided. The solution was just a few miles away.

If only this damn dreadnought hadn't shown up.

God! We're only a couple of miles out. Turns out the sheriff was right . . .

It did not matter. He needed to complete the job. Looking back to the main deck, he saw that Roger had switched the lights on. He had the detonator in hand. He extended the antenna, activating the LED light. On the side of the device were two settings, one for remote activation at the touch of a button, the other for a timer.

"No! Roger, stop!"

Roger lifted one of the barrels on the dolly, then with Bobby's help, lifted it onto the transom.

Alex reached into his jacket and pulled out his .38 Smith and Wesson revolver. "I said STOP!"

Both men looked up at him. Roger's hand went for his rifle.

"The hell are you doing pointing that thing at me?"

"We're not dropping those here."

"The hell you talking about?! The dreadnought's down there! You said we were out here to kill it. It's down there right now! We have our chance."

"Yes . . . no . . . I mean—"

Roger tilted his head, his cheeks, nose and brow wrinkled. "You mean what?"

"This . . . we . . ." There was no good way of getting out of this lie. The sweat lubricating his palm made the handgun feel slippery as ice.

"What the hell is going on?!" Roger shouted. His anger was on full display now. Worse, it was no longer directed at the dreadnought, but at Alex.

"Oh, I warned you about this," said the drunken Bobby to Alex.

"Warned him about what?" Roger said. He glanced back and forth between Bobby and the captain. Bobby swallowed, realizing his bibulous slip of the tongue. "Warned about what? Why did you bring me out here?"

"We needed an extra hand. Someone who'd come on short, immediate notice," Bobby said.

"To do what?"

"To blow up the place where some idiot plant manager has been dumping their shit," Bobby said.

"Douglas!" Alex snapped.

"What?" Bobby took another sip of the flask. "He was gonna figure it out anyway."

Roger sneered, hand clutching the barrel of his rifle tighter. His other hand held the detonator.

"Put it down," Alex said.

Roger scowled. With the .38 trained on him, he knew he could not be the faster draw. But there was one other option.

His thumb moved over the trigger.

"No . . . DON'T!" Roger said.

"Listen!" Bobby threw up his arms, accidentally flinging the flask into the water. He looked in the direction of the splash, dumbly more concerned about that than the current predicament. "Aw, man . . . anyways, listen. Boss, we can drop one barrel. That should be enough to do the trick, right?!"

Alex took that consideration to heart. Who'd have known that the intoxicated Bobby Douglas, who could barely stand up straight, would be the most level-headed of the bunch? He was right, though. One barrel should kill the monster, and the other five would likely be enough to get the original job done. Who knows? Maybe they would be considered heroes upon return.

"All right, maybe—" When Alex returned his focus to Roger, he noticed he was standing on the starboard side, with his rifle now pointed at him. Those ten seconds of deliberation were enough for the enraged fisherman to change the dynamics of the standoff. "Wait, Roger. He's right. We can . . ."

"You took advantage of me, you prick." There was no bothering with negotiation. Roger squeezed the trigger. Simultaneous to the *crack* of the gunshot was a sudden hot pressure in Alex's lower left torso. A seemingly invisible force knocked Alex backward. He landed on his back, spitting blood. When he looked down at himself, he saw a red stain in his sweater rapidly expanding.

Roger racked the bolt, then looked to his right. Bobby Douglas was shivering, and not because of the booze. He had his hands raised.

"I . . . I warned him against it. I . . . Don't shoot me, man."

Roger pointed his muzzle at the crewmate's chest.

Bobby twitched. A dark stain formed over his crotch. He looked down at himself. "Oh, man . . ." He looked back at Roger. There was no turning back. His mind was lost. He had gone the path of the homicidal maniac. Now that the first step was taken, there was no going back. He chambered the next round, his finger twitching against the trigger.

Bobby shut his eyes. "I guess this is better than being eaten alive."

A splash of water struck him from behind. Bobby stumbled forward, his wet clothes hugging his body, then turned around.

Red, leathery flesh glistened in the deck lights. Like the head of a hydra, the huge tentacle stretched over the *Trident*. Two rows of suckers lined its length, each one protruding dual hooks.

"Oh . . ."

In a blur of motion, he was snatched, constricted, then lifted ten feet over the deck. He screamed in horror, then in pain. Hooks pierced his flesh while the pressure snapped his arms, ribs, and spine. Yet, death took its sweet time.

Bulging eyes beheld the sight of a mountain of water lifting beside the ship. More tentacles arose, lashing at the air as though angry at the world above the ocean. Or, at least, the land dwellers that inhabited it. The very creatures that destroyed its habitat with their filth.

Each arm was connected to an enormous mass that nearly matched the length of the ship. Two huge eyes stared at the helpless human. Like flower petals, the arms parted, revealing something made of bone. A jaw—a beak, almost as long as Bobby himself! Behind that beak was a fleshy tongue, as nimble and flexible as the tentacles that protected it. Unlike the tentacles, it was not lined with hooks, but with teeth.

The sheriff had stated it was an intelligent creature. It seemed impossible to Bobby when he first heard that. But now, he was staring into the eye of the beast, who was literally taunting its prey with his fate.

"No . . . NOOOOO!!!!"

The tentacle lowered Bobby into the beak, where he was promptly cut down the middle, then ground into bits.

During this time, Roger froze. Even his hatred of the dreadnought could not overcome the intensity of seeing such a creature in the flesh. Only when the tentacles lashed at him did he snap into focus.

He fired the remaining bullets in his rifle, then lunged for the two shotguns. He snatched one up and raised it at the head of the beast, only to be struck by one of its flailing arms.

Roger fell against one of the drums, bumping it against the one next to it. The device wobbled on its edge, then fell. It landed on its side, the *clang* matched with the *beep* of the three-minute timer being activated.

The ticking of the countdown could not be heard by Roger's ringing ears. Repeated shotgun blasts shook his body with their recoil. There was no technique or strategy to his attack. It was kill the creature at all costs.

When one shotgun ran dry, he went for the other.

Blast, pump, blast!

The tentacles merely twitched when struck by the buckshot. The beast displayed little concern for the limited bodily damage caused by the human weapons. Each tentacle searched the vessel, looking for the perpetrator.

One of them swept the length of the deck, like an angry chess player knocking the pieces off the board. Its tip struck Roger, toppling him and the barrels.

A crushing pain in his knee made him yell out. He leaned up and saw his knee bent in the opposite direction, a drum lying on top of it. His attempt to move it caused lightning bolts of nerve pain.

Slithering across the deck like snakes, the dreadnought's arms converged on their target.

"To hell with you, you damned devil!" Roger drew his revolver and fired all six rounds into the crowd. Numerous dull clicks followed, after which he discarded the revolver and extracted his machete. The blade plunged into the tip of one of the arms. The laceration did not stop its advance. It contorted over his arm, the hooks digging into his bicep and forearm. The dreadnought yanked, intending to lift its prey high off the ship. Only, it yanked too hard.

Roger stared at his empty shoulder and the blood spurting from it. Up above him was his limb, clutched in the squid's grasp. He watched his arm with an odd fascination. The fingers were still gripping the machete handle.

"Swallow it," he muttered, then chuckled. Blood loss and madness turned that chuckle into hysterical laughter. Lost in psychosis, Roger did not even feel the sensation of being lifted off the deck. Only when his ribcage was crushed, preventing his laughter, did he realize the end was near. Right then, the psychosis came to an abrupt halt. It was replaced by a horrible understanding, leading to fresh hatred.

Roger was looking at the mouth of the dreadnought. Like with its previous victim, it taunted him with his fate. He had failed. The creature that killed his sons had bested him. Terror and rage came together in one final scream, cut short once he came into contact with the beak. The jaws came down, severing his other arm and part of his leg. Not enough to kill him instantly, thus forcing him to endure the slicing of his entire frontside, from his thighs all the way to his face. The tongue raked his body, peeling the flesh from the bone. The beak mashed the rest.

Seeing no additional movement aboard the vessel, the dreadnought submerged. Jet propulsion launched it far away. It had healed from its burns and was on the warpath to kill any human traveling these waters.

Alex Kelley faded in and out of consciousness. Pain and blood loss took their toll. Only sheer will kept him from blacking out entirely. Though he did not witness it, he knew his two crewmen were dead. He smelled the ammonia dripping off the dreadnought's many arms. The gunfire had come to a sudden halt. Now, he was left on a quiet ship, with nothing but explosives to keep him company as the end came.

Even in such excruciating pain, even with the energy slipping away, Alex could not shake the desire to get the *Trident* to Popham Furrow.

Maybe I can still get the boat out there. Maybe if I stay alive long enough to finish the job, they'll give the money to my boy.

With a groan, he sat up and looked at the main deck. Blood covered the ship, the explosive drums were everywhere, but intact. There was no sign of the squid. All that remained was a weird ticking sound. Like a clock . . .

Or a countdown timer.

Squinting, he noticed a red glow coming from the port quarter—the same direction that ticking came from.

006 . . . 005 . . . 004 . . .

Alex reached out, wishing his arm would stretch the length of the boat and stop his impending doom. A doom caused by his own fall from grace. Manipulation and brute force had a price to pay. His last thoughts were of his failure, and how this tactic had ensured his son would never get his treatment.

"N-n-nooo!"

003 . . . 002 . . . 001 . . . 000

All six charges erupted, erasing Alex Kelley and the *Trident* from existence.

CHAPTER 29

"Dakota! Dakota! Wake up!"

At first, Siena's voice sounded far away, as though she was calling from the other side of a football field. Each time, she was louder. Then came the sensation of rocking back and forth.

Dakota opened his eyes, then winced. The morning sunlight stung almost as bad as the blow that had knocked him out.

His wrists ached, as though they had been squeezed for hours on end. He saw the bruises, then the ropes lying on the pavement. The bastards had hogtied him in case he woke up early.

Kneeling beside him was Siena. She breathed a sigh of relief and hugged him. "Oh, thank God. You're okay."

"Yep. I'm good. Just, uh, you mind letting me breathe?" Siena did not release him. "Uh, Doc?"

"Oh!" Siena released him. Dakota sat up and rubbed his head. Standing around him were a half-dozen deputies, a few onlookers, and Glenn.

"Dad, you all right? How are you feeling?"

"Well, I got a full night's sleep by the look of it."

Siena and Glenn shared a glance, then a phrase: "He's all right."

"Hey, man," Deputy Zolnai said. "We were all worried about you."

"I'm fine, I'm fine." Dakota stood up and looked at the crowd. "Jesus! Did the entire town show up? I'm not dead yet."

"A dock worker found you," Glenn said. "What the hell happened? We found your truck over there."

Dakota rubbed his head again, then recalled last night's events. "I butchered last night's dinner . . ."

"Big surprise," Siena said.

". . . and headed out for takeout. I see that the lights around here went out. I stop, hear something, then I find the trailer. Then I get jumped by . . ."

"Alex Kelley and his crew," Glenn said.

Dakota looked at the dock. The *Trident* was nowhere to be seen. "Yeah, I guess that was easy to deduce."

"Didn't need to run a trace on the trailer," Glenn said. "There was an explosion last night. Coast Guard responded. Pieces of their ship was found."

"There were traces of secretion on some of the debris. They encountered the dreadnought," Siena said. "Glenn called me during the night after some of the wreckage was brought in. Then he got a call that you were found while I was inspecting it."

"Hard to believe they would resort to this," Zolnai said. "Why would they do this? I can see Bobby Douglas getting drunk and wanting to kill the thing, but it's hard to imagine Art Palley going along with such a deed."

Dakota scratched his head, replayed last night's brawl in his mind, then turned to face him.

"No. Art wasn't there."

Glenn perked up. "No? You sure?"

"Alex would need at least two men to help unload that trailer quietly," Zolnai said.

"It was Roger Wilkerson," Dakota said. "He was with them. From what I saw, there was only the three of them."

"Odd," Siena said. "What was their motivation? Go out and kill the squid for revenge? To get the sheriff to allow fishing boats back on the water?"

"I'd say yes, except it's odd that they managed to obtain so many explosives," Dakota said. "Those things aren't cheap."

"Or legal," Glenn added.

"Considering both Roger and Alex's financial situations, I doubt they obtained the finances to acquire that much TNT in a short time frame," Dakota said.

"What are you implying?" Siena asked.

Dakota looked at his son. "Glenn, you were right. I think somebody hired them to go out there. Somebody with deep pockets and local knowledge."

"Why would somebody pay them to kill the squid when we already have the Coast Guard here to do it?" Zolnai asked. "Wouldn't that bring unwanted attention to yourself?"

Glenn nodded. "It would. There's no gain to doing that . . . unless they were going out there to blow *something else* up."

"Something else?" Siena was starting to read between the lines. "Covering up evidence. The waste site!"

"It's got to be fairly close—close enough to travel out and possibly return before daybreak," Dakota said. "If Glenn's right, they were hired by somebody, set out under the cover of night, then encountered the dreadnought before they could reach their destination."

"Maybe the squid got killed in the blast," Zolnai said.

"No, we'd know by now. After this many hours, its corpse would have floated to the surface," Siena said.

"Sheriff? How far out did they get?" a fisherman shouted from the crowd.

"Only a couple of miles," Glenn said. "Please, for the love of God, *do not* go out on the water."

A series of nods answered his request. Now, it was all the more real to the townspeople. Someone had disobeyed the order and paid the price. All at once, the town understood that Sheriff Glenn McCullough's heart was in the right place and his judgement was sound on this matter.

"Why would Roger go out with them if not to kill the squid?" Siena asked. "My understanding is that he was grieving, obviously. Would he really be motivated by money to cover up evidence? For the people responsible for the dreadnought being here, no less?"

"I know Alex would," Glenn said. "Bobby, definitely. I know Art Palley. He's the more sensible one. I can imagine him refusing such a job. Maybe he did, and Alex needed another crewmate. My guess is he needed to act quickly."

"Meaning whoever paid him knew we'd be searching for the waste site," Dakota said.

"Considering Roger's state, he was probably easily manipulated. Maybe given a good lie about hunting the squid itself," Glenn said.

"Makes sense, but how can we confirm this?" Zolnai asked. "At the moment, we're just spit-balling here."

"First step would be to find Art Palley," Glenn said. "I want a unit at Alex Kelley's house. See if there's anything we can find. Let's go. Move it!" The deputies dispersed and got into their vehicles. Glenn looked at Dakota, who was perked up, alarmed. "Dad, you all right? Need to go to the hospital?"

"Oh, no. I just remembered that I might've left the stove on last night."

Siena face-palmed, then chuckled. "Considering it's you, I'd say it's highly likely."

CHAPTER 30

Twenty minutes later, Glenn received a call to respond to Alex Kelley's residence. There, he found his deputies going through the house, dusting for prints, and bagging Scotch bottles and glass fragments for evidence. Downstairs, EMTs were tending to Art Palley's head.

"Got a few glass fragments here," one of them said.

Art Palley winced, rubbing his wrists and ankles. The EMT pulled another fragment.

"Ow! You dumbass! Isn't this a job for a surgeon?"

"You said you didn't want to go to the hospital," the EMT said. "Now hold still."

"May as well save the doctors for Alex and Bobby. When I'm through with them, they'll need a whole OR team."

"More like a DNA kit," Glenn said.

"Huh?"

"They're dead. Them, and Roger Wilkerson."

Art sat up, then winced in pain. "Ow!"

"Damn it. I said hold still," the EMT said. He looked at the sheriff. "There's little fragments in here. He's gonna need to see a surgeon."

"They smashed him hard," the second medic said.

"Bobby did it. Obviously, they didn't want me spilling the beans on what they were about to do." Fed up, Art brushed the EMT's hand away. "So, they're really dead? Did they encounter the squid?"

"Looks like it. Somehow or another, those explosives they were carrying went off in the process." Glenn sat on the couch opposite him. "Did Alex or Bobby say anything about hiring Roger Wilkerson?"

"No. In fact, that was going to be my next question."

"Then my suspicions are likely correct," Glenn said. "Unfortunately, we'll never know for sure. The more important thing is the 'who' and the 'where.' I'm assuming Alex told you about the job and you refused."

Art smirked. "I'm glad to know my honorable reputation precedes me. Yes, that's what happened. Then *smash*!" He made a splattering sound and waved his hands at the floor.

"What other details did Alex give you? Was the purpose of the mission to erase evidence?"

"Correct."

"Did he say who hired him?"

"No. After I refused to do the job, he wouldn't say anything more."

Glenn threw his head back. "Damn."

"He did slip up and say where, though," Art said. Glenn was leaning forward again, listening. "He mentioned Popham Furrow. Some gorge in Jordan's Basin. I'm not sure where it is. I usually use buoys and wreck sites for markers."

"I don't have the first damn clue where that's at, either," one of the deputies said.

"There are all sorts of little geological areas across the entire Gulf with names," Art said. "Most of them aren't even on any map. Alex apparently knew where it was—probably given the location from the 'client.'"

"I'm assuming the explosives were provided by the 'client' as well," Glenn said.

"Yep."

"Doesn't mean anything," another deputy said. "I'm looking up every map of Jordan's Basin I can on my phone. So far, I can't find anything about some furrow."

"Unless we find who was initially dumping it, we might never find it," said another.

Glenn smiled. "Have you guys no faith?" They all looked at him, thought about it, then smiled, too. "There's one guy who knows these waters as well as anyone, which is hilarious considering he spent most of his career on land." He stood up, phone in hand, and dialed his father's number, who picked up on the first ring. "Hey, Dad. How you feeling? Better already? That's good . . . Yeah, Siena about had a heart attack when she heard the call. I figured she'd volunteer to be your nurse. Guess she's not as capable of distancing herself from you as she thought . . . Hey, since you're feeling well, can you meet me at Falk's Tale? I'm meeting with Linda Berman, and it looks like we're gonna need your help . . . Great, thanks. See ya there."

He hung up and clipped his phone to his belt. "Art, go to the hospital and get that looked at."

"Fine," Art said in an exasperated tone. Glenn started up the stairway. "Oh, hey? Sheriff?"

Glenn stopped and looked back. "Yes?"

"Just curious—how far out did Alex get before he encountered the squid?"

"Roughly two miles. Probably twenty-to-thirty minutes after departure, depending on the speed."

"Good God," Art muttered. "I'm sure glad I talked him into returning to port after we first heard the emergency alert."

"Me, too," Glenn said. The two men shared a nod of mutual respect. Afterward, Glenn was off. Next stop was Falk's Tale. If the Falks didn't like him showing up on their property, they would just have to live with it. There were more important matters at hand.

CHAPTER 31

When Jacob Falk saw the sheriff's department SUV, Dakota's truck, the Coast Guard cutter a hundred yards off their main dock, and its lieutenant commander being boated toward his shoreline, his heart leapt into his throat.

"What's this? What's going on? Oh, shit . . ."

Tris approached from the kitchen. "What's the matter?" Jacob pointed to the gathering in front of one of the cottages. Tris looked, then immediately returned to the kitchen, unbothered. "That's the scientist's cottage. Dr. Lehnert's out there, too. They're probably just meeting her regarding the squid."

"You heard what happened last night, right?"

Tris proceeded to whisk some eggs. "Why don't you offer them some coffee? I just finished brewing a full pot."

"Beg your pardon?"

Tris shot him a look that successfully ended any potential protest. Jacob grabbed a collection of mugs by their handles, snared the coffee pot, and went out the door.

Aside from the group of officials, the beach area was mostly empty. Cottage Seven was still occupied. The client who rented it simply wanted a week of peace and quiet, staring at the water. If anything, the dreadnought situation worked to that guy's advantage. Almost all the other clients left early. No point in being here if they couldn't be out on the water. The only other occupant was here on business.

Linda Berman stood on the beach with Lieutenant Commander Louis Fredrick, Siena, and the current and former sheriffs.

"Yeah, we found Art Palley at Mr. Kelley's house," Glenn announced to them.

Jacob's heart jumped again.

"Did he have information on who hired Alex?" Fredrick asked.

The coffee mugs tapped together in Jacob's quaking hand.

Glenn shook his head. "No."

Jacob eased up.

"He did tell us where Alex was going, though. Popham Furrow. That's why I called you here, Dad. Please tell me you know where that is."

"I do," Dakota said. "It's a little gorge in Jordan's Basin. If you let me ride along, I can show you where it's at."

Those mugs started tapping again at a much faster rhythm. Beads of perspiration glistened at Jacob's widow's peak. His stomach tightened, his bladder and bowels threatening to humiliate him in front of everyone.

Jacob looked back at his house. The blinds were down on the left living room window. There was a small gap between two of the slats. Though he couldn't see her, he knew Tris was behind those blinds, looking through that little gap.

"Ah, it's *you*, Mr. Falk." Glenn spoke loudly, sparking a jump from the business owner. He didn't know what to say or do. What did the sheriff want?

"Uh, I'm just . . ."

"Whoa! Listen, man. I didn't mean to alarm you," Glenn said. He looked equally as nervous.

With all the tension rushing through Jacob's system, he had forgotten the incident a few days back. Then it made sense—Glenn was uneasy around him after being caught tailing him the other day. The sheriff wasn't sure if Jacob was pissed about him daring to set foot on the property.

For a moment, Jacob thought about taking advantage of that power, but immediately reconsidered.

Last thing I need is to draw any kind of negative attention to myself.

"No, no, Sheriff! Actually, I thought I'd offer everyone some coffee."

Siena stepped forward. "I won't say no to that."

Linda Berman was right behind her. "Me, neither." The rest of the group followed. Jacob passed out mugs and filled them with coffee.

"Looks like something serious is going on," he said.

"Very serious," Fredrick said. "That creature's on the warpath. There's no coexisting with it. There's only one option, and I hate to say this about a thought-to-be extinct species, but we have to kill it."

"We're in agreement," Linda said. "As much as it pains me to say it. But this thing is responsible for at least a dozen fatalities. You'll have no qualms from the scientific community."

"This is also a criminal matter," Glenn said. "We need to go out today and find that site."

Lieutenant Commander Fredrick shook his head. "I agree that it needs to be found, Sheriff, but not until the dreadnought is killed."

"I disagree, sir," Glenn said. "We now know the company responsible is hiring people to go out there. Considering the financial situation of many fishermen, it's logical to think someone else will try and go out there."

"I agree," Dakota said. "For someone to even want explosives dropped on Popham Furrow, implies there's something down there that might identify the chemical plant."

"Or the people they originally hired to dump it," Glenn added. "Either way, more people are sure to be killed if we don't uncover it, and fast."

Fredrick put his hands on his hips and looked at the ocean. "We can boost patrols, get more units out, but that might take another day or two for them to get out here. The whole community knows they can slip through our barrier. Who knows? Another might try tonight." He slowly respired, irked by the maddening reality he faced. "All right, Sheriff, I'm inclined to agree."

"We'll need to use the *Century Cross*," Linda said.

"Down there? With that creature swimming around?" Dakota said.

"We can use my drone," Siena said.

"We can try, but it'll be dark down there," Linda said. "Probably around fifteen-hundred feet, to be exact."

"That's about right," Dakota said.

"We'll lose the drone signal," Linda said. "There's no choice. We need to use the *Century Cross*."

"We don't have a crane to lower the sub," Fredrick said.

"Then we'll bring the *Tenacious Seeker*," Linda said.

Fredrick flinched at the thought. "You'd be heading out into dangerous territory, Doctor."

"There's no other choice," Linda said. "The sheriff's right. If we don't find the deposit first, the company will reach out to someone else desperate enough to try."

"Do you speak for everyone aboard your boat?" the lieutenant commander asked.

All eyes turned toward Captain Karl Hubert. He was halfway through his cup of coffee, barely bothered by anything he heard.

"I'm willing to go. I'll speak to my crew, give them all the option," he said.

"All right. Then I'll escort you with my cutter and response boats," Fredrick said. "I'm ready to depart whenever you guys are."

"I'll have foot patrols on the docks to discourage anyone else from attempting to go out," Glenn said. "Boat patrols will remain in place, for what it's worth."

"We fueled up yesterday," Karl said. "Give me the word and we'll set sail."

"The word is given," Glenn said. "Let your crew know the risks. They have five minutes to decide."

“Exactly the time frame I was looking at,” Karl said. He handed his mug back to Jacob. “Well, what are we waiting for? Let’s get aboard!”

CHAPTER 32

Tris watched the group board a small motorboat and depart for the research vessel. Even with the window open, she struggled to make out what they were saying. It was no big deal, since she'd sent her husband out there. The look on his face as he returned said it all.

His foot was barely in the door before the rapid-fire questions came out.

"What's going on? Do they know? Why is the sheriff boarding the research boat? You didn't say anything stupid to make them suspect us, did you? Come on, spit it out! Is your tongue tied or something?!"

Jacob stared at his wife and wondered what happened to the calm, relaxed woman who sent him out to eavesdrop.

"They don't know about us, but they do know about Popham Furrow."

Tris turned around and clasped her hands behind her head. "Oh, no." Her hands, still as ice at first, began to tremble with the rest of her body. Initially, it was the kind of vibration akin to an anxiety attack, which quickly escalated into an outburst of anger. Tris spun back and smacked the mugs out of his hand. Ceramic fragments of varying colors spread across the floor.

Jacob yelped as his heel came down on one. He had backed up after that same hand that smacked the mugs came at his face.

Tris held a finger an inch from his eye. "You stupid idiot! I warned you about this."

"Warned me?" he said. "This whole arrangement was *your* idea! You're the one who accepted that meeting with that CEO, what's her name? . . . Gail! Gail Shingle!"

"You remember what was happening at the time, Jacob?" Tris said. "You remember how business was two years ago? You remember how we had mold in Cottages Six and Seven? You remember how what's-his-name who vacationed here got sick and was about to sue us? Such a thing would have been a death blow to a business like ours. We needed the cash . . . and the lawyers. And someone willing to bribe the plaintiff's lawyers." Jacob's silence only agitated her further. "Remember?!"

"Yes! I remember! God!" Jacob threw his hands up, then stomped past her. He went into the kitchen and poured a couple of shots of rum into his orange juice.

"Yeah, drink it up," Tris said. "Hell, suck it from the bottle, Jacob. If you weren't so careless, it wouldn't matter whether they found it."

Jacob slammed the bottle down, ready to take the argument to the next level. Except—there was nothing to say. All he had were his memories and the regret that came with them.

It was six months ago when he prepped ten barrels of sludge, provided by Orion Plastic Company, to be delivered to the drop spot. It was three in the morning, and he was operating on only two hours of sleep. That previous evening, he had been working late, doing repairs on one of the cottages, which was scheduled to have a new occupant the next day.

Tired, hungry, and uncoordinated after abruptly waking from a short but deep sleep, he tried to load the first drum onto the dolly. He opened the overhead garage door, ready to sneak the drum to the boat. Everything went to hell, for in his haziness, he only had the drum halfway onto the dolly. It toppled over, spilling its filth onto a pallet full of merchandise. Kayaks and paddles, all marked with the Falk's Tale brand logo, were covered in toxic sludge.

Time was short and options limited. With no other choice, Jacob put on thick rubber gloves, attached a chain and weight to the items, and with his pallet jack, took the pallet of items to the boat. That morning, it was dumped along with the sludge shipment. The only thing that went well that morning, other than not getting caught, was that the pallet managed to keep most of the spillage from touching the floor.

To this day, those items rested in Popham Furrow, where they would be discovered with two years' worth of drums. Metals, plastics, electrical waste, dioxin, sludge . . . and stupid kayaks that were in the wrong place at the wrong moment.

Jacob stared at the rum while he reflected on his discomforting memories. He added a third shot, then downed the glass.

"We're screwed. And when they come back . . ." This time, it was his turn to have an outburst. He threw the glass across the room, shattering it on the far wall. Life felt like a big 'gotcha moment' right now. When the sheriff got busted for tailing him, Jacob was sure he and Tris were in the clear. Any further investigation, legal or illegal, would be seen as harassment by the public.

Unless something undeniably incriminating turned up.

Taking Tris' advice, he took a drink straight from the bottle, then marched to the garage.

There, he gazed at the drums that had arrived Saturday night. With everything going on in town, he'd never had an opportunity to ship them out. It hadn't seemed like a big deal. 'Just store them until the coast is clear,' he'd told himself on a few occasions. But eyeing the drums now, he realized he was looking at his own prison sentence.

Making matters worse was the presence of two other drums that were not part of that shipment. Curious, he walked over to one of them and removed the lid. Black bars, six inches long, filled the drum. These were not chocolate bars. He picked one up, felt the plastic texture, and dropped it after seeing the wire extending from it. Each bar had the same wire, all linking to a single electronic device. A tiny word was etched into the frame: *waterproof*.

"What the—" He turned around as Tris entered the garage. "What is this? When did these arrive?"

"Last night," she said. "I made some calls after I caught wind of the blast."

"I don't understand," he said. He moved to the front window and took a peek at the research boat. Its engine had started and its anchor was hauling up. The two forty-five-foot Coast Guard response boats had arrived from the south and were approaching the *Tenacious Seeker*. Up ahead, the cutter was pointing its bow out to open sea. "Don't know what you're planning, but it doesn't matter. They're starting to leave right now."

"Good. Let them," Tris said. Her voice was ice, her stare burning fire. Jacob felt the urge for a hundred more drinks.

"What are you going to do?"

"*We* are going out there."

Jacob stumbled back as though shoved by her words. "What?! Are you insane?" *Who am I kidding? My wife has gone NUTS!*

"Am *I* insane? Ha! You're the one who seems content with sitting around waiting for them to come back and arrest us."

"Which is guaranteed to happen if we go out there," Jacob said. "There's no way out of this. We're done! We're screwed. Up shit creek. Thoroughly fucked!"

This time, Tris' slap caught him on the jaw. "Pull yourself together, idiot!" She pointed a finger for the second time. "I'd rather take a chance than resign myself to prison."

"We could run," Jacob said. "Pack up a bag, withdraw everything from the bank, use cash only . . ."

"Give me a break. The time it would take to pull our funds, sign the papers, the state police would be at the door by the time we left," she said.

"Fine. Tell me your grand plan," Jacob said.

"It's simple. Not easy, but simple," she said. "We wait till they're a couple of miles out. During that time, we load this stuff onto the boat and depart. I already recommended a great restaurant to our only guest, courtesy of Falk's Tale Resort. He eagerly took up the offer and will be heading out in the next five minutes. Once he's gone, we put this stuff onto the boat and head out."

"And dump it into the water right in front of the Coast Guard and sheriff?" Jacob said. "Not sure you thought this through."

"You saw the shipment I picked up last night," she said. "Luckily, the cops were busy at the beach, so I was able to meet the middleman unseen."

"What is this?"

"TNT. More than enough to do the job," Tris said. "It'll close Popham Furrow and bury everything we dropped. Assuming you dropped everything into the same spot as you were supposed to."

"I did."

"Good."

"Still doesn't solve the issue of the Coast Guard," Jacob said.

Tris laughed. "It's easy, really. We know the frequency. And we know these waters pretty well. We'll make a radio call, diverting them away. They're bound to go wherever we tell them, as long as they believe the poor fishing vessel," she made air quotes, "was being attacked by the dreadnought. Once they're gone, we move in."

"That still leaves the others," Jacob said. "No way will the Coast Guard let them tag along for that."

"No. That's, well . . ." Her next laugh carried a trace of nervousness. "You're not gonna like this next part. See, I ordered an additional toy from our sponsor . . ." She moved behind the explosive drums and pulled a heavy metal case that Jacob had not seen.

He watched as she opened it, then jumped back after seeing what was inside.

"You are absolutely insane! How did you get that?!"

"Gail has deep pockets and a lot of connections, including military applications."

"You even know how to use that?!"

"They showed me. It's not hard." She lifted the RPG and propped it over her shoulder. "Point and shoot. Boom. Down goes *Tenacious Seeker* and all its hands. When the Coast Guard arrives, the obvious explanation will be that they encountered the dreadnought."

Jacob shook his head. "But what if the police boats see us leave?"

"They won't. They're gathered at the main harbor. They're at least two miles away. They're not gonna waste time patrolling on the north side. Reputable people, like us, are not exactly who they're worried about."

Jacob took many deep breaths; he bent over to vomit, but regained control at the last second. He pulled a chair and took a seat.

"If we do this, and it goes south, we're screwed."

Tris closed her eyes, tired of repeating herself. "If we wait, we're guaranteed to be screwed."

"I've never killed anyone before," Jacob said.

"Wanna go to prison?" Tris asked. He shook his head. "Then take that dress off, end this tea party, and man up!"

CHAPTER 33

The *USGCG St. Helens* kept pace one hundred yards from the *Tenacious Seeker's* port bow. Behind the research vessel were the two response boats, both maintaining a fifty-yard distance from the stern.

Dakota watched the armored military ship from the bridge, admiring the big gun on its bow and the men moving across its deck. It provided a small sense of security knowing there were high-powered weapons on standby in case the dreadnought appeared.

A small sense.

Captain Karl Hubert and two crew shared the bridge with him. The captain did not seem like much of a talker at first. Dakota accurately pegged him as a 'quiet until he gets to know you' kind of guy. The former sheriff had quickly grown tired of standing on deck, and the research crew had a meeting in the lab discussing things he did not understand, so he figured he'd wait in the bridge. Karl was polite enough, offering a hello and minor small talk, but after that, it was mainly awkward silence for the first twenty minutes. It was Dakota's joke about the scientists and his lack of comprehension of their research that broke the ice.

"You ever find yourself in a chit-chat with the science majors?"

Karl laughed. "Unfortunately, yes. I appreciate the work they do and the employment their university has provided me, but damn it, all the terminology and chemistry gives me a physical headache sometimes. Being no stranger to the sea, I get the gist, but the fine details of their field of study are beyond my IQ."

"A little bit of it sticks with me, particularly the wildlife part," Dakota said. "But like you said, much of it goes over my head."

"Speaking of your head, how's it feeling?" Karl said, pointing at the bruises and cuts.

"The Tylenol's kicked in, thank God," Dakota said. "It's been a while since I've been in a good fight. I'm just glad I didn't slip my disc in the process." He looked at the *St. Helens* again. This time, instead of its weaponry and crew, he studied its armored hull. "Kinda wish they sent us two of those boats."

"I'm glad just to have the unit we have," Karl said. "Believe me, there've been plenty of occasions in which I would've loved to have this escort."

"By the way you said that, I'm assuming you've done other work than commanding mid-sized research boats," Dakota said.

Karl took a sip of his coffee, then offered a mug to Dakota, who accepted.

"Cargo ships," he said. "I used to work for the Atlantic Container Line. I operated large freight shipments between the U.S., Europe, and a few nearby countries in the Mediterranean."

"Doesn't sound so bad," Dakota said.

"Before that, I worked for Matson, Inc."

"Oh." Dakota could sense a lack of enthusiasm in the mention of that company's name. "Where'd you ship for that one?"

"Alaska, Hawaii, Japan, India, some places in the South Pacific."

"Let me guess. Pirates."

"On two occasions," Karl said. "First time my crew was able to repel them. Second time, we weren't so lucky. Long story short, it was a hostage situation. Navy got involved. A SEAL team had to board the vessel. Snipers took out the guy on the bridge, another on the aft deck. Had to infiltrate the boat to clear out the rest." He went to the coffee pot to refill his mug. "Ever since, I've taken joy in watching military ships engage pirate vessels on the internet. That twenty-five- millimeter gun would've made short work of the craft that approached us."

"We can only hope it'll make short work of the dreadnought," Dakota said.

"Absolutely," Karl said with the utmost confidence.

Dakota nodded, then watched the *St. Helens.* "Listen, you know a lot more about boats than I do. You saw the sunken fishing boat in the Submarine Canyon."

"Through a computer screen, but yes."

"That squid managed to bite through its hull and peel the ship apart. That was a pretty big boat—almost as big as ours, and as that cutter. Would the *St. Helens'* hull be able to withstand the creature's bite?"

"Ha!" Karl resisted the urge to poke fun at Dakota for what he thought was a ridiculous question. "Have you seen the armor on those ships? Even on the smaller ones, those things are practically tanks on water."

"Then I hope the squid isn't the equivalent of armor-piercing infantry," Dakota said.

"Listen, there's no chance."

"But what if it did?"

"Then the next sound you'd hear would be that of me blowing my brains out, because if that thing sinks the *St. Helens*, then we're *really* fucked."

Dakota tried to smile, then turned away, knowing he looked as uncomfortable as he felt. He was not sure if the captain was joking or not. Generally speaking, he seemed to be a very confident and professional man, and oddly enough, that made Dakota suspect he was serious. A professional knew when he was doomed.

Hopefully, I'll never have to find out.

Dakota cleared his throat. "Well, thanks for the chit-chat and coffee. I'm gonna see what my son's up to." He handed the mug back then returned to the main deck. The cool Atlantic air embraced him. He watched the waves caressing both sides of the *Tenacious Seeker*, each one causing slight vibrations under his feet. Seasickness gave a brief warning of its existence, then dissipated.

Thank God for Dramamine.

On the mid-deck was the *Century Cross*, secured by chains and locks. A few ship crew moved about.

Surprisingly, it was not hard to find Glenn. He was standing on the fly deck on the port side, watching the main deck in the same manner as his father.

"Hey, Sheriff."

Glenn looked over. "Dad."

"Feeling all right?"

"Yeah. Took some Dramamine this time. Could've used it a few nights ago."

Dakota walked over to his side, then leaned on the guardrail. It was like hanging with the captain all over again, with the initial meeting consisting of awkward silence. Only this time, it was worse because it was his son.

"Hey, uh, tell me more about this Orion Plastic Company." It was the best he could think of.

Glenn looked at him and chuckled. "The CEO has been busted for illegal disposal of toxic waste. This newer company has plants in Nova Scotia and Maine, among other places, of course. If I'm right, God knows where else she's dumping. The interesting thing is the addition of electronic waste, carbon fibers, and metals. You saw the slivers in the tentacles, right?"

"I did."

"Siena said it probably fed on some of the waste itself. I think that's how the piece of fiber got in the orca's jaw, back on the Falks' property. The dreadnought tried being a scavenger, eating the crap in the canyon, getting sharp fragments in its tentacles. Then it came here, got in a fight with a pod of orcas; one of the orcas bit its arm, got a piece of metal and wire covering lodged in its jaw in the process."

"You've gotten quite good at putting pieces together," Dakota said.

"You've gotten quite good at getting your ass kicked," Glenn replied. Dakota punched him in the shoulder.

"Smartass." He smiled, rubbed his bruised forehead, then watched the ocean. "What I really need to get good at is keeping my nose out of official business."

"Miss it?"

"Maybe a small part of me does," Dakota said. "But then again, overall, not really. I knew I was done. I just thought a man at my age didn't need direction. But coasting through the days like I have this past year . . ."

"You need new direction," Glenn said.

Dakota shrugged. "I guess."

"Good thing the new direction found you." Glenn tilted his head down, not at the deck, but who was below it. "You both blew it last time. She has ownership in it, too, and she knows it. The ball's in your court."

"I don't know, bud."

"Dad, you don't need this town holding you back. I know how much you think it needs you, but the people will move on. Just like every community does with all great leaders."

Dakota turned and faced him. "You think I'm staying just because of the town?"

Glenn smirked. "Come on, they've got an incompetent sheriff, low morale, a bad economy."

"It's not their first rodeo," Dakota said. "All places fall on tough times. I have to acknowledge that, you have to acknowledge that, *they* have to acknowledge that. And you're wrong about the 'incompetent sheriff' part."

"Oh, please."

"Snap out of it, Glenn. You've made the right calls. Someone in Saw Ridge is doing this. The townspeople, who hated you for grounding all boats despite the economic ramifications, are second-guessing their judgement." He took a breath and leaned on the rail once more. "You and I have one similar issue. We need to stop feeling sorry for ourselves and fix our issues. You need to believe in yourself. I, on the other hand, need to learn to let go."

"All you need to do is go with Siena. Kiss this place goodbye."

"I will miss this place, but that's not what's really holding me back," Dakota said. He faced his son again. "You're my only son, Glenn. It hurts a little to think I'll be far away from you. When you moved out, it was one of the toughest days of my life. I got over it, happy you were at least nearby, plus you worked in the department. But if I move to Florida . . ." He took a shaky breath. "Maybe I'm just afraid of change."

Glenn stared, dumbfounded. All this time, he was sure his dad stayed because of his lack of confidence in Glenn's ability to run the department. Dakota always felt he owed something to the town, so it made sense.

"But by doing this, I've shattered your confidence. My very presence is a shadow over you. It's my fault you've struggled so far."

"Dad . . ." Glenn put a hand on his shoulder. "You've been my biggest supporter. And a good supporter gives hard truths. Now, I think it's you who's being hard on yourself. You think you've held me back? You've been there for me from day one. You weren't the one who ran out on me . . . on *us*. You had my back way back then, and you've got my back now. I've just never appreciated it."

He looked away for a moment. Such talk was uncomfortable for guys, especially with other guys. Doubly uncomfortable between fathers and sons. But necessary, nonetheless.

"I hate to admit it, but a week ago, I would've loved for you to have moved. Right after the transition, even. But then I wouldn't have appreciated what big shoes I had to fill. Prior to that, I was just a deputy who thought it'd be neat to take over his dad's position. Had you not been here, I would've been even more lost than I was. Not only in my job, but in my life. You're the best friend I ever had, and when I thought I was gonna die Sunday morning, the one I thought of was you. I can't tell you how glad I was when you showed up—then again, I was so shit scared, I probably would've been equally as happy if a freaking alien ship arrived to abduct me. As long as I was getting off that damn boat."

They both chuckled.

"But now, Dad, I still want you to leave, but for the right reason this time. Time to focus on you. I'm a big boy now. Took a while to get there, but I'm there. I promise. You've got a second chance at a good thing." He nodded to the deck again. "Don't blow it."

Dakota tapped the rail, unsure of how to respond. Reality was kicking in. He always wanted to help Glenn in any way he could. Now, the best way to help him was to move on. Let the kid make his own mistakes and find his own way.

"Well, I haven't heard of any sea monsters in Florida so far . . ."

Glenn laughed again. "There you go. Another reason to go with Siena." Finally, they hugged each other tight.

"Love ya, kid."

"Love ya too, Dad." They broke it off. "Now, if we can survive this little expedition."

"As long as nothing else comes out of left field to further complicate things."

CHAPTER 34

Ben Denham arrived at the beach, his sinus pain not quite alleviated. His infection was improving, but his current stress aggravated the symptoms. Instead of painkillers, he needed peace and quiet.

His morning consisted of a two-hour argument with his wife. Ever since he quit the department, she'd hounded him, angered by his abrupt decision. Denham made the point that he would not work for an unethical and incompetent sheriff. His wife's response was 'Who cares?' Next was the point of seeking new employment before quitting his current position. The only thing more ethical than his decision was keeping a paycheck flowing into the household.

His last few applications had gone unanswered so far, adding to the stress. He reminded himself that these things usually take time and that it had only been a couple of days.

"Certainly burnt my bridge here," he said to himself. While he stood by his decision to quit, he did wonder if he'd gone overboard by going to the newspaper. His splitting headache had definitely affected his decision-making at the time. He was short-tempered, just trying to get through the shift. "Maybe a little overboard. I could've just had a direct talk with Glenn instead of dragging his name through the mud."

He walked onto the beach. It was vacant. Not many people bothered to come over here. Swimming wasn't allowed and knowing there was a man-eating creature somewhere in that water, most people did not consider this an appropriate area to sit, stare at the ocean, and relax. It worked for Denham. The solitude, the lapping water, soft breeze, and clear skies did well to quell his stress.

The ocean was perfectly blue. Looking at it, there was little indication that it was poisoned. Birds flew overhead in search of fish. There were less of them these days. Made sense, considering the situation. No fish, less reason to fly here. He watched the tiny flock fly to the north, disappearing from view. It reminded him of a call he received while on boat patrol once. A group of fishermen were complaining because a large flock of seagulls was swooping down and stealing their bait.

"What the hell do you expect me to do? Arrest the birds?" Denham had said. Every cop had a story of some ridiculous request. A campus cop he knew told him of a story while he was parked in one of the many vehicle lots on the community college campus where he worked. A woman had pulled up next to him, demanding his help. She wanted to pick up her son but was not sure of his class schedule or location. As expected, the reply was "What the hell do you expect me to do? There are five thousand people on campus at any given time. You don't even know what time he attends." Apparently, he was the bad guy for pointing out that basic truth.

Denham smiled at the memory of that story.

More seagulls darted overhead, also going northward. The farther they went, the more they decreased altitude. The way they moved indicated something interested them.

He stepped to the edge of the beach, the toes of his shoes cleansed by the waterline.

A half mile to the north, he saw what was attracting the seagulls. A large vessel had set out and was heading into open ocean. Tiny white dots hovered above it, in hopes of sneaking bites from a fishing boat's catch.

Denham wasn't sure if that was a fishing boat or not, but what he did know was it was not part of any first responder team.

"Oh, great. Someone else is probably heading out to get themselves killed." Instinctively, his hand went to his collar to grab a speaker mic that wasn't there. *Not a cop anymore. This is getting harder to get used to than I thought.* He grabbed his phone and scrolled through the contact list until he found Zolnai's name. Knowing him, he was probably out on the water.

***

Zolnai was aboard Boat Two, slowly cruising north from the main harbor, when he felt his phone buzzing. He was surprised to see Ben Denham's name at the top of the screen.

"Hey, man! What's up? Bet you've been sleeping in."

Denham's response was as unenthusiastic as usual. *"Eh, not so much. Wife's pissed at me."*

"Aw, she'll get used to it—"

"Hey, I'll get straight to the point. Are you out on boat patrol?"

"You know me well."

"There's someone heading out, not too far from . . . this might sound weird . . . but near the Falk's Tale Resort. They're already about a half-mile out."

"You sure they're not part of the response crew? Glenn went out with the Coast Guard and research team."

"No, I saw the research boat. This definitely isn't that."

Zolnai pushed the throttle and flashed his lights. "Thanks for the heads-up. I'll go check it out."

"Be careful, man. You'll be heading out into open water. Don't become food for that thing."

"Ha!" Zolnai looked at the shotgun and rifle in the open gun case. "I think I'm well prepared in case that big bastard shows up. Who knows? Maybe I'll come home a hero and get a hero's welcome from my wife." He laughed at the fantasy.

"Dude, don't play around. You saw that thing for yourself. It almost took down Dakota's boat. Yours is nothing. Just intercept those idiots and come right back."

"Yeah, yeah, dude. I'll be fine. Gotta go. Got work to do." He hung up. "Good lord, such a worrywart." He clipped his phone and picked up the boat's radio mic. "Boat Two to Dispatch?"

"Go ahead."

"I'll be heading to the northside, near the Falk's Resort. Got a tip about an unauthorized departure of a local vessel." Saying that out loud made him feel like an imperialist. 'Can't do anything unless I say you can.' But, as proven by Alex Kelley, going out there was certain death, and the county could be held liable.

"Do you require assistance?"

"Nah, I think I can handle it. Keep the other two units near the harbor and southern oceanfront residences. Last thing we need is one of them feeling brave while we're all bunched up with this call."

"Ten-four. Keep us informed."

After several minutes at top speed, he passed Marigold Beach where that movie had been filmed, *Waterspout*. There were only three people on the beach. Two were walking south, a husband and wife by the looks of it. He raised his binoculars to look at the third.

Yep, Ben Denham, looking as irritable as ever. He was looking back at him, pointing his finger forty-five degrees out. *The boat went that way.*

Turning his eyes east, he saw a little black speck on the horizon. There it was, heading out with intention.

"Son of a gun." He pointed his bow at the vessel and sped after it. Minute after minute, the boat gradually took definite form. It was larger than most of the fishing boats. In fact, it wasn't much smaller than the *Tenacious Seeker.*

Only one person on this side of Saw Ridge had a boat that large.

"That's not the Falks' boat . . . is it?" After crossing several hundred feet of distance, he could make out the name on the hull: *Great Valley.* "No shit! What the hell are they doing out here?"

He blared the sirens and turned the radio knob to Channel Four.

"*Great Valley,* this is the Garrison County Police Department. Turn your boat around immediately. I will escort you back to your dock."

***

When Jacob Falk saw the flashing lights in the distance, he was starting to sweat. When the sirens roared, he felt the urge to vomit. He remained at the helm, unsure of what to do. Being caught meant certain doom.

"Keep going," Tris said.

"No, Tris. We can't outrun him," he said. He watched the police boat steadily get nearer. "Screw this." He hopped down to the main deck, passing Tris on his way to the two rows of barrels.

"What are you doing?" she said.

"I'm dumping the barrels over the port side before he gets too close," he said.

"You fool. It's not like you're throwing a gram of cocaine out a car window," Tris said. "Those things will make a hell of a splash. I'll take care of the issue."

She marched to the transom where she'd placed the RPG.

"Dude, you do that, you'll have the whole state out on the beach. We still have to *return* after we attempt your stupid stunt." He took the bungie cord off one of the barrels. "I can't believe I let you talk me into this. Dumping this crap was one thing. Now you're trying to shoot missiles at boats."

"How 'bout I aim it at you?" she growled. "You've been a thorn in my side ever since we started this."

"No shit, bitch." Jacob glanced at the police boat, now only a thousand feet out and rapidly nearing. "Oh, Jesus."

"Jacob, DON'T!"

He dumped the first barrel. Green sludge formed a thick mist under the water's surface.

"Great!" Tris shouted. "Like he won't notice that! It's only a couple hundred feet deep over here." She watched the cloud expand. "You dumbass. It looks like you've unleashed a Marvel Studios backlot's worth of gamma radiation."

"Hey!" This time, it was Jacob sticking a finger in Tris' face. "I didn't want to do this in the first place. I would've rather filed bankruptcy."

"Yet, you went along with it."

The police speakerphone blasted through the air. "Stop the boat now. This is your last warning. Any more items discarded from the boat will be added to your list of charges."

Tris slapped Jacob's finger away. "Nice going, idiot."

Jacob nearly retaliated, but instead redirected that aggressive energy to the next barrel, kicking it hard enough to rock the entire row.

"We should've left town when we had the chance."

"Just shut up and let me do the talking," she said. She looked to the sky, took a deep breath, then went to the starboard side. The police vessel was just a few meters off. She recognized the deputy at the helm. "Andrew! Sorry, we were below. I didn't see you come up."

Zolnai did not smile. "Tris, Jacob, what are you two doing?" He stood on his tiptoes to get a better view of their deck. He could see the tops of the barrels. He thought that's what it was they had dropped but did not want to believe it. The toxic mist under the water confirmed the contents.

His jaw dropped. Not the Falks. They were such nice people who did great things for the town. They were loved by everyone. Literally everyone, to the point that the town nearly revolted after Glenn's GPS scandal was revealed. Had the same thing happened to any other average Joe, it still would not have gone well, but there would not be nearly the same degree of passion.

"I can't believe you guys!"

"Listen, Deputy," Jacob said. "We can explain."

"I can't believe the sheriff was right about you," Zolnai said. For a moment, he questioned if he was in a lucid dream. What was happening before his very eyes seemed too fantastical to be real. "This is unbelievable. You people realize what you've done?! I'm sorry, I'm gonna have to call this in."

"We'll pay you a hundred grand to keep this quiet," Tris said.

Zolnai looked up from his radio. "A hundred—" He was immediately disgusted with himself. He may have been a goofball, but he believed in integrity. The fact that he considered that offer, even if for as brief as a millisecond, made him feel dirty. "No. You can go to hell. Both of you, stay where I can see you. I'm gonna notify the sheriff and state police. You're gonna be boarded and thoroughly searched. If either of you do anything stupid, if you turn around—I don't care if it's only to sneeze—I'll start blasting holes in your boat." He snatched his rifle by the muzzle and held it up, displaying his resolve.

He reached for the console, keeping his eyes on the suspects. Finding nothing but the dashboard with his fingers, he finally looked down. The stupid mic fell from its rack. He knelt to pick it up.

Well, this sucks. If anything good comes from this, I'll at least impress my wife with finding the perpetrators who poisoned the Gulf of Maine.

Jacob and Tris looked at each other. Both were eager to spout blame at the other but didn't. Anything said would serve to incriminate them further.

Tris broke eye contact. Her hands twitched nervously. She was now wishing she went with Jacob's plan to flee town. For her to admit, even in the depths of her own mind, that Jacob was right and she was wrong, was as painful as being arrested. Her half-cooked scheme had failed before it even started.

She looked past the police boat to watch the water, the victim of her actions. There was something haunting about those gentle waves. Something peculiar. At first, she thought it was her overactive imagination.

Looking further out, she noticed the rest of the ocean was calm. Yet, that one spot, right in front of the police boat, was coming alive. It was darker, too, but not from the toxic drum, whose contents were out of reach.

That 'darkness' took definite form. A silhouette, as large as the police boat, arose. Ten limbs, many times the length of the body, danced under the water.

Tris grabbed her husband's arm and backed up.

"Hey! What did I tell you?!" Zolnai shouted at them. Tris ran to the helm and gunned the throttle. Zolnai pressed the transmitter. "Dispatch, I—"

The windshield burst, showering his face with glass fragments. Zolnai staggered backward, the mic falling from his hand. The sight of towering arms, riddled with metal slivers and dual hooks, lashed at his vessel. Panic clouded his senses.

Simple tasks became unbearably complicated.

He aimed the rifle and squeezed the trigger. It wouldn't budge. He had left the safety on. His frenetic mind could not comprehend the task of simply flipping the lever. He threw the weapon at the tentacles, then reached for his pistol. A new issue arose. His shaky hand could not unclip the strap.

The dreadnought tightened its arms around the bow like a lasso, crushing it like tinfoil. Two others wrapped around the transom and pulled the boat and its inhabitant below the water.

Zolnai looked back and forth. There was nothing but water all around him. The *Great Valley* was already several hundred feet to the east, abandoning him to the demon.

There was no chance to shout curses at them. One of the tentacles snatched him off the boat. Next thing he knew, he was underwater. He was pulled through a maze of writhing tentacles, which peeled apart to make way for their master.

The sun's rays shined on its dark red body. Two eyes, yellow except for a black slit in the middle, gazed upon the puny deputy. A beak, like a parrot's but a million times larger, parted. A tongue, pinker than the tentacles, stuck out at him.

Zolnai flailed uselessly against the tentacle that held him, the panic so strong, he didn't register the hooks in his abdomen until he twisted his upper body.

"Maybe I'll get a hero's welcome from my wife . . ."

He knew it was too good to be true. The thought ended along with his life when the beak and tooth-lined tongue processed his body into ground meat.

The dreadnought gorged itself on the tiny snack before tearing apart the vessel. Its beak pierced the keel. Like a rabid canine, it ripped a shred of hull away, spat it out, then bit again. Meanwhile, its ten arms went to work on the rest, snapping the bow like a twig and splintering the body. The wreckage sank to the ocean floor, disappearing under the mist of waste.

Neither its hunger nor its anger was satisfied. There was only one drum here and no others in the wreckage. The scent of the waste, which drew it here from its hunting grounds farther south, was not limited to here. Traces of its scent attracted the dreadnought to the east, where the larger vessel fled.

The beast rose to the surface. Its eyes, accustomed to seeing objects in the black depths, could see far and wide in this brighter world. The boat was far in the distance, the sound of its motor vibrating through the water.

Remaining in this poisoned water was suicide. After previous encounters, the dreadnought had learned not to suction in the substance. Only its superior immune system allowed the giant to survive. That did not prevent some of the mist from entering the opening in its mantle, where water fed through the gills. Its nerves fired alarm signals to its brain. It had only taken in a limited dose, but if it did not vacate the polluted area, more poison would inevitably enter its bloodstream.

It fluttered its fins, located on the rear of its mantle, to slowly steer itself out of the toxic cloud. That was the only downside of its evolution. The dreadnought, more immense than any cephalopod that ever lived, was not gifted with the largest of fins. Nature had intended its jet-propulsion to be its primary means of transport, and for the fins to help with steadiness when attacking and feasting. Nature had not accounted for the possibility of inhaling man-made poisons. However, in addition to size and strength, nature had gifted the dreadnought the power of intelligence. It was capable of learning from its new environment and from its mistakes.

Slowly, it cleared the death cloud. Once in clear water, it allowed itself to fill its mantle slightly and generate more distance. It found a place to rest far from the area. Its senses were hazy, a consequence of the toxin that successfully entered its bloodstream. Its three hearts ached, its other organs signaling various malfunctions. The immune system went to work siphoning clean water through its body. It expelled all waste and forced regurgitation, leaving behind a red and black mixture in its wake. Pieces of the human and the clothing he wore drifted in front of its face, the boots quickly sinking to the seafloor.

A period of rest followed, until its brain gave the all-clear. Detecting the trail from the large vessel, the dreadnought traveled east in pursuit.

Survival was a genetic trait, as ancient as the first single-celled organism. Vengeance was new. Even newer was the pleasure that came from enacting it. Like hunger, it was a driving force that demanded action. Unlike hunger, the dreadnought could not satisfy it. But not for lack of trying.

***

"Oh, my God. Oh, my God." Jacob could not stop repeating that phrase. Earlier that morning, he'd thought his heart was racing to the point he feared it would lead to cardiac arrest. Now, he would kill for that heart rate. It was impossible to stand still, let alone think clearly. The only coherent thought worsened his anxiety. Their antics had led to the death of Deputy Andrew Zolnai, someone whom he'd personally golfed with on two occasions, whom he'd hosted a birthday party for on his beach after his wife arranged it.

Mrs. Zolnai . . . Such a good woman. She'll think I'm a monster when she finds out. The whole town will. How did I let this happen?!

"Oh, my God."

He looked over the portside where he'd dropped the barrel. Bits of sludge covered the side of the *Great Valley*. Little dark green drops slid down the hull and entered the water, like condensation on a drinking glass. "Oh, my God."

"Will you shut the hell up?" Tris said. She kept the boat moving at top speed.

"I can't help it."

"We're far away. If it was chasing us, it would've caught up by now."

"It's not that! We killed Deputy Zolnai. And now we have this crap coating the side of our boat."

"That's your doing," Tris said. "We'll wash it off later. And regarding the deputy, what's your issue? You forget our plan is to sink a boat with both Glenn and Dakota McCullough on it?"

"Maybe we should rethink this . . ."

"Too late. Time to enact the next phase of the plan." Tris picked up her radio, changed it to the Coast Guard channel, then cupped her hand around her mouth to disguise her voice. "Mayday. Mayday. This is the fishing trawler *Abigail Beasley.* We're under attack by some sea creature!" She waited for the Coast Guard response. She looked at Jacob, who stared back in confusion. She held the mic away and whispered, as if that made any difference. "I know the owner. She just retired and plans to sell the boat."

"You . . . arranged this?"

Tris shrugged. "Absolutely."

The receiver squealed as it received the transmission. *"This is the USCGC St. Helen. Give us your location."*

"Oh, thank God! We're about two clicks southeast of the Ammen Rock."

"Copy. We're coming your way."

"Please hurry." Tris smiled and placed the radio down. "That'll get them out of the way. By the time they return, we'll be halfway home."

CHAPTER 35

"This is it," Dakota said. "This is Popham Furrow."

Glenn turned back and forth to look at the surrounding ocean. "Uh, Dad? Is there a street sign or something? Looks all the same to me."

"We're past the Eastern Maine Coastal Current," Dakota said. "Jeffery's Bank is that way. We entered deep waters about an hour ago. Three clicks that way," he pointed to the northwest, "was a buoy for the *San Antonio* wreck. If you use your binoculars, you'll see weather buoy eighteen straight out to the east, dead ahead."

Glenn smiled. "I'll take your word for it, Dad."

"You could've just used the ship's depth reader," Linda Berman said. She laughed on her way to the submersible.

"I figured someone with your education would appreciate skill," Dakota said.

"Oh, I do. But I also believe in working smarter, not harder."

"Funny, coming from someone who's going down in a submersible where an ancient squid, known for sinking ships, has been known to lurk."

"Wish I had a deep-water drone available, but when we set up this operation, we weren't planning on looking out for man-eating monsters." She laughed again. "I'm sure I'll be fine. Come look at the hull of this thing. This has armor that can compete with the hull of a Navy destroyer. Much stronger than the hull of the *Alexandra Yale.* Ever try to bite down on an acorn? It'll be like that for the squid."

Dakota winced. "No, I haven't. Last I checked, I'm not a squirrel."

"Wish I was," Pedro said. The PhD candidate was wiping his brow with a towel. Parts of his shirt were soaked with sweat. Between that and his inability to remain still even when standing, it was not difficult for Dakota to figure out the kid was nervous.

"You all right, bud?"

"Oh, yeah. Sure . . ." Pedro looked at the submersible with the uneasiness of somebody afraid of heights who had been coaxed into boarding a roller coaster.

"You agreed to come," Linda said.

"Really, Doc? All you gave us was a five-minute pep talk," he said. "After a half hour, I realized I was an idiot for coming along."

"I wish I could go!" Ann Driver said.

"Why can't you?" Glenn asked.

"Don't have the training yet. I'm more of a tech-support gal at the moment."

"Hey!" Pedro said. "You're free to go! Experience is the best training there is."

"Don't worry about it," Siena said. "I'll be going."

It was as though Pedro and Dakota had switched personalities. Now, the PhD candidate was at ease, and the former sheriff was on the verge of an anxiety attack.

Dakota approached her. "You're going down there?"

"I'm the only other one who knows how to pilot the submersible."

"Siena, you could be killed," he said.

"Nice how nobody's sweating over the fact that *I'm* going," Linda shouted from the sub's hatch.

Siena watched Dakota's expression then laughed. "You have the same look you do when you're attempting to cook."

"The look of a confident man?"

"The look of an embarrassed goofball who doesn't know what the hell he's doing," she said. "You're trying to say something, but don't know how to say it. Plus, you have an audience here, so you're extra nervous."

He looked over his shoulder at the others. As luck would have it, they were snooping like teenagers. Particularly Glenn, who had a shit-eating grin on his face. Dakota could practically read his son's thoughts.

Do it, old man.

He faced Siena. "Wanna get a bite to eat if we live through this?"

She smiled. "Where?"

"I was thinking of this restaurant I need to try out. I hear it has a crab and lobster stir fry. What was the name . . . Snappers! Right?"

"Snaps," Siena corrected him.

"Right. Why don't you show me that place?"

"How can I do that? It's in Florida."

"Oh, that's right," he said. "Looks like we have quite a drive, then."

Siena stood silent, slowly reading between the lines. Knowing the clown Dakota could be, she didn't want to respond too quickly.

"You . . . want to go to Florida?"

"I hear that's where everyone wants to move after they retire."

"It is great, minus the humidity."

"Not so bad if we're on the coast," he said.

"No, it's not." She put a hand on his shoulder, the other on his face. "You serious?"

"Well, first I'll have to call Ally, see if she can talk me into staying."

Siena cocked her head back. "Ally? Who's Ally?"

"Oh, I never told you about her . . ." Dakota said.

Siena started turning red. A few choice words came to mind. He had another woman in his life, but had the audacity to sleep with her? Of all people, she never thought Dakota McCullough was the type to be a pig.

The smirk on his face made it all come together. She looked down, laughed, then looked back at him.

"Only *I* can have an imaginary date."

"Oh, really? Is that how it is?"

"Damn right." She pulled him in for a lengthy kiss. For Dakota, it was the greatest buzz he ever experienced, and it did not require an ounce of alcohol. When the kiss concluded, he half-expected applause from the group behind him.

"What the hell is this shit? What the hell's going on?!" Linda said.

"This is weird. That's not supposed to happen at all," Glenn said.

The lovers looked at each other, their passion shifting into confusion. They turned toward the group and saw them looking out to sea, northeast. Gradually, their gazes turned to the right, following the path of the *St Helens.* It was moving southward at full throttle. Additionally, the two response boats had broken formation and were accompanying it.

"Where the hell do they think they're going?" Dakota said. Right away, he, Glenn, Siena, and Linda raced to the bridge. There, they found the captain on the radio.

"Aye, sir. We'll hold position here."

"If you deem it necessary, Captain, you can return to port," Lieutenant Commander Fredrick said.

"Might be best if we hold tight. Knowing the doc, she'll want to make her investigation."

"Now's the time to do it, now that we have a location on the dreadnought."

"Copy. Good luck."

Linda stepped forward. "Karl? What's going on?"

He put the mic down and leaned on the console. "The Coast Guard just received a Mayday signal from a fishing trawler. The dreadnought's attacking as we speak."

"You're kidding!" Siena said.

"Nobody should be anywhere near here," Glenn said. "Who is it?"

"Fredrick didn't specify," Karl said. "All I do know is that they're several miles away. Fredrick commanded all units to respond, in hopes that they can catch it in time and kill it."

"What does that mean for us?" Dakota asked.

"He's given us the opportunity to head back or continue on our objective," Karl said. "Dr. Berman, ball's in your court."

Her response was immediate. "We didn't come here for nothing."

"Doctor, you sure?" Glenn said.

A snigger of ridicule was directed at him. "According to the transmission, the creature's miles away. Besides, we came out here knowing the risk."

"We were hoping it'd be sixty miles behind us," Glenn said. "Siena's told us about these creatures. Even small ones can travel long distances with their jet propulsion. I can only imagine how fast the dreadnought is."

"It's true, Linda," Siena said.

"Maybe we should wait for word from the Coast Guard," Glenn said. "If they kill it first, then we can operate freely."

"I say we do this now," Karl said. "Get that sub in the water while we know for sure the dreadnought is in a separate area."

"My previous point still stands," Glenn said. "Not to mention, we're hovering over the deposit. I'd hate for that thing to mistake us for the boat that's dropping the stuff. If it's as smart as you biologists have suggested, it might put two and two together and believe we had something to do with the poisoning of the canyon."

"You yourself said it's imperative to solve this issue before someone else tries to bury the evidence and possibly get themselves killed in the process," Linda said.

In need of fresh air, Glenn stepped outside. He moved to the starboard rail and watched the *St. Helens* disappear into the horizon. Something about this was off. His gut was screaming at him. He wondered why. They were heading toward the dreadnought. For all he knew, this was a good thing. They might actually get an opportunity to kill the beast and end its reign of terror.

"It's attacking a fishing boat," he muttered. "Word has spread. Everyone knows they're not supposed to be out here, including trawlers that are beyond George's Bank."

He hurried back inside. "Captain Hubert, I'd like to speak with the *St. Helens*."

"Be my guest." Karl picked up the mic. "*Tenacious Seeker* to *USCGC St. Helens*. The sheriff would like to speak with you."

"Put him on."

Karl handed the mic over.

"Lieutenant Commander, just a quick question: Who made that call?"

"Is it important?"

"Yes, actually it is."

"What are you getting at, Sheriff?" Linda asked. Her voice conveyed impatience. She was eager to get in that submersible and go to work.

"Shh." Glenn awaited the lieutenant commander's answer.

"Vessel is called Abigail Beasley."

"Did the caller state their name?"

"Negative. There was another attempt to make a call, but the signal was full of static."

Glenn lowered the mic. "How convenient."

"Convenient? They're getting attacked by the dreadnought," Siena said. "They're lucky if they're still alive."

"Maybe. No name and a 'muffled' signal, though?" He turned to Karl. "Can I get on my department channel with this thing? We're too far out for my personal radio."

Karl adjusted the frequency, then turned the channel knob to Garrison County's.

"Here you go."

The receiver picked up the second half of a local transmission. *". . . direct your patrols northward."*

"Copy, Dispatch."

"Boat Two, come in."

Glenn knew the tone. It was not the first time she tried calling for that patrol unit. Something was going on.

"Unit One to Dispatch?"

"Go ahead, sir."

"I need . . . actually, first, what's going on with Boat Two?"

"Deputy Zolnai went to check on a boat departure this morning. Never returned. Won't respond to transmissions."

"A boat departure? Have we figured out who?"

"Negative. Our other units were busy with other matters."

"Understood." Glenn looked to his dad, who was equally concerned. That gut feeling was looking to be more accurate than Glenn had hoped. "Dispatch, I need you to look up a boat for me. *Abigail Beasley.* Trawling vessel. Tell me what results come up."

"Just a moment, sir." The next two minutes passed in agonizing silence. Even Linda Berman was listening intently, her concern with the sub diminished. *"Sheriff, that boat belongs to a fisherman from Falmouth, Massachusetts."*

"Call the local police department. See if that boat's there."

"Sir?"

"They've made a call that they're in the Gulf. They've claimed that they're being attacked by the dreadnought. I think it's a fake call."

"Ten-four. Give me a few minutes."

More excruciating minutes of silence followed.

"I don't get it," Siena said. "Why would they lie?"

"To divert the Coast Guard away from here and keep them from finding the evidence."

"Nothing to keep them from coming back," Dakota said.

"Sure. Unless the plan was to come here while the CG was distracted, bury the evidence, and get out of dodge before they got back."

"I don't know," Linda said. "If you're right, then the person had to have known the Coast Guard wouldn't let us tag along to a hostile situation."

"Dispatch to Unit One."

"Go ahead."

"Just got off the phone with Falmouth Police Department. That boat's still in the harbor."

Karl's eyes widened. "What the hell is going on?"

"Something strange, that's what," Glenn said.

"Good Christ. This is too much for me to comprehend. I need more coffee." He went for the pot.

"Let's get this straight," Linda said. "Somebody actually lied and claimed they were on a boat being attacked by the squid. Who?"

"That's what we were coming out here to find out," Glenn said.

"Whoever it is, they would have to know we were coming out here in the first place," Dakota said. "We made this decision on the spot."

"That's a good point," Glenn said. "Nobody should know. Hell, nobody was on the beach with us when we talked about . . ." His voice trailed off as he watched the captain fill his coffee mug. "Coffee . . ."

Karl turned. "You want some, Sheriff?"

"No . . . we were drinking coffee when we discussed it."

"Son of a bitch," Siena said. "Mr. Falk?"

"Dispatch said a boat had departed on the north side of town," Glenn said. "Not too many residences north of the filming location. Biggest one is their resort."

"If the Falks are on their way here, they're coming with intent," Dakota said. "They're gonna drop explosives on the deposit."

"And if they find us here, they'll get desperate," Glenn said. "Desperate people are the most dangerous."

As soon as the words left his mouth, the captain's two-way radio went off. *"Captain, we have a vessel rapidly approaching from the west."*

Everyone in the bridge raced outside to get a look. There it was, quickly approaching, a vessel a hundred feet in length.

"*Great Valley,*" Glenn said. "It's the Falks."

"Goddamn, Glenn," Dakota muttered. "You were right this whole time."

"I wish I wasn't." Glenn looked at Karl. "Captain, get the Coast Guard back here ASAP!"

"On it," Karl said.

The *Great Valley* closed within seven hundred meters. With the use of binoculars, Glenn and Dakota could see the cargo stacked on its deck.

"You see what I'm seeing?" Glenn asked.

"Yep. Filthy jackasses," Dakota said.

They took the stairwell to the main deck.

"They've got to see us. Yet, they're still coming this way. That's got me nervous." Glenn turned and cupped his hands around his mouth. "Captain Hubert! Tell them to haul ass!"

"What do you think they'll do, exactly?" Siena asked. "I mean, yeah, the Falks are in deep shit. But you really think they'll resort to murder?"

"All this time, they've managed to trick everyone—including me—that they were stand-up citizens," Dakota said. "Who knows what they're capable of. Like Glenn said, a desperate person is the most dangerous kind."

One of the bridge crew stepped outside. "Coast Guard responded. They've turned around and are headed back at full speed."

It was the best Glenn could hope for, but not good enough. The *St. Helens* was currently out of sight, while the *Great Valley* was now at five hundred meters. They could clearly see Tris at the helm. She was moving about, repeatedly leaning down as though sorting something.

At four hundred meters, they slowed and angled their boat to the left.

Glenn, with his hand resting on his sidearm and his police radio on the *Great Valley's* channel, approached the stern. "Sheriff McCullough to *Great Valley.* Tris, Jake, explain yourselves."

There was no reply. Tris knelt once again. They could see her head and shoulders shifting like something heavy was being lifted. She slung a long, narrow object over her shoulder and positioned it over the side. A cone-shaped tip was aimed directly at the *Tenacious Seeker.*

Finally, she gave a brief reply. *"Hate to do this, guys."*

By the time Glenn could comprehend the weapon he was looking at, his ears registered the sound of a sharp hiss, like a fuse rapidly burning. There was a whip of air as the projectile passed overhead, then a thunderous *boom* on the portside of the structure.

Fire and debris spat from the bridge. Panic swept the deck as quickly as the tremors. Crew dashed back and forth, some going for fire extinguishers, others simply fleeing below to get to their life vests.

Glenn drew his Glock and raced to the stern, only to stop after three steps. Tris had already loaded the next RPG round and was aiming it. He turned around and took cover behind the sub.

An explosion engulfed the rear of the ship. When he peeked, he saw smoke rising from behind the transom. She had damaged the propellors and rotors, leaving the *Tenacious Seeker* dead in the water.

Captain Karl Hubert and his crew stumbled out of the smoking bridge. The smoke had cleared enough for everyone outside to see the gaping hole in the side of the structure. Karl gagged for breath, one hand clutching his right ear. His teeth were clenched, his eyes open just enough for him to see where he was going. He was reaching out with his other hand like a blind man.

"Radio's dead," he shouted. "Get to the lifeboats."

"You got any weapons aboard, Captain?" Dakota shouted.

"What?!"

There was no sense in trying to communicate with someone whose ears were ringing. Dakota ran across the deck toward a crewmember who was prepping a lifeboat. He grabbed the panicked man by the vest.

"Are there weapons aboard?"

"No. We are not authorized to carry arms," the crewman said. He pushed the former sheriff away and resumed readying his escape.

Overhearing this, Glenn knew he had no choice. He emerged from behind the *Century Cross*, pointed his pistol, and squeezed off several rounds in Tris' direction. She ducked for cover. Glenn caught brief glimpses of her head and shoulders over the gunwale. She was at the ladder now, heading down for the main deck.

Then it dawned on him: *Shoot the damn barrels!* He adjusted his aim and fired. There was no explosion, just a splatter of brownish sludge. *Son of a bitch. I was right about that, too! That semi-truck* was *carrying toxic waste.*

Tris emerged, visibly panicked. She quickly pointed her weapon at the ship. Glenn fired first, rapidly squeezing the trigger. Only one shot went off before the slide locked back. That shot struck the edge of the guardrail, making Tris twitch just as she fired the round. The rocket went wide, exploding in the water a few yards from the ship's portside. The resulting shockwave sent a wave crashing into the port quarter. The *Tenacious Seeker* began to fishtail, the stern swinging to starboard.

Glenn ducked behind the transom and reloaded his pistol, then readied himself to take the next shot. The roar of the *Great Valley's* engine made him pause. He peeked and saw that the ship was starting to circle back to the west. At the helm was a frantic-looking Jacob Falk.

At the ladder was Tris. She was not so much frantic as she was enraged. The only thing louder than the boat's engine was her voice.

"Hey! What the hell are you doing?!"

***

Tris ditched the RPG and ascended the ladder to the flybridge. "Jacob, you cowardly prick! Turn us back around!"

Jacob kept the bow pointed west and the engine on full blast. He looked back at Tris with an open mouth, dry from hyperventilating.

"I'm sorry, Tris. I can't go along with this."

"You don't have a choice, Jacob."

"I'm not a murderer."

"Too late! These assholes have at least one breach in the hull," Tris said. "They're going under. Now, it's a matter of whether you want to be tied to this event."

"Let's just flee town. Change our names, move to Canada." With that in mind, he turned the boat north.

Tris ran up to him. "You're a limp dick coward!" She grabbed the helm and turned it further to starboard in an attempt to circle back around. Jacob fought against her, pulling the wheel in the opposite direction. Accepting she was not going to give up, he finally planted a hand on her chest and shoved her backward. Tris fell on her rear, briefly teetering backward. She was inches away from the gap in the wall where the ladder met the bridge.

She shifted her weight forward, caught her breath, then turned her eyes back at Jacob. *Traitor.* In her mind, it was as grave a betrayal as if he had bedded another woman or stolen their finances. He had gone this far with her, only to turn tail in the eleventh hour.

Her judgement was folly, wrought with emotion. She sprang to her feet and leapt at him. She was on his back like a wild beast, wrapping one hand over his eyes and clawing at him with the other. It did not matter that she hardly resembled a human in this instance. Anything to get the bastard's hands off the helm.

Jacob squealed, blind as a bat, arms whipping wildly.

"Tris! Stop! Get off me, you damn psycho!" He staggered away from the wheel, then squealed a second time when the crazed woman slipped three fingers into his mouth and pulled at his cheek.

There was no tactic to their struggle, simply wild instinct equivalent to frenzied back ally canines fighting over scraps.

No longer seeing her as his wife, Jacob threw his head back, repeatedly striking Tris in the nose. The assault left them both dazed but was enough to weaken her grip. Jacob rammed an elbow into her rib cage, pried her arms loose, then threw her against the console. She pushed off the console and came at him again, only to be grabbed by the shoulders and thrust backward.

The fight slowed to a standoff, the combatants staring each other down from opposite sides of the flybridge. Jacob's hands were clenched into fists. He had never dreamed he'd ever strike a woman, especially not his wife, but at this point he was ready for anything.

Except the thing rising behind her.

Tris paid no mind to the fact that he was not looking at her but *up over her*, or to the shadow that swept over her, not even to the droplets of water sprinkling down on her shoulders.

Only when one of the tentacles rose behind Jacob did she react.

Shrieking, she jumped to the main deck. The tentacle behind her lashed, smashing the console.

Jacob attempted to follow her. He reached the edge of the flybridge and leapt. In freefall, he braced for the heavy impact. It never came.

For a moment, he seemed to be frozen in midair. When the hooks sank into his stomach, he knew the truth.

"No! No-no-no-no! No—aghhh!"

The tentacle compressed his midsection, sending blood and stomach contents bursting out through his nose and mouth.

Tris watched her husband convulsing in the dreadnought's grip. His upper chest and lower abdomen swelled like balloons as the center torso's contents were squeezed.

Simultaneously fascinated and horrified by the sight, she did not realize the ship was tilting to port until the deck was at a forty-five-degree slope. Pieces of the *Great Valley* were torn free. Slimy tentacles clutched the sides of the vessel, which trembled as they tugged at it. The bow started to dip. Beyond it, a huge red mass, shorter in length, but many times the width of the tentacles, rose to the surface.

Two yellow eyes emerged, then were quickly obscured by the horrible jaws. The beak parted like bolt cutters, then closed over the keel.

Crunch!

The hull cracked as easily as a can opener piercing a metal lid. The incision quickly widened. More bites followed. In seconds, the front of the *Great Valley* was unrecognizable.

The jaws released the mashed remains of the bow but did not submerge. Kept afloat by its mantle fins, the dreadnought awaited the arrival of something tastier than boat hull.

Still alive, Jacob was delivered to his final destination. His last scream came out as a gargling of his own insides, dripping like sauce from a burrito, right onto the creature's tongue. Enticed with the taste, it eagerly fed on the human hors d'oeuvre.

Tris stepped back, the tension having taken its toll. Despite the violent final moments between her husband and herself, it was nonetheless horrifying to see him crushed, then reduced to bits like cheese through a shredder.

The deck split across the middle. Behind her, tentacles were pulling on the stern, while others were pulling down on what was left of the bow. Metal drums toppled over, some of them spilling sludge, metal, and electrical waste. The contents formed a stream which spilled into the ocean.

A new poison cloud took form.

Learning from its past mistake, the dreadnought released the vessel and propelled itself several hundred feet back. It was just as well; the boat was fatally damaged and taking on water. The dreadnought's objective was complete, and it was ready for the next.

Another large vessel drifted nearby, directly above the evil poison cannisters. The lack of poison containers on its deck indicated that this ship must have already dropped its supply. It would pay for the deed with its life. Better yet, this artificial creature carried many more humans than the other. It was a great bonus for a creature ill-intent on wiping out all human-operated watercrafts. As far as the dreadnought was concerned, they were all the same.

It filled its mantle and raced at the new enemy.

"Oh, shit. IT'S COMING!" Dakota shouted.

Like a gigantic red bullet, the creature zoomed under the water at incredible speed.

The panicky crew had assembled near the lifeboats, which were moments from being lowered. When they saw the enormous swell coming at them, they broke apart and retreated for the hatches.

"Holy mother of God!" Linda shouted. Her fascination with the dreadnought ceased with the sight of multiple hundred-seventy-foot arms extending all around the *Tenacious Seeker*.

They went to work attacking the bridge, the deck, and most importantly, the edibles running across it.

Karl Hubert shouted in horror as one of the arms passed right in front of him. It seized one of his crewmen and yanked him over the side. A few meters beyond the edge of the boat, that crewman erupted into a cloud of blood and shredded clothing. The dreadnought had raised its head and exposed its jaws, eager to demonstrate to the others the fate that awaited them.

Another tentacle snatched a crewman by the leg. One lesson the dreadnought could not seem to learn was to know its strength—like it had done with last night's victim, it yanked too hard. The leg snapped off, leaving the crewman writhing in a pool of his own blood. Another tentacle snatched him up and reunited him with his appendage.

Each tentacle acted as an individual lifeform serving the same purpose. Some tore at the deck; others chased the lifeforms darting about.

One of them swept across the deck, smacking the *Century Cross* in the portside. The submersible rolled toward Glenn, who had a split-second to dash for safety before getting pancaked against the deck. He ran to the center deck, only to turn tail and run back the way he came to avoid a lashing tentacle.

The leathery arm smacked the deck, failing to grab ahold of the sheriff. It briefly continued pursuit, then whipped to the side in favor of a nearby crewman. Again, the dreadnought failed to limit its strength. The tentacle smacked the crewman's head clean off his shoulders like a golf ball off its tee. The body quivered in place, blood spurting from the stump, then finally fell. It continued to twitch even while the tentacle carried it to the beak, finally stopping after the serrated tongue did its work.

Several crewmen jampacked themselves against one of the hatches, pushing each other for turns to get below. Their effort to escape only made things easier for the dreadnought, who picked them off one after another. One crewman free-fell down the aft hatch, the pursuing tentacle slithering in after him. Instead of searching the inside of the ship like an eel exploring a cave, it bent around the edge of the hatch and pulled outward. A chunk of the deck came off the ship. Other tentacles followed the example, plunging into any orifice in the vessel. Pieces of deck, hull, and structure came free.

Like rodents driven from the safety of their burrow, the surviving crewmen tried making their way topside again. One was seized by the waist and hastily yanked up. The arm did not slide through the widened opening; rather, it burst through another section of the aft deck, imploding the sailor's skull in the process.

Glenn turned on his heel, looking every which way. Nowhere on this ship was safe. The dreadnought's tentacles were everywhere, tearing at the vessel, yanking its occupants off the deck as though they were refreshments from a cheese platter.

Dakota and Siena fled into the structure's main entrance, stopping briefly to yell at him.

"Get in here, kid!"

The only one who ran faster than Glenn was Pedro, who reached the door in a blur of motion. Ann Driver was right behind him, her confident demeanor lost behind a curtain of panic.

"Wait for me! Wait for me—AHH!" Like a cowboy lassoing a steer, the dreadnought seized her with one of its tentacles.

"No!" Linda shouted. She was right behind Glenn, hands pressed against her face. Once again, the creature's sinister side was unveiled. It waved its prize over the others, crushing her in the process. Linda's hands covered her ears, and she squeezed her eyes shut. She did not need to witness the next part.

Ann was carried to the beak and tossed in. Her final scream was cut short by the squelching sound of pulverization.

Glenn grabbed the scientist by the shoulder and forced her to the structure. "Keep going! You can't help her now." They raced through the doorway, stopping after ten feet. Smoke from the bridge had traveled down the inner stairwell and filled the passageway. Dakota, Siena, and Pedro were already coughing and gagging, as was one of the bridge crew who sought refuge down here. Each breath was like inhaling fire, and every foot down the passageway, the worse it was.

They were stuck between a rock and a hard place. Staying here meant guaranteed suffocation; going outside meant getting squeezed and eaten.

The dreadnought spared them the toil of deciding which fate to go with. Its tentacles speared through the doorway, the hooks sinking into the frames. With a few quick tugs, it widened the entrance.

"Get back!" Dakota shouted. The crewman, who was too busy screaming, failed to heed his instructions. He was snatched first and pulled outside. He reached for the jagged edge of the bulkhead, secured a hold, then screamed again. The dreadnought continued to pull, the crewman refusing to let go. A *popping* sound filled the room. Then tearing fabric. The third sound was a thud of the arms hitting the deck while the crewman was hauled away. They lay in the sunlight, the flesh on the stumps stretched like wet tissue paper.

Other tentacles reached inward.

Glenn fired his pistol. Nine-millimeter rounds stung the invaders but failed to deter them. The beast was familiar with the pain of such weapons and knew they were not fatal.

The magazine ran dry. With no time to load his last one, Glenn turned and pushed Linda and Siena toward the passageway. "Go! There should be a stairwell that should—"

"Oh shit!"

Glenn looked at his father and the tentacle that coiled around his midsection. He reared his head and yelled as the hooks pierced his hips and belly.

"NO!" In a frenzy, Glenn pointed his pistol, then remembered it had run empty. Trembling fingers located his other mag, only to clumsily drop it. "Shit! SHIT!"

He staggered to the side in search of it, bumping into the wall in the process. A metal object clanged against his shoulder. He turned around and saw the fire extinguisher, dangling by a hook. A momentary flash of memory took him back to his first encounter with the creature.

Glenn yanked the extinguisher from the wall and pointed it at the tentacle. "How 'bout a little seasoning!" He sprayed the contents, filling the room with a chemical mixture. The tentacle unraveled and retreated into open air, dropping Dakota onto the floor. Glenn chased it out into the open, firing the remainder of the cannister. "Aww, too much kick for ya, asshole?"

"You trash-talking a giant squid?" Dakota groaned.

Glenn turned around and looked at his father. "Damn right I am." Dakota sat up and groaned again. The clothes on his midsection were red with his blood. Siena was by his side checking his wounds.

"It got you pretty good," she said.

"I'll live . . . I hope." His attempt to smile was cut short after some of the chemical entered his mouth. He coughed and gagged. "We need to go further back. Hurry up." He stood up and put his arm over Siena's shoulders. After stepping into the passageway, he looked back at Glenn. His eyes widened. "Glenn! Look out!"

Glenn looked over his shoulder and saw the tentacle darting into the widened entryway. Completely disregarding the sting of the chemical cloud, it seized him and pulled him outside.

"NO!" Dakota shouted. Despite Siena's pleas, he raced onto the main deck after his son.

Glenn pounded the tentacle with his fists, kicking his legs in defiance. The stabbing in his lower back and abdomen sparked intense pain. Pressure followed. Glenn wheezed, feeling his lower ribs and hips on the verge of imploding.

Directly in front of him was the creature's jaws. Dangling from its tooth-lined tongue were thin strips of fabric and flesh from its previous victims. The huge yellow eyes stared at its next victim, studying him, determining why this one looked so familiar.

Chemical dust coated the red arm. This was the one from several days ago. His death would be the most pleasurable so far.

Dakota yelled helplessly as he watched the arm carry his son toward the jaws. Those screams were obscured by thunderous cracks which echoed across the sky. Water erupted around the dreadnought. Holes were punched into the side of the vessel and the creature's mantle. Blood and flesh splattered into the air. The creature dropped Glenn and darted under the water, trailing blood and ink.

The loud cracks ceased. The survivors grouped outside and beheld the return of the *St. Helens* and two support boats, which were racing from the south.

"Thank God," Siena said.

Dakota raced to Glenn's side. "You all right?"

Glenn moaned, then checked his midsection. "I guess you and I will have matching scars."

Pedro staggered onto the main deck, coughing uncontrollably. "Where—where is it?"

"Did they kill it?" Glenn said.

"I doubt it," Siena said.

"I don't see it," Linda said.

The *St. Helens* neared the *Tenacious Seeker*. The muzzle of its twenty-five- millimeter cannon was smoking after Fredrick stepped outside its bridge with a megaphone in hand. "You guys all right?"

"We're dead in the water," Dakota shouted. "Rotor control is dead. No radio function."

"Explains why our latest transmissions went unanswered," Fredrick said. He studied the side of their vessel. "Sorry to punch additional holes in your boat."

"Not at all," Glenn said. "In fact, I appreciate it."

"I thought you might. Just hang tight. My units and I are gonna find this thing and make calamari out of it."

The *St. Helens* moved west. Fredrick returned to the bridge and hovered over the sonar operator's shoulder.

"Where is the bastard?"

"It's moving all over the place, sir. It's fast."

"Retreating?"

"Negative. Moving in zigzag formations. Currently, it's thirty degrees off the port bow . . . strike that, ten degrees, two hundred meters off the starboard bow . . . moving again."

"Jet propulsion," Fredrick said.

"Sir?"

"Dr. Berman stated the thing travels with jet propulsion. That's how it's moving so fast." He lifted his radio. "Thirteen and Twenty-two, be advised: hostile is still in the area. Moving rapidly. We can't predict what's its next move will be, but rest assured that, having been wounded, it is likely even more aggressive."

"Thirteen to St. Helens. We've got movement on our nine. Zero-three-zero of your position."

"Target depth at fifty meters," the sonar operator said. "Ascending rapidly."

"Rotate the gun thirty degrees starboard," Fredrick ordered.

"It's coming at us!" Thirteen's helmsman cried out.

Like fabled sea serpents, the dreadnought's many arms extended from the ocean. The three guardsmen aboard Boat Thirteen panicked. One fired his M16 while the machine-gun operator pivoted the weapon on its swivel. Gunshots discharged, unleashing dozens of rounds in less than ten seconds. Bullet holes exploded in the tentacles, sending blood and meat drizzling into the water.

Fredrick watched as the main gunner was yanked off the deck. The creature did not bother pulling him into the water—it simply rammed his head into the side of the boat. When the guardsman was pulled away, his head was gone, his arms and shoulders crumpled, giving him the appearance of a turtle that retracted its head into its shell. The dreadnought tossed him away and went for the next.

The guardsman with the M16 was snatched under the arms by one tentacle, then by the legs with the next. He was pulled apart like a bread loaf, entrails spilling onto the boat underneath him.

The helmsman panicked, attempting to speed out of the group. The propellors kicked up water, but the boat remained in place.

More tentacles gripped the boat and pulled it down. Near the bow, the creature's mantle rose. Mountains of water peeled aside like theater curtains, making way for the ocean's grand star.

The beak plunged into the hull, splintering the smaller boat. Repeated bites reduced the boat to fragments. Each time it opened its jaws, it spat the inedible parts out, then continued for the next. It ate through the vessel in twelve seconds, the guardsman backing up the entire time until his rear was against the transom.

The final bite came down directly on him.

"Goddamnit! SHOOT THE FUCKER!" Fredrick yelled.

"Sir, we have guardsmen over there . . ."

"They're dead! Open fire."

The MK-38 unleashed its fury. Firing at one-hundred-and-eighty RPM, the gun pounded the dancing tentacles. Several rounds hit one of the arms thirty feet from its tip, sawing across the limb and dropping its forward segment. Like a huge worm, the severed appendage drifted across the surface.

"That's it!" Fredrick said, fist pumped. "Keep hitting it."

More rounds cut into the creature, punching through its tentacles and nicking its mantle. One grazed its beak, chipping off a small sliver along the upper jaw.

Spurting blood from its severed limb, the dreadnought retreated under the surface. More rounds plunged into the ocean where it had been. The gunner rotated the gun, firing along the trail of blood and ink.

"I lost visual."

Fredrick turned to the sonar operator. "Talk to me."

"Stand by . . . It's still out there. Twenty-meter depth and rising. Closing in on our starboard side. Zero-nine-zero."

The lieutenant commander aimed his glasses ninety degrees to starboard. "I don't have a vis—holy shit."

Its tentacles and blood resembled the tail behind a comet. Propelled by thousands of gallons of water, it hurled itself into the side of the vessel. A thunderous sound of impact resonated through the ocean.

The *St. Helens* rocked to port. The crew on deck lost their balance, several falling against the portside guardrail.

In the bridge, Fredrick clung to the console. The bridge crew, however, fell out of their seats. Alarms blared.

"Turn that shit off," Fredrick groaned. Seeing the dismay in the bridge, he approached the instrument panel and flipped the appropriate switch himself. "Jesus, how the hell am I supposed to focus with that damn racket in my ear?" The ship shifted violently to starboard, then back to port.

Tentacles slithered over the bow, ripping sections of the guardrail off. With the starboard section came one of the fifty-caliber machine guns and its operator.

"Full reverse. Get the other fifty out there and hit the son-of-a-bitch. Twenty-two, where the hell are ya?"

"Fifty meters off your starboard quarter."

"Then what are you waiting for? Shoot the damn thing and get it off of us."

"With pleasure, sir."

Twenty-two's gun operator pivoted the M60 on its swivel and fired. The dreadnought took little notice of the vessel, even as rounds punctured its arms. Its attention was on the larger ship and the crew it carried. It snatched one off the deck and threw him against the bridge. He struck with the force of a four-hundred horsepower sports car, splattering against the frame of the upper deck. Bits of guardsman spilled down the cracked windshield.

The forward deck turned into chaos. Crewmen ran for safety, including the handler of the second fifty-caliber, who abandoned the weapon and sprinted aft. His cowardice did not serve him well. He was nabbed by one of the arms, impaled by its hooks, crushed into pulp, and tossed into the water.

The MK-38 gunner remained. He turned the weapon to starboard, aimed down, and fired at the tentacles. Clouds of blood burst across the deck. The dreadnought released its grip and jetted over a hundred meters northwest. The gunner followed the blood and ink trail with the muzzle of the chain gun, firing the entire way.

Unable to see through the drape of blood on the glass, Fredrick stepped outside. He watched the red shape shrink in the distance. At two hundred meters, it surfaced again.

"This is our chance! Keep hitting it."

Boat Twenty-two sped to the northwest at twenty-knots. The M60 was mounted on the bow rail, firing toward the creature.

Small explosions of water popped all over the target area. Empty cartridges spilled across the deck, while a belt fed fresh ammo into the receiver.

"Sir?"

Fredrick stepped into the bridge. "What is it?" The sonar operator pointed at the screen. Fredrick didn't need to look at the screen, for he saw the brief blur of red coming at the ship.

The dreadnought struck with enough force to drive the *St. Helens* backward. It turned around and attacked for the second time. Its tentacles did not bother rising over the deck. Instead, they clung to the outer hull. Water sprayed along the port bow.

As it did, the ship rotated to starboard, the chain gun still firing off.

Fredrick watched the path of bullet impacts on the water and what lay ahead of it. "Oh Christ! Cease fire!"

It was too late. Before the gun operator understood what was happening, his aim was forced in Boat Twenty-two's direction. Dozens of twenty-five-millimeter rounds shredded the vessel and its three crew. The gunner slumped over the guardrail, one hand still clutching the M60. The other two were spread out all over the console and aft deck.

The gunner stared at the vessel, contemplating the aftermath of his accident. Those were men he knew. The gunner went to boot camp with him in Cape May. The other two he had known from the station in South Portland. The shock numbed his senses, thus preventing him from hearing the lieutenant commander's warnings blaring through his headset.

He finally snapped out of it . . . after the dreadnought's tentacles coiled around the gun and himself. The gunner squealed, feeling his body get pressed tighter and tighter against the weapon station. His shoulders locked against the stirrups while the rest of him was pushed against the machine. Bones splintered, tendons snapped, and muscles ripped. Finally, his shoulders bent back like butterfly wings. The tentacle resumed constricting, crushing the crewman against the weapon. It shook the MK-38 back and forth, then with all its might, it gave a mighty yank. The gun was torn from the boat and tossed into the Atlantic with its handler.

With no further risk of chain gun assault, the dreadnought invaded the *St. Helens.* Its tentacles stretched across its length, picking off crewmen and tossing them in its beak.

Fredrick slipped back into the bridge. "All engines full ahead."

"We can't, sir. We're locked in place."

"Left full rudder. Turn us to port."

"Negative, sir. Same problem."

The bridge crew ducked as one of the tentacles burst through the windshield. Its cobra-like tip expanded, the suckers revealing their talons. It lashed, pancaking one of the crew against the bulkhead, then snatching the sonar operator. Fredrick grabbed the man's hand, but his captor outmuscled him a million-fold. He watched through the busted glass as the crewman was carried over the starboard side. The beak emerged, spat out its tongue, and milled its snack.

"Get a Mayday signal out. Give our position and . . ." Fredrick turned around and saw that the remaining crew had abandoned post.

***

Tris stretched one arm ahead of the other. She grabbed a fistful of water and pulled it toward herself. With the surrounding chaos, she was not sure what direction she was going or if she would even make it to safety. The last several minutes had been comprised of muscle strain, terror, and explosive sounds.

This can't be real. This has to be a dream.

Something splashed a few feet in front of her. Tris stopped and squinted. Long red rope-like objects stretched from a mass. She saw yellow eyes staring back at her. A Coast Guard crewman, wearing a life vest, had been torn in half and tossed aside. His entrails continued to unwind, his blood and guts forming a brownish-red cloud under the water.

"Oh, God!"

Another splash sent bloodied water crashing into her face. Tris was ready to scream. Was the thing launching bodies at her on purpose? Did it know she was the one partially responsible for destroying its home?

"Grab on, you idiot."

Tris opened her eyes and looked ahead. An orange-white donut floated in front of her. Tied to it was a rope which connected it to the *Tenacious Seeker.* Dakota McCullough stood where the transom had been, his hands grasping the rope.

"Better hurry up. I'm tempted to change my mind."

Off to her right, somebody screamed. Tris looked and saw the *St. Helens.* The squid was mounting the ship, its mantle flopping over the forward deck. The tentacles snatched a sailor, lifted him high, and squashed him like a cherry tomato. Even at this distance and with the water splashing her face, she could see the steady red stream trickling from the grip.

Not me!

She grabbed the donut and held tight.

"Why the hell am I doing this?" Dakota asked himself.

"Trust me, I'm asking the same thing," Glenn said. He grabbed the rope and helped his father pull Tris aboard. She walked up the hull, then raced onto the deck as she cleared the side.

"Oh, God! Holy shit." She doubled over, caught her breath, then looked up. "Thanks for . . ."

Dakota punched her in the jaw, flattening her against the deck.

"Cuff her, will ya? If I keep going, I might not be able to stop." He walked off.

"Same here," Siena said.

"With pleasure." Glenn pulled out his cuffs and grabbed Tris by the arm. She waved her arms, ready to fight back. The sheriff quickly outmuscled her and locked her wrists behind her back.

"Ow! Listen! It wasn't supposed to go this far!"

"Shut up," Glenn said.

The others shifted their attention from Tris to the *St. Helens.* Linda Berman covered her mouth. Like a car wreck on the side of a highway, it was impossible to not watch, despite the horror and bloodshed.

The dreadnought used its immense strength to tilt the ship to port, exposing the keel. It worked its way into place, extended its beak, and bit. Its entire body shook with the effort. They heard a squeal of metal, like gears being grinded in a direction they weren't meant to.

A minute of struggle ensued. The dreadnought moved, mounting the mid-deck. Before gravity righted the ship, the onlookers beheld the sight of the gaping hole where it had bitten. Their imaginations went to work. It did not take a high IQ to know the ocean was making its way through the lower decks and engine room.

"Impossible," Linda said.

***

". . . I repeat, Popham Furrow. Send chopper units at once."

"You're breaking up, St. Helens. Please repeat position."

"Goddamn radio! I say again, we're taking on water. Biologic has penetrated the hull. We are sinking. Require immediate air rescue."

He waited for a response, but only received static. He wondered if the dreadnought, as intelligent as it was, had destroyed the comm system on purpose or by accident. Either way, his predicament was the same. The *St. Helens* was defeated. The bow was up thirty degrees, the stern plunging twenty feet. The waterline climbed, consuming the vessel at five feet per second.

Lieutenant Commander Louis Fredrick raced outside. What remained of his crew were being waved around by tentacles. The rest were bloating somewhere under the water or inside the dreadnought's gullet.

He climbed to the forward deck. There, he found the second fifty-caliber machine gun. He grabbed the weapon and went as far as he could. As soon as he reached the front of the vessel, the ship was halfway into the water. The dreadnought was mounted over the bridge. It squeezed with its arms, imploding the structure.

Yellow eyes stared him down. It had eaten the other crewman as he retreated.

Fredrick sat on the edge of the deck, propped the fifty cal. on its stilt then looked the beast in the eye. On his belt was his two-way radio. He switched the channel to the Garrison County Sheriff's Department.

"Sheriff McCullough?"

"Fredrick! Try and swim over to us!"

Fredrick chuckled at the thought. He wouldn't even make it off the boat before being snatched.

"Do me a favor. I sent out a Mayday, not sure how much they got. That said, try and survive this. Then make sure the people who awoke this thing are under the jail. You hear me?"

A short pause followed.

"Yes, sir."

Fredrick dropped the radio and squeezed the trigger. By the sixth gunshot, the tentacles were on him.

The dreadnought snapped its beak shut on the lieutenant commander, savored the taste, then rode the *St. Helens* down into the water.

***

"Oh, no. It freaking sank the *St. Helens*!" Pedro shouted. "Oh, my God! We're going to die!"

His panic worsened when he saw the dreadnought's red color traveling under the surface.

"Stay cool, man. We're not going to die," Glenn said.

Pedro turned and pointed a finger at the sizzling water. "Did you not see what just happened?!"

"Not to make matters worse, but it *is* coming," Siena said.

"We're screwed. If we hide in the ship, it'll just sink it. Or dig us out, whichever it prefers," Pedro shouted. "It's not scared of anything. I knew I should've settled for my master's!"

"Has anything driven it back?" Linda asked.

"The chemical fire extinguisher did. Something about that chemical mixture, it doesn't like," Glenn said. "Are there any more?"

"All over the boat," Linda said. Glenn and Dakota went below, found several cannisters in the passageways, then returned to the deck.

The water behind the ship was foaming.

Pedro was backing up toward the structure. "Hurry! Hurry! Hurry!"

Siena and Linda took a cannister and joined the men in meeting the threat head-on. The dreadnought emerged, tentacles sprawling, dripping blood from their many wounds.

The firing line sprayed their cannisters. The combined mist engulfed the dreadnought and its arms. The dust found its way into the mouth, eyes, and injuries, stinging the creature into oblivion. Spraying water already stored in its mantle, the dreadnought retreated.

Seawater, smelling of squid innards, drenched the survivors. They backed away, physically spent, their hands trembling.

Oddly enough, the only one at ease was Pedro, who stepped from his hiding place behind the submersible. "Oh, wow! It's gone. Thank God!" Nobody replied. What was there to celebrate? A few extra minutes of life? The fact that the *St. Helens* and two supporting boats were sunk? The fact that the *Tenacious Seeker's* engine and radio were dead and it was taking on water? Not to mention the area was inhabited by a carnivorous creature which held grudges.

Pedro took in all of these considerations, then shrugged. "Well, instead of freaking out, I can try to look at it this way. Can't get much worse, right?" He attempted to smile.

A gunshot rang out from the bridge, making him cringe.

The group ascended the stairs and entered what remained of the bridge. On the floor, with his pistol in his mouth, was Captain Karl Hubert.

Pedro followed them, then looked at the dead captain. It was back to panicking for him. He retreated to the main deck, ranting incoherently.

Linda fell against the bulkhead. Siena caught her and helped her outside, leaving the McCulloughs in the bridge.

Dakota pried the pistol from the captain's hands. "I guess he wasn't kidding."

CHAPTER 36

Thirty minutes passed. Enough time for the adrenaline rush to wear off. Mostly.

The infirmary's contents had spilled all over the place during the attack, making the simple task of finding bandages tedious. Siena removed Dakota's shirt and undid his belt buckle for a better view of his injuries.

"Sexy, right?" he said.

She shook her head. "You're damn lucky. They're just flesh wounds. Though the one in your back might've torn some muscle tissue."

"Yeah. It feels like I've spent five hours doing core exercises after six months of sitting on the couch," Dakota said. He lifted his arms, waited for her to apply the bandages, then stood up. Grabbing his shirt, he entered the passageway. Streams of sunlight stretched through the holes created by the dreadnought.

Up on deck, he saw Glenn peering over the starboard side. His waist was bandaged up, already stained red. His stiff posture indicated either muscle damage, or worse, damage to the L5 lumbar region.

"Talk to me, Sheriff."

"I think it's safe to say we're taking water in a few different places," Glenn said. "We've got an hour before this thing takes a dive."

"Will the choppers get here in time?" Pedro asked.

"Assuming they even heard Fredrick's Mayday signal," Glenn said. "Right now, we have to assume we're on our own."

"So, what's the solution?" Siena asked. "Put on lifejackets and hope someone comes?"

"Yeah . . . screw that idea," Pedro said. "What about the lifeboats? Or that little inflatable floating out there?" He pointed southwest where the *St. Helens* had gone down. The Yamaha 90 drifted, several hundred feet from the starboard quarter.

"It has a motor, but it won't be enough to get us back home," Dakota said. "If anything, we'd be in a worse situation. If help is coming, and we're not here, they might assume we're dead. Even if they don't, they still won't know our exact location. Besides, we still have to address the bigger issue."

"It doesn't matter what we do after this boat sinks. We'll be slim pickings for that squid," Siena said.

Linda held one of the remaining extinguishers. "I doubt these will keep it at bay for long." She sighed and looked at the water. "It's licking its wounds and waiting . . . waiting for this ship to sink. Make its work easy for it."

"Why doesn't it just finish the job?" Glenn asked.

"It took a significant amount of damage and spent much of its energy during its fight with the Coast Guard," Siena said. "My guess, considering how smart it is, is that it's thinking 'why bother?'"

"It's a mean prick," Dakota said. "I think it likes knowing we're suffering the mental anguish of awaiting our doom."

The jitters made an unwelcome return to Pedro's nerves. "Oh, really? Is that right? It's trying to scare us, huh?" He hurried to the edge of the vessel and shouted to the ocean. "You happy now?! We're scared! You've won!"

"Pedro!" Linda grabbed him by the shirt collar and yanked him back. She smacked him across the face, stunning him. "Get a grip! I get you're freaked, but honestly, your constant complaining is not helping the situation. So knock it off, or I swear, I'll finish you off before the squid has a chance to eat you."

Pedro looked at her, dumbfounded. Strangely, she was more intimidating than the squid. He had worked with her long enough to know when she was kidding— and when she wasn't.

He nodded. "Yes, ma'am."

She released him, then patted him gently on the spot where she had struck him.

Pedro looked to the sheriff. "Do we have a plan?" he asked, in a much calmer voice. "Not that my vote matters much, but the idea of waiting to sink and be eaten doesn't sit well with me."

"The only way we'll survive is to kill it," Siena said.

"Yeah, but with what?" Pedro asked. "Unless we plan to spear it like Captain Ahab, we've got nothing."

"What about poison?" Dakota asked. "Can we get anything out of the infirmary or the lab and make something to inject into its tentacles?"

"Yeah, but we have nothing to inject it with," Linda said. "Keep in mind, it's hard for a nine-millimeter to penetrate its skin. Most of my needles will snap before I can inject a cocktail. Not to mention its size and ferocity, and how close we'd have to get to inject it."

Dakota's face deflated. "I don't suppose you have any tranquilizer guns or anything like that?"

Linda chuckled. "No. I'm a marine biologist, not a dog catcher."

"So, poison's out of the question," Dakota said.

"Can we burn it?" Glenn said.

"No," Dakota said. "Best we'd be able to do is singe it. The thing would just wait underwater, safe from the fire, and attack once the ship goes under. A slow burn won't do the trick."

"What about an explosive?" Glenn said.

"We don't have any on board," Dakota said.

A collective light bulb lit up. All five of the group looked at the submersible, then at their prisoner, who sat cross-legged on the staircase. A piece of duct tape had been placed over her mouth. Their hatred for her was so great, that if she were to say the wrong thing, it would put them over the edge and spark the most homicidal tendencies that any human could reach.

Glenn knelt in front of her and ripped the tape free. "You and Jacob were going to blast the furrow, yes?" Tris nodded. "What kind of explosives?"

"Doesn't matter," she said.

"What was it?" Dakota asked.

"TNT," she said. "Again, it doesn't matter. How the hell are you going to get the explosives? They're sixteen hundred feet down."

"Bitch, my toy still works," Linda said, waving her hand at the *Century Cross*. "Sheriff, I can take the thing down there, locate the barrels, then bring one up to the boat."

"Dr. Berman, down there, it'll be like trying to find a flea on an elephant's ass," Glenn said.

"Not necessarily. The explosives went down with the Falks' vessel. All I need to do is look for the wreck and the drums should be nearby."

Glenn still did not like it, but he couldn't deny that she had a valid point. He studied the arms on the sub. No way would they be able to cling to a hundred-fifty-pound barrel. "All right. Say you find one. How will you bring it up to the boat?"

"We have heavy duty lifting bags, intended for bringing up our findings from the Submarine Canyon," Linda said. "I'll take the sub down, locate the explosive barrel, then guide it up to the surface."

"And if the dreadnought is waiting for you down there?" Dakota said.

"It's waiting for us anyway," Linda said. She turned and strutted to the *Century Cross*. "Come on. We're wasting time."

Siena jogged after her. "I'll go, too."

"No. I'll go alone," Linda said.

"Give me a break, Linda!" Siena said. "You won't be able to steer the sub and work the arms at the same time."

"Sure I can! I'm *that* good at this," Linda said. "Besides, I need you at the monitor to watch my back while I'm down there." She opened the hatch and ran a systems check. The sub had taken a tumble during the attack. “Everything looks fine. Battery is fully charged. Pedro, I’ll need you to operate the crane for me.”

“Doc, I don’t think this is a good idea . . .” Pedro watched his mentor’s facial expression harden. “On the other hand, you are the boss.”

“Damn right I am.”

CHAPTER 37

To get the crane to work, they needed to start the engine and divert power. Dakota and Siena followed the passageways into the engine room. Dakota stopped, overwhelmed by the assortment of gears, cannisters, tubs, and instrument panels. A boat this size was much different than what he was used to.

Siena had gone into the engine room and started the additional generator to supply electrical power. She didn't bother with most of the safety checks. Getting the engine running was all that was needed. Dakota started the lube oil pump to get lubrication flowing through the system. The next step was to turn the ship's flywheel with the turning gear. She then prepared the starting air system. The engine was started by means of compressed air. After a few resolutions, she disengaged the turning gear.

They conducted the air-blow. The engine was now running.

Up on deck, Pedro was at the crane's manual control. "We've got power."

Linda placed her headset on and climbed into her sub. Secured in one of its claws was the airlift bag, waiting to be strapped to its target. An air cannister was rigged to the *Century Cross* and was linked to the bag through a tube, which would transfer the air at the touch of a button.

Linda harnessed herself in, started up the engine, and sealed the hatch.

Linda gave a thumbs up to her assistant. "The moment of truth has arrived. Pedro, take me up, please."

Pedro bit his tongue to keep himself from asking if she was sure she wanted to follow through with this plan. A glimpse at the water reminded him of the stupidity of that question. The stern was starting to dip, the waterline eighteen-inches higher than it was before.

"Up, up, and away," he said. The crane lifted the sub, swung it over the side, and gently lowered it into the water.

Glenn stood on the gunwale. He wore a black harness over his shoulders that was attached to a tether. Once Pedro placed the sub in the water, he grabbed the tether like a climbing rope.

"You sure you wanna do this?"

Glenn slowly leaned forward. The sight of the water and floating debris bumping against the hull triggered a need to piss.

"Don't make me think about it too much."

"I can help," Tris said.

"Yes, you can," Glenn said, "First, you'll help by being quiet. When I'm done with this, you're going to tell me everything you know about the people who hired you." Giving Pedro a thumbs up, he slowly walked down the side of the vessel.

Linda steered the sub near him, limiting his chances of ending up in the water. Glenn stepped atop the submarine and detached the cable.

He knelt and tapped on the glass. "You're a-go. Be careful down there."

"Don't worry. The deep ocean and I are old friends," Linda said. Glenn walked up the side of the boat like a rock climber until he was back on deck.

"Testing. Testing. You guys hear me?"

Below deck, Siena and Dakota had entered the lab. *"Yeah, I read you. And see you,"* Siena said.

"Looks cramped in there," Dakota added.

"It's not so bad once you're used to it." Linda watched the water lapping around the glass. She was amazed to realize she wasn't scared. She was thrilled. Better than thrilled—mischievous. She was entering a world that nature had prohibited her from exploring. Yet, through technology and determination, she was going down anyway.

"Wish me luck, guys. Commencing descent."

After listening to the series of 'good lucks' that streamed through the receiver, Linda flooded the ballast tank. The *Century Cross* disappeared under the crystal blue surface and followed a gradually darkening path to the bottom. At two hundred feet, the ocean had darkened by seventy percent. At four hundred feet, she was in total darkness.

She resisted the urge to blast her forward lights, instead monitoring the depth reader. Not only did she want to preserve the sub's energy, but she did not want to risk attracting the dreadnought. At the bottom, there would be no choice.

At a thousand feet, it was as though she was in outer space, except with no stars. This was the point where Pedro started getting jittery, and when Linda really felt thrilled. At fourteen-hundred feet, she switched on the lights. It turned out to be a good choice, after she saw the giant rock formation directly in front of her. It was the peak of a large crevice that made up Popham Furrow.

She swerved right to avoid plowing into the thing, then slowly approached the bottom.

"I'm here. You guys read me up top?"

"Yep, we hear you," Siena replied. *"I've been steadily checking all camera angles. No sign of the dreadnought so far."*

"How's Pedro doing?"

"I'm doing fine, Professor," he said.

"He's visited the bathroom twice," Dakota added.

"Oh, jeez, Pedro. You're not even down here."

"It's still scary as hell. How the hell are you not crapping yourself after seeing what that thing did?"

"I guess some of us live for the thrill," she replied, smiling to herself. That smile disappeared when she followed the groove to the west. "Hey guys, ask Tris how much her soul was worth."

***

Everyone was inside the research lab, crammed together by the desk to watch the monitor. The ocean floor was littered with barrels, many of which had spilled their contents into the Gulf. The spotlights showed discolored rocks and decomposing bodies of thousands of fish. Sludge, heavier than the water, formed tiny rivers. Dead crabs were slumped by this dark green river, having mistaken the contents for something nutritious.

On top of that, there were all kinds of metal, plastic, and electrical waste. Rusted pieces of factory machinery had broken into jagged fragments. Electrical equipment decorated the rocks and crevices, the carbon fiber layers peeled backward and shredded.

They watched Linda travel for hundreds of feet, all of which were completely dominated with waste.

Dakota leaned forward. "What is that?" Dakota asked. "Hey, Dr. Berman? Pan left fifteen degrees, will ya?"

The sub rotated to port. Lying among the trail of barrels were two large lumps. In the darkness, they resembled fallen trees in a forest. The light swept the tail ends. Flukes, chipped and stringy from decomposition, lay against the sediment. Extending from the sides were large flippers, equally as broken down as the tails. They were humpback whales, the larger one nearly fifty feet long. Their flesh was intact but decomposing. They had been dead for at least a month.

One was much smaller than the other, less than half the size. Siena zoomed the camera in closer, then looked away in disgust. "Fuck." She turned the camera away. No need to look at a dead calf nuzzled against its mother. Her imagination and knowledge of whales painted a picture of what had happened. The mother had probably fed on shrimp in this area, was infected by the toxins, then died. The calf, uncertain of what to do, stayed with its mother, either drowning or starving. Either way, this was the work of humans, not underwater predators.

Glenn turned to Tris, whom he had brought inside with him. She kept quiet, her face pale. She seemed determined to look anyone in the eye, especially when she could sense their heads turn toward her.

"I actually am curious," Siena said. "How much?"

"Does it matter?"

"Yes, actually," Dakota said.

"Enough to save our business and save for retirement," Tris said. "You look at where I am now and say 'Oh, the Falks are doing well,' without actually knowing the struggles we faced."

"Well, we know how ethically you handled those difficulties," Glenn said.

"Give me a break. It's not like I knew it would piss off a giant prehistoric squid," Tris said.

"But you did know what it would do to the ocean," Glenn said. "I'm no tree-hugging conservationist, but goddamn, all it takes is the tiniest bit of human decency to take a minute and think 'Hey, polluting the Atlantic might not be the best way to solve my financial troubles.'"

"Lay off, Sheriff. I've suffered enough. In case you forgot, I lost my husband today."

"I haven't forgotten . . . how you nearly killed him," Glenn said. Tris looked away again. "Yeah, I saw it. And also, there's the part where you tried killing us with an RPG, just to keep your little secret under wraps. To think you were so fouled-up in the head to think you could sneak past the patrol lines, distract the Coast Guard, sink us, drop your bombs, then return as though nothing happened—is beyond me. Speaking of which . . . what happened with Andy Zolnai?"

"What?"

"My department said he went missing after checking on an unauthorized departure—which was obviously you." He tucked his thumbs under his duty belt. It was a way of self-restraining. Part of him already knew the answer and it made him want to strangle her right then and there.

"I don't know what you're talking about . . ."

One hand came free and grabbed her by the arm. "Stop lying to me!"

"All right! It wasn't my fault!" Tris shouted. "The squid attacked! It killed him, not I!"

"You might as well have," Glenn said. His grip on her arm tightened. He was seething, tempted to fracture the bone. Only his father's hand on his arm put him at ease.

"Don't," Dakota said, his voice calm and comforting. Glenn nodded and released the suspect. Dakota looked at Tris, then back at his son. Glenn knew that behind that seemingly neutral expression was a man who would also love to embrace the dark side and break all four of her limbs.

Glenn paced for a moment, then found a desk to lean on. Arms crossed, he gave Tris another piercing stare. "Who hired you? I want a name. Are they the same ones who provided you with explosives?"

"Yes." Tris' voice was barely audible.

"Louder."

"Yes! Same ones."

"Name. Now."

Tris watched the room. Dakota's calm demeaner was starting to fade and match Glenn's. She might not be able to count on him to intervene if Glenn lost his temper again. Worse, Siena and even Pedro looked as though they would jump her at any moment.

Tris feared her client, but that fear meant little now compared to the clear and present danger in front of her.

"The CEO of Orion Plastic Company," she said. "Shingle. Gail Shingle."

Glenn threw his hands in the air and turned away. "I knew it! Damn it!"

"Son of a bitch," an astounded Siena said.

"They hired the *Alexandra Yale* from Nova Scotia as a cheap means of disposing waste from that plant, and the Falks to clear up the Maine plant," Glenn said. "Gail Shingle is doing the same shit she was doing in Georgia. Destroying environments to save a buck."

"Hey, guys?" Linda said.

Everyone except Tris returned to the monitor. Siena turned up the volume. "Go ahead."

"I've successfully narrowed my search."

At first, the large structure on the screen resembled another rock formation. When she drew closer, the shape of the *Great Valley's* remains came into focus. Barrels were scattered around the wreck, some of them leaking green fluid and brown fluid. The vessel itself had split in two. The bow was essentially a heap of battered steel resting seventy feet from the main body.

"Tris, are there any markings differentiating the explosive barrels from the others?" Siena asked.

"They're plastic," Tris said. "The sides are more rounded than the metal ones. More egg-shaped than tubed."

At least they got that answer without a fight. For Tris, it was about survival. Though she had no interest in prison, the will to live still reigned supreme. Going along with their plan was her only hope.

Linda circled the wreck, inspecting several barrels. With one, she accidentally opened it, spilling a mixture of melted plastics. Her curses came through the comm.

Traveling farther west, she found a few more barrels. She steadied her light on one and studied its shape.

"Finally! I think we have a winner."

Glenn guided Tris to the monitor. She looked at the image and nodded. "Yeah, that's it."

"How will we set it off?" Pedro asked.

"Are they set with a fuse?" Dakota asked Tris.

"Correct."

"We need something to light the main fuse from a distance. The initial blast will be enough to set off the rest of the payload," Dakota said.

"How 'bout a flare gun?" Glenn said. "There's bound to be one in the bridge."

"That should do it," Dakota said. "I'll get the flare gun. You guys go up top with poles to bring in the airlift bag when it comes up."

"Got it." Glenn goaded Tris to the doorway. "You're going up, too. If you think about doing something stupid, think again, then don't do it."

***

Linda carefully worked the mechanical arms. She successfully had the airlift bag placed over the drum. Keeping it in place while securing the straps was the annoying part. The current down here was mild, but enough to make the bag fall off its place.

Using the arms, she stood the drum on end, giving her full access to the sides. She tightened the thick straps around it, then gently laid the drum back down.

With a flick of a switch, she provided air flow. The bag quickly inflated, resembling a hot-air balloon. The drum slowly lifted off the ocean floor.

"I'm coming up," she said into the radio. A feeling of triumph came over her. Once again, she had outsmarted Mother Nature. She took no personal joy in killing a nearly extinct organism, but the fact was this thing was waiting to kill her and her friends. She took an impossible scenario and gave them a fighting chance. That was something worth drinking to once she was on dry land.

She ascended with the package. One thousand feet. Eight hundred. Six hundred. The sub slowed several times for decompression. The inner mechanics did their work, monitoring the ocean pressures and distance from the surface.

At four hundred feet, she could see the first shades of light. At three hundred, she could see the shape of the *Tenacious Seeker*. The bag had floated ahead of her and was moments from reaching the surface.

"Damn, I am good at this."

"Dr. Berman, there's something coming up on you. On your six."

Before Siena finished speaking, a heavy impact rocked the sub forward. Slithery tentacles, still bleeding from their bullet wounds, came over the forward glass. Hooks scraped the hull and cockpit, leaving thin marks in their wake.

Linda pulled the joystick left and right. She was moving, but not of her own free will. The dreadnought had her in a tight grip and was shaking her about. The straps dug into her chest and shoulders. She felt as though she was on a spaceship going through reentry.

"Linda! Can you shake it off?" Siena cried out.

She tried again but was helpless in the squid's grasp. "Fuck!" A high-pitched sound traveled through the water. The sub shook, then jerked to the side. The squid had pulled off one of the arms.

A crunching sound behind her made her throat tighten. Something crunched, then snapped. *The beak.* The blaring alarms and flashing warnings did not help.

Rudder failure.

Pressure alert.

Propulsion system failure.

It wasn't the water pressure that triggered the second warning.

Linda felt her forehead moisten. She wasn't the type to sweat easily. That was true . . . even now.

Tiny impacts exploded over her head, making her look up. That wetness was not perspiration, but water dripping through the cracked hatch.

Her eyes went to the glass visor. The tentacles squeezed tighter and tighter. More cracks formed around the cockpit. In moments, they resembled the lines in a puzzle.

One segment burst free, flying past her head like a bullet. Following it was a heavy stream of water.

Another segment flew in. This time it, and the stream of water behind it, struck her in the face. Linda screamed at the sensation of glass hitting her eye and being pushed inward by the ocean.

Blood ran down her face and chest. All confidence and mischievous joy ceased. Her hands came off the controls and shook frenziedly. Pain and panic overcame all reasoning.

The cockpit flooded, the electronic sensors flickering, then dying. The hull closed in around her.

It was worse than imploding miles under the water. There, a breach in the hull would instantly crush anything inside. Up here, less than three hundred feet down, she was forced to feel the tightening of the submarine.

Like a parent punishing a mischievous child, nature had tracked her down.

The glass imploded entirely, filling the cockpit entirely. Drowning was the least of her concerns.

The overhead and bulkheads closed in around her. A slow, punishing death followed. Bones cracked, organs exploded, her spine snapped, and finally, as the sub was packed into a tight metal ball, her skull imploded.

***

"Stay here. Don't move."

Tris kneeled by the crane and watched Glenn and Pedro race aft. The waterline was two feet from the deck and climbing. The research assistant snatched the lifeline and donut and waved it like a lasso. Ten meters out was the parachute.

"I don't know if I can snag it with this," he said. "We'll have to take the lifeboat out."

"We'll never make it," Glenn said.

"We have to try."

Behind her, Dakota was ruffling through the bridge in search of the flare gun. Siena emerged from the research lab and ascended the steps to the fly deck.

"What are you doing up there? Where's Dr. Berman?" Pedro shouted at her.

"The dreadnought . . ." Siena stuttered. "It killed her."

Pedro dropped the lifeline and stepped back. "Holy shit! She's dead!"

Glenn picked up the lifeline and took a crack at lassoing the airlift bag. The donut fell a few feet shy. He tried again. Same result.

"Damn it!"

Each toss fell short. Making matters worse, the thing was starting to drift away from them. Repeated attempts only caused frustration. The donut landed ten feet away from the target. Then twelve. Fifteen. Additionally, there was the realization that there was no way to snag the thing with the rubbery floatation device.

Glenn threw the lifeline down and shouted to the heavens. "Give us a fucking chance, will ya!"

A high-pitched hiss streamed high into the air behind him, concluding with a roaring burst. He looked up and saw the big red fiery cloud above him, and then his father standing on the fly deck alongside Siena.

Why the hell did he waste a flare?! He was happy he didn't embarrass himself by asking that question out loud. *He wouldn't.* Glenn looked to the north. In the horizon, three dots gradually grew nearer. Rescue choppers.

"I think he heard you," Siena called out.

"Fredrick's message got through! Bless that guy," Glenn said.

A metallic echo rumbled under the water, drawing his attention.

The beast emerged like the spawn of Satan climbing from the crevices of hell. Elongated tentacles, dripping ammonia, slime, and water, lashed at the boat, securing a hold. The *Tenacious Seeker* trembled in its grasp, quickly tilting further to stern.

The dreadnought was ready to finish its task.

Glenn grabbed a screaming Pedro by the shirt and pulled him up the deck, away from the creature's dancing arms. Its head appeared behind the stern, the huge yellow eyes setting sight on its victims.

Fire extinguishers rolled past their feet and over the side where the transom had been torn off. There would be no repelling the beast this time with chemicals.

Just as it had done with the *St. Helens*, it dragged the vessel into the ocean, savoring the panic in its victims' body language. They retreated further up the boat, as if that was some sort of safe haven—as if the fly deck would not meet a watery grave with the rest of the boat.

Tris watched the chaos around her and the approaching helicopters. They were a thousand yards out, rapidly closing in. All she needed to do was get up to the fly deck and hope they arrived in time.

Even now, with her nerves shot, and death staring her in the face, she still thought of the aftermath. Not only did she want to live, but she wanted to have a life. Prison was no life. Being rescued today only meant a year in court and a lifetime behind bars.

The climbing water did not help her nerves.

Her eyes turned to the sheriff. He was still backing up the slope, a few steps from her. She eyed the pistol on his hip. He had one magazine, if she remembered correctly. Enough to take care of the witnesses and prevent herself from going to prison.

Her frantic mind came to the only logical outcome. *Eliminate them right now while the choppers are too far out to witness it. Get rescued, play the victim. The chopper crews probably don't know my involvement with all of this. Just pretend to be a volunteer on the clean-up project.*

There was not enough time to think twice. Her window of opportunity started now and would last about twenty seconds.

Tris slipped her cuffs under her knees, stood up, then charged the sheriff. Glenn looked over his shoulder in time to see her connect. Tris snatched the gun from his holster, then rammed the grip into the back of his head. His senses in a haze, Glenn stumbled down the slope . . . toward the dreadnought's tentacles. He stopped after a few steps, not by his own will, but with the help of the man he'd saved moments prior.

Pedro's teeth were clenched, his fear doing its best to get the better of him once more. The slithering tentacles creeping up the deck only strengthened the paralysis.

It worked for Tris. The creature would eat them, and she could eliminate the other two on the fly deck. All she needed to do was be on point with her shooting. She turned on her heel and aimed the gun up at the former sheriff.

She heard the *CRACK!*

Impossible. She had not squeezed the trigger.

Next was the sensation of heat and pressure in her ribs. She looked at the bullet hole in her torso, then at Dakota and the smoking pistol in his hand.

Her ten-second planning had failed to account for the late Captain Hubert's personal handgun.

She stumbled backward, her legs weakening. They buckled, then gave way. Tris fell backward past Glenn and Pedro, directly into the tentacles. Any that were not gripping the vessel lunged at her like hungry larvae. They fought for a grip, one snagging her left leg, another her arm, while a third planted itself over her head.

A wet suction cup oozed over Tris' face, the edge muffling her scream. The double hooks protruded, directly in line with her eyes. Tris convulsed, her eyes popping like grapes, the hooks arching around the upper edge of her sockets. Next came the sensation of stretching.

The flesh around her neck stretched like warm mozzarella cheese. With a *pop* and some tears, her head came off her shoulders. It dangled at the tip of the tentacle, which tossed it aside like worthless garbage. Her headless corpse was fed into the dreadnought's natural grinder.

"Glenn! Pedro! Get your asses up here, for god sake!" Dakota shouted. Like mountain climbers, the two men scaled the deck until they reached the stairwell. Just a few feet behind them, the deck splintered under the wrath of the squid's tentacles.

The water was past the mid-deck, flooding the ship's lower sections. The added weight and increased pull by the tentacles doubled the speed of sinking.

The survivors moved around the bridge to the bow. The tentacles ravaged the structure, peeling the overhead and sides off and tossing them aside.

At the foredeck, the group huddled together. Ten feet of ship remained between them and their fate.

The wait was over. The dreadnought raised its arms to bring a slow, torturous death to the humans.

Rapid gunshots struck its mantle. The arms retracted and lashed at the flying objects circling above.

Two of the Coast Guard choppers hovered above the creature. Their fuselage doors were open, allowing a guardsman with a high-powered rifle to blast the target.

Bullets penetrated its thick flesh, sparking nerve pain. Alarmed, the creature submerged and propelled itself out of the firing line.

With the danger momentarily out of the way, the third chopper descended. A diver descended on a harness and landed on the bow.

"Lieutenant Ed Dowl. Nice to meet y'all. We don't have much time. I need to bring you up one at a time," he said.

Dakota pushed Siena into his arms. She looked back, ready to protest, but the rescue diver did not waste time. He placed the harness on her and gave the hand signal to the crew to hoist her into the chopper.

"Dakota!"

"I'll be right behind you," he replied. He waited for Siena to enter the chopper before he pushed Glenn forward. "After you're on board."

"Dad . . ."

"No time to argue," Lieutenant Dowl said. The harness came back down. He grabbed it, placed it over the sheriff, then signaled for his team to lift him up. "Halfway done."

Dakota smirked. He could hear Siena telling the crew to hurry up.

Lieutenant Dowl cocked a grin while reaching for the harness. "When a man puts his woman ahead of himself, that's how she knows he loves her. When a woman is mad about it, that's how he knows she loves him."

"You always a romantic during rescues?" Dakota said.

"Small talk helps me focus," the lieutenant said. "Besides, it's refreshing for me to see. Half the time, the spouses are fighting each other for the harness. Had one try and push her husband overboard because he wanted to go first." He grabbed the harness and strapped it over Pedro's shoulders.

They watched Pedro get lifted into the chopper. The sound of gunfire drew their attention to the west. The choppers were a hundred feet above the water, firing at the serpentine arms.

It had surfaced again, the whipping of its tentacles demonstrating its rage.

"Almost done," Lieutenant Dowl said. "Once I get the harness on you, I'll clip it to me and we'll be lifted at once."

Dakota watched the choppers. "Tell them to pull up!"

"Don't worry about them," the lieutenant said. The harness came down. "It's your turn. Arms out. Come on, the water's almost up to our feet."

"That thing has a reach of nearly two-hundred feet. Tell them to pull up now!"

***

The dreadnought watched its new enemies, intrigued by their capabilities. They were above the air, yet they moved like cuttlefish. It had seen small, white creatures that flapped appendages resembling fins, but nothing as large as these things.

Intrigue only lasted for a few moments. These flying objects were operated by humans—humans who were committed to killing it. Invisible projectiles stung its flesh, drawing blood.

It absorbed the pain in order to watch and study their movements. These attackers maintained a constant circle, hitting its mantle and arms with their weapons. Predictable movements from targets that were well within reach.

The dreadnought sprang into action. Fluttering its fins, it pushed its head out of the water for maximum reach. The tentacles whipped at the nearest machine, snatching the gunner from the opening in its side with one, and wrapping two others over the tail.

The chopper tried to lift from its grasp. The men inside panicked, the one in its grip pounding his fists.

It did not pull the chopper down right away. Intrigued by the blur of motion overhead that generated a downward gust, the dreadnought watched. Finally, it realized that motion was generated by a mechanism, somewhat similar to the blades that pushed the large floating objects.

The discovery brought out its devious nature.

With a winding motion, the dreadnought cocked its tentacle back, then chucked the human into the blades. His body burst into a red cloud from which spat fabric, bone, and meat.

The panic inside the chopper amplified.

With all its might, the dreadnought swung the chopper in a downward motion, releasing midway. The chopper flung to the east, tilting to starboard. The pilots' attempt to gain altitude were futile.

Nineteen-thousand pounds of steel struck the ocean. The rotors snapped on impact, whipping across the air like massive shurikens.

***

"Holy shit!" someone shouted from the chopper.

Dakota and Lieutenant Dowl, hand on the harness, jumped as the sound of crashing metal and ocean reached their ears. Fragments of rotors zipped past them, threatening to carve them in two in the blink of an eye. Dakota spun, lost his balance, and hit the water.

One of the fragments grazed the underside of the chopper, another hitting the nose. The pilots lifted, hoisting the lieutenant off the now-submerged *Tenacious Seeker.*

When Dakota emerged, the chopper was circling to the north.

"Great! Just great!"

The chopper hooked back and lowered to its fallen companion. Meanwhile, the dreadnought was in combat with the third chopper, slashing the air with its arms.

A piece of wreckage drifted in front of Dakota. He pulled it under his belly and watched the carnage play out.

The second chopper attempted to ascend, almost successfully evading the dreadnought's attack. One of the tentacles stretched to its full length, slapping the chopper under the nose.

It went into a spiral, the engine stalling. The dreadnought struck again, this time barreling the chopper, which crashed upside down. This time, the attack backfired, for some of the rotor shrapnel sliced into the creature's own tentacles. Pain forced a retreat. A split-second later, the dreadnought was under the water.

Dakota squeezed the edge of the wreckage. The creature was not done. In a minute or two, it would return to finish the job.

There was not enough space on that chopper for all these survivors, and help would not arrive in time for the remaining guardsmen. It was a doomed situation . . .

. . . *Unless we kill that damn thing.*

Drifting toward him was a red object, which at first resembled a parachute. The airlift bag. The crashes had sent the explosive barrel drifting west instead of east.

Dakota pulled the flare gun from his waist. He had only one cartridge, the others lost in the chaos.

"I'm as good as dead anyway. Might as well go out with a literal bang." With that in mind, he paddled as fast as he could, gradually closing the distance.

His situation improved when he noticed one of the lifeboats from the *Tenacious Seeker* drifting forty feet to his right. He adjusted his course, then reached the inflatable boat, and flung himself inside.

It was a big improvement over that piece of deck. Unfortunately, there was no paddle or motor, forcing him to scoop handfuls of water to reach the barrel.

Determination strengthened him. Little by little, he made his way to the bag. He shot a glance to the chopper, which hovered over one of its companions. The pilot, rightfully so, was wary of descending, worried that the dreadnought would attack at any moment.

His arms burned and his stomach ached. As Siena enjoyed pointing out, he was out of shape. All that takeout was coming back to bite him.

"I swear, if I somehow survive this bullshit, I'm going to learn how to properly cook."

The frustration fed strength when determination faltered. The floatation bag grew larger and larger, until the rubber hull brushed against it.

Dakota heaved the heavy drum onto the raft. "Whew!" Sweat mixed with seawater in a strange, extra-salty combination that dripped off his forehead.

He pried the lid off the plastic drum, revealing the explosives inside. The fuses were set. All they needed was a flame.

Dakota looked at the flare gun. "This is *really* gonna piss Siena off." He smiled. "I guess that means she really loves me."

The trap was in place. Now, he needed to draw the squid in. He removed the lid and slapped it against the water.

"Come on, you oversized Japanese cuisine! Got a hot snack waiting for ya!"

***

The dreadnought watched the floating mechanical corpse above it. More importantly, it watched the third machine hovering above it. It was within reach but was at an altitude where it could easily evade its surprise attack.

During its wait, new vibrations attracted its attention. These were from repeated impacts on the water's surface, relatively small, but indicating struggling movements.

For several moments, the dreadnought ignored them. When the flying machine above refused to descend any lower, the dreadnought lost patience. It needed to kill something, but it did not want to waste its efforts on the humans inside the wreckages, for they were the bait to lure the third flyer.

Its urge got the better of it. The dreadnought gently moved away to inspect the sound of the noise.

A few hundred feet away, a tiny boat floated in the water. It was red in color, easy to spot. A human hand splashed. A fleeing human? It did not matter, for it was an easy target. The dreadnought moved in, not eager to satisfy its hunger, but its bloodlust.

***

"There!" the Coast Guard pilot said. He pointed at the red mass moving under the water. "I told you it was waiting down there for us!"

Lieutenant Dowl was standing over his shoulder. "Where's it going?"

"It's going for him!" Glenn said. He squeezed past the lieutenant and pointed at the raft. "Dad's there! He's drawing it in."

"We have to go down for him!" Siena said.

"We can't," the pilot said. "We go down, that thing is sure to knock us out of the air."

"What the hell's he trying to do?" the lieutenant said.

Glenn noticed the barrel in the raft and the floating bag drifting away from it. "He's got the explosive. He's gonna blow it up."

"No, Dakota . . ." Siena pressed her face to the passenger window to see him. "You stupid prick. You're not supposed to leave me like this."

"Get down there," Glenn said. "Drop the harness. Let him grab it and lift off."

Lieutenant Dowl closed his eyes, cursed himself mentally, then tapped his pilot's shoulder. "Do it."

Cursing under his breath, the pilot swept down.

Glenn raced into the fuselage and helped the other crewman ready the harness. Off to the side, Siena watched, hands cupped together in prayer.

***

Dakota could see the creature moving under the water like a huge freight train. He smacked the water once more, then tossed the lid aside in favor of the flare pistol.

Breathing shakily, he braced for the arrival of those tentacles.

A gust of wind swept over him. He looked up at the Coast Guard chopper. Dangling from its side was an empty harness. Directly above it, his son peered down at him, anxiously pointing at it.

"Dad! Grab onto it! Hurry!" Suddenly, Glenn's face lit up with fright. "DAD! HURRY UP!"

The tentacles emerged around him.

"Oh, SHIT!" Dakota grabbed the harness and clung for dear life. Glenn gave the signal to the pilot, who lifted straight up.

Dangling fifty feet high, Dakota looked down at the arms. They were chasing him, ready to snatch him out of the air. In the middle of the horde was a bobbing raft and its payload.

Dakota aimed the pistol straight down, squinted one eye, and hoped for the best.

"Eat *this.*"

He squeezed the trigger. A ball of fire spat from the muzzle, skidded off one of the tentacles, and landed on the explosives. The fuses lit, burned to their caps, and triggered the TNT.

The raft disappeared under a huge orange ball that stretched for over a hundred feet. Those outstretched tentacles departed from their source, their meaty stubs spraying ammonia and blood. Huge chunks of dreadnought flew across the ocean like meteoric fragments, trailing smoke until they hit the ocean.

After a few moments, the fire dissipated. Smoldering in its center was the ravaged mantle, the head and arms missing, the remains resembling a crushed tomato. Its severed tentacles floated across the water in squiggly formations, their reign of terror at an end.

Glenn and the crewmen hoisted Dakota into the chopper and were hastily pushed aside by Siena. She wrapped her hands around Dakota, squeezed him, then released him so she could slap him.

"You crazy bastard! You scared the shit out of me!" She hugged him again. Dakota hugged her back, then winked at the lieutenant.

"That's a good observation."

The lieutenant gave a thumbs up, then got back to work. It was time to rescue the rescue team.

Dakota sat down with his love. Glenn took the seat across from him.

"You all right?"

"Yep. Thanks to you."

Glenn shrugged. "Just doing what you would do. What any good sheriff would do."

Dakota smiled. "That's how I know Garrison County is in good hands."

CHAPTER 38

"This just in. The CEO of Orion Plastic Company was served an arrest warrant by state police this morning after an investigation headed by Garrison County Sheriff Glenn McCullough produced findings of hazardous waste disposal. This company, with plants in Canada and the U.S., has dumped hundreds of toxic barrels into the Atlantic, which experts suspect awakened the spectacular, but violent, Dreadnought squid which wreaked havoc on the coastal town of Saw Ridge.

"It really is a sad situation, but there is a happy ending to it all. Recovery efforts are underway in the Gulf of Maine and the deep canyons beyond it where Gail Shingle's contractors had polluted the ocean. Garrison County, and the East Coast at large, is deeply thankful for the sheriff's valiant efforts in bringing an end to this contamination. As we speak, he is working with the EPA and Coast Guard in overseeing the cleanup effort."

It was the first television broadcast Glenn would see as the new owner of Dakota's house. His father had spent the last week clearing it out. The television and entertainment center remained to be included with the sale. Most of the household items were packed, donated, or left for the new owner.

Glenn grabbed the box of photos at his feet, then carried it to his dad's truck. "Only keeping the essentials, I see."

"Where I'm going, there's already furniture and dinner plates," Dakota said. He was dressed in a short-sleeve button-down shirt tucked into new jeans. It was a special occasion. It was bittersweet. He had lived in this town the better part of his life so far, but it was time for a bright new chapter.

Standing in the yard next to him were several deputies who were offering their farewells. They shook hands with their former boss, then returned to their vehicles.

Deputy Ben Denham, on his second day back on duty, gave Dakota a hug. "See you, man. I'll sure miss ya."

"Likewise. Stay out of trouble."

"Nah. I think we're in good hands." Denham shook his hand once more, nodded his appreciation to the current sheriff, then returned to his vehicle. "See you at the office, Sheriff."

"You betcha, Deputy. Stay safe."

Glenn smiled, then placed the box in the bed of the truck. Dakota secured the tarp, then stood in his front lawn. He looked at the property where he raised his son, then gave one final look at his boat. It wasn't truly the final time he'd see it or the house. For Glenn, there were benefits to being the son of Dakota McCullough, especially when he didn't feel like going through the hassle of selling his property to a stranger.

"How's packing on your end going?" he asked.

Glenn shrugged. "I do it when I can. Work has been busy lately. At least the attorney general's off my ass." He smiled. "Soon enough, I'll be moved in. Frankly, I'm just glad the house is staying in the family. I guess I'm as sentimental as you."

They watched the water and the numerous fishing vessels departing for sea.

"Don't take too many joy rides on the *Pilgrimage*," Dakota said. "Fueling her up is a pain."

"Already got that covered, Dad. All I have to do is install flashers and a siren, then the County will handle fuel costs."

Dakota chuckled. "You're ahead of the game."

"Just like your father," Siena said. She stepped out of the garage with an air fryer in her hand. "How is it you own this, a griddle, several pots and pans, and a George Foreman, and *still* don't know how to cook?"

"I guess I hoped a good woman would enter my life and fill that void."

Siena tossed the item in the backseat and kissed him on the cheek. "Looks like you're in luck." Arm around his back, she gave the place a final glance. "Is that everything?"

"Yep."

"Any regrets?"

"Nope. At least I know I have somewhere to go if you dump me again."

"Don't jinx it, old man," Glenn said.

"Old. Jesus." Dakota shook his head. "Wait till you get there, kid."

"Oh, knock it off. You're not even fifty," Siena said. She admired the ring on her left hand. "And you better not jinx it, since I'll have my hands full the next several months planning the wedding."

"Could just go to the courthouse," Dakota said.

Siena sneered. "*That* would be jinxing it."

They laughed, then spent another minute admiring the property. There was no more putting it off. It was time to depart.

Dakota faced his son. "I guess this is it."

"Never." Glenn looked at Siena. "Make sure you guys visit once in a while."

"You have my word."

The three of them shared a group hug. Dakota and his fiancée entered the truck and started the engine.

Dakota rolled the window down and bumped fists with Glenn. "See ya, Sheriff."

"Enjoy the warm summers, Dad."

Dakota placed his sunglasses over his eyes, gave one more kiss to Siena, then drove out his driveway for the last time. Off to start a new chapter in his life, full of purpose.

Glenn waved them goodbye, then approached his sheriff's vehicle. A committed law enforcement officer, it was time to get back to work.

The End

Printed in Dunstable, United Kingdom

78854715R00137